CONRI

BOOK TWO OF
THE WHITE DRAGON

CONRI

SAMANTHA DAVENPORT

atmosphere press

This book is dedicated to my Papa Cooper,
Bramma and Poppy

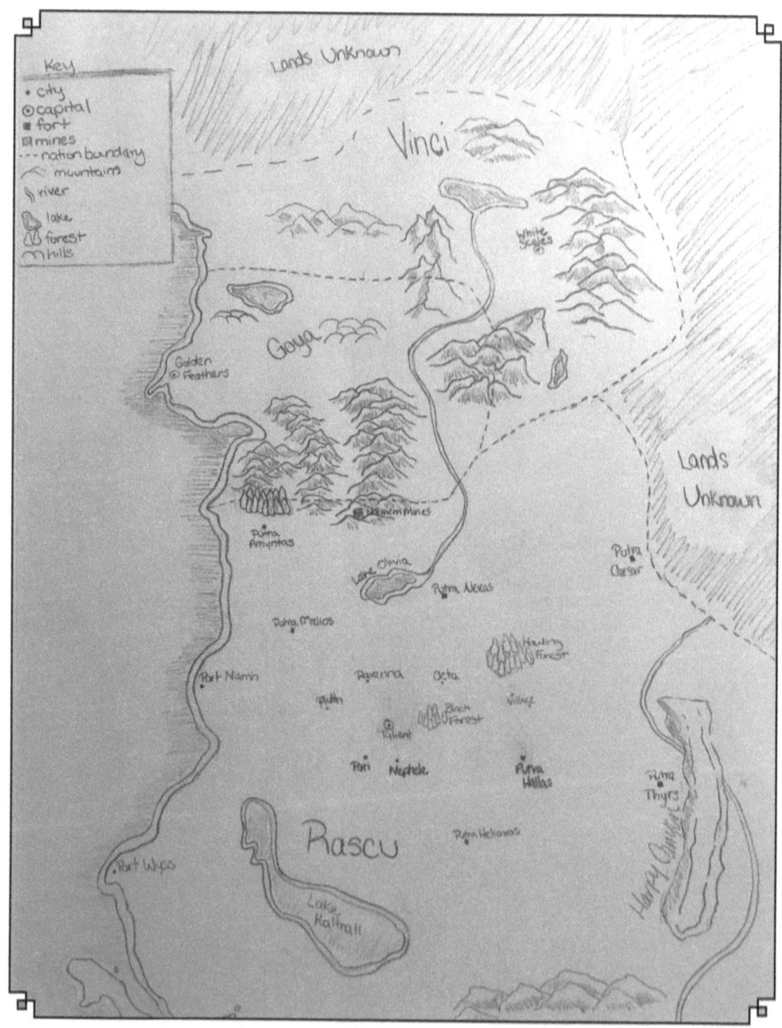

Key
city
capital
fort
mines
nation boundary
mountains
river
lake
forest
hills
Lands Unknown
Vinci
White Scales
Goya
Golden Feathers
Northern Mines
Putra Amyntas
Lake Olivia
Putra Nexas
Putra Melios
Port Niamh
Ravenna
Octa
Plyth
Silent
Hauting Forest
Village
Black Forest
Pari
Nephele
Putra Hellas
Putra Helianos
Rascu
Lake Rathrall
Port Whps
Putra Thyrs
Putra Caesar
Lands Unknown
Harpy Channel

CHARACTER LIST

MAIN AND SECONDARY CHARACTERS

Amaranth "Ami" Rose [AY-mee]: the main character. A free Dragon and a foreigner, Ami tiptoes the line between standing up for herself and risk shunning her male counterparts. She has a deep fear of being deported back to Vinci. While she refuses to tell why, it is clear someone is after her. She has Goyan connections with the twin princes Lunar and Solas as well as the head advisor's son, Ethru. Stubborn and knowledgeable, she often acts older than her physical age. She bears the burn scars from the dorm fire.

Blaine Savage [BLAYN]: a blond male Werewolf with bright blue eyes. He and Ami used to court until he mysteriously disappeared. A gang leader, he is ruthless in his methods. Ami is the only one who sees the softer side of him.

Blejan [BLEH-jen]: a female Dragon slave. Fiercely loyal to Ami and in a secret relationship with Sir Fraster, she is a rebel amongst the slaves. She feels the Bond between her People stronger than others and doesn't seem to be affected by the slave Bond. She holds little respect for her elder Reshmi.

Flander of the Goldmanes [FLAN-dur]: a brown Centaur with green eyes. Rikardi added him to Ami's cover as part of her alliance with the Centaurs. He regrets his actions against Ami when he was a cadet. He is curious and strives to impress Ami.

James Atorra: a male Elf with dark eyes. He is part of Ami's cover. Somewhat cold and analytical, he wants Ami to uphold

his image of a leader. He doesn't get close to People as a way
to protect himself. He is a surprisingly good storyteller.

Jasmine [JAZ-min]: a female Elf with brown hair and light
brown eyes. The first female dictator since the queens, Jasmine
is ambitious and ruthless. Ami often talks her down when she
gets tunnel vision. She will manipulate People as necessary to
obtain her goals. She regards Ami as her only friend and true
ally. Socially awkward, she can be too blunt and rub People the
wrong way. She and the generals do not get along.

Lee: a male Werebobcat. A former police chief and detective,
he is one of the generals in the Rascal military. Sly and with
no qualms of blackmailing to get what he wants, many feel
uncomfortable in his presence. He is unsure about Ami and
worries her secrets will start another war. He investigates
Putra Hallas for 'low morale.'

Leila Moonbeam [LAY-la]: a black female Werecat with dark
blue eyes. She's Ami's best friend from Roy. She of one of
many Royian families fleeing from Roy to Rascu after rumors
of military coup.

Mason [MAY-sun]: a male gray Werewolf. The youngest and
newest general, many of the older cadets joined due to Mason's
heroic acts in the Third Centaur War. He is desperate to please
his older peers and comes off as awkward. He is suspicious of
Ami and the lack of details of her file. He is Ami's superior
officer.

Rikardi [Ri-KAR-dee]: a blond male Centaur. A fairly young
general, he is often seen frowning. He is protective of his soldiers, especially Ami. He is usually found in his office, surrounded by paperwork that never seems to end.

Salvador Dali [Sal-VA-door]: a male brown Werewolf with amber eyes. Cursed by Conri at birth, he struggles with the burden of turning into Conri on his twenty-first birthday. He is fascinated by Ami and firmly believes she can help him with this curse.

Shayne [SHAYN]: a male brown Werewolf. He is observant and a deep thinker. He becomes Ami's second-in-command and leads the gang when Ami is out of the capital. He is good at spying and often keeps an eye on Blaine and his activities.

Smaragdos "Ados" Fallenleaf [A-dose]: a male Elf with green eyes. He is part of Ami's cover. He is a nervous Person around Ami. He eventually grows to admire and respect her. He hopes Ami can help with a problem of his.

Uriah Lakeshore [yuw-RIE-ah]: a male Werewolf with sky blue eyes. He is part of Ami's cover and becomes her second. Not easy to trust, he is cautious around Ami. Snarky at times, he thinks outside the box.

OTHER CHARACTERS

WERES

Ba: a male Werefox and one of Belladonna's minions. He replaces Tso as a puppet.

Black: a male Werewolf Knight.

Bojan: a male Werewolf, commander of Putra Thyrs.

Bru Fonte: a male Werewolf at Putra Hallas, he was severely demoted by Hector due to an incident.

Caleb Dali: a male Werewolf. Also known as Lord Dali and father of Salvador and Deena.

Deena Dali: a female Werewolf and Salvador's sister.

Douglas: a male Werewolf and second in command to Hector at Putra Hallas.

Dr. Elderflower: a male Werewolf. He replaces Dr. Moore at the Common Grounds hospital.

Electra: a female Werewolf and Logan's mother. She handles the trading and business side of the Black Orchids cafe. Chastity is her best friend and business partner.

Gemma Blackhill: a female Werewolf and mother of Viovel Blackhill. She often holds parties at her home in the Spring District for lower Nobles to make connections.

Katha: a female Werewolf. She is one of Dr. Moore's nurses.

Lady Pera: a female Werewolf. Sister to Myst and Sylvia. The current mayor of Ravenna.

Logan: a male Werefox. Ami's favorite coffee maker at the Black Orchids café.

Luke: a male Werewolf, commander of Putra Nexas.

Luther: a male Werefox and Salvador's godfather. He detests priests.

Margaret Masques: a female Werewolf, mother of Myst, Sylvia and Lady Pera. She was a well-known sculptor for depicting important scenes and figures from the holy book.

Mark Tremors: a male Werewolf and first generation Noble, he meets Ami as Lord Sieghild at a Blackhill party.

Michael For'une: a male Werewolf and Captain of the Knights. Stan is his superior officer.

Myst Dali: Salvador and Deena's mother and Caleb's deceased wife. Her sisters are Sylvia and Lady Pera.

Philip: a male Werefox. A hard worker, he usually gets food for the gang and makes sure Rune is taken care of.

Prudence Dali: Caleb's mother and grandmother to Salvador and Deena. She's never forgiven Caleb for marrying Myst and holds tight control over Deena's education.

Sable Warden: a female Werewolf. A second generation Noble, she meets Ami as Lord Sieghild at a Blackhill party.

Sabrina: a female Werewolf. She is one of Dr. Moore's nurses.

Stan LeRoy: a male Werewolf, he is the Commander of the Knights. He often spars with Ami. Michael For'une reports to him.

Sylvia Masques: Myst and Lady Pera's sister. She died shortly after giving birth to her twin sons when her husband was murdered during a gang attack and their Bond broke.

Theo van Gogh: a male Werefox from Roy, he is an apprentice Healer and Ami's physical therapist.

Tso: a male Werefox and head general of the Rascal military, he is strict but competent in his position.

Viovel Blackhill: a male Werewolf with violet eyes and the son of Gemma Blackhill. He meets Ami at his mother's party as Lord Sieghild. He is fascinated by Ami's audacity to go against typical Rascal traditional mannerisms.

CENTAURS

Benton: a male Centaur. The oldest in the gang and knows the streets of Talient the best. He has a crush on Ami.

Clarence: a male Centaur Knight.

Corrie: a female Centaur, she sought Ami at the military ball for help.

Hector: a male Centaur and commander of Putra Hallas.
Dragons

Reshmi: a female Dragon slave. One of the ten Elders, she is over the Dragon slaves in Talient.

Sela, Avani, Callie, Patti, and Fran: female Dragons who serve under Reshmi as seamstresses.

ELVES

Boniface: a male Elf, head priest over the temple in Octa.

Casimir: a male Elf, a high ranking priest in the temple of Octa. He serves under Boniface.

Chastity: a female Elf and business partner with Electra at the Black Orchids café. She handles the café and customer service with Logan.

Elizabeth McCoall: a female Elf. She is the heiress to the McCoall family.

Gabriella Kniles: a female Elf. She is the heiress to the Kniles family.

Isabella Winters: a female Elf. She is the heiress to the Winters family.

Maria: a female Elf and Roger's niece.

Perry: a male Elf Knight. He helped Ami style her hair.

Priscilla Laymate: a female Elf and second generation Noble. She meets Ami as Lord Sieghild at a Blackhill party.

Roger: a male Elf innkeeper at the village near the Howling Forest.

Rune: a male Elf. The youngest in the gang, he adores Ami. He can sneak into any place without getting caught.

Toussaint: a trainee priest who doesn't get out much. He serves the temple in Octa under Boniface.

WITCHES

Belladonna: Jasmine's eldest sister and right-hand to their mother. She wants to get rid of 'the pest' that interferes with her evil plans.

Jeanne: a follower of Belladonna and one of her lieutenants.

Priya: one of Belladonna's lovers, lieutenants, and followers. She uses her sculptures to house evil spirits.

TABLE OF CONTENTS

PROLOGUE

The hospital wing was silent. The smell of bleach hugged the walls and floor. Numerous beds with uncomfortable mattresses and thin white bedsheets lined in neat rows. All except one. At the back wall was an occupied bed. The machines surrounding the bed's metal frame made the appropriate noises as they monitored heart rate and oxygen levels. A bag of saline water hung nearby like a guard. The patient was completely covered in bandages. One could easily mistake her for dead if it wasn't for the slight chest movement. A young Werewolf stood at the foot of the bed.

Shayne stared at the bandaged body of Sigrid. He remembered it as if it happened an hour ago. He was helping out at the Black Orchids Cafe. They still had customers, despite the late hour. The atmosphere was cheerful. He was happy that it was almost time to leave. Then shouts came from the streets. People were pointing at something in the sky. Shayne, Chastity, Electra, and Logan went to see what was happening. Everyone saw the fire demon and the silver Dragon fight in the sky. Then the shrill sounds of the hospital's alarms filled the night. The doctors and nurses from the city hospital raced to the Inner City.

All Shayne could think was, *What's happening? What's going on?*

"Do you think Awesome is okay?" Logan asked worriedly, looking at Chastity.

"Everything will be okay," Chastity said unconvincingly. Her eyes were glued to the silver Dragon flying and fighting the fire demon. Then a faint roar was heard, and the two mighty beings disappeared. Everyone around them whispered and murmured about the strange occurrence. Where did the beings go? Did the Dragon win? Was it hurt?

"Shayne, are you available for a morning shift?" Electra asked. People started to move back into their homes.

"I am. Can you make breakfast?" Shayne asked.

"I'll have it ready for you." Electra nodded. Shayne smiled. He liked the female Werewolf. She made good food. Shayne said his goodbyes and left for the Winter District. The remaining gang was waiting for him at the warehouse.

"Did you see the fire demon?" asked Philip, a Werefox around Shayne's age.

"And the Dragon?" added Benton, a dark brown Centaur. He was three years older than all of them and had been on the streets the longest.

"Everyone saw it. I don't know what's going on. Sigrid didn't mention any magic training," Shayne said. Glancing around, he inquired, "Where's Rune?"

"You know how nosy he is," Philip answered with a sigh. "As soon as he saw the fire demon, he snuck into the Inner City."

"And you didn't follow him?" Shayne nearly shrieked.

"All the Knights were on alert. They would've speared us first and asked questions later," Philip said defensively.

Just then, Rune ran in. He was breathing heavily. The smell of smoke surrounded him like a fog. The young Elf looked terrified. "It's bad! Really, really bad!" Rune screamed hysterically.

"What is?" they demanded.

"Sigrid is hurt bad! Like really, really bad!" Rune exclaimed, collapsing in front of them.

Shayne and Benton helped Rune sit up. The Elf's head hung limp, his chest heaving up and down rapidly.

"Take some deep breaths, Rune," Benton spoke gently. Rune attempted several deep breaths. The panic in his eyes didn't fade.

"How hurt is Sigrid?" Shayne asked.

"She … She had a thing in her chest," Rune gasped.

"What thing?" Philip asked.

"A piece of wood. Like a big piece of wood. And her … her face is melted," Rune added, wheezing.

"Melted?" Shayne whispered.

"Yeah, it's really, really bad." Rune coughed.

"Where is she now?" Benton asked.

"They took her to the big house with lots of doctors and the frowning Centaur," Rune answered. His breathing was normalizing.

"She's more than likely in surgery. We won't hear anything until morning," Benton said sagely.

Shayne sighed. "Let's get some sleep. I have an early shift."

The next morning, Shayne woke up feeling sluggish. He changed into fresh clothes and tiptoed over the still-sleeping males. He made it to the café just as Electra was unlocking the front doors.

"Breakfast is ready in the kitchens," she said. Shayne smiled. He went behind the bar and into the kitchens. Chastity and Logan were making their plates.

"Hey, Shayne. Hungry?" Logan asked cheerfully.

"Always." Shayne grabbed a plate and began to stack pancakes and eggs on it. They went back to the bar and ate. Logan was happily chattering about his dreams and who he hopes will come in for coffee.

"I wonder if Awesome is going to stop by. She said she would," Logan said.

Shayne swallowed hard. "She was hurt last night."

"Hurt?" Logan's whole body swerved to face him. "What do you mean?"

"One of my brothers saw it. I think she fought the fire demon," Shayne said.

"How injured is she?" Chastity asked, her right hand over her heart.

Shayne paused. He didn't want to tell gory details to Logan. "She's in surgery."

"Oh, no," Chastity whispered.

"What's surgery?" Logan asked.

"It's a very delicate procedure. People only get them when they have deep injuries that can't be Healed," Electra explained carefully.

Logan's ears laid flat, then erected again. This occurred several times as the young Werefox pondered over the information. "She'll be all right," Logan said matter-of-factly. "She's Awesome, so she's going to get out of surgery."

After eating, Logan took his plate to the kitchen. Shayne heard the young Werefox begin making coffee for Electra. The two females were talking quietly about what needed to be resupplied and what to serve for lunch. That was when they heard it. A wolf howl from the Inner City. Rune told them of a large tower that echoed in the Inner City. Benton surmised that Werewolves would use it to howl messages.

Shayne listened to the message: *Warehouse Guardian Amaranth Rose is dead.*

The door to the kitchens swooshed softly. Shayne saw a statue-still, wide-eyed Logan holding a saucer with a cup full of coffee. His ears stood straight up. Like an approaching earthquake, his hands began to shake. They shook so hard that the cup and saucer fell to the floor. The sound of shattering ceramic snapped Electra out of her shock.

"What? What did it say?" Chastity asked fervently.

"Amaranth ..." Electra swallowed. "She's dead."

"No!" Logan shouted. His declaration made them jump.

"She's not dead! She just came back! She's not. She's not ..." The young Werefox burst into sobs. Chastity and Electra swiftly went to his side, hugging each other. They were crying as well.

Shayne didn't know what to feel.

"Shayne," Electra said, her voice surprisingly clear. Tears continue to fall down her furry cheeks. "The café will be closed today. You may leave after eating."

Shayne didn't feel like eating anymore. He left his plate and exited the café. As he walked the city, he saw the normally stoic Knights display emotion for the first time. The Weres howled their mourning. The air echoed their messages in a haunting tone. The Centaurs were listless. Many didn't seem to pay attention to those entering and exiting the city's gates. The Elves cried and shouted in despair. No matter how many times they dried their tears, more seemed to appear on their cheeks. Shayne met up with the rest of the gang.

"Did you hear?" Shayne asked quietly.

"I heard the wolf howl, but didn't understand it," Benton admitted.

"Sigrid is dead," Shayne announced deadpan.

"Dead? As in ..." Rune trailed off.

"Yeah." Shayne sniffed.

Philip made a sound between a cough and a sneeze. It wasn't until his shoulders were shaking that they realized he was crying. One by one, they all began to cry. Rune was the loudest, being an Elf and the youngest. Shayne felt conflicted between howling his heart out and curling up into a ball and sobbing. Eventually, they ended up sitting on the cold warehouse floor in a rough circle.

"I miss her already," Rune whispered in a watery voice.

"Why do you miss her?" Benton asked. His tone was one of curiosity.

Rune wiped his running nose with his sleeve. "She always made sure I had food and wasn't hurt. She asked a Knight named Grayson to look out for me."

"She had a Knight look out for me, too," Benton added.

"I think she did for all of us," Philip murmured.

A moment of silence filled the air. In the distance, Shayne could still hear wolf howls.

"I remember when I first really met her," Rune said, sounding wistful. "I accidentally ran into her while she was walking with the boss. The boss looked like he wanted to kill me. Sigrid asked if I was okay and helped me back up. The boss said something like he was going to make sure I didn't do something so stupid again, but Sigrid was like, chill out. The boss tried to charm his way out, but she was firm that I didn't need to be punished, and she said, like, if she heard a whisper of him punishing lads for silly things, he would have to deal with her form of punishment."

The three males stared at him.

"What was her punishment?" Philip asked eagerly.

Rune shrugged. "Never found out. The boss didn't say or do anything to me after that. I guess he didn't want to find out either."

"Whoa." Benton let out a breath, his eyebrows raised high. "Never thought Boss would submit to a female."

"I've watched Sigrid for over a year with the others. I've seen how she interacts with other males," Shayne commented. "With the cadets, it was with patience. With the Knights, it was like a mentor. With the boss, they were the same. With us ..." He paused. In a low tone, he said, "To me, she's like a mom."

Philip gasped at his admittance. Benton stared at him like he had grown another head. Rune nodded.

"I got that, too," Rune agreed.

"A mother?" Benton hissed.

"She always looked out for us," Shayne hissed back defensively. "She always made sure we had clean clothes, had food, and that the boss wasn't hitting us. She cared about us."

Benton's lips twisted as if he couldn't decide if he wanted to snarl or sneer. He hmphed loudly, crossing his arms. Then he abruptly stood up. "I'm going to get food." He grunted as he left.

"Do you think he sees her as a mom but doesn't want to admit it?" Rune asked innocently.

"I don't know. Centaurs are weird," Philip stated.

"How did you see her, Philip?" Rune asked.

Philip flinched at the question. The Werefox's ears went flat. "I, um, I had a crush on her."

"You didn't," Shayne gasped.

"I wasn't the only one," Philip hurriedly said. "Benton had one on her as well."

"But he didn't act like it," Rune pointed out.

"Trust me. I've seen the way he looked at her sometimes. He gets this gooey-eyed look and blushes every time she talks to him," Philip said.

"Did the boss notice?" Shayne asked.

Philip winced. "With a few of the obvious guys. And the ones who thought she was, um, easy."

"Easy? As in getting along with easy?" Rune asked. It was at times like this Shayne realized how young Rune really was.

"No," Philip said slowly. "As in 'doing adult stuff with' easy."

"Oh. Oh!"

"Yeah, Boss did a number on them."

"Is that why he beat the crap out of Boris?" Shayne asked.

Philip nodded. "Yeah. The boss heard Boris call Sigrid a cheap fling, and the boss tore into him."

"Caused him a permanent limp," Benton added, carrying in food from the deli. The Centaur passed out the containers and sat to join them.

Shayne loved the deli. Patsy and Howard adored them and always gave them good food. They ate in comfortable silence. Philip was the first to finish. He collected the trash and deposited it in the trash can outside the warehouse.

"Did you have a crush on Sigrid?" Rune blurted, facing Benton.

The Centaur turned pink all the way down his neck. "What?"

"You heard me." The Elf was smirking.

Benton huffed. "A little," he mumbled.

"How so?" Shayne asked.

"Why do you care?" Benton snapped.

"Cuz I had a crush on her too," Philip admitted. The inside of his ears were dark pink.

Benton grumbled under his breath. "I thought she was cute."

"I liked her hair. It looked soft, and she didn't do weird things to it. She kept it simple," Philip admitted, his furry cheeks heating at the confession.

"I liked her ears," Benton confessed. "They were adorable."

"You guys had it bad." Shayne chuckled.

"Shut up," the two chorused.

"I'm going to bed," Rune announced.

"Me too." Shayne got up and followed the Elf to their shared room. He got under the covers and fell asleep quickly. The next thing he knew, someone was shaking him. Opening his eyes, he saw Philip looking frantic yet excited.

"What's going on?" Shayne asked sleepily.

"The wolf howl came again from the Inner City," Philip spoke passionately. Shayne sat up. The other two males were awake as well.

"And?" Shayne asked impatiently.

"She's alive," Philip said in awe. "Sigrid is alive."

Shayne snapped out of his memories. A month had passed with no change. Shayne visited every morning before working in the café to keep Logan updated. The young Werefox continuously pestered Chastity and Electra for him to visit, but the two females remained firm in letting Sigrid rest. They promised to visit when she woke up. Shayne wondered when that would be as he left for work.

One of the Werewolf nurses came by to check on the still-unconscious female. She sighed as she documented the same results as her last round. Two months have passed since the warehouse fire. A shudder ran down her spine as the nurse recalled the horrible events. Never in her years as a nurse had she seen such horror. She could still hear the cries for help of the injured cadets. Some of them were so traumatized they refused to come back. She didn't blame them. Of all the patients, Rose was the worst off. Tears threatened to fall as the memories of that night materialized.

The little female had a piece of plywood in her chest. Dr. Moore remained calm throughout the entire procedure, determined to save Rose. They spent over eight hours operating on the young female. Even though she and the other nurse, Sabrina, could see Dr. Moore beginning to tire, he refused to give up. It didn't matter. Rose's body couldn't take any more abuse. After several attempts to bring her back, Dr. Moore called the time of death in the most monotone voice she had heard him speak.

The doctor left the surgery, taking off his blood-soaked gloves and apron as he walked. When he reached his office, he shut the door. Both nurses chased after him. They both stopped when they heard sobs coming from the doctor's office.

"Go clean the surgery room, Katha. I'll make the announcement," Sabrina said wearily.

"I hate this," Katha whispered, tears already filling her eyes.

Sabrina hugged her tightly. Katha hugged her back.

She hated remembering that day. A day of pain, suffering, and grief. Then, Rose returned to life. She was alive.

Although, Katha wondered as she stared at her immobilized

patient, *was it really worth coming back? Was it worth coming back to the world in so much pain?* Setting down the clipboard, she left to recount the medicine stock.

Salvador remembered that day as he ran as if his life depended on it. His frequent nightmares refused to allow him to forget. The soldiers he shared a room with for the past three months were sympathetic, but he could tell they were getting annoyed. He took a deep gulp of air and continued, never breaking his stride. Ami taught him how to run properly. Ami taught him the history of the different nations. Ami taught him to never give up on hope. He ran on that hope as the sunrise began to turn Talient's skyline pink and orange. He didn't stop until he saw the northern gates ahead of him. He slowed down to a walk. His heart drummed in his chest fiercely.

"Back again?" asked a Centaur Knight. Salvador kept forgetting his name. He always greeted Salvador with a smile.

"Yes. Any news?" Salvador asked eagerly.

The Centaur shook his head sadly. "I can only pray that she's in the coma for healing, and it's better that she's not awake to feel anything."

Salvador nodded. He walked into Winter District comfortably. The first time he ran back to Talient on his day off, he was wary. Many gangs called the Winter District home, and from what he heard, they were ruthless. Several gang members surrounded him on his first trip. The leader, a scrawny Werewolf who introduced himself as Shayne, offered their protection through the district.

"Not that I don't appreciate it, but why?" Salvador asked.

"You're one of Sigrid's friends," Shayne answered. "Until she recovers, we will maintain the business as usual."

"Sigrid?" he asked.

Shayne frowned. "Her last name is Rose."

"Ami?" Salvador was shocked. How many names did Ami have?

"Sounds about right." Shayne shrugged.

"Um, thank you. I'll take your offer," Salvador agreed.

From that day forward, the gang members quietly escorted him to the front of the Inner City. They always disappeared before he could thank them. The Knights greeted him with polite nods as he made his way to the mansion and eventually to the hospital wing. When he saw Ami, no matter how many times on his days off, the memories of that day came back in force.

When the news of her death came, he lost feeling in his legs. Later, the nurses and other cadets told him he was in a daze they couldn't snap him out of. It wasn't until he heard of Ami's miraculous revival did the feeling return to his nerves. By then, he was on his way to one of the forts. He couldn't remember the name of the fort, only its location. It was a day's run to Talient, which suited him. He, along with the rest of the fresh cadets, listened to the rules. When their superior asked if they had any questions, Salvador asked, "What can we do on our days off?"

His superior, a dark gray Werewolf, shrugged. "As long as you don't create mischief, you can run to Talient and back for all I care."

Salvador took him to his word.

Ami lay in the hospital bed. Salvador silently approached. He pulled a nearby chair to the end of Ami's bed. He sat there and began to speak. He told her of his new duties as a guard and kitchen aide. He told her of how his superiors and bunk mates were curious about his outings on his days off since they didn't know where he went. He reassured her that he would return to the fort before his day was over to avoid trouble. He talked about his nightmares and how he wished she was awake so he could see she was truly alive and not in this state. During his talks, one of the Dragons provided sandwiches and tea.

Salvador ate the lunch provided. After eating, he talked about his family. His father and sister worried about him. They worried about the curse getting stronger and Ami not being able to help them find a cure. Before he left, he gently grasped Ami's feet and prayed. He prayed for healing and for his friend to come out stronger than before.

"You got this, Ami," Salvador whispered. Then he turned and left.

Jasmine stared at the wall of her room. The room symbolized her ambition. Her position as dictator symbolized her power over the military. It was something her sisters never accomplished. For the past three years, Jasmine felt secure in her plans. While it was an uphill battle to get the males to acknowledge her, she managed to gain a few grains of respect from Tso. While Jasmine wished she could say she earned it all by herself, she knew she would never be where she was without Amaranth.

Amaranth, her most powerful ally, her confidant (somewhat), and her political mastermind, was a free Dragon!

"How did I miss that?" Jasmine whispered to herself. The Vincian gave nothing away. Then again, Jasmine wasn't looking for a free Dragon. Suddenly all the puzzle pieces about Amaranth she had collected seemed to fall into place. At least some of them. The way the Dragons deferred to Amaranth instead of Jasmine, how they seemed to obey her without question, Amaranth's own way of dealing with People.

Doubt crept into her mind as she thought over the puzzle pieces. Perhaps it wasn't so obvious after all. She saw the way Amaranth treated People, and it was consistent. The Dragons replied over the top due to their oppression. She felt their happiness every time Amaranth interacted with them. She saw how Amaranth treated them as if they weren't enslaved. It was how she was. Jasmine smiled, a chuckle rising in her throat as a memory surfaced.

The two were debating something. Possibly one of Jasmine's plans that Amaranth thought was too aggressive at the time. The memory of the debate, the sarcasm, exchanged barbs had tears falling down Jasmine's cheeks. She missed Amaranth. No matter how aggravating she was, Amaranth was her only friend and true ally. She was the one who challenged Jasmine and forced her to see the whole picture when she got tunnel vision.

Amaranth was her power.

The whirlwind events with the fire demon made her suck in a shaky breath. She couldn't recall much except when she entered the hospital and saw Amaranth dead on the operating table. She barely managed to contain her magic. She wanted to put as much of her magic in the corpse to bring her back. The realization of death halted her. The finality of her friend's life made her falter. Then, all of a sudden, Amaranth was proclaimed alive by the Dragons.

They celebrated.

Jasmine hid in her room.

That was four months ago. Jasmine worked tirelessly on the new cadet dorms. She wanted to make sure this never happened again. She consulted books on warding, shields, and numerous protection and safety spells to cast on each part of the new building. She will not have this incident repeated. She will not lose her friend to an illegal mage again. Looking at the clock, she noted it was midnight. She stood up from the lace-winged chair she often sat in when Amaranth ate with her. Her heart squeezed painfully. Taking in a deep breath, she exited her room.

The thought of someone seeing her in her pajamas didn't bother her. A level of apathy had crawled into her heart, and she found herself not caring what People thought anymore. She barely read the missives from the members of Old Congress who criticized her handling of the situation.

Weak cowards, she thought coldly. *They complain and complain, yet when it's time to actually make a real decision, they cower like rats in a sewer.*

She entered the hospital. Amaranth lay unresponsive. The consistent beep of the machines helped against the battle of silence. Jasmine sat in the chair on Amaranth's right side and stared at the wall until dawn.

Blejan woke up screaming. The other Dragons came to her side, trying to calm her down. Blejan trembled in her bed, the nightmare still fresh in her mind. In her dreams, they completed the mourning ritual and buried Angel according to Dragon customs. Later, Blejan went to visit Angel's grave with white lilies. She stopped when she noticed something off.

The grave was disturbed.

She cautiously approached the grave, hoping she was just seeing things. As she came closer, she noticed drag marks going away from the fresh grave.

Grave robbers! She thought. She followed the drag marks

until she came across the body of her dearest friend. Only her friend was breathing. She was alive. Then it hit Blejan.

They had buried her alive.

That was when she woke up screaming. Bleddyn hugged her tightly. Blejan was limp with exhaustion.

"When will they stop?" Blejan whispered.

"They may never, or they may when Angel wakes up. We don't know," Bleddyn answered.

"I need to walk," Blejan mumbled as she scrambled out of his clutches and into the hall before anyone could stop her. Tears flowed down her cheeks as she stumbled down the corridor. The next thing she knew, she was in the hospital room, staring at Angel.

From what she heard, Angel's wounds were healing slowly. Too slowly for a Dragon, in Blejan's opinion. Angel didn't fight for consciousness. She didn't resist the medicine like she used to whenever she got injured during her sparring matches with the Knights. Her dear friend was unchanged. That was odd. Dragons were powerful self-healers. Even demon fire healed relatively normally for them.

Something isn't right. Blejan thought. *I need to speak to Reshmi.*

She darted out of the hospital and used the secret hallways to Reshmi's room. She banged on the door urgently. Reshmi answered with sleepy yet wary eyes.

"What's the matter?" Reshmi demanded. "Do you realize what time—"

"Something is wrong with Angel," Blejan blurted.

Reshmi stopped speaking. She motioned for Blejan to enter. The room was still dark. Reshmi muttered for her to stay put. A moment later, a candle illuminated the sparse room. It contained a small dresser, a bed, and a side table where the candle sat.

"Explain," Reshmi ordered stiffly.

"It has been five months, and Angel hasn't woken up. Her injuries also haven't healed. If she was enslaved, I would

believe our master was purposely delaying the healing as punishment," Blejan started. "As she is free, she should've woken
up by now."

The elder looked deep in thought. "I will ask the doctor
and nurses about the *mayakar*'s progress and proceed from there."

"She is no longer *mayakar*," Blejan stated firmly.

"Then what is she?" Reshmi inquired.

"She is *ya'puris*. For she is free."

Reshmi regarded Blejan for a long minute. Blejan thought
the elder would protest. The elder closed her eyes and took a
deep breath. When she opened her eyes, Blejan was surprised
to see acceptance.

"For she is and will be known," Reshmi said. "Go to bed. I
will start in the morning."

Blejan sputtered a good night and slowly walked back
to her corridor. When she returned to her dorm, the other
Dragons were already asleep. She quietly slipped into her bed
and stared at the ceiling, praying for her friend.

Rikardi remembered that day six months ago. He remembered the heat from the demon fire. He remembered the cries
of injured and scared cadets, desperate to escape the inferno.
The smell of burning flesh mixed with wood and magic seared
itself in his nostrils. Seeing the small figure of Rose jumping
to escape the fire demon still made his heart leap with fear.
Nightmares of him not catching her kept him up at night.

All the slaves in Talient thanked him profusely. Blejan, the
slave Ami had befriended, came to him with a pot of tea days
after the catastrophe.

"If you hadn't unlocked the door, we would've suffocated," Blejan answered after he asked why she was still thanking him. She poured him a cup of tea. "This is *ya'puris'* favorite tea."

"Who is *ya'puris*?" Rikardi asked.

"You call her Rose. I call her Freedom," Blejan answered.

Rikardi checked on Rose every day when the sun set since she was proclaimed alive. The halls of the mansion are quiet during this time. All the generals were eating dinner in their rooms, relieved the day of meetings and paperwork was over. When Rikardi arrived at the first floor, Reshmi stood there to greet him. That was new.

"Hello, General." The slave bowed respectfully.

"Greetings." Rikardi nodded back. "Is there a concern?"

Reshmi looked over her shoulder. "Do you have a moment to speak?"

Rikardi felt slightly annoyed at the possibility of his routine being interrupted. The look of apprehension on Reshmi's face forced the irritation away. "I do."

Reshmi motioned for him to follow. She led him to the slaves' dorms. He was shown into an area he believed they used for dining due to the lack of beds. All seventy slaves were in the room. There was barely enough room for Rikardi's horse body to enter. He saw Blejan in the crowd. The kitchen slave gave him a kind smile. Rikardi turned to Reshmi.

"Why am I here?" Rikardi asked coldly.

Reshmi flinched. "We are worried about *ya'puris*. Even with the damage she took with the wood beam and fire, she should've been awake by now. There is something wrong."

Rikardi straightened his spine. "What exactly is wrong?"

"The doctor and nurses won't let us use our magic to see," another slave answered, a male with a deep voice. "They also don't believe she is a Dragon."

"She has a horn and tail," Rikardi pointed out.

The male shook his head. "They still treat her like an Elf when she needs Dragon healing."

"All of us will need to be in the hospital to use our magic," Reshmi added.

"Why?" Rikardi asked.

"Part of the magic requires each Dragon to give a part of their magic. We all must be present to add to *ya'puris* and help her heal. If we do not, she will fade in the night," Reshmi said grimly.

Rikardi's heart leaped to his throat. Fury and determination filled his chest and legs. He briskly exited the room, knocking down several slaves. He barked for them to follow. He heard them scramble to follow. He entered the hospital room just as Dr. Moore and his nurses were checking on Rose.

"Rikardi, what's going on?" Dr. Moore asked, alarmed at the sight of the slaves.

"I'm ordering you to allow the Dragons to heal Guardian Rose," Rikardi said icily.

"I cannot allow that. This is my hospital, and as the head doctor, I can and will overrule your orders, General," Dr. Moore snarled.

Rikardi leaned over until he was inches away from the Elf's face. "Guardian Rose is a Dragon," the Centaur snarled back. "She requires Dragon healing, an area you have no expertise. You will allow them to do their healing, or else you will be working for the city's hospital before the night's out. Am I clear?"

Dr. Moore tried to speak, but nothing came out of his mouth. Satisfied, Rikardi stood up straight. "Perform the healing," Rikardi ordered.

Reshmi came to Rose's left side. The slaves clumped together. Each of them laid a hand on the shoulder of the slave in front of or to the side of them. The one next to Reshmi placed both hands on her shoulders. Reshmi held her hands several inches over Rose's chest and closed her eyes. At first, Rikardi couldn't sense anything. A pressure began to build in his ears. He winced when they popped. The slaves then began to glow.

It wasn't a light surrounding their bodies. Looking closer at the slave nearest to him, the Centaur realized it was their skin that was glowing. Then he looked at Reshmi and Rose. Reshmi's hands were surrounded by dark blue magic. The magic sank like fog into Rose's chest. Ten minutes into the healing, the slave at the end of the line let go of a slave's shoulder. After another ten minutes, the one who was second to last released their grip. This continued every ten minutes until Reshmi was last. The slave lasted twenty minutes before the dark blue magic disappeared.

Rose took a deep breath, her arms flailing wildly. Reshmi and another slave held her arms down while speaking in their native language. Rikardi came forward. The slaves near the bed moved aside. The Centaur came to Rose's right side. Relief filled his lungs and limbs when he saw the amethyst eye he feared he would never see again.

"Welcome back, Guardian Rose."

CHAPTER 1

Ami felt her body slowly shutting down. The magic the Dragons gave woke her up, but it wouldn't last long. She knew what was wrong. All her Bonds were gone. Nothing was anchoring her to anyone. While she knew the Bond with her mother was still connected, it was so faint she wouldn't be surprised to see it vanish. Her head felt empty. When she was coherent enough to think, she called out to the voices.

Nothing. Hollow, vast emptiness greeted her back. She wept. Her heart ached painfully from her wounds and loneliness. Even though they had been planted, they were her only friends that she could confide in. Then she remembered Blaine, and her heart nearly tore. The Bond they shared, once vibrant and colorful with beautiful colors, was now frayed, shriveled, and snapped. It made her wonder if he felt their Bond snap.

Was he coming here? What's stopping him? She half expected to feel his powerful magic swirl around him as he marched through the mansion. She half smiled. She would've loved to see that. But the few days she was awake, she heard and felt nothing.

I was nothing but a fool for him, Ami thought bitterly. More tears went down her cheek. She didn't have the strength to wipe them. Between her heartache and aching wounds, she could barely keep her eye open. Thankfully, her hearing was intact. What she was hearing from the doctor was foreboding. Dr. Moore walked more stiffly and talked more agitated than usual. The nurses gossiped more, usually demeaning things about Rikardi. Ami hoped the nurses didn't spread these stories to the soldiers.

"I just don't understand," Dr. Moore muttered to himself as he paced in his office.

"What's wrong, Doctor?" Sabrina asked.

"What the slaves did. Before, her body could take the liquid IVs to gather her strength. Now, her body is rejecting them! I don't understand how that's possible," Dr. Moore explained frustratingly.

"Do you think what the slaves did is blocking her body's ability to absorb nutrients?" Katha asked.

Dr. Moore's pacing stopped. "That's it!" he exclaimed excitedly. "She needs surgery."

"Wait, what?" Sabrina shrieked.

"Doctor, she's too weak—" Katha started.

"Listen, listen!" Dr. Moore urged. Ami imagined his face maniacal, like a mad scientist discovering a forbidden formula. "The main issue she faces is her burns, correct?" The nurses didn't say anything. "We should be able to peel her burns and use healing magic to promote new skin," Dr. Moore said confidently.

The nurses hummed. Ami couldn't tell if they agreed with him or not.

"Who'll perform the healing?" Sabrina asked.

"That would be Katha," Dr. Moore answered.

"Me? But I haven't taken my Healer's exam," Katha protested.

"See this as a practice run for your exam. You will have to heal burns in your practice. I know you have the skill," Dr. Moore said encouragingly.

"I don't know about this, Doctor," Katha said weakly.

Dr. Moore took a step toward the nurses. Ami's eye was still closed. She imagined he put his hands on her shoulders by what he said next.

"You are one of the most capable Healers I have ever apprenticed. I know you can help our patient. I believe in you," Dr. Moore said in a way that sounded creepy to Ami.

"I believe in you too, Katha," Sabrina said.

"Thank you," Katha said in a weak voice. "All right," she said, her voice more assertive, "what do we need to do?"

"First, we must gather the necessary lotions for the new skin and prep the operating room for complications. Katha, I want you to review chapters twenty-four to twenty-seven of your medical book. There are ideas and suggestions for prepping, preparing, and performing delicate surgeries. We will go over every likely scenario and plan on how to counter them. Sabrina, gather the necessary lotions from the pharmacy or make them yourself. Let me know what it is owed. I'll keep an eye on our patient and monitor her levels. Dismissed," Dr. Moore ordered.

The nurses left in a hurry. Dr. Moore came to her bed. Ami didn't dare open her eye.

"This is the best option," Dr. Moore whispered.

Would I return to where Gramps and Grammy were? Would the Shadow King capture me? Ami thought. Her thoughts turned morbid. *Is it considered bad luck if I die in the same operating room twice?*

Helplessness overwhelmed her, and several tears escaped her eye. Her emotions overcame her senses. Then a large hand covered hers. It wasn't Dr. Moore or the nurses. It was warm and comforting. As her feelings ebbed, she became aware of Blejan muttering something. Before she could form a question, she felt it.

A Bond string.

She grabbed at it greedily and connected it as quickly as

she could without regard. At that moment, she didn't care who it belonged to. The wave of relief and feeling somewhat whole filled Ami. She relished in the feeling until she came down from the high. Her mind was clear. She looked at the Bond more closely. The string of the Person was colorful with greens, yellows, and light purples. Thin strands of her dark purple and black blended in where they connected. A sensation of a strong, stubborn male with iron determination created an image in her mind. She opened her eye.

Rikardi was next to her as if he had been jolted awake. Questions swirled in her mind. *Why did he form a Bond with me? Did he know how? Does he intend to break my hand off? When will he let go?*

Rikardi appeared to be deep in thought. Then she felt him gently grab the Bond and let out a pulse. Ami's eye widened with surprise and amusement. Copying him, she sent a pulse back. He visibly relaxed. Then he noticed their hands. He carefully untangled them, gave her a nod, and left. Inwardly, Ami crowed in delight.

I'm not going to die! I have a Bond! I'm not going to die! Tears of joy ran down her cheek.

Hours later, Dr. Moore and the nurses retired to their rooms. Blejan snuck in. When Ami saw the gang members, her eye widened, and the visible part of her lips spread upwards in a half-smile. They stopped several feet from her bed, unsure what to do. Blejan sat next to her.

"I'm sorry it took so long to fix this," Blejan whispered. "They've agreed to create a Bond with you." She motioned for one of them to come to the other side of Ami's bed.

Shayne was the first to move to the other side of the bed. He carefully clasped her bandaged left hand. Ami listened carefully to Blejan softly explaining to Shayne how to create a Bond. Ami held back a snort. Blejan was making it too complicated. From her explanation, it seemed more like a ritual than a Bond. Poor Shayne was trying to follow Blejan's instructions. The Werewolf closed his eyes in shrewd concentration, almost as if in pain. Ami gently moved her bandaged hand to grip Shayne's furry one. Closing her eye, she concentrated and brought forth her string.

Shayne connected without hesitation. The exchange of energies was different. Ami wasn't as desperate but still greedy for the Bond. Shayne's colors were sky blue and navy blue. The feeling of an early morning mist glided over Ami's face. The pain from her burns lessened for several seconds. Shayne stared at her as if she glowed with holy light when she opened her eye. Carefully, she released his hand. The broken connection snapped Shayne out of whatever was going on in his mind.

He walked back to the eager males. All Ami could hear were incoherent mumbles. Whatever was said, Rune bounced to Ami's side. Ami offered her hand. Rune, despite his excitement, grabbed her hand gently. Ami repeated the method with Rune. It took several seconds longer due to Rune's inability to focus. Finally, she gathered enough of his attention to form a Bond. Hyper green energy filled her body, making her giggle. This led to a coughing fit. Blejan gave her a small glass of water. Ami gratefully drank it. The taste of water was like heaven dancing on her tongue. When was the last time she drank water? Honestly, she couldn't remember.

"Are you okay, boss?" Rune whispered. The Elf looked like he was about to cry.

"I'm fine," she croaked out. Her voice reminded her of rough river rocks.

Satisfied, Rune released her hand to allow Philip to take his place. The Werefox blushed dark pink in his ears when he took her hand. Ami half-smiled in amusement. Philip mock-glared at her apparent delight. His Bond colors were dark yellow, dark blue, and tan. He, too, gave her a similar look of awe.

Then it was Benton's turn. The Centaur blushed down to the top of his shoulders when he took Ami's hand. If she'd had the strength, she would've teased him. His Bond was orange and teal. Unlike the others, Benton refused to look at her. His blush turned from dark pink to scarlet. Ami could feel his awe through the Bond. Then she noticed he was trembling.

"Are you all right?" she asked, her voice less rough than before.

"I-I'm f-f-fine," Benton stammered. He carefully untangled their fingers. His back legs buckled a few times before he could retain his balance.

"Thank you. All you," Ami rasped. Exhaustion seeped into her bones, and darkness overcame her.

The next couple of days were tense. The Dragons heard about Dr. Moore's desire to operate on her and rotated in shifts to prevent the doctor or the nurses from being near her. Reshmi and Dr. Moore argued endlessly about her being a free Dragon or an Elf. Reshmi helped by using her magic on Ami's still-bandaged wounds, and the other Dragons helped redress them when there were enough guards to watch the doctor.

She wasn't sure when the night of the event happened. Her best estimate was roughly a week after she gained Bonds from the gang and Rikardi. She winced at the soft sound of the hospital door opening and closing with a quiet click.

It appears tonight is the night. Ami thought. She held back tears. *I don't want to die again.*

Her heart started to race the closer Dr. Moore and the nurses got, the beeping of the machine alerting them of her wakefulness. Just as Dr. Moore got within arm's distance, a form dropped onto her bed, blocking her view. The weight of the Person made Ami bounce painfully. A growl came from the unknown Person. At first, Ami thought it was Egan. Then she saw the form was solid, unlike Egan's shadowy outline. Dr. Moore started to say something, but then he yelled in pain. The form lunged forward towards the doctor, tackling him to the floor. The nurses attacked the Person, their claws out. The dark Person dodged them effortlessly. The Person blended in with the shadows of the hospital. All Ami could see were the two nurses desperately trying to sniff the attacker out. Dr. Moore moaned from the floor. Then the two nurses disappeared from Ami's view. Their cries of surprise were the last thing she heard.

Silence filled the room. Even Dr. Moore didn't make a sound. Ami's heart pounded a tattoo against her breastbone. She hastily looked in her mind for her Bonds. Swiftly finding Rikardi, she grabbed it hard and urged him to come. It felt like hours before the Centaur appeared with ten Knights. The blond Centaur had his sword ready to strike. He gasped, his green eyes staring at the floor near the end of Ami's bed.

"What happened?" Rikardi demanded with a frown.

"They came to perform surgery," Ami said roughly. "Someone stopped them."

"Who?" Rikardi asked, his voice quieter.

"I don't know."

"Search the mansion. I want this Person caught. Send for the slaves to clean this mess up," Rikardi ordered. The Knights obeyed without question.

"What happened to them?" Ami asked.

"They're dead," Rikardi said deadpan.

"Your bedside manner is wonderful as always, sir," Ami commented.

"How are you feeling?" Rikardi asked.

"Still in pain."

"I meant ..." Rikardi paused. "The doctor and his nurses are dead."

"Relief," Ami answered.

Rikardi sat opposite where he had created a Bond with her. His frown was deep. His arms were crossed tightly across his chest. Finding their Bond, she gently pulsed calmness. He jumped at the sensation.

"What are you doing?" he nearly shrieked.

Ami couldn't suppress her snorting giggles. "I was trying to comfort you."

Rikardi looked away. "Thank you," he mumbled.

"You're welcome."

The next four days were interesting. None of the Knights found anything about the stranger who protected Ami that night. From what she heard, the manner of death of the doctor and the nurses was unnerving. They had no scratches, stab wounds, or signs of strangulation. Aside from a sizeable deep bruise on their chests, they appeared to drop dead. Ami wondered if magic was used. The news didn't deter Rikardi from guarding her from evening to dawn and the assignment of Knights outside and inside the hospital until a new doctor was assigned. It greatly reminded Ami of the bleach incident.

Rikardi was not getting enough sleep. Ami tried to persuade him to allow another Knight to take over guard duty, but the stubborn Centaur refused.

"Until it becomes clear that this stranger will not harm you, your safety takes priority," Rikardi argued.

"I thought it was clear they were protecting me," Ami retorted.

"That has yet to be seen," Rikardi muttered.

"If they wanted to harm me, they would've done it sooner than when the doctor tried to kill me. Or allow the doctor and nurses to continue what they wanted to do. Why protect me if they want to kill me?" Ami reasoned.

"There may be enemies who wish to deal with you themselves," Rikardi said. His tone seemed like he was speaking from experience. "I will not argue about this anymore. It is done, Guardian Rose," Rikardi said firmly when she tried to object.

Ami fumed about his overprotectiveness. At least she was able to get some answers from the blond Centaur surrounding her death and resurrection. She found out that Gabriella managed to escape from the enflamed dorm with no injuries. The anxious weight that pressed on Ami's heart lifted when she heard the redhaired Elf was safe. Rikardi and a few of the Knights recalled their surprise when the three male cadets turned out to be heiresses. Rikardi contacted their families despite their pleas for him not to.

"How did you figure out they were heiresses?" Ami asked. She didn't think the females' appearance would change that drastically when the Oath broke.

"It became obvious that they were female," Rikardi said with a look.

"Puberty hit them like running into a brick wall?" Ami asked rhetorically.

"Although the screams we heard were more female than the males that uttered them," Rikardi said. His lips tried not to smile. His green eyes held mirth. Ami suppressed her laughter as much as she could, making gasping noises instead. It still hurt to laugh.

The next day, Lius visited when Rikardi was in meetings. The Dwarf apologized profusely about not visiting sooner.

"I'd been lookin' all o'er for the stuff to make this balm for ya. This is me People's specialty. It's good against demon fire and should help ya heal quicker, lass," Lius explained.

"You've dealt with demon fire?" Ami asked, impressed.

Lius nodded. "Aye. We Dwarf folk live in the mount'ins. Sometimes, we dig too deep and find unpleasant things. One'f being demons."

The paste was off-white and smelled like mint and burnt pine. Reshmi confirmed the paste was authentic and asked Lius for the recipe. The blacksmith was happy to give it. Reshmi and another Dragon carefully removed Ami's bandages on her head and face. The sad look Lius gave told her how bad the damage was.

"This will help, lass," Lius reassured. Carefully, Lius applied the paste.

It was smooth. Ami was surprised. The smell gave the impression the texture would be rough. A few spots, particularly near her left ear and the back of her head, still pained her, despite how gentle Lius was. After covering her face and head, one Dragon applied fresh bandages while Reshmi undid the bandages on her arms and hands. Lius used the paste there as well. Then Reshmi applied new bandages while the other Dragon undid the bandages on her feet.

"Bless ya, lass," Lius hissed when he saw her feet. "Did ya kick its face while up there?"

"No. I ran," Ami admitted.

"Could've fooled me," Lius mumbled under his breath as he also applied the paste to her feet.

Once he was finished, Reshmi and the other Dragon reapplied fresh bandages.

"Thank you, Lius," Ami said gratefully. She would take a paste over surgery any day.

"Yer welcome, lass. I'll be back tomor'ow to see how ya feel," Lius said with a smile. Ami watched him leave with a small smile.

"*Ya'puris*, are you hungry?" Reshmi asked.

Ami's stomach growled loudly. "Yes, I am."

Reshmi and the Dragon smiled widely. They left and came back shortly with a bowl of broth and bread. Reshmi broke the bread into manageable pieces while the other Dragon stirred the broth. Ami dipped the bread into the broth until it was soft enough for her to swallow whole. She ate slowly. Before she knew it, she ate all the bread pieces and drank all the broth.

"I'm still hungry," Ami announced.

Reshmi and the Dragon looked excited. "Do you want more broth and bread?" Reshmi asked.

"Can I have that onion soup and bread?" Ami asked.

"Of course! We will get that for you," Reshmi said excitedly.

Ami ate several bowls of onion soup and two loaves of bread. She had to convince Reshmi and the other Dragons who came to watch her eat that she was full and couldn't eat anymore. The Dragons present let out a sigh of relief. Ami leaned back in her hospital bed. Being full of food gave her a feeling of comfort and joy she hadn't felt in a long time.

Without realizing it, she let out a content purr.

Jasmine hummed happily as she read a report in her lace-wing chair. While she hadn't been able to see Amaranth, knowing her friend was alive made her elated. The dorms were taking longer than she thought. It didn't matter. They would be safe this time.

Never again, Jasmine reminded herself.

"Master, you have a guest," a Dragon interrupted her thoughts.

Jasmine mentally went through her agenda for the day and frowned slightly. She didn't recall having any meetings with anyone today. However, one of her allies may have learned something.

"Show them in," Jasmine ordered.

The Dragon nodded. When Jasmine saw her guest, the blood drained from her face. It was the last Person she would've thought to visit and her least favorite Person. Belladonna, her oldest sister, waltzed in wearing a form-fitting black dress with a slit up to her thigh. The black heels made her legs look longer than they were. Her silky black hair was down and wavy. Pale skin from lack of sunlight, she was beautiful in a deadly sense. Jasmine didn't understand how males could fall for such a cold Person. Belladonna's dead, dark eyes glinted with malice when she looked at Jasmine.

"Hello, little sister," Belladonna greeted her in a silky voice.

"Hello, eldest sister," Jasmine greeted back, trying to be cordial.

"I'm impressed," Belladonna stated in a slightly amazed voice. "You actually managed to do something properly."

"I am our mother's daughter," Jasmine said tersely.

"True. We were worried that your father's stain was too deep. But now it seems like you may actually be something to be proud of," Belladonna said with fake sweetness.

Panic was threatening to bloom in Jasmine's chest. *No, I can't let her get to me now. I have to be polite and somehow get her to leave,* Jasmine thought.

"I wasn't aware you were in the area. Your latest project seemed to take up a lot of your time," Jasmine said, changing the subject.

Belladonna smiled in a way that made Jasmine feel sick. "My latest project was a failure. Mother was worried about you, so I came to see how my youngest sister was holding up on her project," Belladonna replied.

"I'm doing well, thank you," Jasmine said.

Belladonna then started to slowly walk around the room. Jasmine tensed as she examined every inch of the space. Jasmine felt more and more unsafe. What if she's bewitching something? Could she be placing spells on various items to hurt or harm whoever touches them? Jasmine clasped her hands together to stop them from shaking. It only spread to her legs and arms.

"I must admit, you did better than I expected," Belladonna admitted. Jasmine was too shocked to reply. Getting a compliment from Belladonna was never a good thing. "Unfortunately," Belladonna added, "your project is taking a long time."

"I anticipated my project to take longer than usual," Jasmine said as politely as possible while being defensive.

"Mother wants it done sooner."

Jasmine gaped before she realized she was doing it. "But why?"

Belladonna's dead eyes lit up in sadistic pleasure. "You have an entire People enslaved to you. They are bound to you. Mother wants them for her rituals."

"They are mine," Jasmine growled.

With incredible speed, Belladonna came to Jasmine's side and slapped her cheek so hard her lips started to bleed.

"Don't forget, little sister," Belladonna said coldly, "that everything we do is for Mother and her rituals. They give us power, and we make her proud. Don't you want to make Mother proud?"

Inwardly, Jasmine said no. She despised her mother. Always had. She'd seen what Mother did to the males she seduced, any sons she bore, and even her daughters. It was disgusting. But she knew she couldn't say no to Belladonna. Her eldest sister was Mother's right hand and the most powerful of her siblings.

"I do," Jasmine muttered.

"Then let big sister help you," Belladonna said in her fake sweet voice. She snapped her fingers.

Out of a smoky magical fog that appeared behind Belladonna came two figures. Both were males. One was a Werefox, and the other was an Elf. Jasmine was shocked at their gaunt forms when they kneeled on either side of her sister. When she saw their eyes, they were gray and cloudy. They stared up at Belladonna with unnatural adoration.

So, these are her latest flavors of minions. Jasmine thought bitterly. "Are they new?" she asked.

Belladonna smirked. "Yes, and the most useful I've yet to acquire. I heard through several grapevines that this head general has been giving you problems, dear sister. Ba will take his place."

"Take his place? Like, possess him?" Jasmine asked.

Belladonna tsked as if she was a toddler claiming something ridiculous was true. "Silly sister. No, Ba will take his form with one of my potions." She petted the Werefox's head mockingly. "I've already set up a place to hold the head general so Ba can help you."

"Wait, you're going to replace the head general with one of your minions? It won't work," Jasmine said.

Belladonna narrowed her eyes. "Jasmine, I'm doing you a favor. Appreciate my effort."

"What favor?" Jasmine asked, dreading the answer.

"Mother has her eye on you," Belladonna stated.

Jasmine's heart dropped. If her mother was watching, it meant more eyes were on her than before. Paranoia started to creep up the back of her mind.

"Why does Mother have her eye on me?" Jasmine asked, her voice shaking.

"There's a pest she needs to eliminate," Belladonna said vaguely. "The pest likes to slither around this city. Mother will send some followers to distract the pest so your project speeds up."

Jasmine struggled to keep her breathing regular. Her mouth was dry, her throat tight. Clearing her throat, she asked, "What about the other?"

Belladonna looked amused. "He will be used to deliver the potion to Ba from the place. He will require payment, sister."

"What kind of payment?" Jasmine asked.

Belladonna grinned manically. "The most valuable kind."

It took Jasmine a moment to realize what she was saying. "Souls?" she gasped.

Belladonna nodded. "You have one million enslaved to you. Mother was pleased when she heard that."

Jasmine started to shake uncontrollably. "I can't give away souls like that!" she shouted.

Belladonna glared at her. "Why, I'll be. Little sister is being selfish."

"You're the selfish one thinking I'd give you souls that I earned if you so-called helped me with a project I didn't ask help on," Jasmine snarled.

Belladonna suddenly smiled. One that was filled with pride. It startled Jasmine. She had never seen that look on her eldest sister's face before. It terrified her.

"There's the little witch we all knew was hidden there," Belladonna purred. "Very well. I won't touch your souls. However, he will need to be paid in either sex or blood. He's good doing both."

Jasmine resisted the urge to vomit. "I'll give him blood. How much is the payment?"

"Half a cup usually does it. He has a thing for licking. Be sure to make it somewhere pleasurable," Belladonna replied with a smirk.

"Noted," Jasmine said, looking at the Elf minion with disdain. Seeing Belladonna's look, she reluctantly said, "Thank you, eldest sister."

"I'm eager to see your project grow, little sister. Do save a few souls for me. I have several rituals I want to try out," Belladonna said as if they were discussing school subjects. In a swirl of gray fog, Belladonna and her two minions disappeared.

Jasmine sat there in shock. When everything became crystal clear, she put her face in her hands and wept.

"Come on, just a little more. You're almost there," Nurse van Gogh gently encouraged her at the end of the ramp. Ami forced her weak legs to move. Her arms shook from supporting her body weight. Inch by inch, she grunted.

Left. Right. Left. Right.

"Only a few inches more," Nurse van Gogh said excitedly. "Come on, come on—"

"Will you shut up!" Ami shrieked. She was already feeling bad when she woke up. The male nurse's peppy attitude and Royian accent grated her nerves.

He merely smiled. When Ami reached the end, she collapsed into the nurse's arms.

"That wasn't so bad, was it?" Nurse van Gogh asked smugly.

"You're annoying," Ami snapped waspishly.

With ease, the nurse picked her up, bridal style. Ami didn't care at that point. Her entire body was sore. Her arms and legs shook from the exertion. Nurse van Gogh exited the physical therapy room and entered the hospital room. He gently placed Ami on the bed.

"You're making great progress," Nurse van Gogh stated. "I'm surprised it's already been five months since we've started."

"It helps that I can eat and not vomit all the time," Ami replied.

"And you don't have to be bandaged all the time. I'm curious about that burn balm the slaves put on you," Nurse van Gogh said.

Lius' balm worked wonders. Ami saw herself for the first time last week after Reshmi commented on how well the skin was healing. The healing hid how awful her original injuries had been. She could detect where the deep burns seared parts of her skull, and her left horn was gone entirely. Due to the missing horn, her sense of balance was off, and she suffered from random dizzy spells. Her left eye was a lost cause. The demon fire burned it to ash, according to the new doctor.

Dr. Elderflower was a brown Werewolf. His presence was warmer than Dr. Moore's, and the new nurses, two female Elves, were nicer and less prone to gossip. She mostly interacted with Dr. Elderflower and Nurse van Gogh.

Nurse van Gogh was an intern from Roy. Ami was surprised, given Leila's notes of skepticism about magic. The nurse was a unique Werefox. Black fur covered most of his body. Reddish, almost blond fur stood out around his ears and hands. Whiskey-colored eyes watched Ami closely as she drank water with shaky hands. He wore light blue nurse scrubs.

"Your hair is growing back. Was it always white?" Nurse van Gogh asked.

"Yes. I hate how it itches," Ami grumbled. Her hair felt like she got a fresh buzz cut.

Nurse van Gogh chuckled. "It could be worse."

"If you jinx me, I'll have your tongue, nurse," Ami growled.

"Please call me Theo."

Ami studied him. He was a few years older than her, around eighteen or nineteen. She didn't dare form a Bond with him. He was her physical therapist, and his internship was only for a year. She didn't want to form another friendship that was long distance. Speaking of which, she hadn't heard anything from Leila. Despite writing in the worst handwriting to explain what happened, Leila was silent. Usually, it took at least a week and a half to get a reply. Ami wondered if the shock of the Bond snapping made Leila reconsider their friendship. A piece of her heart felt hollow. She missed Leila.

"Amaranth? Are you all right?" Theo asked.

"Just missing my best friend," Ami admitted.

"Who's your friend?" Theo asked.

Something caught Ami's attention at the entrance of the hospital.

"Sal!" Ami called out. The Werewolf had somehow gotten taller and bulkier, yet maintained the softness of his face.

"Ami," Salvador grinned when he got close to her bed. "How are you?"

"Better. Not great," Ami answered.

"You'll get there," Salvador said encouragingly. "When I came in, I saw you walking, so that's progress, right?"

Ami huffed. "Not enough."

"You're improving every day," Theo said. "I'm surprised

you're able to speak, much less walk."

"Why?" Salvador asked, looking at the Werefox.

"From my experience, People who are severely burned by fire don't recover as fast as Amaranth has. She's defying everything I was taught," Theo answered with a wide smile, showing teeth.

"And is that a bad thing?" Salvador asked defensively. Ami glanced between the two. Why is there tension all of a sudden?

"Oh, quite the contrary. She's a *trilliaisha* in my book."

Salvador stared at him blankly. He glanced at Ami. "He says I'm a walking miracle."

"Oh."

"By the way, I'm Theo van Gogh, Amaranth's physical therapist." The Werefox extended his right hand.

Salvador awkwardly shook it. "I'm Salvador Dali, Ami's friend."

"Nice to meet you, Salvador," Theo said, busying himself again.

"What have you been up to?" Ami asked.

Salvador grabbed a nearby chair and sat down, telling her what happened and why he hadn't been able to visit the last few months. She smiled when he complained about Pitir getting in trouble and the entire dorm being punished. He told her more about his added responsibilities of being a kitchen hand.

"Are you learning any new recipes?" Ami asked eagerly.

Salvador's ears went up and down. "I'm learning how to make food I'm familiar with. Does that answer?" He grinned at Ami's nod. "I really like being in the kitchen, but I'd rather scout. I like being outside and tracking."

"You're good at it," Ami commented. Theo handed her a fresh cup of water. Ami murmured thanks before sipping on it.

Salvador blushed. "Only because you taught me some tricks."

"But you used them," Ami insisted. "I can tell and show

you many things, but it's meaningless if"—she paused to sip her water—"you decide not to use it."

Salvador blushed dark pink.

"How long are you here for?" Ami asked.

Salvador grinned. "I managed to get three days off. I'll be staying with the Knights if they'll have me."

"I'm sure they will. I believe they have a few spare cots in the back," Ami said.

The Dragons brought dinner, somehow knowing Salvador was present. Theo chatted about medical articles he had read and found fascinating. Ami and Salvador nodded and hummed politely in the right places. Ami and Salvador passionately talked about training and sword techniques. Theo repeatedly interrupted with questions. Salvador started to look annoyed. Ami tried to remain patient and answer Theo's questions. Ami switched the topic to books. Theo started to rave about medical textbooks while Ami inwardly groaned. Did the Werefox not read anything else? From Salvador's exasperated look, he felt the same.

Ami finally found a piece of literature they could talk about that wasn't in a medical book. A well-known play, *The Bard's Flute*, was Royian in origin but gained some popularity in Rascu. Salvador was also familiar with the play. They talked about the story, their favorite characters, and their favorite and least favorite scenes and debated about how the play should've ended. The original play was a happy ending with the main character, Travis, ending up with the female lead, Penelope.

Ami argued that Travis didn't deserve a happy ending due to his horrible treatment of his ex-fiancée, Viola. Salvador agreed for the most part, except he believed Viola should've gotten her revenge by falling in love with Travis' best friend, Victor. Theo agreed that Travis was a piece of trash of a character who didn't deserve to be happy. However, he thought the play would've been better if Penelope and Viola had become best friends and ditched Travis. Ami was intrigued by both males' different interpretations.

Dr. Elderflower cleared his throat. He tapped his wristwatch with a deadpan look. Realizing the time, both males apologized.

Ami waved them off. "I enjoyed our discussion. Will you be here tomorrow, Sal?"

"Of course. I'm here for you," Salvador grinned widely.

"We have physical therapy tomorrow, Amaranth," Theo reminded her.

"Party pooper," Ami grumbled.

"What time is the physical therapy?" Salvador asked.

"Usually after breakfast," Ami answered before Theo. "It'll last until lunch. I'm hoping to walk on my own tomorrow."

"You can't push yourself too hard, Amaranth. It'll undo all the progress you've made," Theo warned.

"See what I have to put up with?" Ami said teasingly, pointing to a pouting nurse.

Ami laid back in her bed when both males left. She closed her eye. The glowing white light of her magic made Ami smile. The one good thing about her death was that it got rid of the shadow threads holding her magic down. The ball of magic was small but growing each day. She couldn't wait until she regained her strength. Already, she recovered much of her memories of her learning and practicing magic with her cousins and tutors. Now when she thought of her cousins, mother, and brothers, their facial features and voices came to her clearly. She cried for a long time when she recalled them. Parts of her heart that she didn't know were hollow, filled with love and longing for their company.

The next day's therapy was promising. Ami managed several steps without holding onto the bars before collapsing. Theo scolded her for pushing herself too far, but Ami was too happy to listen. Salvador joined them for lunch. Ami immediately sensed something was wrong.

"Did you sleep all right, Sal?" Ami asked.

"Um, I guess. I've never slept in the Knight's Quarters before, so it was a lot of new smells and sounds to get used to," Salvador said half-heartedly.

Ami sensed he was omitting something. She glanced at his hands. The rings weren't glowing, but she saw markings on his fingers that weren't there before.

"I walked several steps by myself," Ami said proudly.

"Really? That's great. Soon you'll be making the Knights run laps like before," Salvador grinned.

"Hmph, I doubt they miss that part of their training." Ami snorted.

"Will you continue being the Warehouse Guardian when you are released?" Salvador asked.

Ami shrugged. "That'll depend if they still want me in the military. I know Jasmine is fighting the generals to keep me here. Rikardi is siding with her as well. Don't know if there's anyone else, but I know there's opposition with me still being here."

"So, what happens if they do kick you out?" Salvador asked as if dreading the answer.

Ami let out a shaky sigh. "Then I'll go back to Vinci."

"But you don't want to go, right?" Theo asked.

Ami shook her head. "I'm not wanted there."

"Will they allow you to remain in Rascu? I don't see why they wouldn't," Salvador suggested.

"I would have to have a Noble fiancé for me to remain, and I doubt anyone would want to marry this," Ami said, pointing to her still-healing face.

"Don't sell yourself short," Theo scoffed.

"I was ugly before. Now, it's more evident," Ami said in a gloomy tone.

"You were never ugly," Salvador blurted. Ami stared at him. "You're beautiful and still are."

Ami felt shocked at the outburst. A gentle fire she hadn't

felt in a long time lit in her chest. It went to her cheeks, turning them soft pink. A shy smile made it to her lips.

"Excuse me, I have to use the washroom," Theo said abruptly, exiting the hospital room.

Ami didn't ponder on Theo's sudden departure. Salvador's compliment repeated in her head.

"I need to tell you something," Salvador said solemnly.

Ami blinked. This was the same tone he used when he first told her about the Dali curse. "I'm listening."

"I had a dream, and Conri spoke to me," Salvador said.

"He did? How? What did he say?" Ami asked urgently.

"I'm not sure how. He said he's coming soon. He's not waiting until I'm twenty-one. The one he despises is getting closer, and he wants to get rid of her," Salvador explained.

"Wait, is he talking about the witch that cursed the Dali line?" Ami asked.

Salvador shrugged. "I don't know. All I know is that he's becoming stronger."

"Who is it?" Ami asked softly.

Salvador shook his head. "He said she was the one who harmed you—"

"The one who harmed me wasn't a witch," Ami interrupted. "It was an illegal mage. Do you think maybe it wasn't a witch who cursed your family but an illegal mage?"

Salvador looked confused. "Is there a difference?"

Ami nodded. "Yes. A mage learns magic recklessly but keeps their soul. It seemed like the mage in the dorm fire was skilled enough to summon the fire demon. Maybe the mage trapped the unicorn that your ancestor stumbled upon and then cursed the late Dali heiress for interfering?"

In Ami's mind, it made more sense. From what Salvador told her, a witch trapped a unicorn, and his multiple-times-grandmother tried to free it. The witch offered a riddle, and the Dali heiress only agreed to listen to the riddle, not solve it. The Dali heiress used a powerful spell on the witch that bound the witch's power as long as the Dali line existed. The witch countered with a powerful curse that turned the Dali heir into Conri, the Great Wolf, by their twenty-first year.

It didn't make sense for the Dali curse to have been placed by a witch. One, she never heard of a witch able to capture a unicorn. Second, witches love to brag, and rumors would've spread by now. So why was this curse not well-known outside the Dali family? Surely the Dali family had allies and were aware.

"He also said you were his ally," Salvador said quietly.

"Ally?" Ami frowned, snapping out of her thoughts. "How did I become an ally to him?"

The Werewolf shrugged. "Maybe it is due to our friendship? He didn't say. But he grows impatient."

Ami hummed to herself. "This is problematic. If Conri comes before the curse states, it may do more damage to him and you."

"What kind of damage?" Salvador asked shakily.

Ami shrugged. "I don't know, and that is what concerns me. Curses have a timeline for a reason. If one tries to delay or rush it, it could do double the damage, or there may be a backup spell tagged along with it. I don't know much about the curse to see if it has such a contingency attached to it."

"I'll write to my father to arrange a time for you to meet with him and the Dali family to discuss the curse in more detail," Salvador promised.

"Ami, you need to rest," Theo said, reentering the hospital wing.

Ami sighed heavily. She couldn't wait to get out of this hospital.

"I'll go write that letter," Salvador stated.

"I'll see you for dinner." Ami flashed him a half-smile before he left.

Later, when Salvador and Theo left after eating dinner with her, a manor Dragon visited her.

"*Ya'puris*, how are you today?" he asked. The Dragon was covered in dust.

"I'm doing better. I managed to walk a few steps by myself today," Ami said proudly.

"That is good news! May I tell my brother?" the young Dragon asked excitedly.

"Yes, you may," Ami smiled. An idea came to mind. "May I ask for a favor?"

"*Ya'puris*, you have no need to ask for favors. What is your wish?" the Dragon asked.

"Tomorrow is Sal's last day before he has to return to the fort. I haven't been able to spend a lot of time with him due to my therapy. Do you think you can distract Theo tomorrow?" Ami asked.

The slave smirked mischievously. "It will be my pleasure, *ya'puris*."

Salvador's last day was filled with Ami telling him various stories without Theo interrupting. Salvador relaxed considerably the more they talked. Then Salvador had to leave.

"I can't tell you how happy I am to see you," Salvador said warmheartedly.

"I'm happy to see you too, my friend," Ami replied sincerely.

The inside of Salvador's ears turned dark pink. His brown eyes softened more. "*Mish kala'o va,*" he murmured.

Ami tilted her head. She didn't know what language he spoke. "Pardon?"

Salvador smiled mysteriously. He gently gripped her feet, gave them a firm squeeze, and left.

That was odd, Ami thought. At that moment, she wondered if she was seeing Salvador or Conri.

Ami took a moment to take several deep breaths. The morning air felt like she had reemerged from being underwater too long. She then began walking slowly out of the Inner City with the use of a walking stick. One of the Dragons had secretly carved the walking stick for her once he heard of her wanting to leave the hospital. Ami conspired with the Dragons to distract Theo so she could go to the café. She alerted the Knights as well. While she knew she had the strength to get there, she wasn't confident she would have enough to return. Even so, it would get her out of the hospital, something she desperately needed to do.

The Knights nodded and whispered blessings to her as she passed. She nodded back nervously. The idea of having her scars visible for everyone to see and whisper about made her irritated and embarrassed. She stopped in the middle of the road, struggling to stop the rush of tears threatening to fall. She had cried endlessly when she started therapy with Theo. She had cried in frustration, anger, and embarrassment. She was so tired of crying.

Finally, she made it to the café. She struggled to open the door. Chastity swiftly helped, welcoming her.

"We are so glad to see you. I'll get Logan," the Elf said giddily while Ami got comfortable at the bar. It was easier than usual. Did it shrink while she was in the hospital, or did having one eye distort her perspective? Chastity went through the door that led to the back kitchens. Ami heard her say, "Logan, we have a special guest."

Logan looked confused when he exited the kitchen with Chastity right behind him. Confusion shifted to shock when he saw Ami.

"Awesome?" he asked softly.

"Hello, Logan," Ami whispered.

Logan gazed at her with sadness. He calmly came around the bar and carefully hugged her as if she was made of glass. She noticed she was much taller than Logan now. The young

Werefox only reached her shoulder. He looked at her current state. Then he said, "You need coffee. And treats." The little Werefox then went back into the kitchens.

"Logan, do you need—" Chastity started to ask.

"I got it, Ma!" Logan said irritably.

Chastity raised her hands in defeat. "He's got it, I guess."

Ami smiled. "I'm glad he's doing okay. I apologize for not writing lately."

Chastity shook her head. "Don't worry about it. We knew you were injured badly. We wanted you to focus on getting well."

"How are you and Electra?" Ami asked.

Chastity gladly told her how the café was getting more popular. She thanked her for sending Shayne to help out. Ami waved off her thanks. Chastity then told her of the different coffees Logan has experimented with and came up with a new one he called Caramel Floating Mocha.

"That sounds heavenly," Ami moaned. "I haven't been allowed sweets since I woke up. My therapist and doctor have boring palettes."

"I'm gonna fix you right up," Logan announced, cautiously carrying a steaming cup of coffee to her. "This is a new creation I call Awesome's Symphony Number One."

Ami inhaled deeply. "I smell chocolate, nutmeg, cinnamon ... and peanut butter?"

Logan grinned. "See, Awesome? You're the only one who can guess my ingredients just by smelling them."

"It's a gift." Ami took a small sip. The sugar rushed up and down her tongue and the sides of her mouth. The feeling was exhilarating. "Logan, I love you."

"I love you too, Awesome. I'm gonna get your treats," Logan said, heading back into the kitchens. He soon reappeared with a plate piled with blueberry muffins, iced cinnamon scones, and a large piece of breakfast casserole with eggs, potatoes, and cheese. The trio sat around the bar, talking and laughing.

It was the first time since she woke up that Ami felt truly alive. She felt her Bond with Logan reconnect, and it flared with happiness. Ami basked in the feeling. Her cheeks soon started to hurt from smiling so much. Electra came downstairs for her cup of coffee. She greeted Ami politely and asked how her recovery was going. Ami was pleased the Werewolf was civil with her.

After several hours, Electra went back upstairs with her third cup of coffee. Chastity and Logan went into the kitchens to get ready for the lunch rush. Ami happily drank her fifth cup of Logan's experiments and ate everything that was on the plate. Her stomach ached badly, but she didn't care. For once, she was happy. Of course, that meant it was short-lived.

"Amaranth!" Theo growled as he stalked inside the café.

She sighed loudly. "Of course, the party pooper has to come now."

"Excuse me," Theo said, nearly hysterical, "I have been searching for you all morning! The Dragons distracted me for two hours, then I found you missing from your room, and Dr. Elderflower had no idea where you were. Then when I tried to get help from the Knights, they literally sent me on a wild goose chase around the city! So, excuse me if I'm not happy to see you right now."

"Can I help you, sir?" Chastity suddenly appeared.

"No, I finally found my wayward patient," Theo said, glaring at Ami.

She pointed to him. "This is Nurse van Gogh."

"Greetings, sir. Would you like a cup of coffee?" Chastity offered.

"No, thank you," Theo said, barely polite. To Ami, he asked, "Why are you here?"

"I had to see someone very important to me," Ami said.

"Who?"

"The love of my life," Ami answered, drinking the rest of her coffee so she didn't laugh at Theo's incredulous face.

"And who is that?" Theo asked quietly.

"That's me!" Logan announced, coming out from the kitchen.

Theo stared at Logan. He whipped his head towards Ami. "You're having me on."

"No, he truly is the love of my life," Ami stated. "There is no one who can make coffee like he can, and that is my heart in a nutshell."

"Would you like a cup?" Logan asked, replacing Ami's empty cup with a new one. This one was plain but still smelled delicious.

Ami reached for the new cup. Theo quickly grabbed it and held it away from her. "How many have you had?" he asked.

"It doesn't matter. I want my coffee," Ami said, trying to grab it. Theo kept moving it away from her. Frustration coiled in her gut. She wanted her coffee. She forced her claws out in her left hand and held them under Theo's throat. He immediately went still. The tension in the café was palatable.

"Do not ever touch my food or drink without permission again. Therapist or not, I will slit your throat," she growled. Theo gave her coffee back. Ami huddled around it, glaring at Theo. He wisely moved one seat over to give her space.

"Dude, even I know not to do that," Logan commented. Shaking his head, he went back into the kitchens.

When Ami was done with her coffee, she conceded to go back to the Inner City with Theo. She hugged Chastity. Logan held onto the longest, not willing to let her go. Chastity managed to convince him to release her. Ami grabbed her walking stick and walked with Theo back to the Inner City. Theo talked endlessly about various medical articles he had read. Ami nodded and hummed in the right places. As they walked past the Knights, she saw their mischievous looks toward Theo. Ami hid her own smile, knowing they were the ones who misled the nurse.

By the time they arrived at the hospital, Ami was exhausted, and her stomach ached horribly. Theo scolded her for eating so many sweets. She ignored him.

It was worth it.

CHAPTER 2

Today was the first anniversary. Rain poured from the skies. Ami stood in the cemetery constructed by the Knights at the opposite end of the Inner City. It was an isolated corner that even the horses dared not step near. In front of her was a large tombstone. Etched on the white granite were the fourteen names of the cadets she failed to save. Her tears mixed in the rain as she stared, wondering how she could've saved them.

I should've been more aware. I should've sensed the mage before they began to cast spells. I should've told Egan to distract them. I should've—

A heavy coat gently covered her shoulders. A familiar smell of hay, tea, and ink filled her nose. She looked up. Rikardi stood beside her with an umbrella, his trademark frown on his face. The umbrella didn't cover both of them. His crisp white shirt began to soak.

"Thank you," Ami whispered.

"It's not your fault," Rikardi replied.

"I should've done more," Ami retorted bitterly.

"You saved more lives with your actions than if you decided not to do anything. The fact you did do all you could in your power speaks volumes to the males," Rikardi explained passionately. Before she could retort, he added, "And you made me proud."

Ami flinched, staring at the Centaur in shock. The gentle vibrations from the Bond proved the general's words were genuine. Emotions she couldn't name filled her chest and crawled up her throat, making her cry more. Rikardi switched his hand grip on the umbrella and rested a large hand on Ami's bony shoulder. She wiped her wet face with her hands.

"Thank you," she whispered shakily.

Rikardi hummed. They stood there for a while, lost in their own thoughts.

"Are you ready to go inside?" Rikardi asked softly. "There is something I wish to speak to you about."

"I need to change clothes," Ami pointed out. "And you need a fresh shirt."

"The Dragons seem to have an endless supply of your clothing in the mansion. You can change there," Rikardi said disapprovingly.

"They insist on making up for the outfits I lost in the fire," Ami said with a lopsided smile.

They left the monument and went to the mansion. One of the soldiers guarding the inside lobby provided towels. Ami watched as Rikardi wiped off the rain and mud gathered in his front hooves. He paused, looking at his back hooves.

"May I assist?" Ami offered.

Rikardi hesitated. Conflict flickered in his green eyes before nodding. Ami took the towel he was using and copied his movements on his back hooves. She handed their soiled towels back to the soldier. They headed up the stairs and into the sewing room.

"*Ya'puris*, how glad we are to see you," Reshmi greeted her.

"Hello, Reshmi. Sela. Avani. Callie. Patti. Fran," Ami greeted back, nodding at each Person she addressed. Each Dragon curtsied when she said their name. "I need fresh clothes, please."

"You need a hot bath," Sela scolded.

"General Rikardi also needs fresh clothes," Ami added, gesturing to the imposing Centaur behind her.

"*Ya'puris*, please follow me. General, please go with Avani and Callie," Reshmi ordered politely.

Ami felt a lopsided smile form as the two female Dragons tried to strip the blushing Centaur of his wet clothes. She could feel his hot embarrassment through the Bond, and his booming protests echoed in her ears. Behind a dressing screen, Ami struggled to get her wet clothes off. Each piece fought vigorously to stay. Their defeat was a satisfying wet flop on the floor.

"You have grown much taller, *ya'puris*," Reshmi commented as she looked at two shirts.

"How much?" Ami asked.

"At least a foot," Reshmi replied.

"Really?" Ami gasped. *So it wasn't my depth perception being off.* "Can you measure me and tell me how tall I am now?"

"Of course," Reshmi said happily.

Reshmi grabbed her measuring tape. Ami stiffened in anticipation as Reshmi carefully measured her.

"You are currently five feet, seven inches," Reshmi announced.

Ami gaped. What else did the shadow threads hold back?

"At least I'm not the shortest Person anymore," Ami said.

"At this rate, you'll probably grow another foot when you reach maturity," Reshmi mentioned.

"Wait, what?" Ami sputtered.

"Dress as I explain," Reshmi ordered, handing her individual pieces. Ami obeyed, keeping her attention on the elder. "Whatever happened before the fire affected your growth. We were getting worried that you weren't maturing at a normal rate. Now, your body is playing catchup. If you have any questions about your body, please ask us. We will answer all your questions."

Ami smiled as she put on the last piece of clothing, a purple shirt.

"I will let you know if I feel strange," Ami promised.

Reshmi bowed with a smile. They left the dressing screen

to see Rikardi blushing darkly in fresh clothes and the Dragons giggling madly. Rikardi swiftly rushed Ami out while Reshmi started to scold the Dragons in their native language. They entered Rikardi's office.

"Has Jasmine told you about your new title?" Rikardi asked as he sat behind his desk.

"No. All I've heard was her dedication to the new dorms," Ami said, sitting in the opposite chair.

Rikardi sighed. "I'm not surprised. The meeting was late last night, and she barely got in the room."

"The head general likes to keep things close to the chest," Ami commented.

Rikardi narrowed his eyes at her. "Be careful with your words. The meeting was about you."

"I'm hot gossip."

"Tso wanted to deport you," Rikardi said solemnly. Ami stiffened in her chair. "I argued against him, as did Jasmine. I was surprised that Lee also argued in your defense."

"That's interesting." Ami nodded. She never interacted with the Werebobcat or knew his motivations. "Did he say why?"

"He argued that having physical scars is not a valid excuse to deport someone, especially since you risked your life for the cadets. He also said if we got rid of every soldier who obtained a scar from performing their duty, there wouldn't be a military," Rikardi explained. "I agreed with him. Jasmine also argued that your actions were what Tso wanted since he helped you obtain the title of Warehouse Guardian. She questioned his motives of advancing her military campaign only to sabotage her."

Ami whistled. Jasmine was blatantly accusing Tso of treason. Bold but a weak attack on the head general.

"Then what happened?" Ami asked.

"After a lot of yelling back and forth, we finally agreed. You will not be deported," Rikardi said. Ami relaxed. He continued, "You will now report to General Mason as Captain. Congratulations."

"You don't sound pleased," Ami said.

"I have my own issues with Mason. Hopefully, he won't project them onto you," Rikardi said mysteriously.

"When do I report to him?" Ami asked.

"He's supposed to send for you in a few days," Rikardi said.

"Who will replace me as Warehouse Guardian?" Ami asked.

Rikardi frowned. "I haven't heard of any nominations. Once I know, you will be informed."

"Thank you for informing me. How are you these days?" Ami asked.

Rikardi blinked at the casual tone. "I still haven't found the Person who killed the previous doctor and nurses. It's very frustrating."

"Have you tried asking the Dragons? Perhaps they noticed something odd," Ami suggested.

"I have," Rikardi sighed. "They claim to have seen nothing."

"Do you doubt them?" Ami asked.

"I think they know something, but are not willing to share. It may be the slave Bond acting up," Rikardi reasoned.

"I can ask," Ami offered.

"No, that is not needed. I will submit my report to Tso and watch for anything suspicious," Rikardi said. He looked exhausted.

"Is there I can help you with?" Ami asked.

"Focus on your health and running. I noticed you managed to run around the Inner City once," Rikardi said.

"Yes, and I didn't feel like I was about to die," Ami said offhandedly.

Rikardi flinched. "Don't overdo it. Dismissed."

Ami saluted and left the office. On her way out, she asked the Dragons to keep an eye on Rikardi and provide him with soothing tea.

Two days later, Mason summoned Ami to his office. It was four doors down from Rikardi's and surprisingly bare. The bookshelves didn't have many books or knickknacks. His desk wasn't swamped with paperwork. It reminded Ami more of the hospital than an office.

Both Rikardi and Mason are relatively new generals. Why is Rikardi allowed to take more responsibility and not Mason? Ami wondered.

She saluted when she came to Mason's desk. Mason was intently reading a rather thick document, not even looking up. Ami stayed in her position. When Mason finally looked up, he nearly jumped out of his chair.

"Son of a—" he yelped. He stared at Ami incredulously. "How long have you been standing there?"

"For approximately three minutes, sir," Ami answered.

Mason was still breathing hard. "At ease," he muttered.

Ami smoothly transitioned to the *ruwa* pose, a stiffer version of the *slucha* pose.

"Your new title is now Captain Rose, and you will report to me," Mason started awkwardly. Ami wondered if this was his first time doing this. "You will be over the Low Ring Unit. Your goal is to bring them to par with other units. Any questions?"

A sense of dread pooled in Ami's stomach. "How long do I have to obtain this goal, sir?" Ami asked.

"You will have three months," Mason answered. "Any other questions?"

"What exactly do I need to train the soldiers in?"

"Respect for ranks. Obeying leadership. Basic survival skills. The first two are the most important." Mason studied her with a mixture of conflicting emotions. Ami didn't care enough to analyze them.

"Yes, sir," Ami said blandly.

"They will be arriving in three days. Once everyone is accounted for, you may proceed with your training. Dismissed," Mason said, staring at Ami.

Ami saluted and left without a word. She went to her room to reflect on her new assignment and title. Mason didn't trust her at all. He appeared to believe that she brainwashed the

Knights with her training. She was not surprised. There were city soldiers that felt the same way. What worried her was the unit she was assigned.

The Low Ring Unit was something no Rascal soldier ever wanted to be a part of. It was the lowest of the low in the military. No matter their rank or reputation, if a soldier was put in that unit, they were about to get kicked out.

He wants me to train the worst of the worst. Ami concluded. She wasn't confident. There were reasons why certain soldiers were placed there. *I guess I'll find out soon.*

Ami rubbed her temples. It was far worse than she had ever experienced, even in Vinci. The training was almost over, and the reports weren't glowing with improvement. She glanced around their camp outside of Talient. There were fifteen soldiers in total. Their ages ranged between nineteen and twenty-two, but their emotional maturities were stuck at age six. Three argued about the correct way to gather firewood, five gossiped like females, and two huddled around the fire while glancing nervously at Ami. She didn't know where the remaining soldiers were. At this point, she stopped trying to find them all. It was like herding squirrels high on *pow-wow*. As she was filled with gloom, she couldn't decide if the males badly wanted to leave the military or if they were just plain dumb. Here's what she had to deal with:

They didn't even make a fire on their first night due to constant arguments about the "proper" way of gathering firewood. Ami spent the first half of the night breaking up fights over this topic. It was a topic that repeated each night to the very end. On the fifth night, Ami and two others who weren't part of the debate managed to gather firewood and start a fire. She directed them to boil the water collected from the creek for at least twenty minutes before adding soup ingredients. They looked at her like she was crazy. All who ate the soup got diarrhea for two days. Ami was the only one who didn't eat it, due to its funny smell. She gathered luria herbs and made teas for the ailing soldiers. Unfortunately, they didn't learn from this lesson and repeated it thrice.

They absolutely sucked at hunting. All of them were awful and refused to listen to Ami's advice or orders. Ami only worked with one soldier who actually asked Ami for help. The problem was he was often too impatient and timed his pounces too early or too late. Ami tried her hardest to help him. Unfortunately, his attention span was so short and his hunting skills were so bad that the prey could be a statue, and the soldier would still somehow miss. Still, since he kept coming to her for help, she freely gave it. He sat near the fire glancing at her nervously.

The other soldier near the fire was an Elf with thick glasses, a weak build, and a timid personality. Ami was astonished he lasted as long as he had. After the first soup incident, the Elf couldn't even muster enough words to ask about the herbs Ami used. Ami waited patiently until the Elf blurted out quite loudly that he wanted to learn from her. The other soldiers, except the soldier who asked for hunting advice, immediately shunned the timid Elf. Ami took him under her wing. Like the hunting soldier, he couldn't find the right herbs and often gathered weeds or other plants instead of herbs. Ami's head throbbed.

If that wasn't enough, she tried to teach them wards. Wards weren't seen as "true magic" by the Rascals due to the lack of spellcasting. Wards were simply runes etched on stone and placed in specific arrays or patterns to surround what needed protection. The different designs and runes determine the strength of the ward and the type of protection. It was easier than spellcasting magic, and almost anyone could learn the bare basics. The soldiers rejected her offer to teach them, calling it "a cheap trick." Ami created basic wards each night to alert her of anyone approaching from outside the ward stones and of anything entering their camp. This led to another incident, with Ami nearly beating each soldier to a bloody pulp.

It started roughly the third week of their training. Ami forced three soldiers to complete night duty each night and rotate. Mostly it was Ami slapping them awake when she caught them sleeping. She was patrolling when she sensed something passing over the ward stones. She carefully made her way to the disturbance. A large brown bear waddled close to the camp, sniffing the ground. Ami mentally groaned. Someone forgot to put their food away properly and attracted a predator. Thankfully, the bear seemed satisfied with whatever had been left out and left the camp without incident.

Ami became suspicious as the bear continued to follow them, no matter the distance they covered during the day, as pitiful as it was. The males were in awful shape and hated to run. Ami whipped the back of their legs with her tail to get them going. She sometimes wondered if she was a captain or a cattle rancher. Night after night, the same bear somehow found them and ate food left out. Ami's suspicions were confirmed when she spotted one of the soldiers purposely leaving out food before returning to his tent. Ami confronted him before he could enter.

"What do you think you're doing?" Ami demanded coldly.

"I was going to sleep," the soldier replied.

"And the food you left outside?" Ami asked.

"I didn't leave any food," the soldier denied.

"Look around you. Who else would leave food out for the bear?" Ami barely contained a sneer.

"You've seen it too?" the soldier asked excitedly.

Ami wasn't amused. "Of course I have. I patrol every night.

Why are you feeding such a dangerous, wild animal?"

"It's not dangerous!" The soldier said defiantly. "He's a cuddly teddy bear."

Ami stared at him. *He can't be this stupid,* she thought. "You will stop feeding the bear this instant. Go and dispose of the food properly."

"Or what?"

"You can be fed to the bear, and I will write to your family about your stupidity," Ami said deadpan.

"But it's not just me!" the soldier yelled.

A migraine began to settle between Ami's eye and nose. "Who else is feeding the bear?"

"Everyone pitches in a piece of their food. The poor thing must be starving," the soldier lamented.

Her anger couldn't be contained. Ami let out a loud roar, waking every soldier. All of them scrambled out of their tents, scared to death. After rounding them up, Ami laid into them so severely that they all burst into tears. She was beyond caring at that point.

They were heading back to Talient today. It filled Ami with relief and dread. She failed the mission and didn't know how Mason would twist this into deporting her for poor leadership. She wrote the truth and wished for the best. When they arrived in Talient, Ami was feeling defeated. The Knights gave her concerned looks.

I must look awful, Ami thought bitterly. She'd rather face a pack of skells in a blizzard than turn in her reports to Mason. *Put your nice panties on and get it over with,* Ami encouraged herself.

She instructed the unit to wait outside the mansion. No doubt they would disobey and wander around. She was too exhausted to worry about that. She entered the mansion and went to Mason's office. The young Werewolf glanced up when she knocked and motioned her to enter.

"You're back on time," Mason commented.

"It was the time limit you granted me," Ami answered.

Mason's ears twitched. "Your reports?"

"Here, sir." She handed him a thick wad of paper.

"That's ... a large report," Mason said.

"I'm a meticulous writer, sir. May I ask where the unit can stay while we await further orders?" Ami asked.

"I believe the Knights have extra cots. Talk to them. Dismissed." Mason waved her off.

Ami saluted and exited the mansion. The scene that greeted her made the dread and hopelessness sink her stomach to her knees. The Knights, led by Michael, surrounded the unit like prison guards.

"Who are you to keep us here? We are free to roam if we wish!" one loudmouthed soldier shouted.

"Your captain clearly gave you an order. We are helping you obey it," Michael replied through gritted teeth.

"Why, you—" The soldier started until he noticed Ami. "Captain, help us!"

"Oh, now I'm your captain?" Ami drawled. She asked the Knights, "Where can the unit stay while we await further orders?"

"You can stay in your room, Captain Rose," Michael said respectfully. "However," he said as he glared at the soldiers, "they still need to learn how to live outside like everyone else."

Ami shook her head. Her head was still pounding. "You heard him. Follow his orders," Ami stated.

"But you're our captain—" another soldier protested.

"The Inner City is run by the Knights. Master-Leader For'une has the authority, not me. Good night," Ami said. She left for her room. As soon as she plopped onto her bed, she blacked out.

For the next three days, she refused to leave her room. She didn't have the energy or the motivation. Even eating what the Dragons made didn't appeal to her. Nothing the Knights or the Dragons said would encourage her to get up. Only Mason's summons got her up. She forced herself to take a shower and dress. Her limbs felt like she was in a bottle of molasses. Gloom filled her chest. Walking mechanically, she made her way to the mansion, ignoring the Knights' looks as she passed. Mason looked alarmed when she entered his office.

He stared at her saluted form for a long while. Clearing his throat, he said, "At ease."

Ami obeyed, forcing down a sigh.

"I've read your report," Mason said slowly, as if carefully choosing his words. Ami remained silent. She stared at the left corner of Mason's chair. It was *fascinating*. "Your attention to detail is refreshing. It gives a clearer picture of the different scenarios, and I appreciated the individual reports on each soldier," Mason chatted.

Just get to the part where you want to deport me. Ami thought bitterly.

"However, I will say I'm disappointed. The mission was a failure," Mason stated. "I will discuss your performance with the other generals to determine where to go. Any questions?"

"No, sir," Ami answered shakily. She was barely holding in tears.

"Dismissed."

Ami saluted and left the mansion. She exited the Inner City. The café was empty despite being lunch. Chastity came from the kitchens to greet her, but stopped when she saw Ami's tearful face.

"Little flower, what happened?" Chastity asked, going over to her. The Elf embraced Ami. When she did that, the floodgates opened. All the stress, frustration, and fear flooded out. Moments later, Logan joined the hug. The Bond pulsed with concern. A warm hand gently pressed on her back.

Ami pulled back to wipe her face. Hiccups squeaked out of her lips. Logan wrapped his arms around her more securely, gazing at her with puppy eyes. Electra carefully removed her hand from her back. The Werewolf was frowning.

"Let's get coffee, Awesome," Logan said softly.

Ami could only nod. Anxiety swirled in her head and chest. Chastity guided her to her usual seat while Logan went into the kitchens. Electra sat next to Ami at the bar. Ami struggled to hold in the remaining tears. Logan came out with a steaming cup of coffee. It smelled like pumpkin. The familiarity of it calmed her some. Her hands trembled as she carefully took a sip.

"Thank you," she said in a watery tone.

"What happened?" Electra asked. "This is the first time you've lost your composure."

Ami told them everything she had to endure the past three months. Electra growled and muttered curses under her breath. Chastity paled in horror. Logan was appalled and swore to serve them the worst coffee.

"Don't damage your reputation for them," Ami said softly.

"It's not my fault if a sardine came to life and jumped into the coffee cup or the fact a jaja pepper happened to follow it," Logan said darkly.

"Isn't a jaja pepper a little too harsh, Logan?" Chastity asked.

"I don't think a plant that tastes like a spicy pile of dung is too harsh," Logan countered.

"Logan!" Chastity scolded.

"Logan, you will not serve any coffee of that sort to our guests, no matter who they are. Understand?" Electra said, her voice firm.

"I can in my dreams," Logan said stubbornly.

"Just don't cross the line," Electra warned. Logan retreated to the kitchens.

"It's just ..." Ami paused, trying to find the right words. "I feel like I can't catch a break. Even though training the Knights was a pleasure, I'm still not taken seriously."

"What do you have to do to be accepted?" Chastity asked.

Ami sighed. "I don't know, and I'm too tired to care right now. I'm thinking of quitting."

"You can come and work for us," Electra offered immediately.

"Thank you, but it's more complicated than that," Ami replied.

"Why?" Chastity asked.

"I'm Vincian. I can't stay in Rascu unless I'm engaged to a Rascal noble or in the military. The only reason I've managed to stay out of the spotlight until Talient was due to my guardian being a Rascal citizen," Ami explained. A brief memory of Blijing popped into her mind.

She remembered when they were running away from Vinci, and Ami asked Blijing where they were going.

"We're going to Rascu, Amissa," Blijing answered.

"Vincians aren't welcome there," Ami pointed out.

"I am a citizen there, so no worries," Blijing retorted with a wink.

"Why don't you apply for citizenship?" Electra's voice broke through the memory.

"Pardon?" Ami asked.

"You can apply for citizenship at the local police department. It'll take about a year, but will buy you time until you decide what you want to do," Electra explained.

A tiny blossom of hope helped some of the gloomy fog lessen in her chest. "Thank you for listening and helping," Ami said. "I must look awful."

"No, no, dear," Chastity said, covering Ami's hands. "Everyone reaches a breaking point. There's no shame in crying out your emotions when they become overwhelming."

"Again, thank you." Ami blushed. "Logan!"

The Werefox poked his head out. "Yes, Awesome?"

She raised her mug like a beer pint. "More of your amazing coffee, please."

Logan grinned. "On it!"

Ami drank two more cups of coffee, feeling better with each flavor. Her stomach growled loudly. Without asking, Chastity made her a turkey sandwich. Ami devoured it. She helped clean the dishes and wiped down the tables and bar. Electra, Chastity, and Logan gave her long hugs. Ami was shocked when Bonds with Chastity and Electra developed right before her. The females didn't show any surprise. Logan's hug was the tightest. The Bond vibrated with concern, affection, and hope. Ami pulsed back her gratefulness. He finally released her, satisfied.

Ami exited the café and walked to the police department. Unlike Nephele, Talient had four police buildings, one located in each district. Ami half-wondered how territorial they were regarding crimes committed in areas where the lines blurred. Entering the Spring District's police station, she glanced around. A bored secretary filed his nails in the reception area. To the left was a hallway with doors on each side and a door at the end of the hall. To the right of the reception area were several benches occupied by troubled individuals. Another reception area, more secured with double-paned glass and slits just large enough to slide papers through, sat next to a set of large double-locked doors. Ami wondered if it led to the local jail.

"Lady Rose?" a familiar warm voice asked.

Ami turned to the voice. It was Chief Marwen from Nephele. The police chief hadn't changed except for a few more worn lines under his eyes. He came from the hallway left of the reception. He stared at her face in shock.

"Let's talk in my office," Chief Marwen said shortly.

Ami followed the Elf down the left hallway to the door at the end. Inside was a large room with offices around the sides and cubicles in the middle. Chief Marwen expertly weaved in and around the noisy room until they reached his office. Ami noticed it was smaller than the one in Nephele and sparser. She sat in the available stiff chair as Chief Marwen closed the door. Only then did Ami notice how much attention they garnered from the other officers.

"Ignore them. They're nosier than my ex-wife's parents," Chief Marwen said with a wave of his hand.

"She divorced you?" Ami gasped.

"It was coming for a long time. She disapproved of my job status," Chief Marwen replied bitterly.

"But being the chief of police is one of the hardest and most honorable jobs. One doesn't get there through connections. It literally takes hard work, blood, sweat, and tears," Ami argued.

Chief Marwen smiled with a blush. "Thank you, but I'm no longer a police chief."

"Were you forced to step down?" Ami asked sadly.

"No, I went willingly," Marwen said quickly. "Being the chief was too much work, and I miss investigating crimes, so I stepped down to be a detective again."

"Are you happy?" Ami asked.

Marwen blinked. "Despite everything, yes, I am."

Ami smiled. "Congratulations."

"Thank you, but when I put you in the military, I strongly believed you would be safe. You do not look safe," Marwen said in a stern tone.

"What have you heard?" Ami asked somberly.

"Surprisingly little. It's amazing how the loose-lipped Knights suddenly can keep a secret," Marwen growled.

"Will you let me explain?" Ami asked. Her voice was quiet.

"I'm listening."

Ami started when she became the Warehouse Guardian and went on until the fire and her recovery. Marwen paled, flushed with anger, growled, cursed, nodded in approval—mostly of how Rikardi handled the cadets involved in the bleach incident—and was on the edge of his seat about her duel with the illegal mage.

"How did you fight them?" Marwen asked, leaning towards her from his desk.

"I'm not sure," Ami said honestly. "I was desperate to save Gabe, who I learned later was not in the warehouse, and I wanted to stop the *gen-gragia* from spreading further. I just forced my magic to obey and didn't really think about it."

Marwen hummed. "I suppose that makes sense. No one knows how they'll react to a dire situation until they're in it."

"That's how I lost my eye and most of my hair," Ami added.

"You're recovering well."

"I'm not doing well."

"What's going on?" Marwen asked, concerned.

Ami told him about her doomed mission and her unhappy position in the military.

"Will you return to Vinci if you resign?" Marwen asked.

"No, I want to apply for citizenship," Ami stated.

"I can help with that." Marwen nodded. Pulling a drawer, he rummaged around until he pulled out several sheets of paper and a manila folder. "The highlighted portions are the ones you fill out. Please print and don't use calligraphy. Us males need to be able to read it." He explained the last part sarcastically.

Ami pouted playfully. "Then how am I supposed to prove I'm female to Rascals?"

Marwen opened his mouth but closed it. A crooked grin grew on his lips. Ami smiled back. She filled out the paperwork accordingly. When she finished, she handed it back to Marwen. The Elf double-checked the necessary blocks.

"Everything looks in order. I will submit it first thing in the morning. It'll take at least three months to process, and then the consideration will begin," Marwen explained.

"The consideration?" Ami asked.

"The references you wrote will be interviewed, and their opinions of you will help your application process either go faster or slower, depending on the interview," Marwen replied.

"Will I know when the consideration is taking place?" Ami asked.

Marwen shook his head. "No, and the interviewees are forbidden to tell they were interviewed until your application process has been either accepted or denied."

"That's nerve-wracking," Ami commented.

"I have faith you will be accepted," Marwen said confidently. "I know of a few you referenced, and they're good People."

"Thank you, sir." Ami nodded.

"Claudius."

"Ami."

The air relaxed around them. They talked and chatted about random topics. Ami learned that Claudius had a passion for history, and they debated for several hours about the reign of Queen Leopolia and the controversy about her many lovers, rumored and verified. Ami left the police station feeling much better. When she entered the Knights' Quarters, Michael and Stan greeted her.

"Are you okay?" Stan asked.

"Do you need anything?" Michael asked.

"I'm feeling better. I think I just needed to be away today," Ami answered.

"Did you get coffee?" Michael asked.

"Yes, and that helped a lot." Ami chuckled.

"Why do you smell like smoke?" Stan asked, sniffing the air.

Ami blinked. "I'm not sure. What kind of smoke?"

"Like *rolly-polly*," Michael said, making a face.

"Isn't that what the police smoke?" Ami asked.

"How would you know that?" Michael asked suspiciously.

"How do you know *rolly-polly*?" Ami countered.

"It doesn't matter. We're just glad you're feeling better," Stan said, interrupting before an argument ensued. "Oh, your nurse is boring us to death about medical stuff."

Ami sighed. "Where is he?"

"He was looking for you. He heard some Knights talking about how you looked when you returned," Stan answered. "He's this way."

Theo was in the area where the Knights typically gathered when off shift to discuss various topics. Many looked bored with glossy eyes. They sharpened when they saw Ami.

"Captain!" they exclaimed happily. They left Theo mid-lecture to greet Ami warmly.

"Amaranth!" Theo's voice called out. The black Werefox somehow slithered his way to her. The nurse looked worried. "Are you all right?"

"I'm better now," Ami replied.

Theo didn't look convinced. "You know you can talk to me, right?"

"I'm talking right now," Ami retorted.

"Amaranth," Theo huffed.

"Captain Rose, Asher, and Gary are debating about Ruthild's poem '*The Lady in the Fruit Cart.*' Wanna join in?" a Knight asked with excitement.

"Depends. Are you debating over the possible color insinuations or that Ruthild was a horrible poet in general?" Ami asked. She started to walk to the gathering area. Theo barely managed to stay by her side.

"Captain, that is mean," an Elf Knight gasped dramatically.

"Truth hurts," Ami said deadpan.

The Knights laughed wholeheartedly. The debate continued until the topic smoothly transitioned to other literary works. Ami relaxed and joined in on the topics she was well versed in.

Maybe I'll be able to sleep tonight.

CHAPTER 3

Sela and Avani fussed over Ami's outfit while Reshmi watched with a calculating look.

"Why am I being dressed up like this?" Ami asked. The dress was fancy, with silk ribbons, see-through sleeves, and a corset. The urge to burn it was intense.

"The master ordered us to create an outfit for you for the military ball she's preparing," Reshmi explained, the calculating look not fading. Ami noted how they referred to Jasmine. Did something happen to the slave Bond?

"That's interesting," Ami muttered. *Jasmine has been busy.* "Why the dress?"

"It is the latest fashion with the Rascal Nobles," Sela said.

"It will definitely make an impact," Avani added happily.

Ami didn't feel their enthusiasm. She watched the Dragons fuss more over her in the mirror. The dress made her look young, like a doll she saw young Rascal females carry with their mothers. Her hair just covered the burns on her skull. It wasn't long enough for any hairdo needed for this type of dress. The ugly burn scar over her left eye was dark pink with specks of purple bruises that refused to heal. It stood out against her pale skin. A deep, dark circle picketed under her right eye, giving her a haunted look. She looked more like a ghost than a Person. She didn't feel pretty.

She looked hideous.

"Please take this dress off of me," Ami ordered politely.

The statement made the Dragons flinch.

"Do you not like the dress?" Reshmi asked.

"No, I don't. I'm not wearing a dress for the ball," Ami stated.

"But you have to!" Sela exclaimed. "The master ordered us to make you a dress."

"I'll talk to Jasmine. Please take this off of me. I feel a rash forming on my back," Ami urged, resisting the temptation to claw the dress apart.

The Dragons quickly took the dress off. Ami took several deep breaths. Corsets were the worst. She dressed in her comfortable clothes, thanked the Dragons, and left. She was halfway down the hall when an out-of-breath Knight ran up to her.

"Captain, I've been looking all over for you," the Knight panted.

"Take a breather, Knight," Ami ordered. The Knight nodded, taking in deep breaths. Once his breathing calmed, Ami asked, "Why were you searching for me?"

"The generals have summoned you," the Knight answered.

Dread sunk in her stomach like a weight. This was about her report and her failure. Thin threads of fear started to crawl up Ami's spine like crawling ivy. She hid her shaking hands behind her back in a false sense of calmness.

"Lead the way," Ami said, her voice wavering. If the Knight noticed her fear, he didn't comment.

He led Ami to the Council of Generals. It was the same as before. The Rascal flag appeared more prominent than what she remembered. Tso sat in the middle. The Werefox looked like he had just swallowed lemon slices on a dare. Lee looked bored. Rikardi was apprehensive. His Bond buzzed with worry.

Mason looked nervous. The faux generals weren't present. Ami wondered where they were.

"Captain Rose, you are here today concerning the mission you were ordered to complete," Tso began. "Your mission was to bring those in the Low Ring Unit back to military standards. We interviewed the soldiers and read your reports. Imagine our surprise when you tried to teach them magic." Tso paused, staring at Ami intently.

Ami stood there with a blank look. Rikardi's Bond slithered like a snake with anger. It was distracting.

After a while, Tso continued. "As a captain, you are responsible for the soldiers under your command. You failed in disciplining the soldiers. You failed to teach them respect within the ranks. You failed to teach them anything."

Each failure Tso mentioned was like a punch to her chest. *I will not cry. He doesn't deserve to see my tears.* Ami chanted in her mind, forcing her surging emotions down.

"Do you have any excuse for your failures?" Tso asked harshly.

It took Ami a moment to push her feelings down again. Rikardi's anger was boiling hot. "No, sir," Ami said so softly she could hardly hear herself.

"As expected," Tso sneered. "As such, your punishment—"

"Head General, you're being unreasonable," Mason interrupted.

Everyone stared at Mason. The Werewolf looked nervous at the attention.

"Explain, General Mason," Tso growled.

"The soldiers in the Low Ring Unit are known for lying, stealing, disrespecting others, and other despicable behaviors not upheld in the military. If the sternest, most discipline commanders with decades of experience at the forts cannot reform these soldiers, how did you expect a fresh leader to do so?" Mason asked.

"Her command of the Knights proved she can lead—" Tso

started, his voice too smooth.

"The Knights were willing to learn from Captain Rose," Rikardi interrupted. His deep voice echoed through the room. "The Knights are also the top tier of soldiers and wouldn't dare disrespect a training master or doubt her ability, especially since the head general is the one who appointed her." The glare Rikardi gave Tso could melt candles.

"I've read the reports Captain Rose wrote," Lee said. "Why didn't you assign a second-in-command to accompany her as required in our guidelines?"

"She had not earned the right to request a second-in-command—" Tso tried to argue.

"Yet, she's earned the right to lead? You can't have it both ways, Tso," Lee interrupted casually. Tso glared at the Werebobcat, his clenched hands trembling. "Captain Rose is not at fault, and you know it," Lee added with a knowing glint in his sharp amber eyes.

"Captain Rose, step outside," Tso ordered.

Ami saluted and exited, shutting the doors behind her. She felt a silencing spell cover the doors. She took a deep, shaky breath. A tear escaped her eye. She quickly wiped it away. Out of the corner of her eye, she saw movement. Coming into the hall were three People she had never expected to see again.

"Ami!" Elizabeth, Gabriella, and Isabella cried. They walked quickly towards her. Without warning, the trio aggressively hugged Ami. She fought against them, struggling to breathe.

"Let go of me," Ami managed to growl out.

The heiresses quickly obeyed. Ami stumbled back. The hallway went askew, and her sense of place shifted. Did the hallway somehow go sideways?

"Ami, are you okay?" Elizabeth asked worriedly.

"Am I standing?" Ami asked.

"Yes?" Isabella answered uncertainly.

"What's going on?" Gabriella demanded.

"Dizzy spell," Ami snapped. Her eye was closed. Her hands

began to shake. Smooth hands tried to take hers. "Don't touch me," Ami hissed. The hands left.

After a few minutes, the dizzy spell left. It left Ami feeling queasy. She wanted to return to her room and not leave her bed. Seeing the heiresses still there, she took a moment to look at them. Their hair was much longer. When under the Oath, their hair remained crudely cut in the boyish hairstyle. They wore simple dresses and heels.

"Your hair is long," Ami stated.

"Yeah, we've been speculating about that," Elizabeth said, twirling a blond strand with her fingers.

"I want to cut it off again," Gabriella grumbled.

"I like my hair long," Isabella said defensively.

"I don't want it as short as it was before, but I definitely don't want it long like it was when we were in school," Elizabeth said.

"I'm just glad mine can grow," Ami added.

"It's growing quite fast," Isabella commented.

"I like the length. I might get mine that way," Gabriella said, eyeing Ami's hair with interest.

"Amaranth, what are you doing here?" Jasmine asked, coming up from behind the heiresses.

"I know it looks weird, but I think I'm enrolled in the military. They even call me 'Captain,'" Ami replied sarcastically.

Jasmine blushed darkly. "You know that's not what I meant. What are you doing outside the Council of Generals?"

"Why didn't you tell me about the military ball? Why haven't you checked on me when I woke up? Why do I have to learn things from the Dragons and not from you? Why are you avoiding me?" Ami shot off.

"You didn't answer my question," Jasmine pointed out.

"And you refuse to answer mine," Ami retorted.

Tension erupted to volcanic levels as the two females glared at each other. At that moment, the doors opened. Rikardi glanced at the two with a deep frown.

"Captain Rose, you may enter," Rikardi announced.

"Thank you, General Rikardi," Ami said politely, breaking the staring contest. She entered the room with the blond Centaur. The doors gave a satisfying thud.

Ami resumed her previous position in front of Tso. Rikardi returned to his seat. His anger wasn't making the Bond throb anymore. She was glad he calmed down.

"After reconsideration, you will keep your title of Captain. The males in the Lower Ring Unit will be dishonorably discharged. For the mission, even though it was a failure, it was explained to me to be a last-ditch effort, and it will not go on your record negatively. Do you have anything to say?" Tso explained. The aggressive tone was gone.

"Thank you, sir. What is my next mission?" Ami asked, her voice firm.

"That will be decided later. You will be notified by General Mason. Dismissed," Tso stated.

Ami saluted and walked to the doors. When she opened them, the heiresses and Jasmine were still there.

"Amaranth—" Jasmine called out.

Ami walked past them without a glance.

The next day, the heiresses came to visit Ami in her room. She was in her bed, still in her pajamas.

"What's wrong with you?" Gabriella asked snidely.

Ami couldn't even come up with a retort. She wasn't even irritated with the redhead.

"Ami, are you okay?" Elizabeth asked.

"Nope," Ami answered.

"Can we help?" Isabella asked.

"I doubt it," Ami sighed.

"Jasmine wants to see you," Elizabeth said.

"Only so she can yell at me about disrespecting her," Ami groaned. She rolled onto her stomach.

"Are you going to see her?" Gabriella asked, her tone curious.

"Why should I?" Ami asked.

"You're her ally, right?" Isabella asked uncertainly.

"I doubt that now," Ami stated. Seeing their confused looks, she elaborated, "You three are obviously on her side since you were with her. Why would she need a Vincian nobody like me when she has the daughters of the three most powerful families? I'm useless to her now."

The heiresses glanced at each other.

"You have more power than you think," Elizabeth stated.

Ami snorted.

"It's true," Isabella added. "Even when our mothers forced us home, your name was whispered with fear and awe."

"How did you come back? Did your mothers allow it?" Ami asked.

The heiresses grinned mischievously.

"Oh, that's a story we gotta tell you," Gabriella said gleefully.

"I'm listening," Ami said, sitting on her elbows.

The heiresses sat down and told their stories. In summary, while Ami was still in a coma, each heiress was trapped in their homes. Their mothers prevented them from leaving for fear they would make an escape. Elizabeth did attempt to escape multiple times. It reached the point where Lady McCoall hired female bodyguards to guard the house.

Gabriella discovered bats in her room and Bonded with them. While exploring the Bond, she uncovered a way to communicate with Elizabeth and Isabella using the bats. She would think of her message, create it in her mouth, and breathe onto the bat's fur. When the bat reached Elizabeth or Isabella, they could inhale the magic in the bat's fur and receive the message. The practice took several months for the communication to work. Isabella was terrified of anything with wings, so it took her the longest to understand and receive messages.

Inspired by Gabriella using magic, Elizabeth and Isabella decided to find out their magical abilities. Elizabeth sneaked into her family's library to read about possible skills she could learn. When she was almost caught, she found out she could shrink the book in her hand. When she was alone, she tried to get the book to go back to its average size. This resulted in the book becoming the size of her bed. Eventually, she managed to return the book back to its average size. It took a lot out of her, and she passed out shortly after. From then on, she practiced on other items, making them enlarged or shrinking them until she got a good grip on her magic.

Isabella's ability was invisibility. She admitted that it was probably how she got Ami's test paper for the Oath from Miss Cragun's filing cabinet since the teacher didn't even talk to her when she sneaked in. She tested this on her parents when her mother came to get her for dinner. She barely managed to reappear when her father came to get her. Once Isabella was confident in her ability, the three began their plan to escape.

The hardest part was getting Elizabeth out of her home. Isabella, invisible, snuck out of her house and into the neighbor's yard next to Elizabeth's home. Gabriella sent out a pack of bats to distract the bodyguards, allowing Elizabeth to escape. They ran to Ami's old home.

"Wait a minute," Ami interrupted. "Why did you go there? How do you know my address?"

"When I got your test, it was in your personal file. In there was your address. I just knew where to go," Isabella explained.

Is this another ability of the Winters family? Ami wondered.

"Low Valley would be the last place our mothers would search for us," Gabriella pointed out.

Ami nodded. "Continue."

"We found your house and your old room. We were going over our next step when the strangest Person appeared," Elizabeth said.

"She was super freaky," Gabriella said excitedly. "Her skin kept changing colors, and her ears would shrink and enlarge. Her eyes wouldn't stay a single color."

"Who was she?" Ami asked. An inkling of memory was at the edge of her mind.

"She said her name was Aisling," Isabella said.

A flood of memories entered Ami's mind.

She snuck a bundle of cloth over the Vincian border from Goya. Once she knew it was safe, she uncovered it to reveal an infant. The infant opened its eyes. Its amber eyes changed to match Ami's amethyst.

The infant was now a toddler. She wore a simple yellow dress. She followed Ami around the palace, spouting gibberish happily. Her eyes remained purple while her skin changed tones and her Elf ears shrank and enlarged. Her hair was white like Ami's.

The toddler was now six years old. Ami was training her on controlling her ability. The child was trying to meditate. Even when she failed, Ami was patient and continued to encourage her.

Aisling was a teenager. She had just passed the test Ami set out for her to complete. Ami was immensely proud of her. They celebrated with nine others that Ami couldn't remember at the moment.

"I know her," Ami exclaimed.

"You do?" Elizabeth asked.

"How exactly?" Gabriella asked in a suspicious tone.

"She's from Vinci. She's good," Ami said shortly. "Then what happened?"

The heiresses looked like they wanted to ask more.

"She teleported us to Talient," Elizabeth said slowly. "How do you know she's good? I thought you were on bad terms with People from Vinci."

"I have a few allies in Vinci. She's one of them," Ami answered.

"You just don't have enough to be safe in Vinci," Isabella stated.

"Exactly. How did you get back into the Common Grounds?" Ami asked.

"Thankfully, the males recognized us and allowed us in. We were trying to find one of the generals when we ran into Jasmine. We explained the situation to her, and she offered an alliance," Elizabeth explained.

"What sort of alliance?" Ami asked.

"We don't know. We rejected it," Gabriella said.

"Pardon?"

"We told her that we could not ally ourselves with her. Our families would not allow it," Isabella said. "We offered to ally ourselves with you and, through you, would be in alliance with her."

"Why me?" Ami asked. She had a bad feeling about this.

"You have more political power than Jasmine," Elizabeth said. She raised a hand to stop Ami's protest. "Jasmine may have the title, but you have the political clout in Old Congress and the military."

"Jasmine is seen as an annoying gnat that gets swatted at when she gets too close. You, however, are seen as an up-and-coming powerhouse making changes without much effort," Gabriella said.

"The Nobles respect you, and some even fear you. You are an unknown who is making the changes they either refused to make or are too scared of angering their allies to make. You are what we need in Rascu," Isabella said.

Ami sighed. "You've given me a lot to think about. Do you mind stepping out? I need to change."

The heiresses left and shut the door. Ami could sense them outside the door. She changed into her running outfit. After thinking for a bit, she decided to go barefoot. She exited her room.

"Where are you going?" Gabriella asked, eyeing her clothes.

"Running. It helps my mood and my thinking," Ami stated.

"Around the wall?" Elizabeth asked.

"Yes. I need to think," Ami said, making her way outside.

She did a few quick stretches. The patrolling Knights nodded at her as they passed. She nodded back. She started at a low jog. It took a while to find her rhythm. Once she did, she began to think.

What am I going to do? she wondered. Her alliance with Jasmine had been stable before the fire. Did her death and return to life do something to Jasmine? Was there something else in Old Congress that Ami wasn't aware of? What about the northern mines? Was that investigated further? Does Jasmine know what happened to the Dragons there?

Does Jasmine feel threatened by me?

If what the heiresses said was true, perhaps Jasmine was distancing herself. Finding out Ami was a Dragon had to shock the dictator. While Ami hadn't addressed it, she was surprised at how little change in behavior there was with the ones she interacted with. Even the heiresses didn't comment on her drooping ears or tail. The Knights did seem to notice her tail. She saw how their eyes darted to her tail, but they said nothing about it. What Ami didn't understand were the Nobles.

She didn't have much interaction with anyone except Lady Pera. Their letters were long, but not frequent. Ami and Lady Pera had exchanged six letters since their acquaintance. Other than that, Ami had no idea how the Nobles perceived her.

Maybe I need to change that, Ami thought. If Jasmine was going to distance herself from Ami, she needed a backup plan. *I will need more allies than the Centaurs. Perhaps the military ball will be helpful. Now I need to find an outfit.*

She managed to make two laps around the Common Grounds during her thoughts. Exhausted but pleased, she took a shower, dressed, and exited the Inner City. She started in the Summer District. She found several boutiques that only made dresses and skirts in materials Ami found irritating.

Where do the males get their clothing? Ami asked herself. As she walked around, she couldn't find a single shop that sold male clothing. Confusion wafted in her mind. Who made male clothing? There were more males than females in Talient due to the military. Was it outsourced from a nearby city? How did Blaine get clothing?

She stopped dead in her tracks. The crates in the remote warehouse. There had to be clothing in there. Then she smacked herself in the face. Of course, Blaine stole clothing! Why didn't she think of that? She turned and went to the Winter District. As soon as she entered, Shayne silently appeared by her side.

"Are you okay, boss?" Shayne asked quietly.

"I was frustrated and then felt like an idiot," Ami grumbled.

"What for?"

"There's a military ball being hosted by the dictator. She wants me to wear a frilly dress I can't breathe in. I want to raid the crates to see what items Blaine has acquired over the years. Will you help?" Ami asked.

"I can help, although I know nothing about fashion. Why does she want you to wear something you can't breathe in?" Shayne inquired.

"I think she feels threatened by me and wants to rein me in. I want to be comfortable," Ami answered.

"You don't think it's odd for a female to wear male clothing?" Shayne asked innocently.

"Shayne, look at me," Ami ordered. The Werewolf obeyed. "Do I look like a female to you? I look more like a male than a female at the moment."

Shayne stared at her intently. She could see the wheels turning in his head.

"You're changing the game," Shayne stated abruptly.

"How do you mean?" Ami asked.

"The Nobles will expect you to be like a typical female Rascal or try to imitate them. The dictator expects you to obey her without question. You're creating new rules in the old game," Shayne observed.

Ami smirked. "Precisely. Why weren't you second-in-command?"

Shayne tucked his head down, his ears flat. He stopped walking. "I wasn't strong enough."

Ami stopped. Stepping closer, she gently raised his chin with her fingers so he could look at her. "Another error to add to the pile that Blaine has made."

The Bond pulsed with emotion from Shayne. The Werewolf looked at her like he had when they created the Bond. Ami released his chin and continued to walk. Shayne followed a step behind her. When they arrived at the warehouse, they began to dive into the crates. This lasted until dusk. Ami was about to give up when Shayne opened the last container.

"Boss, I think this is what you were looking for," Shayne announced happily. His tail wagged proudly.

Ami purred when she looked at the contents. This was going to be fun.

Rikardi sat at his desk. The stack of paperwork never dwindled to a reasonable size. Occasionally, he would pause and look at the Bond he had made with Amaranth. It was fascinating. He didn't have many Bonds, but this one kept his attention for some reason. Almost as if the Bond itself was trying to say, "Look at me! Focus on me!"

A knock broke his concentration. "Enter."

Lady Jasmine entered with several folders. Rikardi was on guard. This was the first time the dictator had come to his office.

"May I help you?" he asked neutrally.

"It's about the Warehouse Guardian position," Jasmine said stiffly. She handed the folders to him. "Here are candidates to consider."

With a frown, Rikardi took the folders. As he glanced at each one, his frown deepened.

"These are male candidates," Rikardi pointed out.

Lady Jasmine raised an eyebrow. "Is that a problem?"

"The Warehouse Guardian is specifically for females. It was how Tso convinced Old Congress to encourage non-heiresses to join the military. From my records, we will have five in the next semester," Rikardi explained.

Lady Jasmine seemed stunned. "I wasn't aware."

"Obviously," Rikardi drawled.

Lady Jasmine glared. "Don't start, General. I'm not in the mood."

"You never are," Rikardi commented casually. The redness of her angered face gave him satisfaction. "I reject your candidates."

Lady Jasmine huffed. "Then do you have a candidate in mind?"

Rikardi's frown lightened. "Why not allow Rose to continue the position?"

The dictator flinched. "No, she needs to be a captain."

"Needs to be?" Rikardi echoed, not liking how this was going. "Why does Rose need to be a captain?"

"That's none of your business," Lady Jasmine hissed.

"It is when it concerns a cadet under my command," Rikardi sneered.

"Former cadet," Lady Jasmine said smugly. "She is now a captain and no longer under your command. I reject your candidate. I will bring you more options later." She left swiftly, snapping his office door shut.

Rikardi pondered this interaction. What was the dictator up to?

The morning of the military ball was filled with chaos. More Knights patrolled the Inner City. Ami was surprised to see Dragons she had never seen before entering with stern soldiers and their commanders. The Dragons wore outfits similar to those of caterers. A sinking feeling began to form in Ami's stomach. When the afternoon started to wane into the evening, Ami went to her room to get dressed.

It took her a while to put everything in order. Remembering a spell, she mumbled, "*Purlos.*"

A temporary floor-length mirror appeared in front of her. Ami straightened her collar and made sure her vest was on correctly. The colors were black and deep purple. The dress shirt, dress pants, and overcoat were black. The vest was purple with an embroidered flower pattern in silver. The tie was also purple. The black leather shoes shined. Ami smirked. This was much better than that frilly monster Jasmine tried to make her wear.

A knock caused Ami to lose concentration. The mirror disappeared in a small cloud of smoke that immediately dissipated. Ami opened the door. It was Michael. He openly gaped at her.

"Captain?" Michael asked in disbelief.

"How many one-eyed captains do you know?" Ami asked teasingly.

"Um, wow. You look great," Michael said awkwardly. "Are you going to do anything with your hair?"

"It's not long enough to do anything with," Ami pointed out.

"Not true," Michael stated. Over his shoulder, he barked, "Hey, Perry! I need your hands!"

The Elf Knight came over with a curious look. "What's up, sir?"

"I noticed sometimes you do something with your hair that makes it spike up. You think you could help the captain with something like that?" Michael asked.

Perry gazed at Ami's hair. "I'm pretty sure I can come up with something. Hold on."

Perry left and came back a minute later with a small container. When he popped open the top, the smell of lavender and pine filled her nose.

"Whatever that is, I already like the smell," Ami commented.

Both Knights chuckled.

"Captain, may I touch your hair?" Perry asked.

"You may, but please be gentle. There are some spots still tender," Ami warned softly.

Perry was meticulous and gentle. She wasn't sure what he was doing. After less than a minute, he withdrew his hands.

"What do you think?" Perry asked Michael.

"I think it looks good. How does it feel, Captain?" Michael asked.

Without mumbling the spell this time, Ami summoned the temporary mirror. Both Knights jumped. Ami stared at herself. While Perry didn't do anything dramatic, it was enough to give her white hair more definition. Random yet well-placed strands were spiked enough to make a statement without her looking foolish. She was impressed.

"I love it." Ami smiled widely. Unbeknownst to her, both males relaxed. "I didn't know this could be done to short hair. After the ball, I will come to you for practice," Ami said to Perry.

"I'm glad my services were well received," Perry said with a sloppy salute.

Ami dispelled the mirror. "Thank you both."

"You're welcome, sir," Michael murmured.

"Anytime, Captain." Perry smiled.

Ami left the Knight's Quarters in high spirits. When she entered the gardens, she slowed her pace. She hid from the edge of the gardens to watch the guests arrive. She mainly focused on what the female Nobles were wearing. Each wife or courter wore a unique outfit. After watching about ten couples enter, she noticed a pattern with the dresses. They were form-fitting and not with corsets. Ami could tell due to how freely the females moved from side to side. Their backs weren't rigid, and they wore high heels.

Seeing enough, Ami exited the gardens. The soldiers looked wary when they saw her. The females looked surprised and intrigued. Ami ignored them as she followed the line to the library. While a strange place to hold a ball, Ami reasoned it would be the largest room in the mansion. She waited on the stairs to be announced, observing the library's new look.

The shelves were covered with red curtains, hiding the books from possible damage. The desks and chairs used for studying were replaced by elegantly clothed round dinner tables. The reception area was converted into a temporary caterer station. The Dragons Ami had seen earlier were hard at work. Finally, it was her turn to be announced. The Knight making the announcements stared at her in shock.

"C-Captain Rose?" Harold, a dark brown Werewolf, asked. His voice was abnormally soft.

"Hello, Harold," Ami greeted him.

Harold looked nervous. "Um, sir. What's your first name?" The Werewolf looked deeply embarrassed.

"It's Amaranth. Amaranth Rose," Ami supplied easily.

"Announcing Captain Amaranth Rose!" Harold's voice boomed.

Ami nodded at the soldier and descended the remaining stairs. Numerous eyes stared at the strange female as she walked confidently around, looking for a familiar face.

"Excuse me, may I have a moment of your time?" a female voice spoke to Ami's right.

It belonged to a female Centaur. Unlike other female Centaurs, this one was not dressed head to hoof with colorful fabrics. She wore a custom dress that was deep green with lace sleeves and lace fringe on the bottom of her dress that covered her horse half. The top part was similar to what any female Elf would wear. Her dark brown hair was in an elegant bun with small pink flowers.

"Greetings, milady," Ami greeted like a male.

"Greetings, *philippias*," the female greeted back.

"Bless you."

The female giggled. "I am called Corrie of the Blackhoof clan. I am honored to meet you."

"We are well met, Corrie. Please call me Ami," Ami smiled. "Did you come with others?"

"No, I wished to come alone, hoping to seek you," Corrie admitted.

"Oh? What for?" Ami asked.

"There's something I wish to discuss with you privately," Corrie said solemnly.

"I can't discuss it at this moment. Unfortunately, I have to find Lady Jasmine. However, after the first song, how about we meet on the second floor, and we can have that discussion?" Ami suggested.

"I understand. Thank you so much, *philippias*," Corrie gushed.

Ami nodded and walked through the growing crowds of People. Whispers and murmurs followed her as she slithered in and out of concentrated groups. She found Jasmine and the heiresses on the other side of the room. The heiresses gasped and immediately started gushing over Ami's outfit. Jasmine stood there, seething.

"I gave the Dragons direct orders to make you an outfit," Jasmine hissed.

"This isn't from the Dragons," Ami replied offhandedly. "They did make a dress. I chose not to wear it."

"And why not?" Jasmine growled.

"Because I am not a doll you can dress up," Ami growled back. She stepped closer to the dictator, instantly noticing the height difference. She looked down at Jasmine.

"You're supposed to be my ally," Jasmine said, her tone hurt. Ami hated it when she tried to make Ami feel guilty.

"Start acting like one, and I will be," Ami retorted coldly. She stepped back and turned to the heiresses. Each was dressed similarly to Jasmine. Elizabeth and Isabella seemed fine, but Gabriella was glaring at Ami.

"Next time there's a ball, I'm going shopping with you," Gabriella grumbled. "Also, what did you do with your hair?"

"Knight Woodsworth assisted with my hair today. I will be asking for his assistance after this," Ami replied.

"I'm so cutting my hair after this. Can I join?" Gabriella asked with puppy eyes.

"Of course."

Ami glanced at the caterers. Food was out, but no one had approached the buffet. Ami went to one of the Dragons. The male jumped when he noticed Ami.

"Are we serving ourselves?" Ami asked politely.

The male Dragon glanced around. He barked something in the Dragon language. Another male Dragon came over. Ami was intrigued. This Dragon walked like a warrior. A deep scar went down the left side of his face. Brown hair streaked with gray was pulled back into a low ponytail.

"The Noble wants to know about the food," the first Dragon said in the Dragon language.

"What about it?" the second male replied with an accent Ami couldn't identify.

"He wants to know if we're serving it," the first Dragon hissed irritably.

"That's not what I asked," Ami said in the Dragon language. All the Dragons stared at her. "All I wanted to know is if I can serve myself. I didn't want to assume."

"Who are you?" the second Dragon whispered.

"I am Amaranth Rose. The Dragons here call me *ya'puris*," Ami answered.

The Dragons gaped at her. Ami wagged her tail enough for them to notice it. She saw their eyes dart to her right temple.

"You are free," the first Dragon murmured.

"Yes. Hopefully, we will all be free," Ami murmured back. "So, is the food available for serving?"

"Of-of course, *ya'puris*. Please help yourself," the second Dragon said with a deep bow. The rest of the Dragons copied him.

"Arise. Continue with your duties," Ami ordered, picking up a plate. Behind her were the heiresses. Ami placed a little bit of everything, eager to see how these Dragons made their dishes. Without realizing it, she started a trend. The heiresses copied Ami. The soldiers and their companions watched and copied them as well.

Ami found an empty table. Realizing she had forgotten a drink, she started to turn when a female Dragon appeared with a glass of water.

"Thank you." Ami nodded. The Dragon kept her eyes on the ground and returned to the caterers. Ami frowned. The bad feeling in her stomach grew.

"May I join you?" Lady Pera asked. The Werewolf was dressed in a strapless, form-fitting navy blue dress. Her high heel shoes made her appear twice as tall. A pearl-stringed headdress adorned her head.

"Of course, milady. I'm pleased to see you," Ami said with a smile. They sat next to each other. "How are you? How is Ravenna?"

"Busy as usual. My new program is growing. Soon I'll be able to send some of my trained People to the nearby cities to train others and set up similar programs. Ravenna's crime rate has dramatically decreased since I was allowed to pass my legislation," Lady Pera explained.

"That's great news. You've been hard at work," Ami said.

"Yes, but that's not why I wanted to speak with you," Lady Pera said. She reached over and gently grabbed Ami's left wrist. "I am indebted to you."

"What for?" Ami asked.

Lady Pera looked surprised. "You saved my nephews from the fire. They are the only family I have left. If I had lost them ..." The female closed her eyes, her ears flat on her head.

Ami placed her free hand on top of Lady Pera's. "You owe me nothing, Lady Pera," Ami said softly. The female Werewolf looked at her, searching her eye for something. She seemed to find it, or at least be satisfied.

Lady Pera chuckled. "As a Rascal, I cannot accept that. If you need my assistance for anything, please come to me first."

"I will." Ami nodded.

"Pardon me. May I join?" Corrie asked, holding a plate full of salad and bread.

"Do you mind, Lady Pera?" Ami asked.

"I don't mind. I don't believe I've had the pleasure of speaking to a female Centaur," Lady Pera replied.

Ami moved a chair out of the way so Corrie could properly lower her horse body to sit at the table. The three chatted about mundane things. Lady Pera and Ami asked Corrie about her dress and complimented her on how well it was made. Corrie blushed darkly. The Centaur, in return, complimented Ami on her outfit. When Ami tried to rebuke the compliment, Lady Pera added her compliments.

"I believe I will start to wear similar items to balls and events in Ravenna. It is refreshing to see females who wear the family's pants actually display them," Lady Pera commented.

"You don't believe it is disgraceful for a female to wear male clothing?" Ami asked.

"You're not trying to be a male," Lady Pera emphasized. "It'll make other females realize that there are other options than dresses, skirts, and, ugh, corsets."

Ami snorted into her water. Corrie coughed to hide her laughter.

"I've never felt good wearing female clothing. It's always looked odd on me," Ami admitted.

"The latest fashions often don't include Centaurs," Corrie said. "It took a long time for me to find a dress style that suited me, so I understand your frustration."

They continued to talk about other things. The three females got into a lively debate about Ami's favorite play, *The Queen and the Bandit*. They were halfway through discussing the hilarious ways the queen turned down the bandit when Jasmine interrupted.

"Amaranth, we need to talk," Jasmine said coldly.

"My apologies, ladies. I'm needed elsewhere," Ami said, getting up. To Corrie, she said, "After the first song."

Corrie smiled. Lady Pera glanced back and forth between them. Ami followed Jasmine to the third floor of the library. When Jasmine went down the fourth corridor, Ami was curious and wary. This section required special permission to even touch one of its books. Black curtains covered them, obscuring the titles. Jasmine stopped in the middle and turned to face Ami with a stormy look.

"Why are you acting like this?" Jasmine hissed.

Ami raised an eyebrow. "You're the one who hasn't been updating me on what's happening and acting like a spoiled brat."

"So are you," Jasmine retorted. "You start barking off questions and then leave before I can explain myself."

"Why didn't you visit me when I woke up?" Ami asked. It hurt when her supposed ally wouldn't even check on her while she was asleep. It hurt even more when Ami started to walk on her own again and still didn't see Jasmine.

"I was busy with the new dorms," Jasmine said, averting her gaze to the floor.

"The new dorms were completed a month after I woke up," Ami pointed out. This time, her tone was like ice.

"I was also busy arranging this ball," Jasmine said weakly.

"How did that come about?" Ami asked.

Jasmine started to pace. "I need females in my military. My entire campaign was focused on allowing females to join and gain rank. I wanted to show you and the heiresses off to show a strong front. Instead, you come dressed like *that*," Jasmine said, glaring at Ami, "and shifted the power structure. Now I have People coming to me to ask about you and your political plans, not mine."

"Basically, you're mad that you're not the center of attention tonight," Ami stated blandly.

Jasmine's magic flared. Ami felt the books on the shelves to her left react.

"I wouldn't use magic in this corridor," Ami warned.

Jasmine didn't seem to hear. "Your personality is different," she said, as if she was sad.

"I came back from the dead. It's a life-changing event," Ami replied. "The shadow threads are gone."

"So this is how you are truly?" Jasmine scoffed.

Ami shrugged. "I don't know. I haven't pissed off enough People yet."

Jasmine laughed unexpectedly. It started hysterical, but she placed a hand over her mouth to silence it.

"You're the most stubborn Person I know," Jasmine muttered, her hand still over her mouth.

"It takes one to spot one."

Jasmine lowered her hand and sighed heavily. "Are we still allies?"

"As long as you continue to have my back, I'll have yours," Ami quoted.

Jasmine sighed. "Can we start over?"

"Depends," Ami said, a mischievous smirk forming.

"On what?" Jasmine asked warily.

"On how many times you will try to seduce me." Ami grinned widely, barely keeping in her laughter.

Jasmine blushed darkly. "That was one time!"

"So, you admit you were trying to seduce me on New Year. And now you're doing it here," Ami said, purposely lowering her voice.

"Huh?"

Ami blinked. "Do you really not know this part of the library?"

"I haven't been down here before," Jasmine admitted.

Ami laughed hard. She doubled over, holding her belly so she wouldn't start rolling on the floor. When her laughter ceased enough for her to talk, she said, "Look at the titles behind the curtain."

Jasmine did. She scoffed. "I don't get why you are laughing over this."

"Of course, I'm laughing. The hardcore stuff is on the top shelves," Ami pointed.

Jasmine magically floated to the top shelf. She pulled back the curtain. Immediately she let go and blushed. "Amaranth!"

Ami laughed again. Jasmine floated back down, still blushing.

"Ahem," Rikardi's deep voice echoed in the corridor.

Ami turned to face him. *Whoa. When did Rikardi jump into the sexy pool?* She thought.

Rikardi was dressed elegantly in his formal military attire. A crisp white shirt and overcoat with shined gold buttons complimented the Centaur's lightly tanned skin. Numerous medals and honor badges adorned the right side of the coat. The bottom part, typically pants for Weres and Elves, was emerald green and designed like a masculine skirt. Ami enjoyed the view.

Rikardi gave her an odd look. "Captain Rose, may I have a moment of your time?"

Ami glanced at Jasmine. She nodded. Ami nodded at Rikardi. He still had the odd look on his face.

Why is he looking at me like that? Ami wondered. As they started down the corridor, it hit her like a gust of cold wind.

He can feel my emotions through the Bond, she realized in horror. A shadow gently cast itself over their Bond. Rikardi jumped as if a snake had snuck up on him.

"What did you do?" he hissed in a low tone, eyeing Jasmine, who trailed behind them.

Ami blinked. "I realized how open the Bond was. I was giving us privacy."

Rikardi let out a shuddered sigh. "Release it."

"Pardon?"

"Release whatever you put on it. That's an order, Captain," Rikardi demanded through gritted teeth.

Ami stared at him for a moment. The shadow left the Bond. Rikardi visibly relaxed. They didn't say anything as they returned to the main floor. Ami glanced at Rikardi, puzzled.

Why did it bother him so much? Perhaps because it's still new? I probably put it on too fast. That makes sense. Ami thought to herself.

Rikardi led her to a trio of males close to the orchestra. All three males were dressed in white and green like Rikardi.

"Captain Rose, this is Commander Luke of Putra Nexas," Rikardi introduced. Luke was a dark gray Werewolf with sharp amber eyes. The top half of his left ear was missing. What struck Ami was the sagging skin around his wrists and neck. It looked like he lost a lot of weight in a short period.

Rikardi continued, "This is Commander Bojan of Putra Thyrs." A dull black Werewolf with dark eyes, he had three noticeable scars on his face. Two went from the top of his head to an inch below his left eye in a ragged manner, suggesting claw marks. The third was from a sword, starting from the bottom of his right ear and disappearing underneath his white shirt.

"And this is Commander Hector of Putra Hallas," Rikardi finished. Hector was a dark brown Centaur with pale skin. Ami didn't like the way he looked at her. He reminded her of dirty oil from several days of frying food.

"I'm pleased to see you recovering well, Lady Rose," Luke said.

"As am I. The stories I hear of your time as a cadet are amusing," Bojan said.

"That depends on who you're hearing it from," Ami replied.

"The cadets we received told conflicting stories," Luke said carefully.

"I think once they were away from certain influences, they could speak their minds more freely," Rikardi said diplomatically.

"I agree. The power structure amongst the cadets—" Ami started.

"How did you do it?" Hector interrupted.

Ami blinked. "Do what?"

"Get the males to fall in love with you. How'd you do it?" Hector asked with a creepy grin.

"I don't follow." Ami frowned.

"Neither do I," Bojan growled. He took a step towards the Centaur.

"The line of questioning is inappropriate, Commander Hector. Drop it," Rikardi ordered coldly.

"Anyway," Luke said quickly, "are you going to be assigned a fort, Lady Rose?"

"I am awaiting further orders," Ami answered.

"If you'd like, I can request for you to come to Putra Nexas. We're further north than most forts, but not close to the border either," Luke offered.

"Why on Torus would she want to be buried in snow?" Bojan argued. To Ami, he said, "Ask to come to Putra Thyrs. We're around the middle entrance of Harpy Canyon. We don't deal with the harpies much, but there are plenty of woods to explore on your days off."

She glanced at Hector and Rikardi. Hector looked constipated at the thought of her coming to his fort. Rikardi frowned.

Ami chuckled. "I appreciate your recommendations. I will recall them if I have a choice."

The orchestra started to play. Ami recognized the song as "My Fair Lady is a Songbird."

"As interesting as this is—" Hector started to say snidely. Rikardi also opened his mouth to speak when Luke beat him.

"May I have this dance, Lady Rose?" Luke asked earnestly.

The males stared at him in shock. Ami grinned.

"Do you want to lead?" she asked.

The males stared at her now. Luke looked surprised. "You wouldn't mind?" he asked.

"I have confidence in your skills." Ami offered her left hand.

Luke took it. They were the first to enter the dance floor. It was a traditional dance with steps that were easy to follow. Ami was pleased to learn that Luke was an excellent dancer. They didn't speak during the song, content with the silence between them. When the song ended, they bowed to each other.

"Were you pleased, Lady Rose?" Luke asked.

"Very. Your skills are excellent," Ami praised.

Luke blushed. "So are yours. Perhaps later we can dance another?"

"If I can be spared. I have to go speak to someone first," Ami said. With a wave, she exited the dance floor and went to the second floor. Corrie was waiting anxiously there.

"*Philippas*, you are true to your word," Corrie said with awe.

"Of course. Shall we?" Ami motioned with her hand towards a corridor. They walked for a bit until they came to an unoccupied corner. Ami liked this part of the library. She sometimes hid here when she needed to get away from the heiresses.

"Before we begin, I need to be honest with you," Corrie said, her hands fidgeting with her dress.

"I'm listening."

"Even though you are well-known and well-thought-of amongst the Centaurs, I didn't realize you were associated with a Roos clan member," Corrie said nervously.

"I'm not aware of what that means," Ami admitted.

"The Roos clan is a departed branch of the Goldmanes. They're considered unpure," Corrie explained.

"Why?"

Corrie started to sweat noticeably on her forehead. "According to the Centaur elders, those who seek to create a herd outside the Centaur clans are considered not a 'true' Centaur and a traitor to the clans."

Ami stared at her deadpan. "I really don't care about who someone's parents or ancestors slept with, whether they be Centaur or another People. What I care about is if someone knows the meaning of loyalty and honor."

"U-Understood, *philippas*. I-I just wanted to inform you how the Centaurs view each other," Corrie stammered.

"Thank you for enlightening me." Ami nodded. "What did you want to discuss?"

Corrie seemed relieved by the change of subject. "My idea is not popular with my People. Mostly due to how long it will take." Corrie took a deep breath. "I would like female Centaurs to enter the military."

Ami cocked her head to the side in confusion. "All non-heiresses are allowed to join."

"You don't understand." Corrie shook her head. "No Centaur holds a Noble title due to the lack of records. We are migratory nomads. All we have are our oral tales, which differ amongst the clans. Even though we are citizens, the Rascals look down on us because we are not their equals."

Ami hummed. That would explain some reactions to Centaurs she witnessed while in Rascu. She always wondered why Rikardi was the only Centaur general and why other Centaurs didn't think of him fondly.

Then how did Rikardi obtain his title? Ami wondered.

A quiet shuffling from several rows down drew her attention. A flash of fabric confirmed her suspicions. Ami huffed under her breath. In a louder voice, she said, "If you're going to spy on me, you might as well get over here and help."

"Who are you—" Corrie began to ask.

Elizabeth, Isabella, and Gabriella guiltily emerged from their hiding spot.

"Who are they?" Corrie asked Ami.

"Nosy females who don't know when to leave me alone," Ami said, glaring at them.

"We were worried," Elizabeth said, fidgeting with her dress.

"We didn't know what was going on," Isabella added.

"You could've entertained us by flirting with her at least," Gabriella complained.

"Jealous, Gabriella?" Ami smirked.

Gabriella flushed pink.

"Since you three are here, you can assist in this endeavor. Corrie, this is Elizabeth, Isabella, and Gabriella, who wants to flirt with you," Ami introduced them with a straight face. Gabriella's blush darkened while the other two snickered. "They are from Noble families and can help trace possible lineages."

"We're doing family trees?" Isabella asked excitedly.

"Yes. We're looking for Centaurs." Ami nodded uneasily. She had never seen Isabella so excited before.

"Oh, I can't wait. When can we start?" Isabella asked, nearly breathless.

"When the library reopens," Ami stated.

"Great! You two," Isabella commanded Elizabeth and Gabriella, "come with me. We need to set up a game plan."

"But—"

"Wait—"

Isabella dragged the two away despite their protesting. Then it was just Ami and Corrie.

"It'll take time, but I'm confident they will provide answers," Ami reassured.

"I trust you." Corrie smiled.

"Let's go hit the dance floor. I hear a good song playing,"

Ami said, offering her arm.

Corrie took it, and they exited. A more formal dance was playing. When they reached the main floor, Corrie left to speak with Lady Pera more. Ami saw Luke and Bojan talking and glaring at Hector in the same spot. Rikardi was frowning more. It lessened when he saw Ami. When the song ended, Ami went to the conductor. She whispered a song request. The conductor smiled mischievously.

The song that played was unlike any song the Rascals had heard. It was fast-paced and something more that belonged at a festival than a ball. Ami rounded up different People, males and females, and danced freely with them. They were stiff at first until they started to move with the beat. Pleased, Ami headed over to Rikardi and the males. The song was making her disregard Rascal formal protocol between military ranks.

"Commander Bojan, dance with me," Ami demanded playfully.

Bojan grinned widely and joined in. Ami felt free when she danced like this. While there were steps, they weren't necessary. All that mattered was how one danced with their partner and that one had fun doing it. Ami and Bojan laughed as they spun each other, clapped their hands, and enjoyed each other's company. Bojan was like a ball of light. The energy he produced made Ami feel light, and she greedily absorbed it. Soon Luke joined in, and they adapted quickly to include him. Luke added a level of playfulness she didn't realize was missing. The trio dominated the dance floor, others joining in. Soon it was a group dance without a designated leader. Everyone danced however they liked. Laughter and giggles filled the air. When the song ended, everyone cheered. The happy atmosphere settled into a relaxing calm.

The three grabbed a drink from the Dragons and returned to their previous spot. Hector wasn't there. Rikardi was talking to Lee in low tones further away.

"That was entertaining, Lady Rose. Thank you for teaching us that," Bojan said boisterously.

"What song was that?" Luke asked.

"It's a festival song called 'The Lady Comes Out at Night.' It's typically played during nightly festivals like New Year or Denarii's Glow," Ami explained. Her chest was achy from being breathless. It felt wonderful.

"That was a lot of fun. You definitely need to come to my fort. You'll make things interesting," Bojan said, still grinning.

A more traditional song started to play.

"Lady Rose, may I have another dance?" Luke asked. The Werewolf oozed charm. Ami was intrigued.

"Of course."

They set their drinks down and went to the dance floor. This dance was different. Ami didn't know the steps.

"Follow my lead," Luke said softly.

"What song is this?" Ami asked, letting Luke guide her.

"It's called 'The Morning Glories.' The famous composer Sir Alrick Cantrell wrote it for his sickly daughter. The only flowers she could see from her window were the morning glories," Luke explained.

"It's beautiful," Ami murmured. The song had a hint of sadness and mourning.

The rest of the dance was in comfortable silence. It had Ami thinking, *When have I really noticed males?* Luke and Bojan were charming in their own way. Luke was quiet but bold enough to ask her for a dance, while Bojan was loud and full of energy. *Am I starting puberty?* Ami wondered. *Or maybe I'm just attracted to males in uniform.* She glanced at Luke. He did look sharp in his crisp clothes. So did Bojan and Rikardi. *I'll wait and see if it's just the uniforms.* When the song ended, they bowed to each other. Bojan approached them.

"If you're not too tired, may I have the next dance?" Bojan asked.

Ami grinned at his enthusiasm. "I don't mind."

The night continued like that. Luke and Bojan alternated dancing with Ami. For the last song, Ami asked the conductor to play the festival song again. Everyone rejoiced and swarmed the dance floor when the familiar beat was heard. Ami somehow got between Lady Pera and Luke. The mayor looked like she was having fun.

The tired guests slowly started to trickle out as the last string played. Ami escorted Lady Pera and Corrie to the Iron Gates. They said their goodbyes with promises to write. Ami whistled while walking through the garden. The ball went better than she thought. Then she sensed Rune coming towards her in a panic. The young Elf emerged out of the darkness, out of breath.

"S-Sigrid," he gasped.

"What's wrong? Is someone hurt?" Ami asked.

"N-No. It's w-worse," Rune stuttered.

"What is it?"

"Blaine is back."

CHAPTER 4

Ami followed Rune through the Winter District. The streets were dark except for the occasional lamppost. The stars shined brightly. The happiness she felt earlier made her calm. Rune's arms were shaking from anxiety. Several times, Ami pulsed relaxing emotions through their Bond. It seemed to help the young Elf from going over the edge. It also helped Ami's own anxiety from overtaking her. They arrived at the warehouse where she was first told her street name. The warehouse was dustier and barren. The crates that had been there before were either gone or pieces of wood now. Blaine stood in the middle, frowning at Shayne, Philip, and Benton.

"Rune!" Blaine barked. "Why didn't you answer my call?"

Rune flinched and ducked his head down. The anxiety from before came back fourfold.

"Perhaps because he had the common sense to let me know you have returned," Ami answered coldly. Her voice echoed eerily in the stale air.

Blaine turned to face her. Ami was irritated at how well Blaine looked. He had gained weight in his absence. Before, the blond Werewolf had been just as skinny as any street gangster. Now with his expensive outfit, he looked far more like a Noble and not at all like a cutthroat gang leader. He was clean, and she noticed he talked differently.

"Who are you?" Blaine demanded, taking a few steps towards her. His attempt to be intimidating was laughable.

"Don't you recognize me, *handsome*?" Ami asked, hissing at his nickname. She looked at him with disgust.

Blaine stared at her. Then horror morphed onto his face. "Sigrid?" Blaine whispered.

Having her street name uttered from his lips made Ami furious. How dare he call her that when he abandoned her!

"It's Rose to you, Savage," Ami snarled.

"But we're courting—" Blaine started to say. The four males growled.

"You didn't feel it?" Ami asked, her voice dangerously soft. "The lack of emotions? The emptiness from the black hole? The never-ending questions circling in your head of 'what did I do wrong?' when it crumbled like dust?"

Blaine huffed. His neon blue eyes took a distant look. A few minutes passed. The blond Werewolf's chest started to heave, his breathing becoming more labored as her words came true. Cold realization washed over Ami. It was true. He didn't notice their lack of Bond until she pointed it out. *I guess that means it wasn't important to him like he led me to believe.*

"W-What? I-I don't understand," Blaine stammered.

"What don't you understand?" Ami asked. Her voice was cold. The four males flinched.

"Why did it disappear like that?" Blaine asked, his eyes full of tears. "Did ... did you sever it?"

Ami stared at him, emotionless. "I had no choice in the matter."

"Did another male force you into a courtship?" Blaine asked angrily.

Ami tsked. "For someone who was once well-informed, you are incredibly ignorant right now."

Blaine looked over his shoulder at the males. They glowered at him. Then he looked back at Ami thoughtfully. "I've heard rumors."

"But you don't believe them," Ami stated deadpan.

"You ..." Blaine looked away, the heavy panting returning. He paced a few steps. He repeatedly ran both hands through the fur on the top of his head. "What happened?"

"Where were you?" Ami countered.

"My father found me. He trapped me in a section of the house where I couldn't use my magic. I just barely escaped when one of the ward stones somehow weakened. Then I made my way back here," Blaine said, his tone sad.

Ami didn't believe him.

"And our Bond? You didn't try to communicate as we discussed?" Ami asked, her voice almost cracking in her anger.

Blaine scrunched up his face. "He cast some kind of spell on me that blocked it."

How convenient. Ami thought sarcastically. "Our courtship is over."

"What? Wait a minute! Why?" Blaine snarled.

"The Bond snapped when I died. Goodbye, Savage," Ami stated matter-of-factly. Turning on her heel, she left the warehouse. Rune, Philip, Shayne, and Benton followed after her.

Ami walked to the Winter District square. The cool night air fought against the angry heat shimmering on Ami's skin. She felt blood rush to her face as she tried not to let the tears fall. She went to the wolf fountain. Using both hands, she scooped up water and splashed her face, hoping to hide the tears that fell. Anger and anguish clawed at her chest, making it hard to breathe.

A fool! That's all I am! A foolish unlovable creature desperate for affection from anything offering promises! she shrieked to herself. She sunk to her knees, her arms hanging over the fountain's lip. Her fingers lightly grazed the water's surface.

Skinny arms wrapped themselves around her shoulders.

Without looking, she knew it was Shayne. She could smell the faint traces of coffee and fresh bread. After a long time—Ami wasn't sure how long—she finally moved to stand. Shayne removed his arms and stepped back to give her space. Her knees popped and groaned.

"Boss?" Shayne asked, his voice soft.

"I'm an idiot," Ami moaned, turning towards him. More tears came down her cheek.

Shayne took a step forward. Using a finger, he lifted her chin up so they were eye to eye. "The only fool is Blaine. Another error to add to Blaine's pile," Shayne said.

Ami let out a watery chuckle. "Thank you."

Two days later, Ami was summoned to Mason's office. It took her longer to reach the Inner City due to being in the Winter District with the four males. They insisted on her being in the Winter District to discourage Blaine from going after them. The gang's anxiety levels were through the roof, and the only thing that calmed them was her presence. She felt them follow her into the Common Grounds. When she entered the mansion, they waited outside.

Mason's door was closed. Ami knocked.

"Enter," Lee's voice answered.

Ami opened the door enough to see inside. Mason was looking at Lee with suspicion. The Werebobcat seemed amused.

"Am I interrupting?" Ami asked politely.

"Not at all, Captain," Lee answered, waving her in. Mason glared at him.

Ami entered and stood in her usual spot. She saluted Mason.

"At ease," Mason commanded softly. Her action appeared to calm him down. "Your next mission is with General Lee. Both of you will be going to Putra Hallas to investigate the low morale in the fort."

"Yes, sir."

"Any questions?" Mason asked.

"When do we leave?" Ami asked, glancing at Lee.

"Tomorrow morning," Lee answered. "Meet me in front of the mansion at dawn. It'll take us all day to reach Putra Hallas."

"Understood, sir." Ami nodded.

"Dismissed," Mason said softly.

Ami saluted and left. The four males crowded her as soon as she exited the mansion.

"Is everything okay?" Shayne asked.

"I've been assigned a mission. I leave tomorrow at dawn," Ami informed them. They walked together towards the gardens.

"Where are you going?" Rune asked anxiously.

"Putra Hallas. It's outside of Talient," Ami answered.

"What about Blaine?" Benton asked.

"What about him?" Ami asked.

"He'll come after us when he learns you're not here," Philip said fearfully.

Ami stopped. The males stopped as well. Their anxiety was giving her a migraine. Then an idea came to mind. "Follow me."

They walked through the gardens. The beautiful arrangements did nothing for the males' anxiety. When they emerged on the other side, the sight of Lius' shack near the Knight's Quarters put a smile on Ami's face. The smell of coal and hot metal lifted her spirits. She entered the blacksmith's shop first.

"Lass! Whatta surprise," Lius greeted her warmly from his workbench. The Dwarf's black hair and beard glistened with sweat in the hot room. His usual soot and grime outfit was only slightly cleaner than his work apron. Ami was now several inches taller than Lius. "Who'd the lads behind ye?"

"Shayne, Benton, Rune, and Philip," Ami introduced, pointing to each male. "Lads, this is Lius. He's a good friend of mine."

Each male gave a shy, murmured hello.

"The lads wanna learn how ta blacksmith?" Lius inquired. His dark eyes looked at them in a calculating manner. Ami wondered if it was to measure their strength by sight alone.

"Actually, I wanted to ask you to give them sanctuary," Ami said. "I'm going on a mission tomorrow, and they don't feel safe outside the Inner City. Can they come to you for safety?"

Lius stared at them thoughtfully. Ami wasn't sure if the blacksmith would allow them to stay. Glancing around, he appeared to have a lot of projects to work on.

"I will on o'e condition," Lius said. "The lads have to help me out aro'nd the smithy and not complain."

"You hear that, lads?" Ami asked.

"Yes, sir," the males answered both of them.

"The lads can come here if they wanna." Lius nodded. "C'mere before ya go. I gotta knife I've been wantin' to show ya."

Ami happily talked to Lius about the long dagger he had made. The males curiously watched from a distance, unsure about the new environment. Shayne was the first to overcome his shyness and come to Ami's side while she was still talking to Lius. She and Lius explained what they were talking about. Eventually, the other three also came closer, although they mostly hovered near Ami. The time spent with Lius significantly reduced their anxiety levels and eliminated Ami's migraine. They left Lius before dinner was served. Ami convinced them to go eat in the Winter District.

"I have to inform the Knights to get cots," she explained. Although still worried, the males obeyed.

Entering the Knight's Quarters, Ami found who she was looking for.

"Knights Trudy, Black, Amos, and Gruth, may I speak to

you, please?" Ami called out. All four Knights, three Werewolves, and one Elf obeyed. "Thank you for looking out for the lads in the Winter District when I was injured," Ami started.

"It was no problem," Trudy, a dark brown Werewolf, said.

"The reason I wanted to talk to you is that tomorrow, I'm going to Putra Hallas—" Ami started before being interrupted.

"Permanently?" Amos, a raven-haired Elf, shrieked. The barn went silent.

Ami frowned. "If you would stop interrupting me, I will explain." All eyes and ears were on her. "I'm going there on a mission with General Lee. I don't know the details. It's not permanent."

A sigh of relief from every Knight filled the air. It made Ami want to giggle for some reason.

"The lads I asked you to watch over. Do you mind continuing to do so while I'm away?" Ami asked.

"Is there something, in particular, we're looking out for?" Gruth, a dark reddish-brown Werewolf, asked.

"Do you remember a blond Werewolf on the streets?" Ami asked.

"His name was Savage, right?" Trudy asked.

"A real piece of work," Amos grumbled.

"Didn't he disappear a while back?" Black, a light gray Werewolf asked.

"He's back," Ami said grimly. "He may want to recreate the business again by using the lads. Could you protect them from him? Please."

"Of course, sir," Gruth agreed.

"We'll protect them," Trudy said, puffing out his chest.

"You can count on us, Captain," Amos said with a salute.

"Thank you. Are there any spare cots available?" Ami asked.

"The lads can stay in the back with us," Black said amicably.

I'm so blessed. Ami thought. Out loud, she said, "Thank you. I can't express my gratitude."

"You can express your gratitude by discussing some literature with us." Amos grinned widely.

"Which works are we discussing?" Ami answered with a smirk.

"Have we talked about Rivera's work *Down by The River?*" Amos asked.

"I'm not familiar with Rivera," Ami admitted.

"Don't worry. You're not missing much," Gruth said offhandedly.

"Excuse me, Rivera is one of the rare authors who express equality in his work," Amos retorted defensively.

"If you define equality as a female convincing a male that he should just worship her instead of attending his duties, sure," Gruth argued deadpan.

The two got into a heavy debate. During one of Amos' rants, she saw Gruth wink at her. Ami shook her head and managed to get to her room without getting dragged into a debate.

Lee and Ami exited Talient the following morning. Besides exchanging morning pleasantries, they didn't speak. Ami didn't know what to think of the Werebobcat. Very little is known about him amongst the Knights. Rikardi didn't mention him or comment about him. She didn't know how long he had been a general. From what she had observed, everyone seemed to be on edge around him. As if he could blackmail them at any time. She wondered if he was a spy in the last war.

"How long has it been since you left the capital?" Lee asked all of a sudden.

Ami nearly jumped out of her skin. She recovered quickly. "I believe it was when I looked for unicorns, sir."

"Unicorns?" Lee asked, intrigued.

"Yes, sir."

"Why?"

"It was a dare, sir," Ami answered.

"From the cadets?" Lee asked, even though he already knew the answer.

"Yes, sir."

"Why?"

"I thought if I completed the dare, I would be accepted, sir," Ami answered honestly. She glanced at him. She couldn't determine what he was thinking.

They didn't talk until they reached the fort at nightfall. The building was like a looming shadow. All Ami could tell was it was tall, bulky, and square-shaped. When they approached, the walls appeared to be made out of concrete. She couldn't wait to see what it looked like in the daylight.

"Halt!" a booming voice sounded when they were about a hundred feet from the fort. "Who comes forth?"

That phrasing is odd. Ami thought. It was said in a mixture of old and modern Ras. Was the soldier a foreigner who learned both dialects and combined them?

"'Tis I, General Lee. My companion is Captain Rose. We come with orders from Head General Tso," Lee yelled back. Ami was impressed with his range.

The familiar sound of a large door being opened creaked in front of them. A soldier holding a lit torch, an Elf, exited. She sensed archers above them. Lee whispered for her to remain put as he met the soldier halfway. The two murmured for a bit. Lee motioned for her to join him.

"Follow me," the soldier with the torch said.

As soon as they entered, the door slammed shut behind them. Ami couldn't tell much about the courtyard they entered as the soldier took a sharp left into a hallway. The halls were dark. The torch held by the Elf was their only light. Loud snoring could be heard through the doors they passed. Ami assumed this was the barracks. Turning right, they entered a hallway with lit torches on both sides. The soldier continued to hold his until he came to an empty torch holder.

"You may stay here, General Lee," the soldier said, pointing to the door on the right. "Captain, you may stay in there." He pointed to the room across from Lee.

"Thank you, soldier." Lee nodded.

The soldier sniffed and walked away without saluting. Ami raised her only eyebrow at the disrespect.

Perhaps it's not only morale we are investigating. Ami thought.

"Captain, after you get settled, I need to discuss a few things with you," Lee ordered gently.

The hair on the back of her neck stood up. "Yes, sir," Ami replied a little stiffly.

Her room was about the size of her own in the Knight's Quarters. The bathroom was slightly larger. Ami placed the knapsack the Dragons had prepared next to the bed. She pulled out her nightclothes and set them on the thin sheets. She desperately wanted to take a shower and go straight to sleep. Fighting against the urge, she went to Lee's door. She knocked.

"Enter."

She opened the door. Lee was also setting out his nightclothes. On the bed were several notebooks and pencils. She saluted.

"At ease. Close the door," Lee ordered, glancing at her as he rummaged through a sack she had barely taken notice of. That made her wary. How could she have missed that? She sniffed deeply through her nose. The sharp scent of enchantments made her sneeze.

"Bless you," Lee responded immediately.

"Thank you," Ami murmured.

"I'm sure you're wondering why we're here," Lee started,

pulling out a folded piece of paper. He placed it in a different pocket of the sack. "As you noticed, the soldiers here don't respect their betters. General Rikardi saw Commander Hector's treatment of you at the military ball and suggested investigating his fort.

"This investigation is two-fold. One, we will act as auditors, ensuring the ledgers align with what we see. During this part, you will ask basic questions of the soldiers. What is their position, how long they've been in the military, and how long they've been assigned to the fort. If they've been here more than three years, ask them what made them choose this fort over others. With me so far?"

"I am, sir," Ami replied.

"The second part is mostly observing the soldiers. How they interact with different ranks, treat each other, and react to you. In addition, listen to what they talk about if you can. These notebooks," Lee said as he motioned towards the bed, "are for our notes. If you run out of paper, let me know. I have more. Any questions?"

"What are we investigating, exactly?" Ami asked.

"Suspicions at this point. A hunch, really," Lee answered cryptically.

Ami held in a sigh. "I understand, sir."

"Anything else?" Lee asked.

"No, sir," Ami answered tiredly.

"After breakfast, we'll start our investigation. Good night, Captain," Lee dismissed her.

Ami saluted, grabbed a notebook and several pencils, and returned to her room. She placed them beside her bag. Forgoing the shower, she dressed in her nightclothes and was asleep as soon as her head hit the pillow.

Sharp knocks woke her up instantly. She groaned. It didn't feel like she had gotten any sleep. Dragging herself out of bed, she went to the door and opened it. Lee stood there, fresh and confident, in his crisp white button-down shirt with green buttons and green pants. He frowned.

"Why aren't you dressed?" Lee asked worriedly.

"I just woke up, sir," Ami answered groggily. "I'll get dressed."

She closed the door and sighed. Today was not going to be a good day. Her new captain's uniform felt odd. It looked like a fancier version of her training clothes: a stiff white cotton shirt and green pants with black sandals. Running her fingers through her short hair, she exited her room. Lee nodded at her.

"Ami?" a familiar voice asked from behind.

Salvador stood there bewildered. He wore the standard soldier attire of a black shirt and gray pants. He was barefoot.

"You will address those above you by their rank, soldier," Lee growled.

Salvador flinched. "M-My apologies, Captain Rose."

"You are forgiven this once, Soldier Dali," Ami answered calmly, "This is General Lee."

Salvador saluted correctly. Lee narrowed his eyes at him.

"Any soldier worth their salt should identify another military personnel by their rank on sight. It seems the current commander has been slacking in that regard," Lee said out loud.

Salvador didn't comment or express any emotion.

"Guide us to the dining hall," Lee snarled.

Salvador glanced at Ami nervously before complying. The uncomfortable silence hovered around them. Ami focused on the lefts and rights as Salvador was leading them. After several minutes of awkwardness, they arrived at the dining hall. All eyes bore into her. Ami ignored them, following Salvador to the food line. Glancing around, she noticed three other cadets she was familiar with. They ignored her.

Lee was vibrating next to her. He was like a volcano about to erupt. The soldiers in charge of breakfast didn't even look at them. Ami wondered if this fort had Dragons.

"I've had enough of you, maggots!" Lee bellowed. All the

soldiers stared at him owlishly. "Twenty laps around the fort!" Not a soldier moved, glancing at each other in confusion.

"The general gave a direct order!" Ami shouted. "Move out!"

Salvador immediately ran out, knowing how strict Ami was. The remaining soldiers moved, albeit slowly, as if they couldn't believe this was really happening. Lee even rounded up the soldiers in the kitchens, hissing at them to get a move on. When they reached the courtyard, all the soldiers stood there. The exception was Salvador, who was already running laps.

"The general gave the order of twenty laps!" Ami yelled. Many of the soldiers rolled their eyes at her.

That sparked her anger. It overrode her exhaustion. She let out a Dragon roar. That got the soldiers running. Ami used her tail to urge them to keep running and her menacing growl to encourage those who wanted to slow down to run faster. Lee stood in the middle, watching them with cold eyes. Salvador finished first, breathing heavily. He stood in the *ruwa* pose in front of General Lee.

"What's going on here?" Hector demanded, coming from somewhere in the fort. The Centaur glared at Ami. "Female, stop—"

"It amazes me," Lee interrupted softly, "how you don't even acknowledge my presence when I have the highest rank here."

At the last lap, Ami guided the soldiers to where Salvador stood. For those who tried to sit down, she grabbed them by the arm and forced them to stand.

"Show respect and salute properly," Ami ordered icily.

Most of the soldiers obeyed grudgingly. For those who didn't, Ami made them perform twenty pushups. Ami took her place slightly behind Lee's left side when all the soldiers were saluting correctly.

"Now that you know how to salute properly, does anyone know what rank I am?" Lee asked.

Salvador half-raised his hand. Lee nodded at him. "You are a general, sir," Salvador answered.

"Really?" Lee asked, his tone dripping with sarcasm. "Because when I got here, I might as well have been a commoner with how I've been treated!" the Werebobcat shouted. Then he whipped his attention to Hector. "And you, Commander, are to blame."

"Excuse me?" Hector asked snidely.

"Captain Rose, enlighten the commander," Lee ordered.

"Not one soldier here saluted nor greeted the general or me properly as our ranks demand. The soldiers did not obey the general's orders to run laps immediately as he directed or take his order seriously. The only soldier who did so was Soldier Dali," Ami stated matter-of-factly.

"Why have you not trained your soldiers in military etiquette, commander?" Lee demanded.

"This is my fort—" Hector tried to act intimidating.

"And I can wipe off your record and send your horse tail packing with a flick of a pen," Lee growled, stepping towards the Centaur. Despite their immense height difference, Hector stepped back while Lee appeared twice as tall. "Captain, get the lads warmed up. The morning air is rather chilly," Lee said cruelly.

"But what about breakfast?" one soldier blurted out.

"Breakfast?" Lee sneered. "You want breakfast? If you want to eat, you'll have to earn it."

"From a female?" a different soldier scoffed.

"I trained the Knights in the Inner City and made them cry." Ami's low tone sent shivers down their spines. "Permission to start, general?"

"Break them in half."

"Get in lines, soldiers!" Ami shouted. For the next two hours, Ami made them do squats, pushups, lunges, planks, and anything else that came to mind. Lee had Hector doing his own sort of workout punishment.

"Halt," Lee's voice echoed in the courtyard. "Now, lads, you've earned breakfast."

"Salute and go eat," Ami reminded them.

The soldiers obeyed without protest. Salvador walked up to Ami. She gave him a disapproving look.

"You're picking up bad habits," she stated. Without a second glance, she joined Lee and Hector.

"Let's go to your office, commander," Lee said in a way that wasn't a suggestion.

Soaked with sweat, the glaring Centaur didn't respond. He led them to his office. It was on the second level of the fort. The space was messy and strangely sparse. Old plates and bowls were piled on the floor, but there was hardly any paperwork or books. The desk was covered in dirty clothes. Moldy food and bold body odor dominated Ami's nose. She tried not to gag.

Lee wasn't doing much better. He kicked the dirty dishes out of his way. They broke against the wall.

"I see your office is the same as the rest of the fort," Lee commented.

Hector glared. Ami was surprised he wasn't baring his teeth.

"First order of business: cleaning this mess up. Commander, leave," Lee ordered.

Hector appeared to obey. Ami watched him. When the Centaur approached the door, he pulled a book out of a nearby bookcase.

"What are you doing?" Ami demanded.

Hector ran. Ami chased after him. Hector got down the stairs when Ami pounced onto his back. She dug her claws into his horse-half's ribcage, making him yelp in pain. The surprise made him trip. When he fell, the book escaped his grasp. Ami followed the book, leaping off the Centaur. She slid on the floor, grabbing the book. Her body slammed into the wall.

"Captain, are you okay?" Salvador asked, coming to her side.

"I'm fine," Ami groaned. She had definitely gained some bruises. Getting up, she saw Lee tie Hector up with rope.

"Put him in the brig until this investigation is over," Lee ordered. As soon as his orders were being followed, he looked at her. "Good quick thinking, Captain."

"Thank you, sir," Ami replied.

"We're going to need backup," Lee huffed.

"It'll take at least a day for a messenger to get to Talient," Salvador commented.

Ami went to her magic. Her white ball of light was a good size now. She focused on a message, forming the letters onto the magic like a musical composition.

"*Payam*," she murmured.

In front of her, her magic took shape. It grew into the form of a large bird. With its wide wingspan, crooked sharp beak, and unusual head feathers, the bone vulture crowed hauntingly before flying off at the speed of light.

"What was that?" Salvador asked curiously.

"A messenger spell. General Mason should have the message shortly," Ami explained briefly.

"That's handy," Lee murmured. Shaking his head, he sighed. "Let's clean up the office and see what else the commander doesn't want us to see."

"Soldier Dali, get us trash bags and cleaning supplies," Ami ordered.

"Yes, Captain," Salvador said. He saluted and went to carry out his orders.

The remainder of the day was spent cleaning the office. Only four other books were found in decent condition, hidden beneath a pile of dirty clothes. Ami counted twelve trash bags piled around the office. Lee was finishing tying the thirteenth bag.

"That's enough for today," Lee said tiredly. "I'm starving."

"Yes, sir," Ami agreed. She wiped the sweat off her brow. She stepped forward to take the bag from Lee.

Pop, pop.

They froze. Slowly, Ami lifted her foot. A piece of hardwood lifted up slightly. Lee came closer and crouched down. Using a claw, he lifted the piece of wood. Hidden underneath were more books. Grabbing one, he opened a random page.

"Our job just got harder," Lee grumbled.

"Let me guess: the real ledger?" Ami asked.

"Yes, and what I'm glancing at isn't good," Lee said, shaking his head. "Let's see if there are more secret compartments around here."

Lee found a secret compartment in the desk. The contents were a mixture of notebooks and letters. Ami inspected the bookshelves. They were empty except for random pieces of trash.

Why did Hector grab the only book on this shelf? Ami asked herself, staring at the rack closest to the door. The book was in the stack they planned to return to their rooms. She turned her attention to the shelf itself. She gently tugged on the shelves themselves. When they remained firm, she stepped back to examine them. There wasn't anything special in the look or design of the bookshelf. If anything, it looked cheap and of poor quality.

"Captain Rose, is everything okay?" Salvador asked outside the office.

Ami blinked. "Just wanting to make sure we didn't miss anything." Glancing around, she noticed all the trash bags were gone.

"I helped take the trash out while you and General Lee were preoccupied," Salvador explained.

"Thank you, Soldier Dali," Ami murmured. "Is dinner being made?"

"Yes, sir. Second-Commander Douglas is overseeing the kitchens," Salvador reported.

"The second-commander is right under the commander, correct?" Ami asked.

"Yes, sir. Second-Commander Douglas is also responsible for the new cadets and running the fort," Salvador added.

"What did Commander Hector do?" she asked.

Salvador hesitated. "I'm not sure, sir. I rarely saw him."

Interesting, Ami thought. "Thank you, Soldier Dali. General Lee, are you ready?"

"Yes, let's get these out of here." Lee sighed. "Go to dinner, soldier."

Salvador saluted and left. Ami gathered the large stack of letters and several books. Lee picked the rest. They placed the items in Lee's room.

"Put them in this sack," Lee ordered. It was the same sack that Ami had trouble remembering was there. Ami obeyed. She wondered who put such strong spells on the bag and why. After Lee put his pile in, they went to the dining hall. Salvador was waiting for them outside.

"You didn't have to wait," Ami said with a small smile.

"I don't mind the company," Salvador replied with a grin.

A tall, dark gray Werewolf approached them when they entered the hall. In a loud booming voice, he announced, "The general has entered!" He then gave a crisp salute.

The screeching of chairs against the floor rang in the air. All the soldiers in the hall stood and saluted. Ami liked this Werewolf already.

"At ease," Lee ordered gruffly. "Rank and name?"

"I am Second-Commander Douglas of Putra Hallas, sir," the Werewolf answered.

"Where were you when we arrived?" Lee asked.

"I was ordered by Commander Hector to make myself scarce during your stay. When I learned of his detainment, his orders were void," Douglas answered.

What does Douglas know that Hector didn't want him to reveal to us? Ami thought.

"I see. Let's eat and discuss some things," Lee said.

"If you'll follow me. I have a separate dinner waiting for us, sir," Douglas offered.

"Including the captain?" Lee asked.

Ami was surprised. She didn't think Lee would want her to dine with them. Douglas looked surprised as well.

"I can have another plate brought," Douglas said slowly.

"General Lee, I'm content to dine with the soldiers," Ami said. She hoped she didn't sound too anxious. "Soldier Dali and I are former comrades and wish to catch up, sir."

Lee hummed. "Very well, Captain. I'll see you after dinner."

"Thank you, sir." Ami nodded. To Salvador, she asked, "Shall we?"

Ami and Salvador joined the line.

"Do you know what they're serving?" Ami asked eagerly.

"I was not part of the prepping, so I'm not sure, sir," Salvador answered.

Ami sniffed the air. "It at least smells delicious."

The food line was set up almost exactly as in Talient. It felt odd being served by soldiers instead of Dragons. Dinner was fried chicken with white gravy, green beans, and mashed potatoes. Salvador guided her to a table in the middle of the dining hall.

"This feels familiar," Ami commented.

It took a second for Salvador to catch on. "The only difference is that the males here don't hate you."

"For now," Ami said, digging into her food. It was bland compared to Talient, but edible.

"You have made an impression," Salvador said.

Ami hummed. "Before we came, what was life like here?"

Salvador shrugged. "Very routine. Trying to get used to being at a fort, honestly."

"Even over a year?" Ami asked.

"Yeah, it took me a while to get used to Talient too. I guess I'm weird like that," Salvador said. He stuffed his mouth with chicken. His ears were pink.

"How are things different?" Ami asked.

It took a minute for Salvador to chew and swallow. "Every day is the same, but ..." Salvador started. He whispered, "There are a lot of things I need to tell you. Privately."

Ami nodded. "I see. You want to hear a tale?"

Salvador's ears perked straight up. "Yes, please."

"Have you heard the story of Qu'uan's first emperor, the Jade Heron?" Ami asked.

"I thought Hideki was the first emperor," Salvador pointed out.

"Not quite. Hideki united the nation, but he didn't rule it. That went to his nephew, Seiji," Ami explained. Seeing Salvador's confused face, she elaborated, "After Hideki united the island, they later discovered that Ryoko was pregnant with her dead husband's child. Since the child was from the Qua clan, he became the first emperor. Hideki and his family managed the administration aspect."

She went to tell the story of the Jade Heron. Seiji, at sixteen years old, had a lot on his shoulders. An introvert with low confidence, he had suffered from anxiety and struggled to socialize with his peers. Hoping to help his nephew, Hideki suggested that Seiji go on an adventure for a year and explore the land he reigned. Ryoko was against the idea, but Seiji agreed. Donning a disguise, Seiji set out on his journey.

On his way through the mountains, Seiji encountered bandits. Outnumbered, they beat him up and mugged him, stripping him of everything he owned. They left him on the mountain road for dead. Not long after, a monk came upon him. However, the monk passed on. Shortly after the monk left, an odd Person came upon the fallen emperor. This Person picked Seiji up and brought him to a cave. The bizarre Person took care of Seiji, feeding and healing his wounds there.

When Seiji regained consciousness, he asked for the Person's name. She replied, "I am Nasrin." When he asked what People she was, she replied, "I am a Dragon."

"Wait, a Dragon?" a soldier exclaimed from the table to their left.

Ami jumped. She didn't realize she had an audience. "Yes, a Dragon. May I continue?"

"Sorry, Captain," the soldier said abashedly.

Nasrin guided Seiji through the mountains. Seiji asked Nasrin to accompany him on his adventure. Nasrin agreed. They came to a river without a bridge. As they debated on what to do, a Merperson surfaced. Seiji asked if they would help them cross the river. The Merperson replied that they must answer a riddle. If they answer correctly, the Merperson will help them cross. After agreeing, the Merperson said,

What is greater than the Creator,
More evil than the inhabitants of the Pits?
The poor have it; the wealthy have no need of it.
If you consume it, you will die.

Ami paused in the story. "Can anyone guess the answer?"

"Could you repeat it, please?" a soldier from Ami's right asked.

She repeated the riddle. All the soldiers had thoughtful looks.

"I'm going to end the story there," Ami said. Numerous groans reached her ears, making her grin. "I'll tell you the answer tomorrow at dinner. It's getting late, lads."

"I'll escort you to your room," Salvador said quickly.

"Thank you. I'm not sure I'd be able to find my way by myself just yet," Ami said gratefully.

The two left the dining hall after cleaning up their plates. Ami noticed they were going a different way. Were they going the long way so they could speak? Salvador slowed to a halt before turning to face her in an empty hallway. Salvador was only a few inches taller than her, no longer towering over a foot above her. Salvador had an indecipherable look on his face. Without warning, he hugged her tightly. Slowly Ami hugged him back. They stayed like that for several moments.

"What's wrong, Sal?" she asked, her voice soft and calm.

"It's getting worse," Salvador said brokenly. He pulled away enough to see her face.

"Is it the witch that cursed your family? Can he sense her?" Ami asked.

Salvador shook his head. "He's so stubborn. He won't tell me who he wants to kill or what they look like."

Ami paused. That was strange. People don't converse with curses. As far as she knew, curses weren't sentient. "I know you said you had a dream about him. Are you saying you're talking to him?" Ami asked.

Salvador shrugged. "I guess? I mean, he's in my head, and I can feel his magic whenever my emotions run hot."

"Your emotions? Any particular ones?" Ami asked, staring at him intently.

Salvador started to blush. "Um, you know, um, anger and stuff."

"What other stuff?" Ami urged.

Salvador's blush went dark red. He released the hug and took several steps back. His eyes refused to meet hers. "That's really personal, Ami," he mumbled.

It took a moment to realize what he was not saying. "Oh."

"A-Anyway, what does that mean?" Salvador asked. He started to fidget with his fingers.

"Well, if the Dali curse truly is a curse, it's the strangest one I've encountered," Ami admitted.

"How so?"

"First off, curses don't communicate with their host," Ami said. "They act more like viruses that can't be healed, and the symptoms get worse. Speaking of symptoms, I'm not seeing the typical symptoms of someone who is cursed."

"What are the symptoms?" Salvador asked, finally looking at her.

"Weight loss, lack of sleep, random bouts of uncontrollable pain, lack of appetite, migraines, I could go on. Some experience hallucinations, others experience boils or rashes. With this curse, if it is one, you aren't experiencing any of it. Even dormant curses do something to their host," Ami explained.

"So," Salvador asked, hope lacing his voice, "this may not be a curse?"

"That's what I don't understand," Ami said in a frustrated voice. "Why call it a curse if it wasn't? Also, if it isn't a curse, then what is it?" Then Ami realized something. "You said you can feel his magic. How do you know it's his magic?"

Salvador looked confused. "Because it's green? And in the stories, that's how Conri's magic is described."

"I know at least four People whose magic is the color green," Ami stated. "It's not unique just to Conri."

"Well, that's what my grandmother always told us. She—" Salvador stopped. He gulped and looked away. "She told me about the Dali curse and made me repeat the story until I had it memorized."

Ami's eye narrowed. She had a feeling she wasn't going to like this grandmother. "Why did she make you memorize—"

"Ahem." Lee stood a few feet away from them. From his crossed arms, he didn't look impressed.

Ami and Salvador immediately saluted the general.

"At ease. Soldier dismissed. Captain, my quarters," Lee ordered.

Salvador left, glancing over his shoulder after he passed Lee. Ami followed the Werebobcat into his room.

"We will need to start our investigation. Your task is to go through the letters. Figure out who Hector was writing to and why. I'm reviewing the ledgers and trying to make sense of this mess. It's going to be a sleepless night," Lee said, his voice already sounding tired. He pulled out the large stack and handed it to her.

"Yes, sir." Ami nodded. She gathered the large stack of letters and headed to her room. Just as she reached the door, Lee said, "Captain, you need to be careful."

"Understood, sir," Ami stated without turning to look at the Werebobcat. She exited and entered her room. Lighting a lantern on the nightstand, she sat on the floor, using the bed as a backrest. Starting with the first letter on top, she began to read.

Screams echoed in the abyss. Hot irons rhythmically pounded into the Shadow, making Ryft scream with each blow. Emyr and Egan watched emotionlessly. Egan was fuming inside. Little mistress was never meant to be harmed enough to be brought to his master's realm without a body. Nor did he expect Ryft to try to attack and kill little mistress. He would've never trained her in the magical arts if he had known she was jealous. Glancing at Emyr, he knew his master was not pleased with Ryft's attempt.

"Master, please!" Ryft pleaded. "Please, forgive me!"

"Forgive you?" Emyr's icy voice rumbled over the Shadow's screams. "You not only failed to bring Amaranth home, but you harmed her to death. Do you realize how hard it was to temporarily bring her soul here? And when I was ready to greet her, she managed to return to the living. Now, she is harder to obtain than before."

Emyr turned and started to walk away. Egan followed. Ryft's screams grew fainter as they entered the Shadow King's home. Emyr sighed heavily.

"She can't be left up there, though," Emyr muttered.

Egan remained silent with a frown. His master was growing more and more agitated ever since little mistress escaped.

He barely evaded whip lashings from his master's tail by shifting the blame to Ryft's failure. He rolled his shoulders. His master gave him several bruises on his back for not protecting his little mistress appropriately. Egan felt he deserved that.

"Egan," Emyr broke his thoughts. "Bring Amaranth home."

"How?" Egan asked hesitantly.

"Bring her whole, body and soul," Emyr ordered. "Use any opportunity you see. She needs to be here."

"Yes, master." Egan bowed and left.

CHAPTER 5

Ami closed her eyes. Her head pounded. She spent the last five days talking to the soldiers and Salvador and her nights studying the letters between Hector and his mysterious pen pal. Her nose wrinkled. She needed a shower. Getting up, she moaned as her legs protested.

The letters were scattered in chaotic yet organized piles across the floor. So far, she couldn't decipher who Hector was possibly writing to or what they were writing about. The commander was intelligent in hiding his actual meaning. Carefully toeing around the letters, she entered the bathroom. Stripping bare, she turned the water to its hottest and greeted the water spray with a half-smile. When steam filled the small area, the pounding in her head slowly went away. Now able to think, she went over what she knew so far.

Many of the soldiers had not been in Putra Hallas for long. It averaged around one to two years, not including the new cadets from Talient. Only two had been at the fort for longer. Sir Tres, an Elf of veteran status, had been stationed at the fort for the past twenty years. He was there before Hector became commander seven years ago. Tres often helped Douglas in running the fort. The other soldier was Sir Kain, who came a year after Hector. Ami intended to speak with him when he had night guard duty. Her mind went back to the letters.

What am I missing? She asked herself. The letters appeared to be randomly written. They didn't have a date, and from the writing, they were from a male. In some areas, there seemed to be flirting between Hector and this mysterious writer. *Were these letters from a forbidden lover?* She wasn't wholly convinced. *I need to look at this differently. First, I need to sleep.*

Turning off the water, she dried off. Three sharp knocks came from her door. Wrapping the towel around her, Ami exited the bathroom. She quickly gathered the letters into one pile and put them out of the way. She then opened the door. Lee stood there in his nightclothes.

"Captain, get dressed and meet me in my room," Lee ordered.

"Yes, sir." Ami saluted and closed the door. Her bed stared at her like a temptress. She dressed tiredly in her pajamas. Grabbing her notebook and pencils, she went to Lee's room. Lee was already at the small round table.

"Close the door and sit down," Lee mumbled tiredly. He looked as tired as she felt. Ami closed the door. She occupied the remaining seat at the table. "Have you been able to decipher the letters?"

"Not yet, sir," Ami admitted.

Lee rubbed his furry face with both hands. Reaching to grab his ears, he sighed. "Tell me what you know so far."

"From what I've gathered, the writer appears to be a male. I haven't been able to tell what exactly they are writing about. Some parts are flirty, though," Ami reported.

"A lover?" Lee asked, making a face.

"It's not confirmed, sir. It could be a ruse," Ami pointed out.

"What do you mean?" Lee asked.

"Given your reaction, would you read more of the letter if you read that part?" Ami asked.

Lee blinked. "I see."

"I've spoken to the soldiers here," Ami continued. "The only ones who have been here for over two years are Sir Tres and Sir Kain. Sir Tres has been here for the past twenty years, long before the commander took command. Sir Kain came a year after the commander. I'll speak to him tomorrow night when he has guard duty."

"Why wait until then?" Lee asked.

"The males are quite nosy and gossipy," Ami said.

"It's because of boredom," Lee said grimly.

"I don't think the Knights are giving them any reason to be bored," Ami said with a half-grin. Mason had sent ten Knights from Talient to assist them the morning after Ami sent the request. The Knights were happy to see Ami again and were eager to "help" the soldiers with their military etiquette. Ami appreciated the temporary break.

"True." Lee nodded. He looked at the stack of notebooks on his nightstand. "I think I'm encountering the same problems you have with these ledgers. Hector used odd language and acronyms I can't make heads or tails of." The Werebobcat rubbed his eyes.

"Sir, may I go to sleep?" Ami nearly begged. She could barely keep her eyes open and felt sick to her stomach.

"You may. I'm going to do the same. Dismissed." Lee yawned widely.

Ami gathered her things and went back to her room. Setting them next to her bed, she blew out the candle on her nightstand, curled under the covers, and instantly fell asleep. In the corner of her room, a shadow shifted. Red burning eyes emerged from the darkness. Like a crocodile in the water, the Shadow extended toward Ami's sleeping form. The young female didn't stir.

Just as the Shadow reached the edge of her bedframe, a Person appeared out of thin air, crouching over Ami protectively. Despite the Person's weight on the bed, Ami didn't stir. The Shadow hissed in warning. The Person, with their dark skin, blended in the darkness. Cornflower-colored eyes shined in the night. From the Person's palm, a ball of light suddenly burst. The Shadow shrieked in pain as it was banished. The Person turned invisible when the Shadow was banished and resumed their guard.

Ami opened her eyes at a light in her room even though there wasn't a window and the candle was unlit. Calmly, she got up and exited her room. Light exposed the fort's hallways without aid from the dead torches. Ami walked down the hall towards the courtyard. However, she realized she wasn't at Putra Hallas when she reached outside.

Snow covered the ground. A light, brisk wind blew her long white hair. Someone yelled a familiar name. Ami turned to the voice. It was a Person. She knew this Person well, yet she couldn't recall their name or defining features. As they continued to yell, her vision blurred. Faintly, elsewhere, someone else was calling her name. This voice was more familiar.

Salvador, her mind supplied. *Why is Salvador calling for me?* As she focused more on Salvador's voice, it grew louder, and the other Person's voice became fainter. She crossed the bridge from dream to reality and woke up with a gasp.

"Ami, wake up!" Salvador begged with tears in his eyes.

"Sal?" Ami asked groggily.

"Ami? Oh, thank the Almighty One," Salvador said, sinking to his knees next to her bed.

"What's going on?" Ami mumbled, rubbing her eyes and yawning widely.

"You've been asleep all day. General Lee tried to get you for breakfast but allowed you to sleep. When we noticed no one had seen you all day, I volunteered to get you for dinner. I called for you from the door, but you didn't say anything. Then I entered and tried to call for you again. Then I started to shake you cuz you-you-you—" Salvador explained. His stutter at the end prevented him from completing his thought.

"I didn't mean to scare you, Sal. I'm awake now." Ami

tried to console the shaking Werewolf. She grabbed one of his large hands. He squeezed it. Several tears escaped his eyes. Ami gently wiped them off with her free hand.

"Captain!" Black the Knight called out as he entered.

"Sir Black, what's the matter?" Ami asked.

"Are you all right, sir?" Black asked.

"I'm awake now." Ami yawned. "I'm going to take a shower and dress."

Both males left the room, shutting the door behind them. She could sense Salvador's anxiety from the door. Ami quickly showered and dressed. When she opened the door, Lee was also outside.

"Greetings, Captain. Have a good nap?" Lee asked.

Ami saluted. "Yes, sir."

"Good. Go eat and continue your investigation," Lee ordered.

"Yes, sir." Ami saluted and went to the dining hall. Salvador and Black followed closely behind her.

Every soldier she passed nodded and mumbled a greeting to her. It seemed like the Knights' lessons were taking hold. Tonight's dinner was just as bland as last night's meal. Ami wondered if it was a fort thing or if the cooks didn't believe in spices.

"Captain, may I ask a question that may be personal?" Black asked.

"You may ask," Ami answered warily.

"Why did you sleep so late today?" Black asked. "Is something wrong?"

Ami shook her head. "No. I've been up for the past five days. I pushed myself too hard and slept more than I intended."

"Five days straight?" Salvador asked.

"Yes. I've been completing what General Lee has commanded me," Ami replied.

Black whistled in a low tone. "I knew he was a *majkeeka*, but I didn't realize how much until now."

Ami snorted loudly. It evolved into low chuckles she struggled to hide under her breath.

"What's so funny?" Salvador asked.

"The w-word he used." Ami snickered.

"*Majkeeka?*" Black asked with a smirk. Ami snorted like a pig. It made Salvador and Black burst into laughter. When he calmed down, Black asked, "What's so funny about it?"

"It ..."—she gasped—"it has a different meaning in Vin." Ami barely managed to reply.

"Oh?" Black asked, his wolf ears forward with interest.

"Instead of meaning 'one whose rear is made of stone,' in Vin, it means, 'one's face which resembles my rear.'" Ami explained. She continued to giggle while the males looked confused. Clearing her throat, she added, "You have to speak Vin to get the reference, I suppose."

"I don't think I've seen you laugh so much," Salvador said fondly.

"It took me by surprise, honestly," Ami admitted.

They chatted as they ate. When Ami realized the time, she excused herself. The fort's layout was confusing for such a simple-looking building. Every time Ami thought she had the floor planned out, something new popped up and challenged her understanding. The only thing she knew for sure was the location of the dining hall and the archer's landing.

The archer's landing was at the top of the fort. Many would think this was the roof, but it was flat to allow archers and soldiers to move freely without the threat of sliding off. Walls enclosed the area from enemy arrows. Cleverly designed slits were carved into the concrete walls to allow archers to fire their arrows while being protected. It was here where Sir Kain warily walked as he performed his nightguard duties. Ami paused at the top of the stairs that led to the archer's landing. Sir Kain, a black Werewolf, glanced over his shoulder.

"Captain." He nodded at her.

"Sir Kain." Ami nodded back.

"I've heard of the stories you tell the soldiers," Sir Kain said, resuming his guard.

"Have you heard of them?" Ami asked. She came to the soldier's side. She stood about a foot away at his right.

"Not the versions you tell. I will admit that I know little of Qu'uan and its stories," Sir Kain replied honestly.

"Then I'm happy to share them. Stories of Qu'uan are some of my favorites," Ami said.

"Too bad there aren't more females like you," Sir Kain said sadly. "The ones I know would never share knowledge and culture so freely."

"You don't want more versions of me," Ami protested playfully.

"Why not?" Sir Kain asked, glancing at her.

"First off, it would be awkward."

Sir Kain chuckled. "How is it working under the general?"

"It hasn't been a week. I can't form an adequate opinion," Ami answered vaguely. "It is different from General Rikardi."

"How so?" Sir Kain asked curiously.

"Mostly their personalities. Each has different approaches to problems. I'm learning as I go," Ami said.

"Understandable." Sir Kain nodded.

"May I ask a question?" Ami asked.

"You may."

"I was taught that soldiers moved forts every two years. How have you and Sir Tres been here longer than that?" Ami asked.

"When one has been in the military for at least ten years, you can choose a fort for permanent residence unless the fort selected is full. Typically, a soldier will submit the top three forts they wish to reside in and seven optional ones if the top three are full," Sir Kain explained.

"That makes more sense. Thank you for explaining."

"Captain?" a soldier whose name Ami didn't know emerged from the stairs. "The general wishes to speak with you."

"Thank you, soldier. Good night, Sir Kain," Ami said, nodding to each male.

Lee was pacing with a thunderous look when Ami arrived at his room.

"Have you heard?" Lee growled.

"No, sir," Ami replied.

"We have traitors in this fort," Lee hissed. His pacing turned into stomping. "*Ta-bo eiretta* no good socks freed Hector!" Lee roared.

"What?" Ami gasped.

"He's gone, and no one knows who freed him," Lee snarled. He stopped pacing abruptly. The Werebobcat was vibrating with rage. "Find them," Lee ordered in a dangerous tone. "Lock this fort down and interrogate everyone. No one is exempt from this."

"Yes, sir." Ami saluted, her eyes hardening.

The next four days were brutal. With the help of the Knights, Ami rounded up soldier after soldier as she interrogated them like clockwork. Even Salvador wasn't spared Ami's interrogation. The Werewolf looked at her like she murdered his whole family before him. She pushed her feelings of guilt aside. Being overly cautious, Ami ordered several Knights to patrol outside the fort in case any tried to leave. It paid off when three were caught going through a secret tunnel and thrown in the brig. The Knights guarded the brig strictly.

She did learn something disturbing. Each soldier told a similar story of an event happening two months ago. A soldier's sister came to visit. Hector heckled and made sexual advances toward the female the entire week she visited the fort. Even with the soldier, other males, and the female telling him to back off, Hector didn't listen. On her last day, Hector attempted to rape her. She was barely saved by her brother, who attacked the commander. The soldier was punished for striking the commander, and his sister managed to leave the fort without further incident. What remained elusive was the soldier's name and why he was punished for defending his sister.

This bothered Ami greatly. Rascals were close-knit and didn't allow outsiders to mess with their families, especially their females. The fact that the soldier protected his sister yet was punished for defending her didn't make sense. The soldiers were leaving out a crucial detail. She needed to find it. First, she needed to know his name and rank. She moved up the ranks in her interrogation. The sergeants told a similar story, but now she knew his name: Bru Fonte. He was a sergeant until he was demoted to night lead after the incident.

"Where can I find him?" Ami demanded.

"He usually has night duty, but he's hard to find," the Elf sergeant answered nervously.

"Why?" Ami asked in a stern tone.

The Elf swallowed hard. "After his demotion, he's been keeping a low profile. Hardly anyone has seen him."

"Not even for meals?" Ami asked.

The Elf shook his head. "He's probably sneaking into the kitchens after mealtime."

"Why was he punished so harshly?" Ami asked.

The Elf started to shake under Ami's one-eyed glare. "H-He's a foreigner. He's not R-Rascal."

"Why was Hector allowed to harass his sister without consequence? I thought Rascals prized females above males," Ami drawled.

"S-She's also foreign and unwed. When she arrived, the commander found out she wa-wasn't engaged," the Elf answered shakily.

Foreigners are easy targets, Ami thought bitterly. *It explains my treatment and lack of punishment of the males for the bleach.*

She asked several more questions about Bru Fonte before dismissing the sergeant. Noticing the time, she stopped interrogating for the day. The next ones on her list were Sir Tres and Second-Commander Douglas. She would get to them later. The two constantly ran around to keep the fort in working order. She had to find Bru and find out what had happened.

She entered the dining hall. The males regarded her with fear and more respect than before. Getting her food, she sat at the table with Salvador. The Werewolf only glanced at her before staring back at his food. They had barely said a word since Ami had interrogated him thoroughly. She wasn't in the mood to appease him. She took a bite of food. Her taste buds wept in mourning. Another bland meal with an awkward atmosphere.

"Captain?" a soldier sitting at the table to Ami's right asked.

"Yes?"

"Can you continue the tale about the Jade Heron?" the soldier asked nervously.

Ami thought for a moment. She didn't have a meeting with Lee tonight. The Werebobcat told her he was writing a report to Tso about his investigation and needed to be alone. She needed to stay up to talk to Bru anyway.

"I don't see why not. Where did I leave off?" Ami asked.

"It was the riddle the Merperson asked," Another soldier at the same table as the first replied eagerly.

"Has anyone guessed the answer?" Ami asked.

"Can you repeat it, sir?" a soldier at a table to her left asked.

Ami did so. After a few minutes, the soldiers were frustrated.

"What's the answer?" asked a soldier.

"Nothing," Ami answered. The soldiers gaped at her, the answer not quite registering. "Think about it: Nothing is greater than the Almighty One. Nothing is more evil than the inhabitants of the Pits. The poor have nothing, the wealthy need nothing, and if you consume nothing, you will die," Ami explained.

"Oooohhh," echoed throughout the dining hall. There were several grumbles about not working out a simple answer.

"Anyway, Seiji and Nasrin did know the answer, and the Merperson helped them across the river," Ami continued.

Seiji and Nasrin came to a small village. The People were wailing and sobbing. When asked, the villagers explained that a witch had come and taken their children. They didn't know where the witch lived, but knew she came from the nearby forest. Seiji and Nasrin entered the forest. Soon, they went to a cottage. A beautiful female came out to greet them.

"Greetings, strangers. Would you like to rest your feet and fill your stomachs with food?" the female asked.

"Don't do it. It's a trap," Ami heard one soldier mutter.

"We were wondering if you had seen a child in your forest," Nasrin replied. "Her parents told us that she went into the forest, but they haven't seen her since. They are very worried."

"I have not seen a child, but I thought I heard someone pass by my cottage earlier today," the beautiful female said.

"Thank you, and good day," Nasrin said. She dragged a confused Seiji away.

Seiji complained about how tired he was and wouldn't have minded resting and eating. Nasrin had to explain to him that the female was the witch. Seiji didn't believe a female of such beauty could be a witch. Nasrin tried to convince him otherwise, but Seiji wasn't listening. Somehow, Seiji managed to get away from Nasrin and made his way back to the cottage.

The beautiful female was surprised but pleased to see him alone. He entered the cottage. He ate her food and drank her tea. Before he could finish the tea, he fell into a deep sleep. The witch bound him with rope and dragged him to her basement, where the villagers' children were being kept.

Nasrin found Seiji's trail and followed it to the witch's cottage. She waited until Denarii shined brightly in the sky. The witch, unable to ignore her evil ritual, left the hut. Nasrin entered and found the entrance to the basement. There she freed Seiji and the villagers' children. They returned to the village. The villagers were thankful and begged Nasrin and Seiji to remove the witch.

"To get rid of the witch, we must pray to the Almighty

One to bring down such evil. Hold tight to your faith and pray for this evil to be banished," Nasrin ordered.

Every villager and child who could speak raised their voices to the Almighty One. As the light of Denarii shone brighter, a thunderstorm echoed through the clear sky. Without clouds or rain, a bolt of red lightning slapped the ground. It shook the earth violently. Once the ground stopped shaking, Nasrin, Seiji, and the villagers raced to where the lightning struck. In the middle of the field, all that remained of the witch was scorched earth. The villagers cheered and celebrated for two days. Nasrin and Seiji were honored guests. During that time, Seiji apologized to Nasrin.

"I'm going to end the tale there for tonight," Ami said, her throat slightly sore.

"There's more?" a soldier asked.

"Oh, yes. We still have three more characters to meet," Ami teased.

The soldiers talked excitedly as they left the dining hall. Salvador abruptly left without a word to Ami. She sighed. Picking up her plate, she went to the kitchen. The cook and assistants were already gone. Ami washed her plate and placed it on the drying rack. She fixed herself a cup of tea and waited.

Bru showed up on her fourth cup of tea. He froze when he realized he wasn't alone.

"You do realize that Hector is no longer at the fort, correct?" Ami asked, sipping her tea. Bru watched her with a calculating look. Ami watched back. Bru was a dark Werewolf. The lack of light made it hard to determine its actual color.

"Hector is gone?" Bru asked. His strong accent suggested he was from the southern desert. It irked Ami for some reason. It sounded fake.

"Yes. Someone helped him escape," Ami said.

Bru seemed more confused than relieved. "Why are you here?"

"I wanted to ask you about your sister—" Ami started.

"You want to mock me too?" Bru sneered. "You *niho koko* are all the same. Just because I'm a foreigner—"

"You must've not heard of me," Ami interrupted coldly. Bru narrowed his eyes at her. "My name is Amaranth."

Bru's eyes widened. "That's a Vincian name."

"Exactly. Now, what happened when your sister visited you?" Ami asked.

Bru immediately launched into telling her everything. His account was more appalling than the water-downed version the soldiers had told her. When he finished, Ami thanked him and left to see Lee.

The light under Lee's door told her he was still awake. She knocked. Lee opened with tired eyes.

"Captain?" Lee asked.

"May I come in, sir?" Ami asked.

Lee motioned with his hand as he stepped aside. She entered. When he closed the door, her magic reached out. A purple sheen covered the walls and floor before disappearing.

"What was that?" Lee demanded.

"Privacy shield," Ami answered shortly. "I may have a lead on Hector."

The Werebobcat turned attentive. "I'm listening."

"When I was interrogating the soldiers, each told a story about a soldier's sister that visited several months ago. While she was here, Hector became obsessed with her. He even tried to rape her," Ami explained. Lee's eyes narrowed dangerously. "The soldier's sister lives in a village a few hours north of the fort. I'm requesting permission to go to the village for further investigation."

Lee hummed thoughtfully. "Do you think he would go after this female?"

"If he was obsessed with her, as I was told, I wouldn't be surprised," Ami said. "I'm hoping to find letters he may have written to her."

Lee's ears perked up. "That would be handy in court. Get

some rest. We'll come up with a game plan after we both sleep," Lee ordered.

"Thank you, sir." Ami saluted. When she exited, the privacy shield fell. She took a shower and dressed in her nightclothes. She got under the sheets and relaxed.

Sleep evaded her that night. Bru's tale of how his sister was treated horrified Ami. She hoped the female was safe and away from Hector. A shift in the air caught her attention. She sat up. Glancing around the dark, she listened. She saw a pair of red eyes from the furthest corner of her room.

"Egan?" Ami called out.

"Little mistress," Egan replied. His deep voice filled the room. She couldn't see his mouth.

"Why are you here?" Ami asked.

"Master wants you home," Egan answered. Strangely, he sounded reluctant.

"Why?" Ami asked.

"It is his demand," Egan said vaguely. "I have orders to bring you home, no matter what."

"And if I don't want to come?" Ami asked. Her magic began to build in her chest.

"You are to come in body *and* soul," Egan emphasized.

"I still don't want to come," Ami retorted.

"Please, little mistress," Egan pleaded. "Don't make this difficult."

"Tell me why he wants me so badly," Ami demanded.

Egan stared at her for a moment before replying, "You don't know?"

Never had the desire to strangle a Person been so strong. "Why do you think I'm asking?" Ami shrieked incredulously.

"We thought he told you. We thought you knew," Egan said. He seemed to be talking to himself.

"If you won't tell me, I'll keep banishing you," Ami threatened.

Egan stared at her. Somehow she could see a war battling in his eyes.

"Look deep in your memories, little mistress," Egan warned solemnly. "It will bring more clarity than me telling you."

Then he was gone.

CHAPTER 6

The journey to the village was exhausting. Ami suffered two dizzy spells that disoriented her to the point where she got lost three times. When she left that morning, she estimated she would arrive late afternoon. Now it was looking like nighttime. Seeing the village in the distance didn't relieve the nauseating sensation in her stomach. It was pitch black when she entered. The scent of smoke, burnt wood, and fear filled the air. As she walked what she assumed was the main road, hardly any of the homes had lights lit or looked to be occupied. Uneasiness became Ami's shadow as she searched for shelter.

After wandering for an hour, she managed to find an inn. From the shattered window, a light was lit inside. The smell of smoke was strong as she entered. The main area was a mess. Toppled tables and chairs were scattered across the dusty floor. Behind the bar were a scrawny female Elf and a slim male Elf. The female Elf squeaked when she saw Ami. She disappeared to the back. The male Elf narrowed his eyes at Ami. Ami was staring at his impressive mustache. It was thick and bushy. She could only recall select Nobles in Vinci having such facial hair.

"Who are you, and what do you want?" the Elf demanded gruffly.

"I'm from Putra Hallas. I wish to stay a few nights, please," Ami answered politely.

The Elf eyed her suspiciously. "You're one of them soldiers, eh? Come to make fun of the foreigners for laughs?"

"What soldiers?" Ami asked, her eye narrowing.

"The ones from the fort you're from. They come and mess with the villagers for kicks and giggles," the Elf said heatedly. "That's all they do. They torment them cuz there's nothing in the books about soldiers messin' around with foreigners and they don't get any punishment."

"I was not aware of this—" Ami started.

"And where were the investigators we were promised three months ago when the bandits attacked?" the Elf continued, as if he didn't hear Ami. "We've been livin' in fear daily, and now they send one soldier? And they wonder why we don't respect them," the Elf huffed.

"Are you through?" Ami asked.

The Elf glared. "I am."

"I am Captain Amaranth Rose. I am here under the authority of General Lee to investigate the harassment and possible assault of Bru Fonte's sister. I was unaware of the soldiers' conduct towards the villagers here or of a bandit attack. However, I will take your statement and any other information the villagers may have on this incident," Ami explained.

The Elf gaped at her. Behind him, she saw the female Elf peek her head out.

"You're the Blessed Rose?" the Elf asked in awe.

The Blessed Rose? What kind of name is that? Ami thought. "I am known as Captain Rose. I do not know of this 'Blessed Rose' you speak of."

"Are you the one who saved the cadets?" the female Elf asked, coming to the male Elf's side.

"I am."

"Thank you for your service," the male Elf said sincerely. "A few of the villagers' sons were saved by you."

"I was doing my duty," Ami replied automatically.

"Maria, put something on for our guest. I'll get a table set up," the Elf ordered.

"Yes, Uncle," Maria answered. She disappeared to the back. The sounds of pots and pans filled the air.

"Please wait one moment," the male said. Going around the bar, he straightened the nearest table and chair. With a rag, he wiped down both swiftly. "Please sit. Your meal will be out shortly." He gestured with one arm.

"Thank you." Ami nodded.

The male left to assist Maria. Ami sat in the chair, her mind in chaos. She rested her knapsack on the floor next to her chair.

What were the soldiers doing here? Was it of their own volition, or did Hector encourage them? Her thoughts swirled to the more significant issue. *Bandits? Here? How did they get so close to Talient without the generals or Jasmine knowing? Why haven't I heard about it? Why isn't anyone talking about this? What is going on?*

Her thoughts were interrupted by the smell of spiced food. Her nose cheered when it detected sweet rosemary, thyme, and garlic. Maria and her uncle came carrying dishes in both hands. The dishes placed on the table made a feast. Grilled chicken with savory gravy sat on top of wild black rice, green beans coated with creamed mushroom soup, and cheesy broccoli sat on one dish. On another platter, slow-roasted beef with chopped carrots and radishes with smooth mashed potatoes. The third contained a pile of small rolls, perfect for dipping in leftover gravy. A large glass of water completed the meal. The two Elves turned to leave.

"Would you join me?" Ami asked. "I can't eat all of this by myself." Her previous appetite hadn't returned, and she hated wasting food.

The Elves looked surprised but happy at her request. Maria quickly got extra plates and silverware. Ami's tongue sang when it tasted the rich flavor of the food. They chatted about safe subjects. The male Elf, Roger, was the only innkeeper in the village. Maria was his niece whom he had raised since she was two. Maria was fifteen and learning about the business to help Roger. Roger left first to prepare Ami's room.

"It has to be intimidating to be in the military as a female," Maria commented.

"Not really. I was in the military in Vinci." Ami shrugged.

"Don't the males make disrespecting remarks and stuff that makes you uncomfortable?" Maria asked.

"I don't really pay attention to it," Ami lied.

You know that's not true. Felicia's voice scoffed.

Ami stiffened a gasp. *Felicia?* No answer. *Blessing? Emotion? Serene?* Silence greeted her. Sorrow filled Ami's heart.

"Are you okay?" Maria asked gently.

Ami blinked away the tears. "I apologize. I thought I heard something." Her voice shook.

"My apologies, milady. You probably heard me rummaging about," Roger answered as he came down the stairs. "Your room is ready."

"Thank you. The meal was delicious," Ami said. She stood up and followed the Elf upstairs with her knapsack in hand.

Her room was the first door on the left at the top of the stairs. It was small and basic. A twin bed was the only piece of furniture in the room. It was fine by Ami. Thanking Roger, she set her knapsack down. Exhaustion punched her in the face several times. She barely managed to change into her night-clothes before passing out.

She looked around. She was dreaming again. It was evident by the deep snow covering the ground. *Why am I here?* Ami wondered.

"Logic!" Emotion's voice cried out.

Ami swirled around. A small figure almost tackled her to the ground. Ami barely kept her balance. The small figure hugged her tightly. Then Ami felt something dampening her shirt.

"Emotion?" Ami asked cautiously.

"Logic! You remembered me!" The small figure cried out. She released Ami. Emotion didn't look like what Ami had imagined. Then again, she didn't really imagine the voices having faces when they were in her head. Emotion was a Faerie with dark blue hair and blue eyes. She wore a blue halter summer dress with bright yellow flowers. From her back came light blue wings shaped like flower petals. They made a buzzing sound as Emotion circled Ami happily.

"Where are you?" Ami asked as she watched Emotion buzz around like a bumblebee.

Emotion landed in front of Ami, a solemn look on her face. "I don't know," she answered in her childlike voice.

"Where are the others?" Ami asked.

"I don't know. All I see is darkness," Emotion said, her voice becoming faint.

Sensing the dream was about to end, Ami persisted. "When you are awake, what do you see?" Ami demanded.

"I see stones. Pretty stones all around," Emotion replied sleepily. Her voice and presence were fading right before Ami's eyes.

"Are you in the northern mines?" Ami urged.

"Mines? No Dragons. Pretty stones," Emotion said before she disappeared completely.

Ami bolted straight up with a loud gasp. Emotion was alive! She was real! That meant the others were real as well. Something solid clicked with Ami's heart. It made her feel more centered and more in tune with reality.

Why is she in the northern mines? Ami wondered. It was the only place she could think that fit what Emotion described. That also meant she would have to kill the witch residing there. *I have to get stronger first. I will have to practice my magic more. Then I will rescue her and find the others.* Ami determined.

Her internal clock told her it was almost dawn. She forced her body to move. All it wanted to do was go back to sleep.

Thankfully the more she moved, the temptation eased. Dressed in her captain uniform, she went downstairs. Maria and Roger were making breakfast.

"Good morn, Blessed Rose," Maria greeted her.

"Please call me Captain Rose. I don't like nicknames," Ami asked politely.

Maria frowned. Before she could reply, Roger intercepted, "Our apologies, Captain. Coffee?"

That piqued Ami's interest. "Yes, please."

Ami sat at the bar, sipping on her coffee. It was delicious, but nothing compared to Logan's skills. Breakfast consisted of eggs, waffles, and cheese grits. Ami doused her waffle with butter and honey.

"This is really good," Ami said with half her mouth filled with food.

Maria gave her a forced smile. "Thank you."

"What are your plans today, Captain Rose?" Roger asked.

Ami swallowed her food. "I hoped to speak to Jeanne, Bru's sister, to get her account."

For some reason, Roger seemed sad. "Very well. When you are ready, I will take you to her."

After eating, Ami went to her room to grab her notebook and pencil. Roger stood by the bar, waiting for her.

"I'm ready," Ami announced.

"Very well." Roger nodded.

The village was worse in the daylight. There wasn't a house or store that didn't suffer some fire damage or shattered windows. Ami scarcely saw any villagers, and those she did quickly ducked back into the battered building they occupied. Ami was confused.

This was from three months ago? Why haven't there been any fixtures or rebuilding? Ami's thoughts swirled.

Roger led her to the most northern part of the village. It was a massive graveyard. Mixed in with the old headstones were numerous new ones. She could still smell the freshly dug dirt. In the distance was a dark, looming forest. It made the Black Forest look cheerful. Ami glanced around, hoping to spot Jeanne. Given the devastating damage and gravestones, she wouldn't be surprised if Jeanne was mourning someone.

Roger stopped at a gravestone. Ami could see etchings on the headstone but couldn't make out what they said.

"Here she is. Jeanne, Bru's sister," Roger said gravely.

Ami stared at him, confused. "What do you mean?"

Roger frowned. "When Jeanne returned from that fort, she wasn't the same. There was a darkness around her that wouldn't let up. Then, two weeks ago, we noticed she was missing. After searching, we found her in the Howling Forest, with a rope around her neck."

Ami was stunned. "Does Bru know?" she asked.

Roger nodded. "He was notified, and he helped bury her."

Shock shifted to confusion. Why didn't Bru tell her that his sister committed suicide? It would've been worth mentioning, especially with the charges against Hector. Also, wouldn't Jeanne have told Bru about the bandit attack several months earlier? Why didn't he mention it? Was he mocked so much that he didn't think anyone would listen to him? She had too many questions and not enough answers.

"Thank you for showing me. My condolences on the villagers' losses," Ami said sincerely.

"Thank you. Who do you wish to talk to first?" Roger asked.

"Whoever will speak with me," Ami stated.

"All right, let's go."

She swore her wrist was going to fall off. If she thought writing proposals for Jasmine was giving her carpal tunnel, it was a cakewalk compared to the notes and stories she gathered from the villagers. Roger was a huge help. His presence helped ease the villagers out of their burnt abodes, and they told numerous stories. What pleased Ami was how consistent they were. Many villagers saw strange activity in the Howling Forest; after the bandit attack, it only increased. She also learned more about Jeanne and Bru.

First, they weren't brother and sister. In fact, they were closer to being lovers than blood relatives. Jeanne had been an Elf of dark beauty that seemed very out of place in the isolated village of Rascu. Bru and Jeanne arrived together roughly three years ago. Jeanne had stayed at the inn while Bru was at Putra Hallas. Jeanne had been friendly but distant. No one knew much about her family, background, or relationship with Bru. The hot gossip was rumored to be that the two were star-crossed lovers who ran away when their families didn't agree to the match. More sensible villagers believed it was more of a business partnership than a love-based relationship.

All the villagers believed the strange activity in the Howling Forest and the bandit attack were linked. Ami had to agree. Unfortunately, she couldn't go and investigate the Howling Forest by herself. If it did house bandits, she would be outnumbered and killed. She needed backup. Then she asked about the soldiers from Putra Hallas.

"When did the harassment first start?" Ami asked.

"They came shortly after Bru was assigned to that fort," An elderly Elf villager barked. "The head Centaur there started comin' more often when he met Jeanne. He had the banging pots and pans for her."

Ami barely hid her shock. "How long would you say they knew each other?" she asked slowly.

"I know they only knew each other for about two years.

The rumor mill had it that they were possibly lovers. I noticed that the Centaur only came when Bru wasn't around," the villager said conspiratorially.

"Interesting," Ami mumbled. "Did they say anything about the strange activity in the forest?"

The villager rubbed his chin with a weathered hand. "Now that I think about it, Jeanne always changed the subject when that came up. The Centaur didn't seem interested. Shouldn't a military Person be interested in stuff like that?"

"They should've been. When did other soldiers from Putra Hallas start to harass the village?" Ami asked.

"There were only like eight that came during their leave. Bru came with them. However, he always immediately went to Jeanne when he was on leave. The soldiers did whatever they wanted." The villager shrugged and shook his head.

"Did you happen to catch their names or ranks?" Ami asked. She jotted down what the villager could remember, although there were two he wasn't sure of. It didn't matter. Ami already had an idea who these People were. They matched up with the other villagers' testimonies.

That night, Ami tiredly ate the hearty meal Roger and Maria cooked. Maria was giving Ami the cold shoulder for some reason. Thankfully Roger was in a talkative mood. After eating, Ami went to her room and fell right to sleep. From the corner of her room, three sets of red eyes watched her.

The following day, Ami awoke feeling refreshed. She only had five more villagers to question before she reorganized her notes. After eating breakfast, Ami and Roger found the last villagers. Their stories lined up with what Ami had heard the day before. The rest of the day was spent in her room at the inn, rewriting her notes in a separate notebook. It was there when the strange activity in the Howling Forest became clearer.

According to the villagers, they noticed flashes of light randomly going off about a month before Jeanne and Bru arrived.

These flashes of light started off as red. Then, several months later, it turned blue, green, and orange. After each flash of light, a strange howl would echo through the air. It wasn't like anything the villagers had ever heard. They knew it wasn't a Were howl or a Centaur's horn. They also knew it wasn't a scream. It sounded otherworldly. Then came the strange animal behavior.

All the animals avoided the forest. The squirrels that used to wander in and out of the forest refused to go near it. Birds no longer sang in the forest's trees. The horses would scream if they were led toward it. After two months, the villagers' animals started to drop dead. Birds and squirrels dropped as if shot with a sling, but none had evidence of being attacked. It was as if they were scared to death. The horses ran away, never to be seen again. Next were the odd weather patterns.

A surprise drought had made for a lean harvest that year. Then in the new year, during the spring planting, a flash flood wiped out everything. The picture was disturbing.

Lee is going to have a field day, Ami thought. Then she thought, *If Jeanne and Hector knew each other before, what exactly happened when Jeanne visited the fort? Was what the soldiers viewed as harassment actually flirting between Jeanne and Hector, and had Bru found out?* She didn't know what to think. What she wanted to know was why Jeanne decided to visit the fort. Was it to see Bru or Hector or both? Why? Are they connected to the strange happenings in the Howling Forest?

I have to report to Lee. There's something weird happening here, and I'm over my head, Ami thought. Then she thought, *I wonder if Jeanne left anything. I'll ask Roger at dinner.*

Roger called her for dinner a few hours later. Tonight's meal was steak and a baked potato. Ami dug into her meal with gusto. Roger served the steak with a homemade dipping sauce that was out of this world. To say Ami was happy was an understatement.

"How's your investigation going?" Roger asked.

"It's going well. I was organizing my notes," Ami replied. "I was wondering, did Jeanne stay here at the inn or somewhere else?"

"She stayed here. Actually, you're in her old room," Roger said offhandedly.

"Oh. Did she leave anything behind?" Ami asked.

"Like what?" Maria asked suspiciously.

"Like anything that would help us contact the family of her passing, or possibly what place she was from?" Ami answered smoothly.

Roger shook his head. "All she left were some clothes. She packed light for such a long stay."

"I see. Thank you for your help yesterday and today," Ami thanked him.

"I don't mind helping the Blessed Rose," Roger smirked.

"I really don't like that nickname," Ami groaned.

"Why not?" Maria demanded snobbily. "I think it would be great to be so famous."

"Not if you knew what price came with that," Ami said solemnly.

"Like what?" Maria asked curiously.

"Fourteen lives," Ami stated. Roger looked crestfallen while Maria gaped at her. "Fourteen lives that I couldn't save. There are no blessings with that kind of loss."

The atmosphere stayed grim after that. Maria stared at her plate, refusing to look at Ami. Ami couldn't tell if she preferred that or the cold shoulder. Losing her appetite, Ami excused herself to her room. When she opened the door, she was shocked to see three weirdly shaped Shadows in her room.

"Who are you, and what are you doing?" Ami demanded icily.

"We are Shadows, little mistress," one Shadow hissed. She couldn't see their mouths.

"I get that. Answer my questions," Ami ordered.

"Egan was right. She is bossy," Another Shadow commented. That voice sounded female.

"One," Ami counted.

"One what?" the first voice asked dumbly.

"Two." She extended her arm out, her palm facing the Shadows.

"Oh, is she counting us? That's cute," the female voice said snidely.

"Three." A ball of light erupted out of Ami's extended palm. The three screamed as they were banished. "This is getting annoying," Ami muttered.

A snort was heard from her left. Ami swirled around, her magic collecting in her chest. She eyed the corners of the room with suspicion. Sensing nothing, she lowered her guard.

I need sleep if I'm imagining sounds. Ami thought to herself. She dressed in her nightclothes and went to sleep instantly.

The silent, invisible guard let out a quiet sigh of relief.

"Do you have to go back so soon?" Roger asked. The two were drinking coffee together at the bar. Maria was in the back, making breakfast.

"Yes. I wish to inform General Lee about what is happening and assign punishments for the soldiers that have been harassing you and the villagers. Such treatment is unacceptable, and they will face the consequences," Ami informed. "Was there anything else that needs to be brought to my attention?"

"You give me hope for this nation," Roger admitted. "Villages like ours are not seen as a high priority. The fact you listened to us means a lot."

"Change will take time," Ami pointed out. "I hope I can change it for the better."

"You will." Roger nodded.

After breakfast, Ami packed her bag. Roger walked with her to the entrance of the village. As they passed, the villagers came out of their homes to wave or call hello to Ami. Her heart warmed at the change. Before she knew it, all the villagers gathered at the entrance, waving goodbye to Ami. She waved back and started on her journey back. Thankfully she didn't suffer any dizzy spells this time. She arrived at Putra Hallas in the late afternoon.

The air around the fort felt heavier, as if a severe thunderstorm threatened to throw its bolts at the walls. The hairs on the back of her neck and on her arms rose the closer she got.

"Halt!" a voice ordered from above. "Who goes there?"

"It is I, Captain Amaranth Rose. I wish to speak to General Lee," Ami shouted back.

There was a pause of silence. Ami wondered what had happened while she was away. After what felt like an hour, the door finally opened. Several Knights motioned for her to enter quickly. Ami barely got inside when the door slammed shut, almost taking the skin off her heels.

"What's going on?" Ami asked.

"Captain, where were you?" Black asked, his voice full of concern.

"I went to the village to the north like I told General Lee. Has something happened here? Did someone get hurt?" Ami asked.

"You need to report to General Lee now," Black advised.

"Where is he?" Ami asked.

"In his room," Black answered.

"Thank you. Excuse me." Ami nodded. She ran to Lee's room. The door was wide open. The Werebobcat was pacing furiously. He looked sick with worry.

"Sir," Ami greeted with a salute.

Lee jumped nearly four feet in the air. Like any feline, he landed on his feet. When he saw her, he stomped like a herd of stampeding horses over to her. His face was one of absolute fury.

"Where have you been?" Lee bellowed.

Ami narrowed her eye at him. "I was in the village in the north like I said I was, sir."

"And why did it take you seven days to return? Why didn't you send any reports of what you found? Why couldn't any soldier find the supposed village you went to? What are you hiding?" Lee roared.

"Sir, I was only away for two days," Ami answered calmly. She supposed the shock calmed her voice because her heart felt like it would beat out of her chest and dance a death tango. "And I found the village."

Lee stared at her as if determining her truthfulness. "That's impossible. No one could find the village. I even sent a Knight several hours after you left when I realized you didn't have a backup. He kept getting lost," Lee explained.

"Lost ..." Ami murmured. She set down her knapsack to get her notebook. Finding the right one, she flipped through it until she found the page she was searching for. One villager mentioned how they stopped getting visitors after the light in the forest turned orange. The only reason the villager noticed was due to her home being in the most western part of the village and generally isolated compared to the others. She knew when certain relatives of particular villagers would visit, but their visits stopped utterly, to the bewilderment of the villagers. Then the villager noticed that they couldn't leave the village. They would go in the morning and return several hours later, confused and shaken.

"Sir, we have a big problem," Ami said shakily.

"Is it Hector?" Lee asked.

"This is bigger than Hector," Ami replied. "Someone or a group of People is experimenting with time magic."

"Time magic? Why?" Lee asked.

"I'm not sure, sir. I suffered from dizzy spells on my way to the village and got lost three times," Ami admitted.

"But you got to the village," Lee pointed out.

"Yes, sir. I'm not sure how," Ami said.

"I want your report now," Lee ordered.

Ami explained everything, even what she found out about Bru and Jeanne. Lee began pacing again halfway through her report. When she ended, Lee walked faster.

"Hector had to have known what was going on in that forest," Lee growled.

"I agree, sir."

Lee stopped pacing. His broad chest heaved with his panting. Ami hoped he didn't suffer a heart attack. A lot has happened in a short amount of time for the Werebobcat.

"Bru is a traitor," Lee surmised.

Ami nodded. "I agree. However, I don't believe he freed Hector."

Lee blinked. "Why not?"

"Hector was a love rival, and he demoted Bru severely. Also, he seemed genuinely surprised when I told him that Hector was no longer at the fort," Ami explained.

"He could be a good actor." Lee shrugged.

"If he is, he's quite excellent to fool me," Ami said.

Lee hummed. "Burns!" he shouted abruptly, making Ami jump.

Hurried footsteps came their way. A Knight poked his head in. "Yes, sir?" The Werewolf saluted.

"Bring dinner for the captain and me. We won't be joining the rest in the hall tonight," Lee ordered.

"Yes, sir." Burns saluted again and rushed away.

"We need to know what the letters and the ledgers are discussing. You and I are not leaving this room until we figure this out," Lee ordered.

"Understood, sir." Ami nodded. "May I go and retrieve the letters?"

"I have them here." Lee pointed to his knapsack. "When you didn't send a report after two days, I gathered everything I could from your room for safekeeping."

Burns and another Knight brought dinner. It was so bland Ami couldn't eat it.

"Is it not to your liking?" Lee asked.

"It's so bland. There are no spices," Ami complained.

Lee gave her a confused look. "It tastes like how the Dragons make it in the capital."

"No, it doesn't. Even when I was in the village, the food tasted normal. The cooks here don't believe in spices, I suppose," Ami retorted.

Lee put down his fork. "How long has this been going on?"

"Ever since we arrived," Ami said.

Lee jumped up and walked swiftly out of his room, barking for her to follow. Ami stumbled to catch up. Lee entered the dining hall. He went to the main kitchen area. Without speaking to anyone, he started opening and closing cabinets he could reach. Then he climbed on top of the counters to open the upper cabinets. Ami watched, wondering what Lee was searching for.

"Captain, what's going on?" Douglas asked, entering the kitchens. Behind him was Sir Tres.

"Aha!" Lee cheered.

"General, is something wrong?" Douglas asked.

"Yes, Second-Commander, there is," Lee hissed in a dangerous tone. "Tell me, when did mercury become a spice?" He pulled out a small vial from the cabinet. Ami couldn't tell what was in it.

"Never, sir," Douglas gasped. "Why is mercury in the kitchens?"

"Do tell, Sir Tres," Lee ordered, looking past Douglas to stare at the tall Elf.

Douglas half-turned to look at him. "Martin?"

Sir Tres' face was like stone. Ami was stunned. Why would

Sir Tres put mercury in the food? What does this have to do with her not tasting the spices?

Sir Tres turned to run. Ami's tail grabbed the Elf's ankle like a rope, making him fall flat on his face.

"Knights, take him to the brig. I'll interrogate him later," Lee ordered.

Several Knights entered to take the limp Elf. Then he started to convulse.

"Tooth tablet!" Lee shouted, jumping down from the counter.

White foam erupted from Sir Tres' mouth as his body continued to convulse. His veins strained against his skin. After a minute, his body went still. His wide eyes were bloodshot.

"Sir, can you please explain what's going on?" Ami asked.

Lee sighed. "Knights, take him to the infirmary."

The Knights carried the Elf's corpse out of the kitchens. Douglas followed them, leaving Lee and Ami alone in the kitchens.

"While you were gone," Lee explained, "I started investigating how Hector ran the fort. During that time, Soldier Dali told me that you hadn't been eating like usual."

"I did come back from the dead. My appetite isn't like it used to be," Ami pointed out.

"Yes, but then he told me how suspicious the kitchen personnel have become. For example, before we arrived, one of his duties was to assist in the kitchens. Then, all of a sudden, his duties changed for no reason. The ones typically in the kitchens were also replaced by Sir Tres. The food changed completely. When we arrived, the food changed again. Then he noticed how less and less you ate. He also thought the idea of you sleeping was weird. Why is that?" Lee asked.

"Before I died, I never slept," Ami replied.

"Never?" Lee asked with wide eyes.

"No, sir."

"Hmmm ... anyway, more and more soldiers were telling me how the food was becoming weird. Like each soldier was given different food like an experiment," Lee said.

"What does the mercury have to do with anything?" Ami asked.

"Mercury is deadly to Dragons. If you had been fatally dosed, you would've gone insane," Lee said solemnly.

"Then why didn't they?" Ami asked.

"I think they tried," Lee said. "Except you were losing your taste buds instead, which probably saved your life from not eating as much food as before."

She fell to her knees. Her chest started heaving. Her stomach rolled up to her throat. She vomited all over the floor. Blearily, she could see silver mercury threads in the few food scraps. Lee was next to her. She could feel his breath against her skin, but not the words he was speaking. The world spun, and darkness took over.

CHAPTER 7

Ami woke up in a cold sweat. Looking around, she noticed she wasn't in her room. From the smell of bleach and white linens, her guess was a hospital room. Slowly, she sat up. She glanced down. She was still wearing the same clothes. On her right, she noticed the sleeping form of Lee. The Werebobcat sat in a hard chair with his arms crossed. His head nodded up and down with his breathing.

"Captain!" Black cried out from the door he entered.

His shout jolted Lee out of his sleep. He glanced around. Not seeing any danger, he glared at the Knight. "Knight, if you value your life, you will never do that again," Lee growled.

"Apologies, General." Black saluted, not sounding sorry at all. Turning to Ami, he asked, "How are you feeling?"

"Exhausted. Confused," Ami stated. "Starving."

"We'll get you some real food in a bit," Black said. The Knight left.

Lee sighed. "Are you okay?"

Ami looked down at the linens covering her lower half. "I don't know."

"Anything you want to talk about?" Lee asked gently.

"Why did Sir Tres try to poison me?" Ami asked.

Lee shrugged. "I honestly don't know. I went through his room and found nothing. There were no journals, letters, or anything. I even asked the other generals if they had heard about him. No one could recall his contributions to the last war. It was as if he was invisible until Hector came."

"That is strange. Did none of the soldiers here witness any odd behavior? What about the second-commander?" Ami asked.

Lee shook his head. "The second-commander didn't interact with Sir Tres until a few months ago. He honestly thought Sir Tres was a new transfer from a fort that became overcrowded. He had Sir Tres assist with inventory tracking when Hector was imprisoned. The second-commander was too busy fixing what Hector didn't do to notice anything odd."

"Then why was I told he had been here for twenty years?" Ami asked.

"Who told you that?" Lee asked.

"I'm not sure. I'll have to look at my notes," Ami said. At that time, Black and Salvador entered. Each carried a tray piled with food.

"Salvador made you a feast," Black announced with a grin.

Salvador blushed dark pink. He shyly glanced at Ami. The food on Black's tray was primarily fresh biscuits, scrambled eggs, and a large bowl of cheese grits. Salvador's tray contained various fruit jams for the biscuits and utensils.

"This looks delicious. Thank you," Ami said sincerely.

They ate for twenty minutes in comfortable silence. Then the door burst open.

"Captain! General!" Sir Kain ran in. He saluted quickly before continuing, "Sirs, someone has broken into your rooms!"

"What?" Lee shouted. He stuffed his leftover biscuit in his mouth before running out. Sir Kain ran after him.

"I'll go and see how I can help. Stay well, Captain," Black said. He left.

Ami and Salvador were alone in awkward silence.

"Are you still mad at me?" Ami asked softly.

Salvador stared at the biscuit in his hands. "A little."

"I'm not going to apologize for doing my job," Ami said sternly.

"I know," Salvador sighed. He sounded defeated.

"Is it Conri?" Ami asked, taking a bite of her biscuit. She filled hers with raspberry jam.

"Yeah. We've been talking." Salvador sighed again.

"Anything interesting?" Ami asked.

Salvador shook his head. "Not really. I think he was comforting me. It was kind of strange."

"How so?"

"It felt ... familiar," Salvador said hesitantly. "It's hard to describe. Like getting a hug from an old friend than someone who detests you. Really unnerving."

This can't be a curse. Ami thought. *Curses don't comfort you or act familiar to their host. I need to find out other avenues.* Hope rose in Ami's chest. *If it wasn't a curse, then that meant Salvador wouldn't suffer when he turned twenty-one.*

Salvador put his uneaten biscuit back on the tray. "I know you were doing your job. I didn't like being treated like everyone else," Salvador admitted. It took Ami a moment to realize what he was back on the interrogation thing.

"If I hadn't, you would be under scrutiny," Ami pointed out.

"What do you mean?" Salvador asked.

"If I show favoritism towards you, the other males would start to shun you, believing that I brainwashed you or you were sent to spy for me. Many still despise me and would rather see me deported. They would've used you against me," Ami explained.

"So, you did it because of that?" Salvador asked.

Ami shook her head. "No, I did it because it was part of my job. I also know how People will twist my words and actions. Since we're friends, you must also know how others will perceive me."

"It's politics," Salvador summarized.

"Exactly."

"I hate politics," Salvador moaned.

Ami shrugged and ate the rest of her biscuit. Still feeling hungry, she reached for another one. Salvador's large hand intercepted hers, placing his hand over hers firmly.

"Sal—"

"I need to tell you something," Salvador said in a tone she hadn't heard before. It made her sit up straighter, her full attention on him.

"What is it?" Ami asked.

"There's something wrong with this fort," Salvador started. His brown eyes glinted green for a moment. When he blinked, they were brown again. "Conri has been on edge ever since I came here. He told me that black magic was being used. I started to investigate after you woke up. That was when Sir Tres changed my duties in the kitchens. Then I began to examine Sir Tres.

"I started to notice how Sir Tres seemed ..." Salvador paused, deep in thought. Ami watched in fascination as his brown eyes flickered from green to brown to green. It was like a racket match with the ball going back and forth between players. "He seemed dirty. Not like physically, but just his presence got dirtier. Does that make sense?"

"Was it his actions or words that made him seem dirtier? Or did he seem to get dirtier the more you saw him?" Ami asked, her suspicions growing.

"He got dirtier every time I saw him. It was like his *lashu* was infected," Salvador confirmed.

"What's a *lashu*?" Ami asked.

"It's a Were term, usually with wolves. It's like your inner self or inner wolf. I guess other People would call it their conscience," Salvador tried to explain. "Does that make sense?"

"I understand. What else did you notice?" Ami urged gently.

"I don't know who, but Sir Tres would sneak around to

meet with someone. I couldn't tell who. I was usually too far away to hear what they discussed, but it was a female," Salvador explained.

"When was this?" Ami asked.

"It was before you and the general arrived. Then they met up only once that I'm aware of, and that was when you went to the village," Salvador said.

Could it have been Jeanne? Then who was Sir Tres meeting after she died? Is there someone else I'm not aware of? Ami thought. "After I left for the village, was the Person female?"

Salvador nodded. "It was the same female. I recognized her voice."

"What did Sir Tres' smell like?" Ami asked randomly.

"Huh?"

"His scent. What did he smell like?" Ami insisted.

"Well, he was like a normal Elf, like grass or whatever. Then when he started getting dirtier, it started to get weird," Salvador admitted.

"Weird, how?"

"Well, it started to have this odd, sweet smell, like wild honey. But then it got musky, overpowering the sweet smell like—" Salvador started.

"A perfume," Ami ended.

Salvador stared at her with alarm. "Yeah. What does that mean?"

"This is more complicated than we realized," Ami stated. As she got out of bed, she said, "Come. We need to talk to General Lee about this."

"What's going on, Ami?" Salvador demanded, standing in front of her.

Ami debated with herself before coming to a decision. "There's a witch in the fort," she whispered.

Salvador's eyes widened. Ami sidestepped around the stunned Werewolf and exited the hospital. She heard Salvador catch up. As they neared the corridor of her room, it was guarded with

Knights on high alert. When they saw Ami and Salvador, they cautiously allowed them through. Two Knights stood outside Ami's room. The door was opened. Lee was studying the room, muttering under his breath. The room was an absolute mess. It looked more like a battlefield than a burglary. Scorch marks covered the walls. Black sludge covered the walls like blood splatter.

"General?" Ami asked.

Lee glanced at her. "Captain, why are you here? You should be in the hospital wing."

"Salvador has brought new information to my attention," Ami stated.

Lee turned to her, his ears fully erect. "Speak."

"I have reason to believe that there is a witch in the fort," Ami stated confidently.

Lee snorted. "You believe those old tales?"

"There's a witch in the northern mines," Ami pointed out.

Lee frowned. "How do you arrest a witch?"

Ami shook her head. "You don't. You kill them."

"We will need to interrogate for more information—" Lee started.

"You won't be able to," Ami interrupted. "This is not a light matter, sir. Witches can and will kill anyone they see getting in their way. It doesn't matter who they are, their bloodline, or their relationship. I've seen witches kill their own family members to further their ambitions. Do not take this lightly."

Lee seemed to take her words into consideration. He glanced around. "Can you explain this?" he asked, pointing to the damage.

Ami walked into the room. Oddly, she couldn't smell anything. She expected to smell remnants of magic or burnt wood. The black sludge appeared to be slimy with the way it shined. However, it was hard when she barely touched it with her fingertip. The scorch marks didn't seem to be made with fire. The more she observed it, the more it looked like blood.

"Captain?" Salvador called out. The Werewolf was pale. His

hands trembled by his sides.

"What is it, Soldier Dali?" Ami asked.

"She's here," Salvador whispered.

"Who?" Lee demanded.

"Where?" Ami demanded at the same time.

Salvador glanced at Ami, who nodded. He led them at a fast walking pace out of the corridor and towards the kitchens. He started to sniff around. Ami, Lee, and a few Knights watched in anticipation. Salvador began to concentrate on a tall cabinet.

"The scent is strong here," Salvador stated.

Lee went over and observed the cabinet. It was odd for the cabinet to be a stand-alone. It was between the pantry and the central cupboard that housed the dinnerware. The Werebobcat kicked the bottom half of the cabinet. The wood shattered as if rotted. Lee kicked it several more times until the cabinet crumbled. He shoved the large pieces of cheap wood away. Revealed was a large hole with stairs leading downwards.

"Get your torches and swords ready. Captain, stay here," Lee ordered.

The Knights and Salvador lit their torches from the gas stove. They followed the general down the hole. Something moved from a dark corner of the kitchen. Ami followed the movement. Someone was sneaking out of the kitchens using the shadows. Stealthily, Ami followed. They exited the kitchens and entered the corridors. After trailing the Person for several hundred feet, the Person swirled around as if noticing Ami's presence. Without warning, Ami let out a bright light spell from her hand. The Person shrieked in pain. The shadows fled, revealing who it was.

"I can't say I'm surprised," Ami stated as her spell ebbed away.

Bru glared at her. "If only you ate your food properly, I wouldn't have dealt with such fools," Bru snarled. His voice sounded like two People were speaking at the same time.

"I live for disappointment," Ami replied sarcastically.

The next thing she knew, she was thrown into the stone wall. The attack left her stunned. Something hissed from her left. Bru stood over here with bared yellow teeth. He looked like he was about to attack her, but thought better. The Werewolf started to run away. Ami knew the direction he was heading. He was trying to leave the fort. Adrenaline rushed through her veins, snapping her out of her stunned state. Scrambling to her feet, she chased after Bru.

The corridors were empty. The torches were half-lit. The scent of sickly-sweet poppy juice filled her nostrils. It lit a flame of rage in her chest. The instinct to hunt her prey boiled in her muscles and sharpened her sight. She zeroed in on her target, who was several hundred feet ahead of her. Bru was shutting the door leading outside the fort.

Ami didn't stop, didn't slow down, and didn't care. She ran faster towards the heavy door. She slammed into it with the force of twenty stampeding Centaurs. The door broke from its hinges, sliding on the slick grass, and slammed into the running Werewolf. Ami and Bru were tossed in different directions across the grass. Ami got to her feet quickly. She pounced on Bru just as he got to his feet.

The two wrestled fiercely. They grabbed and squeezed whatever was within reach, twisting body parts in hopes of pinning the other down. Bru bit Ami's right shoulder. Ami replied with a sharp bite of her own on Bru's collarbone. Bru yelped, releasing Ami's shoulder. Ami didn't let go despite Bru biting her repeatedly around the bite mark he made. If anything, she made her sharp needle teeth go in deeper. Bru then clawed at Ami's head. He managed to grab enough hair to yank her away from him. Then he punched her in the face.

Ami's head snapped back. The Werewolf somehow got on top of her and punched her face repeatedly. Ami wrapped her tail around Bru's neck and threw him away from her. Blood oozed out of her bloody mouth, lips, and nose. Blearily through her swollen eyelid, she saw Bru running away. The rage lit up again, more ferocious than before. Her magic joined the frenzy, filling her with energy. Absently, she noticed the swelling on her face disappear as her focused sight sharpened even more. She chased after him.

The air around her was electrifying. Sparks blew around her as she steadily caught up to Bru. The Werewolf made a wild motion with his right hand.

SLAM!

Ami landed on her back, and the air zapped out of her lungs. Sitting up, she saw Bru enter the village through frosted glass. With her chest heaving from the exertion and adrenaline, she stared at the obstacle in her way. It was a magical dome. Shaped and frosted like glass, it covered the village like a prison. She stood up. All she could think about was how her prey was getting away.

"Captain!" a voice that sounded like Lee shouted from a distance. Ami ignored it. She pulled back her arm, her hand shaped into a fist. "Captain, wait!" Lee's voice urged desperately.

Her fist collided with the magical dome. The dome cracked and spider-webbed where her fist impacted. Gathering all her strength, Ami pulled her arm back again. When she punched the same spot, a portion of the dome shattered, leaving a large enough opening for Ami to run through. She sprinted after Bru. She caught up to him in the middle of the village.

"You are the most annoying little brat," Bru hissed.

Ami couldn't speak. All she could focus on was killing her prey. Bru started to chant. Ami charged, hoping to distract the Werewolf. Bru backhanded her, throwing her into the nearest house. She broke through two walls before slamming into the back wall. Her head ached. She felt blood dripping down her face. The rage in her chest grew. Staggering to her feet, she stumbled out of the broken house. The stench of black magic blanketed the air. Then, as Bru continued to chant, chunks of his skin began to fall off. Ami watched in horror as Bru disappeared, piece by piece, to reveal a female Elf of dark beauty.

"Jeanne," Ami growled.

Jeanne smirked cruelly. "Oh, surprised by my beloved's appearance? He was such a darling until he realized I preferred Hector over him." Ami glared. Jeanne pouted. "Now, don't look so worried. He filled his purpose just like dear Hector did. And like all the villagers here will as well." She let out an evil laugh.

Ami mustered all the magic she had in her chest. Before she could unleash it, a long Shadow formed behind Jeanne. It crept taller and taller above the witch. Jeanne didn't seem to notice. Two large red eyes appeared. Somehow, Ami could see more definition in the Shadow as a horse muzzle with sharp crocodile teeth emerged.

"I don't think I gave you permission to harm the little mistress." Egan's deep voice echoed in the air.

Jeanne turned to the Shadow in surprise. She glared at him. "I don't need your permission, Shadow," she sneered.

Egan's horse mouth smiled, showing more teeth. "Wrong."

His mouth latched onto Jeanne's shoulder with a disturbing crack. Jeanne screamed. Using her free hand, she discharged a purple sphere at Egan. It passed through the Shadow. Egan clamped harder with his mouth. Ami saw her window of opportunity. Extending her claws, she ran towards Jeanne.

The witch tried to cast another spell, but Egan twisted his head, almost ripping her arm off. Ami plunged her claws into the witch's chest, piercing what remained of her heart. Jeanne's body went still, then limp. Ami ripped her bloodless nails out. Egan released Jeanne's now dead body. It crumbled to the ground like a broken doll.

"Little mistress," Egan said, his bloody mouth not moving, "burn it."

Ami somehow knew what he meant. She took a few steps backward, not averting her gaze from the dead witch. She took in several deep breaths, each one larger than the last. Magic pooled into her lungs like magma. Heat emanated from her lungs. The smell of sulfur filled her nose. Then she exhaled as if trying to blow up a balloon. Out of her mouth erupted white flames. They engulfed the witch entirely. She didn't stop spewing fire from that exhalation until the witch was nothing more than ash. When it was done, she inhaled and choked. Blood coated her throat. She coughed and hacked nonstop. Egan came to her side. He mumbled something. Whatever it was, it stopped her coughing. Ami inhaled and exhaled as if breathing for the first time.

"Ami!" Salvador's voice rang.

She turned to the voice, and the next thing she knew, she was waking up in a crumpled house. The ceiling had a large hole. Jolts of sharp pain raced across her shoulders and upper back. She hissed as her nerves lit up like winter candles during a Goyan opera.

"Ami?" Salvador called out from another room. Rustling noises were heard until Salvador entered the room. Dark bags hung under his eyes. He appeared thinner, and the rings around his fingers pulsed green light.

"Sal?" Ami croaked. "Where are we?"

"We're in the village," Sal said, reaching her side. He sat cross-legged next to her. "The general and the Knights are searching for clues about the villagers. We don't know where they've gone."

"Everyone is gone?" Ami asked. She gritted her teeth as she forced her body to sit up.

Salvador nodded. "The dome is still around with the hole you made. And ..." The Werewolf suddenly turned nervous.

"What is it?" Ami asked.

"The priests are here," Salvador whispered, as if they could hear them.

"From where?" Ami asked.

"Apparently, there's a large temple near the city of Octa,

which is the closest to here. Lee sent for them to look at the dome," Salvador explained shakily.

Ami moved to get up. Salvador grabbed her by the unharmed arm with his large hand, stopping her.

"They know about Conri," Salvador said through gritted teeth.

Ami cocked her head to the side. "I don't understand."

"They think I'm cursed because of my mother," Salvador hissed. Ami stared at him. Never in the years she'd known him had she seen such anger in his brown eyes.

"Explain," Ami ordered.

"They believe that I have Conri because of my mother's past sins," Salvador explained in a frustrated tone. "But that's not true. I don't believe that."

"Neither do I," Ami stated. "Have they said why they don't believe it to be a witch's curse?"

"I don't know exactly. They always dance around it and never give a full answer," Salvador sighed.

"How long was I out?" Ami asked.

"For a day and a half."

"All right, let's go," Ami said, getting out of Salvador's grip and standing up.

"Where are you going?" Salvador asked, standing as well.

"To see General Lee and irritate some priests," Ami grunted.

She found Lee as soon as she left the house. The Werebobcat was speaking to several Knights several feet from the entrance of the crumpled house.

"Captain!" the Knights greeted her happily, interrupting whatever Lee was speaking about.

"Captain." Lee nodded at her. His sharp amber eyes looked at her up and down. "Are you well?" he asked.

"I'm alive," Ami replied dryly. The pain was dull and half numb now. "Have you found the villagers?"

Lee shook his head. "All we found was that they left in a hurry. I don't think they had a choice."

"I heard we have priests here?" Ami asked.

Lee frowned. "Yes, they're investigating the magical dome. So far, all they've been telling us is how we're going to the Pits when we die, and our souls are doomed for housing a witch."

"But we didn't know we had a witch in our presence," Ami pointed out.

One of the Knights, an Elf, snorted. "That doesn't matter to them. They believe if you're holy enough, you ought to be able to find a witch by determining her soul."

"Witches don't have souls," Ami said slowly.

"What do you mean?" Salvador asked.

"It's why they're called witches. They sell their soul to the Lord of Lies and Darkness in exchange for dark magic. It is why they are so ruthless and manipulative," Ami explained.

"A simple explanation for the plebian," a male voice commented.

An Elf dressed in white robes outlined in gold thread walked towards them. He had short dark hair and brown eyes shadowed by his oversized glasses and walked with the arrogance of an idiot who believed his lies. Ami grinned.

"Then explain it in the way Nobles can understand, dear priest," Ami said sweetly. "I'm sure their vocabulary is vastly different than mine."

Salvador and the Knights hid their chuckles with coughs. Lee hid his grin behind his hand.

The priest looked confused. "There are no Nobles here."

"Are you calling the fellow males here non-Nobles? Their mothers would disagree," Ami said.

The priest sneered. "The only ones called Nobles are females, and there are none here."

Ami cackled. "How would you know?"

"What do you mean, how would I know?" the priest sputtered.

"Granted, I don't know much about the priests and the ways of the temple, but I do know that you're not allowed to marry or venture out of the temple often. If you're not allowed to marry or interact with People, and all you see are males, how do you know if someone is female?" Ami asked.

"Females are obviously different from males," the priest scoffed.

"How so?" Ami asked.

"They have different parts."

"Like?" Ami nearly sang. The priest blushed dark red, glaring. "So, you do know what a female looks like," Ami said in a playful accusatory tone. "Oh, dear. Someone's been staring out the window too long instead of studying."

"Why, you—" the priest started to yell.

"Oh dear, what is going on here?" a different male voice interrupted.

Two more male Elves came their way. Both were much older than the bespectacled priest and wore the same robes. One had slicked black hair and calculating blue eyes. The other had long gray hair and laugh wrinkles around his eyes and mouth. Gentle brown eyes gazed at the group.

"Head Priest, this heathen was questioning our conduct," the priest with the glasses said heatedly.

"Which one?" Ami asked, examining her nails as if bored.

"Pardon?" the slick-haired priest asked.

"I asked him which order of conduct I questioned," Ami stated.

"It's a matter of principle." The priest with glasses gulped.

"It's astonishing how easily you accuse someone without sufficient evidence and base it on your own insecurities," Ami said offhandedly.

The priest with glasses glared at her. If looks could kill, she would be ash. His face turned purple with rage. Then the priest with gray hair laughed.

"Toussaint, I believe the lady is, as they say, riling you up," the gray-haired priest said with a chuckle. "Allow me to apologize for his behavior. As you said, priests do not leave the temple often, and Toussaint is still learning."

Toussaint hung his head, his face going back to red in embarrassment.

Ami smiled. She liked the old priest. He sort of reminded her of Gramps. "I took no offense. I was hoping for him to learn how different People are outside the temple and may not be as he perceives them," Ami replied diplomatically.

"I agree. I am Boniface, Head Priest of the temple in Octa," the gray-haired priest said with a respectful bow.

"I am Captain Amaranth Rose," Ami replied with a matching bow.

"Amaranth?" the slicked hair priest asked. Ami looked at him coolly.

"Something wrong, Casimir?" Boniface asked.

"It depends," Casimir muttered.

"On what exactly?" Lee asked. Ami almost forgot they were there.

"If what the common folk is praying is true, then she is who they call the Blessed Rose," Casimir said with a deep frown.

Ami shrugged. "I've been called that."

"Surely such a name will condemn you to arrogance. You must humble yourself—" Toussaint started heatedly.

"I cannot control what People call me," Ami interrupted in an icy tone. Cold amethyst stared down at the young Elf. "I did not tell the People to call me such a name, and I have politely told those who tried not to. Do not assume me filled with arrogance when your own ignorance can be translated as such."

Toussaint sputtered while Casimir scowled. Boniface nodded approvingly.

"I have heard stories of your good deeds even within the temple, young lady. May the Almighty One continue to bless you," Boniface said warmly.

"If I may butt in," Lee said, "but have you had time to inspect the dome?"

Boniface frowned. "Yes, and it was created by someone of great power."

"Obviously, a witch," Casimir sneered.

Does he not have any other facial expressions? Ami wondered. "It wasn't the witch," she said out loud.

All eyes were on her.

"Black magic is everywhere, female," Casimir hissed.

"If it was the witch, it should've collapsed when she was destroyed," Ami pointed out.

"The witch could still be around, hiding," Boniface said with a slight frown.

Ami jabbed over her right shoulder with her thumb. "In the middle of the village, you'll see what's left of her."

"You can't kill a witch," Toussaint scoffed disbelievingly.

"She did," Lee confirmed.

"And she wasn't the first one I've killed either," Ami added.

"How did you kill her?" Casimir asked. For once, he wasn't sneering.

"Dragon fire."

The priests stared at her with owlish eyes. The Knights smiled proudly. Lee nodded approvingly.

"The captain was the one that alerted us to the witch in the fort. She personally pursued it and got rid of it," Lee explained.

"Would it be allowed if we could examine the witch's remains? It may hold clues of which coven she belonged to," Boniface asked.

Ami had never thought of that before.

"I don't see a problem with that," Lee said. "Davis, Cullor, go with them."

Two Werewolf Knights walked with the three priests to the middle of the village. Ami turned her gaze to the Howling Forest.

"Sir, has anyone tried the forest?" Ami asked.

Lee's ears flickered nervously. "The furthest we can reach is the graveyard. There is something powerful around that forest that is beyond us."

"What happens when you try to go near it?" Ami asked.

"It's like a pressure," the Elf Knight answered. "It feels like gravity intensifies until you can't breathe."

"You said it was time magic," Lee stated.

Ami nodded. "What you are describing fits from what I know."

"How do you know time magic?" Lee asked.

"There was a young soldier in Vinci who was proficient in magic. He became obsessed with time magic and its theory. I was often sent to dispel his wayward spells," Ami explained.

"Then you can dispel this one?" Lee asked hopefully.

Ami shook her head. "Not at this time."

"Why not?" Lee huffed.

"Sir, I have been poisoned, sleep-deprived, bitten, and just killed a witch. I'm in no state to deal with time magic," Ami said exasperatedly.

Lee sighed. "Fine. Let's wrap this up and get back to the fort. I got a report fit for the Pits to write to Tso."

"What about the villagers?" Salvador asked.

"It wouldn't surprise me if they were in the forest," Ami said sadly. "Somehow, they got caught or forced to go into whatever is going on there."

"I agree. Let's move out," Lee ordered.

Belladonna stared at the chessboard she created. Her pieces, black warped mangled versions of her minions and pets, were strategically placed on her side of the board. Her opponent, however, remained unknown. Solid white blocks represented the other side. She didn't know what they looked like or their positions. Despite missing a few pieces, they stood like a solid wall against her.

Belladonna adored chess. She especially loved devouring her foes. This chess match was different. The pest that Mother worried about was crafty and unpredictable. The problem was also ruthless in hunting her sisters and followers. She froze when her magic jolted down her back.

"No," Belladonna said in a low tone. Standing up abruptly, she rushed over to her crystal ball. The ball swirled with a storm of black and red clouds. A beam of white light shined from within, making the clouds disappear.

"No!" Belladonna bellowed. One of her followers was killed by the pest. She knew exactly which one it was. "Jeanne, you had so much promise," Belladonna said mournfully. Jeanne had embraced black magic as a child embraces their parent. She had been crafty and diligent. When Jeanne had told Belladonna her plans with the villagers, she crowed in delight.

"The pest," Belladonna hissed darkly. The villagers were already lost to her if Jeanne died before performing the ritual. *She had to use the energy from the forest to power up the ritual to get to the villagers. Now that she's gone, I won't be able to get to the forest because of the time magic going out of control.* Belladonna's thoughts rampaged.

Unlucky for her, time magic was something out of her element. It wasn't dark magic. Therefore, it never interested her. Jeanne, however, knew the theory. Now she was gone.

And I'm back to my standstill with the pest, Belladonna thought heatedly. As she stared at the chessboard, an idea came to mind. It calmed the wrath threatening to unleash.

"I still have my pet general. That will occupy the pest for a while," Belladonna murmured with a wide grin.

His wrist ached. Lee leaned back against his chair, closing his eyes. His report was one of the largest he had ever written. It took him six days to finish it. Not only did he have to include what happened in the village, but he also added the captain's notes and observations from the fort. Who would've thought a simple mission about low morality would lead to discovering a witch and someone tampering with time magic?

What he and the soldiers discovered down in the tunnel was fuel for nightmares to come. They found what was left of Hector. The Centaur was unidentifiable except for the message written in his own blood. It stated, "Here lies a traitor, undeserving to be a Rascal. His name is Hector."

That led to more questions. Did the witch kill Hector and write that to distract them? Did a soldier find where Hector was hiding and kill him in a rage? Lee wasn't looking forward to that conversation with Tso. After reading the report, he could see the Head General foaming at the mouth. His account resembled a novel.

His thoughts went to Rose. He wasn't sure about her. He couldn't pinpoint what it was that put him off. At first, he thought she was nervous and bound to make mistakes. Her reports and attention to detail told him she had previous military experience. She knew how to write an efficient essay, which took at least a few years for cadets to learn. Then he thought she had something over the Dali heir.

The way the Werewolf deferred to her spoke of submission. Lee noticed how Dali glanced at Rose for confirmation, even when Lee gave the order. Was there blackmail involved? What was it? What did Rose want with the Dali family? Who was Conri?

Finally, he knew Rose had secrets. Who didn't? However, Lee was concerned that Rose's secrets were dangerous. Her knowledge of witches, magic, and military experience made Lee bite his nails at night as he paced. The odd incident of her robbed room didn't sit well with him. His room was what he expected: papers strewed about, bedding on the floor, mattress flipped over and cut into. The strange black smears weren't normal. If he was a believer, he would say they were supernatural.

Lee sighed heavily. He and Rose were leaving for Talient in the morning. Gathering his report, he placed them in his protected knapsack.

CHAPTER 8

When Ami returned to Talient, she was trapped in the hospital with Theo and Dr. Elderflower. Ami wasn't pleased with being Theo's test subject for learning how to heal, but she did allow it so the nurse would shut up about the unscientific method. Ami and the doctor became smug when Theo accessed his magic and healed Ami's wounds. The Werefox stared at his hands for the longest time, as if seeing them for the first time. Ami was pleased that Theo's magic felt relaxing, and her magic didn't reject it.

Once released, she visited the Winter District to check on the gang. The males told her what had happened during her absence. True to her suspicions, Blaine tried to recruit the males by intimidation. The Knights defended them whenever they could. However, Blaine started to recruit others to join his business. He tried to intrude on what the males' determined as 'her territory,' aka the Winter and Spring Districts, but the males fought back fiercely. The males started their own recruiting to secure her territory.

"I don't know what you expect me to do," Ami said, eating in the eating hall. It was after breakfast for the cadets. The non-cadet males had joined her for a hearty breakfast. Blejan was happy to serve them.

"You're Sigrid," Shayne said dumbly.

Ami shook her head. "I was only Sigrid because of Blaine. I don't know if I can run a business and keep up with my military duties. Especially after what Lee and I discovered at the fort."

"What did you find?" Benton asked.

"We found a witch," Ami answered.

Rune sucked in a breath through his teeth. Benton hissed like a cat. Philip looked troubled. Shayne appeared thoughtful.

"Witches are bad. Like really, really bad," Rune stated.

Ami nodded. "Yes, and there was a bandit attack that Hector didn't alert the generals about. I don't know what we're going to do about that." She rubbed her face with her hands in frustration.

"Sounds like a lot is going on from something so simple," Philip commented.

"I agree." Ami finished her plate of eggs and biscuits.

"Ya'puris?" Bleddyn asked hesitantly.

"Yes?" Ami answered coolly. Even though she wasn't angry at him or the others, she didn't like him.

"The master wishes for you to meet with her," Bleddyn replied, looking at his feet.

"Very well. Tell your master I'm on my way," Ami said with cold politeness.

Ami and the males got up. Ami glanced at Shayne. The Werewolf was deep in his thoughts. When they exited the warehouse, Ami pulsed a question to Shayne through their Bond. Shayne snapped out of his daze. She pulled Shayne to the side.

"Is everything all right?" Ami asked worriedly.

Shayne stared at her, the cogs in his mind turning. "I'm thinking of a solution to the Blaine problem."

"I'm not strong enough to kill him," Ami pointed out. It wasn't an option she wanted to have, but she kept it open just in case. Territory wars were bloody, and Blaine was ruthless.

"Not yet," Shayne countered. "I'm thinking of other areas to push back."

"Like what?" Ami asked.

"Allies," Shayne stated.

"I've been thinking that as well." Ami nodded.

"How so?" Shayne asked.

"Jasmine doesn't trust me, and I'm afraid our alliance may not last. I will need allies also to maintain my stay in Rascu," Ami explained.

"You mean leaving?" Shayne looked horrified at the notion.

"Tso is looking for any reason to deport me back to Vinci. I will need more allies besides the Centaurs to secure my place in Rascal society," Ami said. "It is tricky to gain allies within the military due to my status as a foreigner and female."

Shayne nodded. "I may have a solution."

"And?"

"I will need to investigate it further to see if it will benefit you," Shayne said vaguely.

"Shayne." Ami gave him a look.

"Please trust me," Shayne pleaded with puppy eyes.

Ami eyed him critically. "Very well. Don't keep me in the dark."

"I won't. I'll speak to you soon, Sigrid," Shayne promised.

"Be safe," Ami warned. Shayne nodded before heading to join the others. Ami made her way to the mansion. She wasn't sure what kind of mood Jasmine would be in. She knocked on Jasmine's door. The dictator opened it, her brown eyes tired.

"Come in," Jasmine muttered.

Ami's curiosity was piqued. The young Elf wore a long sleeve plain brown dress with white lace at the bottom hem. Her hair was completely down in lanky curls. Looking closer at her, Ami saw the beginnings of dark circles settling like black cats under Jasmine's eyes. She looked pale, as if seeing a ghost continuously. What had Jasmine been dealing with to leave her in this state? Jasmine waved her hand. A tray of tea appeared. Ami was disappointed by the lack of food. Jasmine poured them each a cup of hot tea. She drank hers pensively. Ami cautiously sipped hers.

"What's wrong?" Ami broke the silence.

"I am this close," Jasmine said, almost pinching her forefinger and thumb together, "to killing the generals and the males in Old Congress."

"Mood."

Jasmine sighed. "I just don't know what to do. Tso undermines me at every turn. If it wasn't for the slaves, I wouldn't even know he was having these secret meetings."

"What are these meetings about?" Ami asked.

"Lately, they've been about you and how to deport you back to Vinci." Jasmine sipped more of her tea.

"Why does he want to get rid of me?" Ami asked.

Jasmine shrugged. "Honestly, I think he's scared of you gaining power and influence in the military, which will threaten his position."

"I am not popular outside the capital," Ami pointed out.

"No, but you are with the Knights, and they've been bragging about you with everyone, inside and outside the military," Jasmine said with a dark chuckle. "At this rate, you could have my job."

"I have no interest in your position," Ami stated flatly.

"What are you interested in?" Jasmine inquired.

"I want to free the Dragons," Ami replied honestly. Jasmine's eyebrows rose to her hairline. "They deserve to be free, and Rascals should never harbor slaves."

"Is that all?" Jasmine asked.

Ami nodded. "That was my primary goal in entering the military."

"What's your goal now?"

"I still want to free the slaves," Ami said. "However, right now, I'm more concerned about the presence of bandits and their influence on the military."

"What about the bandits?" Jasmine asked, her tone dangerously solemn.

Ami paused. "Have you spoken to General Lee or read his reports?"

"I haven't seen him."

"It'll be best if you read the reports. They are far more detailed than what I can explain," Ami said. "Also, it will have his investigations as well as mine."

Jasmine eyed her suspiciously. "Why aren't you telling me?"

"It is General Lee's report. I don't know the whole story," Ami replied. It was true. She still couldn't find out who told her Sir Tres had been at Putra Hallas for twenty years. For some reason, she didn't write it down in her notes. She also still didn't know why he tried to kill her.

Jasmine stared at her for a moment. "All right. I'll talk to Lee later."

"Thank you. Any new drama from Old Congress?" Ami asked.

"Ugh," Jasmine groaned. She poured more tea into her cup. "Gilbert, one of Jona's cronies, is trying to get a piece of land under his family's land. Unlucky for him, no one is buying his stupid claim."

"Why is he trying to claim it? What history does his family have with it?" Ami asked.

Jasmine shrugged. "Honestly, it wouldn't surprise me if he was making the whole thing up just to have the land in his family's name."

"What kind of land is it?" Ami asked.

"It's this forest near this no-name village. It's called Wolf Forest or something," Jasmine said with a wave of her hand.

Chills went down Ami's spine. "Is the village near Putra Hallas?"

"Yes. How'd you know that?" Jasmine asked, looking at her suspiciously.

Ami jumped out of her seat. She rushed out of the room,

ignoring Jasmine's shouts. She knocked frantically on Lee's door. The Werebobcat answered.

"Are you busy, sir?" Ami asked quickly.

"What's the matter?" Lee asked, opening the door wider.

"Amaranth!" Jasmine shouted. She stomped her way toward Ami. She huffed when she reached the white-haired female.

"May we come in, sir?" Ami asked.

Lee glanced between the two warily before nodding. Beautiful walnut bookshelves filled neatly with thick leather-bound books covered both sides of the office. The dark wood desk was slightly messy but organized. Lee sat in a plush leather chair. He motioned for the two females to sit on the velvet ones before his desk.

"My lady, please tell General Lee what you just told me," Ami asked politely.

Jasmine barely hid her uneasiness and explained the happenings in Old Congress to Lee. The Werebobcat's ears were fully erect.

"That is worth investigating," Lee purred. He sounded excited. "My lady, may I look into his claims with your permission?"

"You have my permission, General," Jasmine replied amicably. "If you'll excuse us, we have more to discuss."

Lee bowed his head. "I'll update you as soon as possible."

"Thank you. Amaranth, follow me." Jasmine stood. Ami followed her back to her room. When the door shut, Jasmine whipped around with a thunderous look. "What was that?"

Ami jumped. "What do you mean?"

"Why did we have to involve him?" Jasmine snarled.

Ami narrowed her eye at Jasmine. "Because the land that Gilbert wants to claim involves a witch."

Jasmine deflated at the word 'witch.' She stumbled backward into her lace-winged chair, her face pale.

"Is that in Lee's report?" Jasmine whispered.

"Yes, and mine," Ami answered.

Jasmine looked at her sharply. "What do you know of the witch?"

"I killed her."

"What was her name?" Jasmine asked shakily.

"Jeanne," Ami replied. Her suspicions grew when Jasmine seemed relieved.

"I need to be alone," Jasmine whispered.

Ami left without a word. *Why did Jasmine seem relieved by the witch's name? Does Jasmine know a witch? Is that how she got to power? Why is she so suspicious of Lee?* Shaking her head, she exited the mansion. She needed coffee.

The heart of the library was an area reserved for dedicated scholars. Five large rooms could be booked for research purposes. One such space was reserved until further notice by the dictator. That is where Elizabeth, Isabella, and Gabriella lived, breathed, and worked on their project. Isabella was still going strong, her passion oozing out of her pores. Elizabeth struggled to read a population census. Her vision kept going double, making her dizzy. Gabriella was snoring with her head on the table and a puddle of drool forming from the corner of her open mouth.

They had made tremendous progress. It led to startling surprises in their own family trees. Gabriella discovered she was a third cousin twice removed to General Rikardi, for starters. While there wasn't an official marriage certificate, it clarified some family gossip Gabriella had heard whenever there was a gathering. While it was humorous, Elizabeth started to notice a different problem.

It started when they went through their family trees from the roots, at the times of the queens, to see if there were Centaur ancestors they could link. Elizabeth was fascinated with how long People lived back then. One of her ancestors, Elizi McCoall, lived until she was six hundred years old. Then, without warning, her family didn't live past one hundred and fifty. It startled her that she went to the history books to see if there was a plague or famine during these times. Not finding anything, she went to the death certificates. They were either listed as "killed in the line of duty" or "natural causes."

How can someone entirely healthy die suddenly at one hundred and fifty when his mother lived to be over three hundred? Elizabeth thought. *Was there some kind of grudge against my family?*

She investigated Isabella's and Gabriella's families as well. Their families were the same. Not believing in coincidences, she made a timeline of when the age of natural death changed. When she was finished, the evidence alarmed her. It all started when the Dragons were enslaved. Slowly, all People began to live shorter and shorter lives.

With all our civil wars, no wonder no one has noticed this. Elizabeth thought bitterly. It led to more questions than answers. Why was it when the Dragons were enslaved? Was it their magic or the slave Bond? Were they Bonded with some prominent families, and it spread that way? Did Ami know this?

"Eli, did you find Thoth the fourth?" Isabella asked.

How does she still have energy? Elizabeth wondered. "Still working on it. I'll let you know."

Gabriella let out a loud snore, waking herself up. The redhead looked around sleepily. Elizabeth shook her head.

Ami didn't hear anything from Lee or Jasmine for five days. During that time, she visited the café, jogged around the Inner City, and kept an ear out for Blaine's movements. Blaine was keeping suspiciously quiet. It made Ami anxious and overwhelmed with the presumed responsibility of a business. Logan was pleased to see her more often, lavishing her with his new creations. Ami's favorite so far was the caramel pecan pie latte.

On top of that, the Shadows were getting bolder. She often saw at least five watching on her way to the café. She wasn't sure why, but she felt it had to do with the Shadow King. Her nights became sleepless once again. Thankfully, Shayne asked to meet with her privately on the sixth day during his shift. Ami was drinking another Logan invention. This one had blueberries and cream. It reminded her of the blueberry cobbler Grammy used to make alongside homemade ice cream. Ami and Shayne left together when Shayne's shift ended. They walked in comfortable silence to the Winter District. The new grunts the males had recruited nodded respectfully at Ami.

The warehouse the males stayed in was clean. In one corner was their sleeping area. Shayne motioned for her to stay put. He jogged to the back of the warehouse, where random crates were scattered. She couldn't see what they contained. Sniffing, she couldn't detect any food. Shayne came back with a fancy envelope in his hand.

"What's this?" Ami asked, taking the offered envelope.

"When you were away, I kept an eye on Blaine," Shayne said. "He always dressed up and went to this specific house in the Summer District. I managed to sneak in and was assumed to be one of the serving staff. There I learned it was a party held by a high-ranking Noble for lesser Nobles. They were networking."

"That was risky, tailing Blaine," Ami commented.

Shayne snorted. "He never noticed me before. Anyway, I saw him flirting and talking politics with the females. I found out a high-ranking Noble was hosting a party in the Spring District and got an invitation for you."

"What's the catch?" Ami asked.

"You will have to go dressed as a male," Shayne said, his ears flicking uneasily.

"I don't mind going as a male. This might be fun." Ami smirked.

"I found an outfit for you, too," Shayne said excitedly. He grabbed her wrist and pulled her toward the back of the warehouse. Ami allowed it, bemused.

When they came to a set of three crates flushed to the back wall of the warehouse, Shayne released her wrist. He popped open the middle crate. He pulled out several articles of pink and black clothing. Intrigued, Ami took the bundle from him and went behind a tower of stacked boxes to change.

The outfit was identical to the one she wore to the military ball. The button-down shirt was a soft pink that Ami liked. The jacket and pants were black with thin pink vertical stripes. The tie and vest were black with black lace. Suspiciously, the clothes fit her perfectly. She came out to show Shayne. From his blush, she may have pulled it off.

"Why does this fit so well?" Ami asked.

"Blaine often used magic on the clothes he stole," Shayne answered.

"Where did he steal them from?" Ami asked, curious.

"I'm not sure. I only know that I saw Blaine several times with a few males when they scored." Shayne shrugged. "The clothes often didn't fit him until he used magic."

That makes sense. Ami mused. "How do I look? Do I look like a Noble male?" she asked.

"There's one more thing," Shayne said. Reaching deeper into the crate, he pulled out a length of cloth that was oddly shaped. When Shayne handed it to her, she realized it was an eye patch. It was black except for the eye covering, which was pink with black lace overlayed. She tried to put it on. Shayne had to assist. Without a word, Ami summoned a full-length mirror. She was impressed.

She didn't think she would ever look good in pink, but enough black in the design made her feel comfortable. Once she asked Perry how to do her hair again, she would be good to go.

"I think I can pass for a male physically. Shall I practice deepening my voice?" Ami asked playfully.

Shayne grinned. "I think your raspy accent will suffice."

"True."

Ami changed back to her normal clothes as Shayne chatted about the café with his back to her. She folded the outfit neatly and returned to the Inner City with Shayne. The Werewolf's ears constantly flickered around, listening for danger. When they reached the Common Grounds, Shayne said goodbye and left. Thankfully, it was dinner time, and the Knights were still patrolling. Ami went to her room. She put the bundle on her bed. The invitation fell out.

When did it get there? Ami wondered. Shaking her head, she observed the invitation. On the outside was the party's address, date, and time. It didn't say who was hosting. The party was tomorrow night. Ami knew the street and had an idea of which house it was.

Things were about to get interesting.

The Spring District was well-lit, particularly the street Ami walked. Glancing at the invitation again, she started to look for the place. A small group of well-dressed Nobles appeared to be heading the same way. She followed. The destination was a large mansion. Intricate iron rods with threatening spikes were the fence around the roomy front garden. Two hired male guards dressed in suits monitored the gate. Ami observed small groups and couples handing them their invitations. The guards glanced at them and then handed them back. After watching them a few times, Ami noticed something interesting.

The guards were using magic. It was subtle and easy to miss. She only noticed that one guard's eyes flashed a different color when he was looking at the invitation. It was a common sign of using magic.

This could be useful if I want to teach the males magic. Ami thought. *Maybe I can practice with the gang first?* She would have to see how they would react. When the crowds thinned, Ami approached the guards.

She handed one of them her invitation. She didn't recognize them, but wasn't sure how far her infamous name had spread. The guard's eyes flashed, and he handed it back to her. Ami nodded and entered the grounds. The mansion was three stories high and styled from the First Gold era, some four hundred years ago. While tall and intimidating, it was also narrow due to being in the middle of the city. Mainly made of wood, the house had metalwork around the windows and roof edges that added a sense of intrigue and danger. From the looks of it, the grounds and the house were well-maintained. Ami wondered if the original family still lived here. She noticed, due to their clothing, many of the Nobles present were not of high rank. She only knew this because the etiquette school in Nephele was only tailored to the Most High and Most Noble families. She followed the groups and clusters ahead of her to the mansion's entrance. The sound of an announcer made it to her ears. She felt intrigued, and her stomach sank at the same time.

What name did Shayne put me under? Ami wondered.

As the line edged closer, the interior came into view. The ballroom was long and tall. Despite the shortened width, the cool colors, numerous windows, and opened doors leading to the lush gardens hindered any claustrophobia. Ami watched various Nobles cluster into small groups of four or five. When it was Ami's turn, she handed her invitation to the announcer. The tall, well-dressed male Elf opened the envelope. His eyes flashed with magic.

"Please welcome, Lord Sieghild." The announcer's voice traveled through the long ballroom.

Ami relaxed as she entered the ballroom. Not many People seemed to take notice of her. That was fine with her for now. She wanted to watch and see what precisely this party was about before making a political move. Also, she wanted to make sure Blaine didn't make an appearance. She didn't want to deal with any drama tonight. A waiter passed by. Ami smoothly grabbed a flute filled with champagne. The gold liquid was bubbly and smelled like blackberries. Taking a sip, Ami was impressed. It was good quality.

Who is the host of this party? Ami asked herself, glancing around. So far, the host hadn't announced their presence. She checked her internal clock and estimated the official party would start in about twenty minutes. She was disappointed when the food wasn't out yet. Ami spotted a part of the ballroom wall where she could observe without being disturbed. She only took several steps when someone spoke.

"Did your partner abandon you?" a female voice asked. The owner was a dark brown Werewolf. She wore a corset-fitted frilly dress. Her long dark brown was pinned up in complicated knots. It looked like a termite mound. She hid half of her face with a cheap fan.

"I did not come in with one," Ami answered coolly.

"I'm surprised they let a foreigner in," the female said snootily.

"Why?" Ami asked curiously.

The Werewolf looked startled. "What do you mean why?"

"Rascu is very kind to foreigners. They can join the military and earn rank, something unheard of in other nations.

Rascals even still trade with Goya despite the tension," Ami answered.

"Hmmm," the Werewolf hummed. "I never thought of that before." She eyed Ami up and down. "I don't believe I caught your name."

"I will once you introduce yourself," Ami replied, taking a sip.

"I am Sable Warden," Sable replied sweetly with a poor curtsey. Ami could hear the criticisms from the etiquette school's head teacher in her head.

"I am Lord Sieghild," Ami introduced her male name.

"Oh?" Sable asked, her tail wagging from underneath her dress. "Well, my lord, may I introduce you to my friends?" Sable asked, her voice still sickly sweet.

Ami forced a smile on her lips. "I would like that, my lady."

The Werewolf snapped her fan closed. Ami wished she would snap it back open. Her gaudy makeup made her look like a clown. Sable looped her arm around Ami's and dragged her to the other side of the ballroom. The only good thing about being on the other side was the more accessible food bar when it opened.

"Hello, *putas*. Did you miss me?" Sable asked sassily.

An equally gaudy-looking female Elf retorted, "As much as I miss smelling a barn; I just figured it was you."

The only male, a Werewolf, didn't seem fazed by this crass exchange. "May I ask who our guest is, Lady Warden?" he asked. His dark brown eyes gazed at Ami curiously.

"This is Lord Sieghild," Sable introduced proudly. Ami became suspicious.

"Sieghild?" the female Elf asked incredulously.

"Does my name bother you?" Ami asked, her voice cold.

"No offense, my lord," the male Werewolf said quickly. "It is an unusual name that hasn't been heard in a long time amongst Nobles."

Ami looked at the male Werewolf with a stony gaze. "And you are?"

"I am Sir Mark Tremors, son of Adrianna Tremors," Mark replied with a bow.

"Greetings, Mark." Ami gave a short, respectful bow.

"You have not asked for my name," the female Elf said, her voice grating Ami's ears.

"You have not offered it," Ami replied deadpan.

The Elf hmphed. "It's Priscilla Laymate."

"Hello, my lady." Ami nodded at her.

"You're supposed to bow, male," Priscilla sneered.

"You're supposed to be polite to foreign guests, lower Noble," Ami retorted icily. Priscilla and Sable flinched. Mark glanced back and forth between the females and Ami. Ami turned to Sable and asked, "I thought you were supposed to introduce me to friends, not be blatantly insulted?"

"My apologies, my lord." Sable stumbled over her words. "I didn't know they would react this way." She glared at Priscilla, who looked ashamed.

"Perhaps we should enlighten our new friend on the current events amongst the Nobles," Mark suggested.

"Excellent idea, Mark." Sable nodded eagerly.

Current events consisted mainly of gossip Ami already heard from the Knights, although they contained far juicier details. During their gossip, Ami picked up information on the trio. Priscilla and Sable were from the lowest rank of Noble, barely attaining the position. Mark was his family's first generation with the status of Noble and was constantly under pressure to marry up. Despite this, the three somehow managed to slither all around the Noble ranks, listening to gossip and paying attention to Noble politics and internal conflicts. One topic, in particular, captured her full attention.

"Have you heard about the Goyans?" Priscilla asked conspiratorially.

"What about?" Sable asked.

"I heard from a Noble's cousin in the military that the Goyans have completely stopped their advances in Rascu. It's like they just lost interest," Priscilla said, grinning widely.

"When did this happen?" Ami asked.

Priscilla thought for a moment. "I would say at least over a year ago, at least. Very strange if you ask me."

Ice went down Ami's spine. *It was because of my death.* She realized. *My Bonds with everyone …*

"My lord, is something wrong?" Mark asked, snapping Ami out of her thoughts.

Ami blinked. "My apologies. I was wondering about the repercussions of this new development."

"What do you mean?" Sable asked.

"I would be concerned about what attracted the Goyans' attention away from Rascu," Ami lied.

"I bet someone died," Priscilla snickered.

Ami gave her a hard look. "I don't see the humor."

Priscilla blushed, hiding her shamed face with her cheap fan. Sable looked embarrassed and irritated. Mark shook his head.

"I need a refreshment," Ami said in an irritated tone. She turned heel and left the group. She passed her empty flute to a waiter with an empty tray.

"My lord," Mark called out, jogging to catch up to her.

"Mark," Ami stated flatly. Her stomach growled. Why haven't the host or hostess announced themselves? Why are they withholding food?

"Please forgive Priscilla for her rude behavior," Mark pleaded. Ami stared at him. The Werewolf continued to blabber, "She's not used to dealing with Nobles of your stature, and she is not the best at social cues. This is her second party, and she's desperate to please anyone of rank."

"If she feels so guilty of her ill speech, it should be her pleading, not you," Ami growled. She raised a hand when Mark started to protest. "A female should be able to recognize and admit she is at fault if she wishes to gain respect from anyone, Noble or otherwise. If not, she will be stuck in her dilemma for a long time."

A horn ran through the ballroom, making everyone jump. A few females screamed in terror. A beautiful middle-aged female Werewolf stepped onto a platform several feet before her. It was tall enough for everyone to see her. She had dark shiny brown fur that was beautifully streaked with gray. Her long hair, also streaked with gray, was pinned up into an elegant bun. Her presence was strong yet calm. She wore a simple emerald silk dress.

"Good evening, my esteemed guests," the female Werewolf spoke, her voice carrying authority. The ballroom went silent. All eyes and ears were focused on the Werewolf. "I, Lady Gemma Blackhill of the Most High Nobles, welcome you to my party. Please enjoy the refreshments provided, and I will greet you personally as soon as I can."

Polite clapping echoed through the air while Lady Blackhill stepped off her platform. Ami managed to walk away from the distracted Mark, found a new flute from a waiter, and hung back at the wall she originally wanted to be. Immediately, Lady Blackhill was swarmed by lesser Nobles hoping to speak with her. Ami didn't blame them. The Blackhill family was notable. They specialized in social gatherings like this and had many fingers in many pies with other Noble families' businesses. Perhaps this was a blessing in disguise for Ami. If she managed to impress Lady Blackhill, she would gain much power.

But what can I offer? Ami wondered. It would depend on whether Lady Blackhill wanted to create a business or alliance with the Centaurs. Her status in the military would mean nothing to a Most High Noble. Glancing at the other side of the hall, Ami sighed heavily. Food was still not being served.

This is a waste of time, Ami thought.

"Are you not interested?" a male voice asked from Ami's left. Ami turned fully to face the new Person. A chocolate brown Werewolf, several inches taller than her, approached her. He wore a steel-gray suit with a soft purple button-down shirt. It brought out his violet eyes. Those eyes stared at Ami's single amethyst. He was handsome, almost making Ami blush.

"Interested in what?" Ami asked, her curiosity overcoming her hunger for the moment.

"You ... We have the same eyes," the Werewolf replied dumbly.

"Well, you have both of yours," Ami retorted playfully.

"Oh, I meant no offense," the Werewolf said quickly, bowing his head.

"I'm not offended, my lord," Ami said with a half-smile.

The Werewolf lifted his head hesitantly. "I apologize for not introducing myself. I am Viovel Blackhill, son of Lady Blackhill," Viovel said, glancing at where his mother was mingling.

"We are well met, my lord. I am Lord Sieghild," Ami replied with a respectful bow.

Viovel appeared thoughtful. "That is an old name in these halls," he commented.

Ami shrugged. "I'm bringing sexy back."

Viovel burst into guffaws. He barely caught himself from falling to the floor in his laughter, hugging his abdomen. His laugh caught Ami, and she joined him in his laughter. Thankfully, they weren't loud enough to gather attention except for those who were a few feet away from them. Those People quickly moved away from the two's open behavior.

"I'm sorry, my lord," Viovel said once his laughter died. "That ... That comment took me by surprise."

Ami barely suppressed her giggles. "If you're that easily surprised, you're in for a wild ride with me."

Viovel wiped his watery eyes, still chuckling. "I haven't laughed that hard in a long time."

Ami smiled widely, showing teeth. "At least it won't be boring. Violet eyes are unheard of in Weres."

The young Werewolf nodded. "My father was from Qu'uan and was albino. Instead of blue eyes, he had violet ones. His coloring was similar to yours, my lord, if he had been a Dragon."

"I look like my mother," Ami said. "Are you in the military?"

"Yes," he answered, "I'm on leave now. Mother wanted me to attend this party."

"Wife hunting?"

Viovel flinched. "I wouldn't be surprised if that was the case." Defeat showed in his slumped shoulders and lowered ears.

Ami shrugged. "Well, while you're single, how about we get this party started?"

"What do you mean?" Viovel asked.

The sound of lids popping off was music to Ami's ears. "First, food."

The two weaved in and around various People effortlessly. Ami was pleased with the variety of finger foods: fried chicken skewers, roast beef and cheese roll-ups, cheese balls with crackers, and cut-up fruit and vegetables with dip, to name a few. Viovel gawked at her piled plate. He continued to stare as he watched her devour it with gusto.

"What?" she asked, mouth half full of crackers and cheese.

"Your manners are appalling," Viovel said aghast.

Ami swallowed. "And you're too uptight."

Viovel looked affronted. "This isn't my first party, my lord."

Ami smirked. "It is with me."

"What do you—"

Ami gave her empty dirty plate to a passing waiter and stalked towards the orchestra, setting up towards the back of the hall. The female Elf conductor was flipping through the music sheets when Ami approached. The two whispered back and forth. The conductor appeared to be nervous about Ami's request. Ami wasn't deterred. Somehow the conductor relented. With a sigh, the Elf stood up straight. The players immediately took their positions, their instruments at the ready. Then the conductor tapped her foot, creating a beat.

The players recognized the rhythm and started to play.

The song was "A Beauty Came to My Window." A sense of being in the country, free from the worries of the city, filled the hall. The violins and drums dominated the tune. Windchimes mimicked the summer breeze at night. Ami gathered random People around and formed two lines. She was in the line with the males. The females were across, facing them. Following Ami's cue, she introduced them to line dancing.

A simple dance compared to many Rascal routines, the Nobles quickly picked up the steps. Ami showed them how to twirl their partner, when to clap, and how many times to twirl with their partner. Laughter, giggles, and whoots rang through the air.

"Trade out!" Ami commanded.

The males dancing exited, introducing fresh dancers. The females copied them. Ami watched from the sidelines, clapping with the beat. Somehow Viovel came to her side, clapping awkwardly.

"Having fun yet?" Ami asked, raising her voice over the dancing, music, and laughter.

"I'm not sure," Viovel answered loudly.

Feeling mischievous, Ami grabbed Viovel by the arm.

"Trade out!" Ami shouted.

With Viovel beside her, the two danced with Priscilla and Sable. Ami was thankful she had Sable as her dance partner. The Werewolf was a good dancer. Priscilla kept stomping on Viovel's toes, making him wince each time. When the song ended, everyone cheered. The air was filled with happiness. Ami felt pleasantly drunk from the atmosphere. Many male and female Nobles approached Viovel, thanking him for creating the dance. Ami slipped away to find something to drink. She smirked, hearing Viovel protesting that it wasn't his idea.

The waitstaff was considerate for providing cold water. The liquid tasted delicious. Cooling down, Ami returned to her previous spot against the wall. As she did, she saw Lady

Blackhill frowning fiercely at Viovel. That sobered Ami up quickly.

"My lady, I don't believe I had the pleasure," Ami said as she approached the older Werewolf.

"We haven't. Unfortunately, my son is making a fool of himself," Lady Blackhill nearly growled.

"Actually, that was my doing," Ami admitted.

Lady Blackhill stared at her in surprise. "You? Why?"

"I was bored."

Lady Blackhill frowned at her. "It is rude to become a host at another's party."

"It is also rude to make your guests wait for over two hours without food," Ami retorted coldly. She sipped her water, gazing at Lady Blackhill emotionlessly.

Lady Blackhill flinched visibly. "How dare you—"

"Lord Sieghild!" Sable sang. The Werewolf ran up to her excitedly. Seeing Lady Blackhill, she barely curtsied before turning to Ami. "My lord, they're about to play a fun song. Will you dance with me?"

"How can I deny such a request?" Ami asked. Nodding at a glaring Lady Blackhill, she followed Sable back to the dance floor. She downed the rest of her water. One of the Nobles offered to take it from her. Thanking him, she turned her attention back to the dance.

"We were talking with Viovel, and he's convinced you are an amazing dancer," Sable explained loudly.

"Has someone doubted his claim?" Ami asked.

"We think you need to prove it," a male Elf, dressed in an outfit so old-fashioned even the elders would deem it ancient, replied. At first glance, she thought she was looking at a younger version of Jona. Then she determined his eyes weren't slimy enough and his attitude was due to spoiled youth.

"How so?" Ami asked.

The Elf smiled maliciously. "You two have to dance, and you have to be the submissive."

"All right."

Ami walked to the clear dance floor, ignoring the stunned male's gaping stare. Viovel stood there uncomfortably.

"My lord, they have challenged us to a humiliating dance," Viovel whispered shamefully.

"It's only humiliating if we allow it to be," Ami whispered.

"What do you have planned?" Viovel murmured suspiciously.

"If we're going to be challenged, we might as well enjoy it," Ami mumbled offhandedly.

Viovel stared at her as if he couldn't figure her out. "I suppose."

"I got this," Ami said confidently. She went back to the conductor. After whispering a request, the Elf seemed to be more receiving. With a nod, Ami went back to Viovel.

The sound of soft flutes filled the air.

"What's going—" Viovel tried to ask.

"Position, my lord," Ami ordered.

"For a submissive, you're quite bossy," Viovel commented.

Ami gave him a feral smile. "What makes you think I'm submissive?"

The soft flutes abruptly erupted into a flurry of snare drums, violins, and trumpets. The song she requested was called "When My Love Comes to Town," and accompanying it was one of the most complex dances in Rascal culture called *phinoa saylor*.

Ami subtly led Viovel along the dance floor, careful in her facial expressions and steps. She was surprised at how easily Viovel let her have control, yet managed to act like the lead. She didn't know what she did to earn that level of trust. The song ended after an exhausting eight minutes. The two bowed respectfully to each other. The room roared with claps and cheers. Suddenly, Ami and Viovel were surrounded by Nobles.

"That was masterful, my lords! I have never seen such beautiful step work," Sable shouted in Ami's ear.

"Please excuse us. We need refreshments," Viovel said

quickly. He easily grabbed Ami's arm and pulled her through the thick crowd of People.

Ami thought he was going to lead her toward the food. Instead, he guided her to the opposite side of the room and into an empty hallway. The hall was narrower than a typical home, but the air was less overwhelming. They stood several feet apart, taking in deep breaths.

"I thought we could both take a breather," Viovel panted.

"I agree."

They stood in comfortable silence. At the same time, they looked at each other. Heated tension filled the air. It was strange to Ami since she didn't feel like fighting Viovel or felt like he had wronged her. This was different and something she didn't understand. Viovel slowly stalked his way toward her. Ami watched with interest. He stopped inches from her. If he inhaled a large breath, his chest would touch hers.

"Why don't we entertain ourselves elsewhere?" Viovel asked, his voice husky and soft.

Ami chuckled darkly. "Darling, you can't handle me."

"Would I impress you if I could?" Viovel asked, undeterred.

"I don't undress at the first male showing interest," Ami warned.

"We don't have to undress to entertain," Viovel answered smoothly.

Ami forced down a half smile at the remark. "Let's get to know each other a bit more before we decide on that, shall we?"

"Is that a promise?" Viovel asked, his violet eyes hopeful.

"We'll see," Ami answered vaguely.

A nearby grandfather clock rang noisily, making them jump. The heated tension evaporated, leaving awkwardness in its wake.

"I'll see you later, my lord," Ami said quickly.

"Yes, my lord. It was good meeting you," Viovel agreed, his ears turning dark red.

Ami walked as fast as she could without running out of

the Blackhill house. A thought hit her as she stalked down the street toward the Inner City.

Was I just offered sex?

CHAPTER 9

"I don't understand why you're not taking the situation seriously, Head General," Rikardi said with a deep frown. All the generals, including the fake ones, were in the meeting room.

"I don't understand how you can trust a word from that female," Tso growled.

Rikardi narrowed his eyes. "Which female do you speak of? There are two in Talient."

"Rose!" Tso snarled. "The one who threatens the entire military reputation we've been trying to preserve for the last thousand years!"

"Tso, breathe," Lee said with a bored tone. The Werebobcat was filing his claws, making them sharper.

"And you," Tso swirled his attention to Lee. "Since when do you carry out investigations for our esteemed dictator?"

"Investigations?" Mason asked, sitting up straighter in curiosity.

"I investigate situations that interest me," Lee answered, not perturbed by Tso's angry attention. "Especially when they intertwine with an interesting puzzle."

"Is this about Hector?" Rikardi asked.

"Yes and no," Lee said. "I'm still searching for information on how and why a witch ensnared him."

Tso scoffed. "You don't believe in witches."

"Not in the supernatural sense, no," Lee admitted. "However, I am concerned with People who believe they are witches of great power and what they will do to obtain that power. Captain Rose warned me of their brutality, and I saw with my own eyes what one Person would do. I hate to see a group of them organizing in our nation like that."

"It would take great skill to hide such an organization—" Tso started.

"Speaking of our nation, you don't seem to hold in high regard, Head General," Lee continued as if Tso hadn't spoken. "Ever since Rose was promoted to captain, you have been pushing and shoving any which way in delaying her from becoming a leader. If we are to uphold these esteemed values you say we've treasured for the last thousand years, we need a female leader that isn't Jasmine."

The two glared at each other.

"Lee, why do we need a female leader?" Rikardi asked, snapping the tense air.

"Call me old-fashioned, but we suck at leadership. Consider our history in the past one hundred years, for example. How many civil wars have we had? Fifty-seven? Fifty-nine? We can barely keep count, and the only way we kept track of how many is naming them after the kind of People the leaders were! Look at the different types of crime in our cities. In Ravenna, Lady Pera has reduced the crime rate by over sixty percent. Compare that to Pari with Lord Button, who can't keep up with the investigations. Even he had to ask Lady Pera for assistance because he was overwhelmed. We need a strong female leader in the military," Lee explained.

"Do you think that leader is Rose?" Rikardi inquired.

"I don't know," Lee admitted. "I have my own reservations about her, but it's not personal." He eyed Tso when he said this.

"What about the bandits?" Mason asked. "I believe this is a much bigger problem than we realized."

"Very astute," Rikardi sneered. Mason glared at the Centaur. "Give Captain Rose a cover."

"A cover?" Grasswind asked dumbly.

"Yes," Rikardi said slowly, "with three or four other soldiers to investigate the bandits."

"Even as strong as Rose is, she can't take down bandits," Mason argued.

"That's not what he's talking about," Lee said, realization in his eyes. "It's a stealth mission."

Rikardi nodded. "We need to evaluate each situation carefully without the bandits knowing."

"Why do you care?" Moss asked nasally.

"Unlike you," Rikardi said coldly, "I care about our citizens."

"Who will want to be on her cover?" Tso asked. His tone had a hint of snide coloring it.

"She will choose from a list of soldiers who are eligible for promotion," Rikardi stated.

"I can't allow that," Tso tsked.

"I am in command of all the soldiers who have trained here and am given the authority of who will be promoted based on their training in Talient. You gave me that power, remember?" Rikardi said smugly.

Tso paled at the implication. "I rescind that use of power—"

"You can't do that without a full vote of confidence from the other generals," Rikardi interrupted.

"I trust Rikardi," Lee stated.

"As do I," Mason added.

"Don't look at us," Playwright hissed. "We're not real generals, remember?"

Tso growled. "Fine!"

The Werefox stood up and stomped out of the meeting room. The faux generals left shortly after. Only Mason, Rikardi, and Lee were left.

"He's changed," Mason stated.

"Quite dramatically," Lee noted.

"I have a feeling a witch is a part of this," Rikardi sighed deeply.

"You think Tso is in with them?" Mason asked in disbelief.

"No. But I believe a witch is involved and doing something with our leaders," Rikardi answered.

Ami and Blejan chatted as they made their way to Rikardi's office. The blond Centaur summoned her around lunchtime, and Ami knew he hadn't eaten yet. The two Dragons made two large platters of sandwiches, veggies for Rikardi and turkey for Ami, with minced pies, sliced vegetables, various fruits, and lemonade. When they entered, Rikardi looked up.

"What's this?" he asked suspiciously.

"Sir, we've brought lunch," Blejan answered.

Rikardi's lips twitched. "And our appetites are the same as Knights?"

"I wouldn't know, sir," Ami said with a small smile. She had missed their banter.

After setting up, Blejan left. Ami and Rikardi each picked a sandwich and started to eat. When he was halfway done, Rikardi broke the silence.

"You are assigned a cover," the Centaur said as if he was mentioning the weather.

Ami slowed her chewing. Swallowing, she asked, "Sir?"

"I have a box of files of potential soldiers for your cover," Rikardi explained. "You need to choose one soldier as your second and two others. Once decided, they will be summoned here and you will learn of your mission."

"Thank you for this opportunity, sir," Ami said gratefully. A spark of hope lit up in her chest. Perhaps she wouldn't need to leave the military after all.

"How is your health?" Rikardi asked.

"Much better. I've managed to run around the Common Grounds three times and keep the Knights on their toes," Ami said proudly.

"And the dizzy spells?" Rikardi asked.

"They appear every once in a while. Mainly, they make me feel nauseous and disorient me for a few seconds," Ami admitted.

"That's unfortunate." Rikardi frowned.

They chatted about literature, mainly poetry. Ami adored Paisley's works, particularly her poem *"Ode to a Meadow."* Rikardi had an odd look when Ami recited the poem from memory. The Bond didn't elaborate on what he was feeling. It did vibrate with sad fondness when Rikardi recited Brooke's poem *"A Lighthouse's Woe."*

"That's ... really sad," Ami said, barely keeping her tears at bay. She didn't know why she was getting emotional over the poem. Perhaps it was the way Rikardi recited it?

"It is," Rikardi said, his face emotionless. His voice and the Bond, however, spoke a depth of sadness.

Ami wanted to ask but didn't think it was appropriate. He was a general and her superior officer. Instead, she stuffed her mouth with a minced pie. Rikardi snapped out of whatever memories he had remembered and changed the topic to short stories. Ami didn't know that many but enjoyed watching and listening to Rikardi speak of something passionately. It was an upgrade from his constant frowning.

He's very handsome when he's like this. Ami thought to herself. The Centaur oozed sexy confidence as he discussed one of Long's works, *The Lady at the Shop.*

"Are you listening?" Rikardi asked, a slight frown forming.

"Of course," Ami said quickly. "You were going on about Long's beautiful courtship with his second wife and how that influenced him to write this story. I hoped you would get to the part where she accepts him and why, since she rejected his proposal twice already."

Rikardi smiled. A bolt of arousal jolted Ami out of her thoughts. Her heart pounded in her chest. Frantically, she tried to force the blush away from her cheeks. *What in the Pits is wrong with her?*

"Are you all right?" Rikardi asked, his tone far too innocent.

Did he do that on purpose? Ami wondered, fully embarrassed. She hoped her face wasn't bright red. "I'm fine," Ami answered, glad her voice didn't shake. "Please continue."

Rikardi did, but Ami only heard half of it. Thankfully, Blejan came in to collect the trays. Ami determined she had spent enough time with the Centaur.

"Sir, where are the folders I must look through?" Ami asked.

"They are here," Rikardi said. Leaning back, he reached for something on the floor. Lifting the open box quickly, he placed it on the desk. Inside were at least thirty folders. "I expect these returned the same as I placed them," he warned.

"I understand, sir." Ami nodded. She saluted, grabbed the box, and went to her room.

When she reached her room, the blush she desperately tried to push down rushed to her face. She mentally screamed. Why did that happen? Was she reaching puberty already? Why couldn't the floor swallow her up at that moment? She placed the box next to her bed. Sitting on the covers, she looked at herself, mostly at her chest. As far as she knew, Dragons didn't grow breasts. However, a memory of her mom popped into her head.

Mom wore a dress for the first time. It was the first one Mom made by herself. Ami knew she was really young when it happened. In the corner of her eye were her little brothers. They were just out of diapers.

"Well, what do you think?" Mom asked, her voice soothing.

*"Purty!" one brother, Gabriel, cried. Her other brother Mikail nod-
ded. The other two, Ezra and Hezekiah, stared at Mom in awe.*

"Lots of lace," Ami stated.

*Mom turned to face Ami. Her mom was skin and bones from lack of
food. Her young face was worn from trauma, yet she somehow managed
to hold love for them. Even though her mom was gaunt, she had breasts.*

But she's a Dragon, Ami thought. Maybe there is a clan that
does? Or does the slave Bond hinder this? She would have to
talk to Reshmi about it. She looked at the box of folders. Her
questions about the Dragons could wait. She needed to find a
team. A thought entered her mind.

Why am I assigned a cover and not a unit? She asked herself. A
unit would more efficiently battle bandits and their typical
guerilla strategies. *Unless I'm not sent for battle but spying.* Ami
concluded. In that sense, her perspective on potential team-
mates altered.

She spent the next three hours carefully looking through
each folder. The stack on her right was her rejection pile. Her
left only had two potentials. Even after relooking at the folders she accepted, she was skeptical. She couldn't pinpoint why
the two stood out. They weren't extraordinary in their training under Sir Fraster. From the forts, they obeyed and didn't
cause trouble. Their families weren't politically influential or
destitute. Overall, they were as expected. Boring even.

But they have the potential to be more. Ami thought. Why she
felt that she had no idea. Her instincts never failed her before.
It had saved her numerous times in Vinci. A nagging feeling
tugged at the back of her mind. She still needed one more to
complete her cover. She went over the rejection pile again. The
only one who stood out was a strict rule follower. His folder
was filled with accolades and awards. She shook her head. No,
she wouldn't be able to handle someone like that. She would
probably maim him.

Sighing heavily, she took a break. She placed the rejected folders in the box and left the accepted ones on her pillow. She exited her room, remembering to shut her door. She nodded at the Knights she passed, and they nodded back. She left the Knight's Quarters. She didn't pause in the garden. She stared at the new warehouse as she walked towards it. It shined like freshly mined silver. It appeared colder, more distant than the old warehouse's warm woods. Ami sneezed when she detected the wards. Jasmine had spared no expense.

The new glass doors opened automatically. Thankfully Jasmine hadn't changed the layout, with the exception of exit doors at the end of every dorm corridor. Blejan told her that there were more exits in the kitchens as well, giving the Dragons more peace of mind. Dinner was in full swing in the new eating hall. She could hear the chatter from the main hall. Ami smiled sadly. She missed this noise. When she entered, the lively chatter died instantly. Ami paused, frowning at the stares. Without looking at anyone, she joined the line. The three males in front of her trembled. Ami took several steps back to give them space.

Blejan smiled when Ami reached her. "Hello, *ya'puris*. How is your day?"

"Much better now that the moon who commands the stars spoke to me," Ami said dramatically.

Blejan blushed. "Don't let your previous instructor hear you say that."

Ami's only eyebrow rose. "Oh? And why's that?"

Blejan squeaked. Her pink blush turned red. "N-Nothing."

"Blejan." Ami gave her a look.

"It's nothing," Blejan nearly shouted defensively.

"Uh, huh," Ami said, unconvinced.

She picked up her tray and scanned for a table. Unfortunately, there weren't many open spots. From the glances, all of them hoped she wouldn't sit with them. Shaking her head, Ami made her way to the furthest wall and sat down. Her tray was balanced on her thighs. Inhaling dinner's scent, she dug in.

I really need to learn how they make this. Ami thought. She couldn't figure out how the Dragons made fried chicken so juicy. The green beans, mashed potatoes with brown gravy, and creamed corn occupied the rest of her tray. Ami mulled over what she just learned. *Blejan and Sir Fraster are seeing each other? I didn't see that coming. I thought he hated all females. As long as he treats her well, I won't break his bones twice.*

"Um, ma'am?" a shaky voice called out. Ami ignored it, focusing on eating. "M-Ma'am?"

Ami swallowed. "Sir. You will address me as sir, Cadet," she stated, her voice carrying over the silence. She glanced up. Around ten or twelve, a young Elf cadet stood at the end of the nearest table. His knees trembled comically. His baby face and mousy brown hair made him look even younger. Only his growing gangly frame spoke of his actual age.

"But you're female," the cadet pointed out.

"I am your superior officer, and you will address me properly, Cadet," Ami replied coldly.

"But—"

"Did I stutter, Cadet?" Ami growled. "Return to your dinner so I may continue mine." She returned her focus to her dinner. A moment later, she sensed someone sitting on her right side. She glanced over. It was a young Werewolf with dark gray fur. He was around ten years old. Innocent yet scared brown eyes observed her.

"May I sit with you, sir?" he asked timidly.

"You may," Ami muttered.

They ate in silence. Low murmuring filled the air. Satisfied and full, Ami moved to stand. The murmurs immediately died when she stood. She returned her tray to the Dragons and left. The gardens were in full bloom. Ami changed her route and went deeper into the gardens. One of the large fountains, surrounded by daffodils and sunflowers, became her destination. Taking in a deep breath, she felt herself relax. She mused over her present dilemma.

She wished she could've picked Salvador as one for her cover. At least she would have someone she trusted and knew on the team. His file wasn't in the box. All the folders contained soldiers who had been out of Talient for at least three years. What bothered Ami was that all the males would be older than her; the youngest was twenty-three. She was almost seventeen, the youngest and only female.

When do Dragons hit puberty? Are there signs for males and females like the Weres, Centaurs, and Elves? When am I supposed to grow breasts like Mom?

She stared at a daffodil swaying in the breeze. She had never really thought about it since she had always been small. She had always said she was twelve because that's what everyone thought. Now that she was taller and finding males sexy, anxiety vibrated in her chest.

I need to speak to Reshmi about this. She did offer to explain things. Ami left the gardens and made her way to the mansion.

Reshmi greeted her warmly. "Come in, *ya'puris*. Do you need a new outfit?" The other Dragons were busy working on various pieces of clothing.

"No, thank you. May I speak to you in private?" Ami asked.

Reshmi nodded. The Dragon elder guided her to a back room where they kept their fabrics. "What is the matter?" Reshmi asked gently.

"A few things. It may be because my memory is faulty, but do Dragon females grow breasts at any point in their lives?" Ami asked.

Reshmi chuckled. "No, *ya'puris*. Dragons have never had milk glands like other People."

"Oh."

Reshmi just smiled. "Anything else?"

"When do Dragon females hit puberty? What are the signs?" Ami asked.

"Usually, females enter what is called a feral state. She starts to notice males as potential mates and shows more aggression toward other single females. Older married females teach them how to control their instincts. If a female fails to control her instincts, she will be shunned and deemed an unworthy mate. After conquering the feral state, single females will learn about courting rituals and what to expect from a male vying for her attention. Once she accepts a courtship, and if it is successful, she will marry," Reshmi explained patiently.

"So, controlling her natural instincts is vital. Why is that?" Ami asked.

"If a Dragon, male or female, can't or won't control their instincts, they will act no more than a wild animal. Our instincts are strong, but a stronger will can overcome them. Have you experienced anything in such a manner?" Reshmi asked.

"I don't believe so. I hadn't lost my composure over a male," Ami said. "I will come to you if I am overwhelmed."

"Please do. There are certain methods that Dragons use that will be helpful," Reshmi urged. "Anything else?"

"You mentioned last time that I might hit another growth spurt. Is it because my growth was suppressed?" Ami asked.

Hesitantly, Reshmi asked, "Do you know what caused your physical body to stop aging?"

"I think the Shadow King had something to do with it," Ami stated.

"The Shadow King?" Reshmi asked, her eyebrows furrowing.

"Have you heard of him?" Ami asked.

"Yes. It is odd for him to interfere with us since he can't stand living creatures. He prefers wandering souls of past warriors," Reshmi explained.

"How do you know so much about him?" Ami asked.

"He is one of the last Dragons from the ancient Diamond bloodline. They are an aloof clan that looks down on others. Hence why there are so few of them left. No one wants to be around them," Reshmi said.

"Interesting."

"It doesn't explain why he decided to intervene with the

living regarding you," Reshmi pointed out.

Ami shrugged. "I have no idea. Who knows what's going on with him."

"True. Is there anything else you have questions about?" Reshmi asked.

"Not at the moment. Thank you for your advice," Ami said gratefully.

"Anytime, *ya'puris.*"

Saying her goodbyes, Ami left the mansion. The anxiety in her chest was gone. Relief filled her lungs. She felt better knowing she hadn't entered the feral stage yet. A growth spurt was easier to deal with than overwhelming instincts to mate. It made her curious. What was her ideal mate? Rikardi popped into her mind. Ami blushed. She dismissed it swiftly. The Centaur wouldn't consider her for a mate. Plus, he was her superior officer, so that was awkward. Although he did look excellent in that uniform.

I need to focus on my cover. Ami refocused her thoughts, still blushing. She walked to her room, greeting the shift-changing Knights as she went. When she opened her door, she paused. A new folder was on her pillow on top of the two she left. Glancing around, nothing else in her room was amiss. All the folders were accounted for. Cautiously, she opened the new folder. Her eyebrow raised with interest.

It looks like she found her third teammate.

The fort was the same as always. It gave the sense of home in a way his mother's house never did. The home his mother claimed was a cage. He was her pet, and being in the military was just a form of entertainment until his mother decided which Noble daughter he would marry. At least at the fort, others were in the same predicament as him.

"Another boring party?" an orange Werefox asked as he walked beside the taller Werewolf.

"Not quite," Viovel answered.

"Oh? Was there a lucky lady who caught your eye?" the Werefox asked slyly.

"Not a lady. A foreign lord," Viovel replied.

"From where? Goya?"

"Vinci."

"Vinci? Why would they travel so far to get here?" the Werefox asked incredulously.

"I don't know, Doran. He definitely made it interesting," Viovel said with a smile.

"He had to if he makes you smile about a party. What did your mother say?" Doran asked.

"She wasn't pleased with how he treated her or how he took over her party. However, it did create more interest. We may invite him again," Viovel explained.

"Wait," Doran said as he stared at Viovel in shock, "he took over a Blackhill party? How?"

"Dancing. He somehow made a new dance right on the spot that was easy to remember. Everyone had a blast," Viovel said, grinning at the memory.

"What's his name?" Doran asked.

"Lord Sieghild."

"That's an old name," Doran pointed out.

"Yes, he told me that he was bringing sexy back," Viovel said, barely containing his giggles.

Doran stared at him as if he had grown another head. "What else happened?"

"I'll ask Mother to invite you to her next party so you can meet him yourself," Viovel said.

"I would like that. I have to get to my post. Later, Viovel,"

Doran stated. With a wave, he walked down a different corridor.

Viovel continued to his room, already finished with his guard shift. Once the door to his room closed, he relaxed. He hated how many masks he was forced to create and wear with different People. It was the Blackhill family motto, *Tieg mala at'tla fo.* Never show your true face. The only Person who came close to seeing his true face was Lord Sieghild, and it was a moment when Viovel had temporarily lowered his barriers. It wasn't hard to do.

Lord Sieghild was the kind of Person one wanted to be around. With his sassy attitude, proper Ras pronunciation, and disgusting eating manners—Viovel shuddered at the thought— it made him an enigma. He strongly suspected Lord Sieghild wasn't a male. No male was that confident in Rascal society, including foreigners. Despite this, Viovel desired the mysterious lord. For the first time in his life, he felt passion. The small fire lit his dead, stony heart, melting away the rusted ore his mother piled on over the years. There was so much he didn't know about Lord Sieghild. Why Rascu, of all places? Why were they here? What were their goals? He would write to his mother and urge her to invite the interesting lord to her next party. If she did, he would attend willingly. That would prompt her to respond readily. After he wrote the letter, he anxiously waited for the ink to dry.

He couldn't wait for the next party.

Ami patiently waited as Rikardi examined the three folders. The box of rejections sat on the floor next to the Centaur's desk. Rikardi flicked through each one thoroughly, his frown deepening. Doubt began to creep into Ami's mind. Was there something she missed? Did she choose wrong?

"Why haven't you chosen a Centaur as part of your cover?" Rikardi asked bluntly.

Ah, the alliance.

"For a cover, stealth is everything. If the area we need to survey is like those in Vinci, the area will be remote, with heavily dense foliage and filled to the brim with traps. Such environments would be difficult to navigate for Centaurs. No offense, sir, but Centaurs are more suited for open areas," Ami explained carefully.

Rikardi let out a little huff. *That shouldn't be adorable, but it is.* Ami thought despite herself.

"Very well. I'll summon these soldiers. When they arrive, General Mason will provide more information about your mission. Any questions?" Rikardi asked.

"No, sir."

"Dismissed."

Ami saluted and left. She exited the Inner City. Many of the patrolling soldiers and Knights greeted her. She waved and nodded back. The café was reasonably busy. The booths were filled with families. The couch and loveseats were occupied by male teenagers enjoying Logan's coffee. She could tell by the unique aromas. From their heated voices, they were discussing a controversial piece of literature. Ami wondered if it was Guang's novel *Pieces of Her Heart* or Flute's novella *Thorn in My Side.*

"Awesome!" Logan greeted her enthusiastically. "How've you been?"

Ami's ears twitched. "Is that a deeper tone I hear? Is my beloved coffee maker growing up?"

Logan blushed, rubbing the back of his head sheepishly. "I can't help it," he mumbled.

Ami smiled warmly. "This is good news, Logan. It means

you're becoming an adult."

"I don't wanna grow up," Logan whined.

"Am I that boring?" Ami asked teasingly.

Logan's eyes widened. "No, Awesome! You're so not boring."

"Good. Then you have no worries of being boring either," Ami stated confidently.

"Coffee?"

"Always."

Logan went into the kitchens. Ami sat two seats away from a male Werewolf drinking black tea. Memories of her first meeting with Logan flooded her mind. He had been so tiny and adorable. He was still cute, but she could tell he would be a heartbreaker when he reached adulthood.

I can't believe he's already thirteen. Where did the time go? Ami thought.

Logan came back with a mug of fresh coffee. Ami inhaled deeply.

"Heavy cream, nutmeg, chocolate, and ..." Ami listed, pausing at the last one. The coffee smell seemed more profound than usual. She took a small sip. "Espresso."

"You got it all in one." Logan grinned.

"You got all that from smelling it?" the Werewolf, drinking tea, asked.

"It's a special talent." Ami smiled. "The espresso was tricky, since it blended in with the coffee." She took a big gulp of it. Warmth spread across her chest.

The Werewolf stared at her with a calculating look. With a blink, it was gone. He reached out with his left hand. "I'm Lord Loran Bright, son of Lady Udea Bright of the Most Noble house."

Ami grabbed and shook his hand. "Captain Amaranth Rose."

"Are you a patron here?" Loran asked.

"Oh, yes. Logan has my heart in a mug," Ami said with a small smile.

"I'm not much of a coffee drinker, but they are excellent tea brewers," Loran commented.

"That would be Ma's specialty. I don't do tea well," Logan said.

"Where is Chastity?" Ami asked.

"Upstairs with Mother," Logan said, glancing at the hallway that led to the stairs. He looked worried about something.

"How's business?" Ami asked.

"Going great. Mother's been busy getting more coffee in. Leandra's been baking the pastries for the morning rush," Logan said, eager for the subject change.

"That's good. Is Leandra working today?" Ami asked.

"She did this morning. She had errands to run this afternoon for her mom," Logan replied.

"Tell her I miss her."

"Will do."

"Unfortunately, I have to return. I'll see you soon, Logan. It was nice meeting you, Lord Loran," Ami said. She chugged the rest of her coffee. The chocolate flavor at the end was satisfying.

"Do you really have to go, Awesome?" Logan whined as he exited from behind the counter.

They embraced briefly before releasing. Their Bond pulsed strongly.

"I'll be back as soon as possible," Ami promised.

"Be careful!" Logan called after her.

With her mood lifted, Ami hummed on her way to the Winter District. As soon as she entered, Shayne silently appeared at her side.

"You're in a good mood," Shayne commented.

"I had coffee," Ami stated.

They walked for a bit before Ami broke the silence.

"I've been assigned a cover and had to select three soldiers to be in it," Ami said. Seeing his confused look, she continued, "A cover is a small group of soldiers, typically four, used to spying."

"Who are you spying on?" Shayne asked curiously.

"I don't know for sure. I haven't received my orders yet," Ami replied.

"But you have suspicions," Shayne stated.

"Yes, but I will have to wait until the soldiers I picked arrive to know what my mission is truly about," Ami explained.

"You have to leave again," Shayne said sadly.

"It's going to be a repeating theme," Ami pointed out.

"I understand, sir."

"Any news on Blaine?" Ami asked. She hated that she had to keep an eye on him. It reopened emotional wounds just thinking about him.

"No, sir. He seems to be focusing on making allies with the Nobles," Shayne reported.

"Speaking of Nobles, I need you and the others to do a few things for me while I'm away," Ami stated. Seeing she had his attention, she said, "Take note of who Blaine is trying to sway. I'll see if I can convince their sons to refuse him if I can. Also, I want you to be my liaison with the Nobles."

"Me?" Shayne gasped.

"Yes, you. You'll do well. I have faith in you," Ami said encouragingly.

"Y-Yes, sir. I-I'll do my best," Shayne stammered. "What exactly will I be doing?"

"When I'm away, you'll be the go-to Person for any invitations for Lord Sieghild. You will write my responses to them when I cannot attend a party or function. If they ask why I can't attend, state I am away on business," Ami explained smoothly.

"I can do that." Shayne nodded.

"Thank you," Ami said gratefully. It pulsed through their Bond, making Shayne inhale sharply.

They walked in silence until they came to an entrance to the Inner City. Saying goodbye, the two parted ways. As she walked to the Knights' Quarters in the shadows, multiple red eyes followed her.

CHAPTER 10

Ami stood in Mason's office, waiting for her cover to enter. She had only been there a few minutes when there was a knock on the door.

"Enter," Mason ordered.

Three males entered. Ami examined them meticulously. The two Elves were around the same height at six feet tall. One was paler than the other. Both had lithe builds and dark brownish-black hair. Ami noticed one had bright green eyes while the other had dark brown eyes. The Werewolf had dark steel-gray fur. It reminded Ami of freshly made swords in Vinci. The sky-blue eyes were emotionless. The three saluted Mason properly.

At least I don't have to teach them etiquette. Ami thought.

"At ease," Mason stated. The males shifted to the *ruwa* pose. "You are called here today because you are being assigned a cover under the command of Captain Rose."

"Greetings," Ami nodded. The three hid their reactions well. Ami barely caught a glimpse of worry from one of the Elves.

"Captain Rose," Mason looked at her now. "Your mission is to return to the village north of Putra Hallas, investigate where the villagers could have gone, and see if there are any more clues about the witch. As soon as you are ready, leave for your mission. Dismissed."

"Yes, sir," Ami said, saluting crisply. The three males copied her. She exited Mason's office. She heard the three males follow her. As she left the mansion, Blejan ran up to her, her yellow bag in hand.

"*Ya'puris*, here are your things," Blejan said, slightly out of breath.

"You packed my things?" Ami asked awkwardly.

Blejan smiled. "Yes, news travels fast in the Inner City."

"Ah, thank you." Ami nodded. Turning to the males, she asked, "Where are your things?"

"In the Knight's Quarters, sir," one of the Elves murmured.

"Retrieve them and meet me at the Iron Gate," Ami ordered.

The three saluted and ran to obey. Ami felt uneasy. She wasn't sure if it was the mission or being alone with three males, but her guard was up. She thanked Blejan and went to the Iron Gate to wait. A few minutes later, the three males ran towards her, each carrying a large knapsack over their shoulder.

Their walk towards the northern part of Talient was silent. The Knights greeted Ami and nodded at the males following her. Ami greeted them back. In the alleyways, Ami saw Shayne secretly following them. Rune and Philip came out boldly, walking on either side of her. Benton remained hidden. The two at her sides didn't say anything. Ami wondered if they were trying to intimidate the three males. Rune and Philip surprised her at the northern gate when they hugged her. She hugged them back.

"Come back safe, boss," Philip said, blushing.

"Please don't get hurt," Rune half begged.

"I'm going to do my best," Ami answered.

Rune's Bond vibrated in a quick, rough way, not happy with her answer. She tried to pulse calm waves. It settled down a bit. Ami beat her goodbyes to Benton and Shayne through the Bond. Benton radiated shyness as he replied through the Bond. Shayne's Bond vibrated almost like a purr. Smiling, Ami led the trio out of Talient. They were barely out of the city limits when Ami broke the silence.

"I guess this is the icebreaker moment," Ami said abruptly. She turned around, walking backward. "I am your captain, Amaranth Rose. I love food, enjoy blacksmithing, and my favorite color is purple. You?" she asked one of the dark-haired Elves.

Panic briefly filled his green eyes before he hid them. "I am Smaragdos Fallenleaf, night guard from Putra Melios. I prefer to be called Ados and enjoy reading poetry; my favorite color is green," Ados answered, uncertainty in his voice.

"Nice to meet you, Fallenleaf. Next?" Ami asked, looking at the other Elf.

"I am James Atorra, a food prepper from Putra Nexas. I enjoy cooking, and my favorite color is blue," James answered, his voice low.

"Well met, Atorra." Ami nodded. She looked expectantly at the Werewolf.

"Uriah Lakeshore, night guard at Putra Helioxos. I like the color black," Uriah replied shortly.

"What do you enjoy doing?" Ami asked politely.

"I enjoy being left alone," Uriah said, barely respectful.

"Too bad. We will be in each other's company for the next week," Ami announced.

"A week?" Ados asked, horrified.

"This isn't a field trip, lads. I'll explain more when we make camp," Ami said firmly. She turned around to walk forward again.

She expected them to start asking questions. Silence greeted her.

Maybe they'll talk more when we make camp. Ami thought.

They made camp just as the sun started to set. Ami glanced around. A few hours' walk to the east would take them straight to Putra Hallas. She estimated they would arrive at the village around late afternoon, perhaps early evening if they didn't get disoriented. Ami ordered Ados and James to set up tents and Uriah to start a fire while she hunted. Grabbing her hunting knife, she set out. When she returned with four large rabbits, the tents were up, and the fire was intense.

"Is that it?" Uriah asked bluntly.

"Is there a problem?" Ami asked coolly.

Uriah briefly looked uncertain. "Don't you think we need more?" he asked.

"Not if you use every part of the animal," Ami concluded. "Come over here."

Uriah's uncertainty extended to his hesitant body language. Cautiously, as if she would attack him at any moment, he obeyed.

"What are you doing?" he asked. He crouched by her side, ready to dart away if she made a wrong move.

"I'm going to show you how to make four rabbits go a long way," Ami answered.

While Ami taught Uriah, Ados and James busied themselves by getting water from a nearby creek and boiling it in the soup pot. From afar, they observed. Ami and Uriah added the meat and pieces of fat to the boiling soup pot.

"Fallenleaf, in my bag, is a bag of mushrooms and herbs," Ami said.

The Elf obeyed, his curiosity overcoming his nervousness. Or maybe it was hunger. Handing the two small bags to Ami, he stayed closer to her than before. James even came closer to see what she was doing.

"This is a common Vincian stew. Me cousins and I would make this during our hunting trips," Ami explained, her accent appearing with her memories.

Byrin, her eldest cousin, brought the rabbits. His wide grin and puffed-out chest made Lushra and Metka roll their eyes. Lushra, the second eldest, showed Ami how to properly skin and cut the meat and fat. Metka watched the fire and simmering water in the soup pot. They worked like a well-oiled machine.

"Puutka, is Lushra grossing you out yet?" Byrin asked aggravatingly.

"No, your face does the job just fine," Ami retorted, her voice monotone.

Lushra and Metka laughed at Bryin's pouting face. Once the meat and fat were cut, Metka took the pieces and expertly put them in the pot. He pulled out a handful of dried mushrooms mixed with herbs from his pouch. From the smell, they were wild sage and limewort.

"Captain?" Ados called out softly.

Ami blinked. All three males were staring at her. Uriah, in particular, had a calculating look. "Sorry. Memories."

"When will it be ready?" James asked, nodding at the pot.

Ami eyed the soup. Inhaling a deep breath, she replied, "It needs about another ten minutes. While we're waiting, I'll give you some background on our mission."

Ami explained the situation of Hector's behavior and the odd things that happened at Putra Hallas. She excluded what she had discussed with Salvador and the mercury incident. To explain Sir Tres' death, she told them that General Lee was about to arrest the Elf when he decided to kill himself. She continued as she poured the finished soup into their traveling bowls.

"Due to there being a witch and with the villagers being gone, we are to see if anything was missed," Ami concluded.

"Why target a fort when the witch already imprisoned a whole village?" Ados asked thoughtfully.

"I don't think the witch created the dome," Ami said, eating a spoonful of soup. It wasn't as good as her cousins', but it was close.

"Why is that?" James asked.

"If the witch created the dome, it should've shattered when she was killed. It was still up after I killed her," Ami pointed out.

"Unless a runic array was set up beforehand," Uriah said suddenly.

Ami's ears perked up. "Then where does it get its power? For as large as it is, it would consume a lot of energy."

Uriah shook his head. "Not necessarily. You stated that someone or a group was doing some kind of experiment in the forest, correct?"

"That's right."

"What if whatever they were doing produced too much energy, and the runic array was set up to absorb that extra energy?" Uriah hypothesized.

"And the witch used it to her advantage," Ami concluded breathlessly. "That is brilliant."

Uriah blushed and looked away. "It's just a theory."

"One that has promise. When we arrive tomorrow, it will be one of the areas to explore," Ami said happily.

She divided up a night watch. Uriah had first watch, Ados second, James third, and Ami last. Even though her lack of sleep was becoming more frequent, she closed her eyes and relaxed. Her ball of magic was much larger than before. Gathering a sliver, she directed it to her senses. Numerous sounds, smells, and sensations assaulted her. A violent sneeze snapped her out of it. The magic backed off yet waited to be called again.

Let's do one sense at a time. Taking a few deep breaths, Ami took a smaller sliver of magic and directed it to her hearing. Her ears tingled at the sensation. To her left was James' tent. The Elf was slowly falling asleep, his breathing deepening. To her right was Ados' tent. The Elf sounded tense. She could hear his muscles tensing and loosening, the motion repeating for a long time.

What is making him so tense? Ami wondered. Perhaps it was the first time he camped? He was with strangers as well. Hopefully, they could trust each other enough for that to go away.

What caught Ami's attention was Uriah. The Werewolf was casually pacing around the perimeter of their camp. Even though his pace was casual, she could sense his alertness. The

Werewolf was muttering to himself. Even with her enhanced hearing, she couldn't decipher most of his words.

Female. What is? How was I? What about the. Lashu doesn't.

That was all Ami could hear from Uriah's mumblings. It piqued her interest. Did Uriah usually talk to himself when he was alone? Then Uriah woke the barely asleep Ados for second watch. She listened for Uriah to enter his tent. Ados paced around the fire pit, his nervousness heightened. Ami debated if she should exit her tent and talk to the Elf.

No, he was nervous enough when we ate together. It has to be first-night nerves. Ami reasoned. She listened to Uriah relax into a light sleep. Before she knew it, Ados was waking James for his watch.

James yawned periodically during his watch, pacing around the camp like Uriah, trying to stay alert. The Elf started to do walking lunges as his silhouette passed her tent. Ami stifled a giggle. Then it was Ami's turn. James reached into her tent and tapped her ankle.

"I'm up," Ami answered.

She exited her tent. James saluted sleepily and returned to his tent. The night was dark. The fire barely had any burning coals. She transferred her magic from her ears to her eye. It became as clear as if it was daytime. She eyed the areas where the males had paced. She could see the different paces each took. A memory of an elderly female from Vinci came to mind. Ami couldn't recall her name but remembered she was eccentric. The white-haired female enjoyed how the old female would rebuke the Vincians and their superstitions by creating or making up her own. She was well known for her talent for reading footprints and determining a Person's state of mind. Most of the time, the female was off the mark, but it was entertaining.

I wonder what kind of personality she would read off their trails? Ami wondered absently.

She removed her magic from her sight, adjusting back to

the darkness. As she did, dawn began to peek over the horizon. Ami turned as Uriah emerged from his tent.

"I'm going to gather more wood," Ami stated.

Uriah nodded. "Are we eating the leftover soup?"

"Breakfast of champions." Ami grinned.

Uriah cocked his head to the side. "What?"

Ami shook his head. "I've got to import movies to show you someday. I'll be back."

She came back with her arms full of thick sticks. James helped restart the fire. The morning was quiet. She wished she had Logan's coffee. After eating, they put out the fire and packed up the tents. Ami led them to the village. As they walked, a tense silence followed them. Even without enhancing her senses, their unease was palpable.

"Ask your questions," Ami stated abruptly, making them jump.

"Why are you in Rascu?" Uriah asked bluntly.

"Vinci wasn't safe," Ami answered shortly.

"Sir?" Ados asked quietly.

"Yes, Fallenleaf?"

"What exactly is a witch?" Ados asked, his voice quivering.

Ami explained, "A witch is a Person who allows their ambitions and earthly desires to consume them. Whether to gain power, esteem, sex, wealth, or to challenge the laws of magic, they open their hearts to the darkness. Once the darkness enters their heart, a demon guides them through a ritual. This ritual must be performed every so often, or the witch will be consumed by the demon and become a Wraith.

"After the Person becomes a witch, they are granted forbidden knowledge that further consumes them. In the pursuit of their ambitions and desires, they will do anything to accomplish it. They will even sacrifice their family to the Lord of Darkness and Lies. They are exceedingly dangerous and never to be underestimated," she concluded.

"What do they offer in return for the ritual?" Uriah asked.

"Their soul for the first ritual. For the repeat, souls of others," Ami answered.

"How do you know this?" James asked suspiciously.

"Witches are prominent in Vinci," Ami answered. "Not including the one in Rascu, I've killed three."

"I thought they were hard to kill," Uriah scoffed.

Ami stopped and swirled to face the Werewolf. He stopped and took a step back, his blue eyes wary. "For someone who has never seen battle, you're very flippant about death." She stared at him.

Uriah's ears went flat. He bowed his head, looking away.

"Let me make this clear: A witch is the most challenging and hardest opponent you will ever face. Let's hope we don't see another one," Ami said crisply. She turned and continued walking.

The café was quiet. The lunch rush had just ended. Shayne glanced at the pile of dishes waiting to be cleaned. He was the only one in the back. Logan was watching the bar and serving the only two customers while Chastity cleaned the booths and straightened the couch area. His Bond with Rune throbbed absently with emotions not his own. The young Elf was missing the boss badly. Strangely, Benton was just as affected, if not more, as Rune. Shayne wondered if it was because of the Bond or a Centaur thing.

He heard Logan talk to a customer entering. His ear flicked towards Logan's direction by the young Werefox's tone. Drying his hands with a towel, he peeked out. A messenger from a high-rank Noble stood at the bar. Shayne noticed a familiar envelope in his hand.

"What's going on?" Shayne asked, exiting the kitchen and coming to Logan's side.

Logan was frowning. "He's looking for someone, but I don't know who."

"What's the name?" Shayne asked.

"I am seeking Lord Sieghild. Lady Blackhill has an invitation for the lord," the messenger replied.

"Lord Sieghild is out of town on business," Shayne answered. He ignored Logan's surprised look.

"You are his messenger," the messenger surmised.

"I am. Please tell the lady that my lord thanks her for her invitation and that he will send a letter when he returns," Shayne replied smoothly. He was thankful the boss had him practice before she left.

The messenger bowed and left. Before Shayne could return to his duties, Logan stood before him.

"Who is Lord Sieghild?" Logan asked suspiciously.

"Someone I run errands for when I'm not here," Shayne answered vaguely. Even though Logan was likable, he tended to run his mouth.

"Is he nice?" Logan inquired.

"He treats his employees well," Shayne replied.

"What do you do for him?" Logan asked.

"I run errands and don't ask questions," Shayne said, his tone hard. Slipping past Logan, he returned to the dishes.

"He worries about you," Chastity said as she entered the kitchen. She grabbed a spare rag and dipped it in the hot soapy water.

"I understand," Shayne muttered.

"Remember, you can always come here," Chastity said with a smile. Shayne nodded. Satisfied, Chastity left.

Shayne sent a message through the Bond to Philip. The Werefox pulsed back. Philip was almost done with his shift as well. Pulsing the Bonds he had with Rune and Benton, they agreed to meet at the deli for dinner. Shayne hesitated. Going to the Bond he shared with Sigrid, he looked at it in his mind. Marveling at its intricate coloring, he softly pulsed how much he missed her.

The village seemed worse than before. The houses appeared to have aged decades. The rotted wood and mold smell coated the air in a damp mist. Even the bricked homes looked like someone took a chisel and hammer to them in anger. Wild foliage grew randomly inside, outside, and around each structure. As they walked further towards the inn, Ami swore she could hear the grass grow as they passed.

Time magic has to be what's causing this. Ami thought. She remembered how Lee and the other Knights couldn't get further than the cemetery. *Maybe I can get closer since I'm more familiar with it.*

"Sir, what's going on?" James asked, looking around fearfully.

"It appears the time magic is aging the village faster," Ami answered. "We will need to be careful."

"How do you be careful with something intangible as time?" Uriah asked.

That's a fair question. Ami answered, "We will need to be vigilant towards each other. If we notice one or all of us aging faster than normal, we must leave and reevaluate our approach in this investigation."

"What signs do Dragons display?" Ados asked innocently.

Ami paused to think. "If I have a sudden growth spurt. Another would be troublesome. What about you three?"

"Elves' hair tends to thin the more we age. Also, our reflexes slow down," James answered. Ados nodded.

"Weres' fur turns gray, and our sense of smell dims," Uriah said, albeit hesitantly.

"We'll keep an eye on each other as we look around. Let's find the inn and get settled," Ami stated.

The inn was in a rougher state. Inches of dust covered every inch of the place. When they tried to straighten the tables and chairs, the wood collapsed in their hands. Somehow the broom managed to survive. Ados was tasked to sweep off an area for them to sit as Uriah and James looked at the kitchen. Ami carefully climbed upstairs to the room she had occupied the last time. The wood held in certain places, making her mindful of her steps. The room was covered in dust, like downstairs. However, Ami noticed something odd. Multiple faint footprints going in and out of the room stood out. Ami kneeled down to look at them closer. The impressions were from large boots with a pointed toe. The shape looked familiar, but nothing was coming to mind. Ami frowned.

I don't remember seeing these kinds of boots in Talient. She mused. Dismissing military footwear, she tried to remember if she had seen something like it at the military ball or the Blackhill party. Nothing came to mind. *Then again, I wasn't paying attention to People's shoes. Perhaps it's a style for travel in Rascu. I may have seen it in passing and can't remember where. Was it at the Harvest Festival? When was the last time I went to one? Two years ago?*

She shook her head and followed the footprints down the hall to a different room. The room was identical to the one Ami had stayed in. The impressions hadn't stayed long in the room from to the lack of activity. She followed them to the room across the hall. The room was more decorated. The homemade quilt was dull, but Ami could still see the faint pattern of flowers.

Was this Maria's room? Ami glanced at the footprints. They went in further to what looked like a dresser. Carefully,

Ami approached the unassuming piece of furniture. She was surprised when the drawer opened. She poked the side of it. It was solid and looked new. Taking note, she looked inside. Random pieces of clothes were haphazardly shoved in the drawer. Ami pulled out each piece of clothing to examine. A dress, a blouse, another dress, a long skirt, and another dress were placed next to Ami. The bottom revealed a bundle of letters and a notebook. Ami grabbed the letters, reading the one on top.

> *My beloved Maria,*
>
> *My heart aches for you. Every day I wish to spend with you. My nights are filled with thoughts of you. Your laugh enriches this dead heart of mine. My old soul becomes younger when I am with you. May your days be fruitful and free. Give my regards to your uncle.*
>
> *Yours always, Bru*

Ami stared at the letter in shock. Reading the other letters, she read the progression of Bru's relationship with Maria. At the bottom of the pile, the first letter started innocent and friendly. It seemed more like pen pals. Bru even asked if he could call her Maria in his letters. By the sixth letter, it switched to pet names when the dead male chose 'beloved' for her. Disgust and revulsion filled her mind. Her stomach twisted painfully. How old had Bru been? Hadn't he been in his twenties, almost thirties? And he was courting a fifteen-year-old? Some pieces started to fall into place. What if Bru hadn't visited the village to see Jeanne but Maria? What if Jeanne had come to the fort to blackmail Bru? That would make sense. Then Jeanne had used Bru in a ritual where she used his skin to impersonate him.

This is so twisted, Ami thought with a shudder. Then she turned her attention to the notebook. Glancing at the pages, Ami saw it was Maria's diary. Scanning random pages, she noted the dates where she mentioned Bru. It matched the letters. Maria was smitten with the soldier, but not so much to lose her common sense. Ami felt relief when she read that Maria told Bru she wouldn't lose her virginity until her wedding night. A particular page caught her attention.

3rd day of Bloch, month of Suvi
My dear friend,

We met a celebrity today! Technically yesterday, but I didn't have time to write then. Her name is Rose, and she's not what I expected. For one, she's quiet. Also, she doesn't like her nickname. I thought it was pretty cool. Then she told me that it was because fourteen cadets died. Really? That's the reason why she doesn't like her nickname? Seems stupid to me. Anyway, she's leaving tomorrow morning. Uncle is sad. He really likes her for some reason. I wonder if she reminds him of his late wife. I never met her, so I don't know how similar the two are.

3rd day of Wenz, month of Suvi
Dear friend,

Things have gotten much weirder since Rose left. Everyone is aging rapidly. Even I look older. I look like an adult! Ugh, an old Person already at fifteen! Uncle appears frailer, and it's hard for him to climb the stairs today. Uncle is calling me.

3rd ---
---Friend,

The village is --- and something is going on with the --- Forest. Uncle is super old and can't ---. Someone is dragging --- to the forest at night, and --- are screams. I wonder when it is our time when --- gets us. I hope we have a swift death.

The last passage was deeply smudged. The pit of Ami's stomach sunk to her toes. Someone or something dragged the villagers into the Howling Forest. Did Jeanne do something to the villagers?

Tomorrow I will investigate the cemetery and see how close I can reach the forest. Ami thought. Gathering the letters and Maria's diary, she carefully went downstairs. Most of the floor was swept clean from dust. Ados looked like he was wearing most of it. Ami grinned.

"Did you lose the battle?" she asked humorously.

Ados huffed. "It was very particular."

Uriah and James exited the kitchens. "Any luck?" Ami asked.

The two males shook their heads. "Everything is either brittle from rust or crumbled when we touched them," James answered.

"I assume all the food is rotted as well?" Ami asked.

"I don't think there's any food left to rot," Uriah replied. "All that's left is dust."

"That's disappointing," Ami sighed. She rummaged through her bag. Relieved, she pulled out several sticks of jerky. "The Dragons gave us jerky. If we ration them, it'll last us several more days until we have to hunt." She handed them each a stick.

"What can we hunt if all the animals have left?" Ados asked.

"We will have to hunt outside the dome. I wouldn't be surprised if these buildings collapsed soon," Ami said. At their alarmed looks, she reassured them, "Spending one night here won't make it collapse. We will camp outside the village start-ing tomorrow."

"Sir, I don't feel safe doing that," Uriah protested.

"Me either, sir," James added.

"I agree," Ados commented.

Ami glanced at their uneasy faces. "I understand. Let's eat and then find a campsite."

"What's that in your hand?" Ados asked.

"I found letters in the innkeeper's daughter's room. She mentions Bru Fonte. General Lee will want to see these," Ami said, placing the letters in her knapsack.

They sat on the less dusty floor chewing the jerky. It was salty with a hint of sweetness. Ami half-wished it was spicy. She missed making spicy jerky with purple devil peppers. The males kept quiet, not even looking at each other. Ami hoped that wouldn't be the case when they got to know each other better.

Once they had eaten, they exited the inn to find a camp-site. They decided on an open area between the village and the villager's house on the western side. Even that house didn't escape from the drastic aging. The walls were sagging, and the roof had already caved in. They silently set up their tents and dug a fire pit. They each gathered a pile of wood from the col-lapsed houses. Like the night before, they didn't speak. Ami hoped it would get better.

The following day, after breakfast of cold jerky, Ami doled out tasks.

"Lakeshore, do you remember where the hole in the dome is?" Ami asked.

"I do." The Werewolf nodded.

"I want you to start a patrol from the hole to the outer edges of the village to here. See if there has been any other activity besides us. Atorra, Fallenleaf, start a patrol inside the village. If anything is salvageable, grab it and bring it to camp," Ami ordered.

"What are you going to do, sir?" Uriah asked.

"I'll be in the cemetery. I was here before and want to see if there are more graves than before," Ami answered. "Let's meet back before evening."

The males saluted. Ami saluted back. They went their separate ways. The path to the cemetery was eerie. As she passed houses, a few started to fall apart when she walked past. Getting closer, she began to feel the pressure Lee told her about. Like when a dark thunderstorm rumbled through the sky. Her temples started to pound with her heartbeat. Taking a deep breath, she focused on her mission.

The cemetery had contained numerous half-dug, half-filled graves amongst the fresh graves she saw the first time. The half-finished graves didn't have tombstones or markers. She went to the other new graves, ones that had wooden markers. Leaning closer to one marker, she tried deciphering the Person's name. She stared at it for several minutes, but couldn't comprehend what was written. She moved to the next one. Despite being carved in a language, none of the markers could be deciphered.

What's going on? Did I lose some of my language when I came back? Ami asked, feeling frustrated. Relief flooded her when she read one of the older tombstones from a year ago. Then she tried to reread the wooden markers. No such luck. Shaking her head, she moved on to the half-created graves.

She stopped in her tracks at one. Something shiny glinted in the sunlight at the bottom. She glanced around the grave. This one was deeper than the others. The coffin couldn't be seen, and she wasn't sure if one was placed in it. A ladder lay nearby. She took the ladder and set it down the dug grave. The ground felt solid. Going down the ladder, she cautiously stepped into the grave. Something was off. It felt like Ami had stepped into a twilight world. The air was heavy and dense. She took one step before she heard in her mind **Get out now!**

Turning to the ladder, she managed to get one foot on the step before an unholy roar filled the air. The earth morphed into sand. Ami scrambled up the ladder. The ladder sunk into the loose soil. Ami got to the top and jumped, landing hard on her chest halfway out of the grave. Something grabbed her ankle. Ami screamed with all her might. She continued to yell as she used her claws to dig into the earth, trying to pull herself out of the grave. The grip on her ankle remained firm. She looked over her shoulder. She wished she hadn't.

A grotesque creature that looked more like a melted blob with multiple eyes and mouths filled with sharp teeth roared from the grave. Hoofbeats rumbled the earth Ami desperately tried to cling to. Strong hands grabbed her wrists and pulled her out of the grave. The creature's grip slipped, releasing Ami. More hoofbeats came. A low hum echoed in the air. The one who pulled her out of the grave held her close to his chest. The smell of hay and fresh rosemary filled her nose. Ami strained her neck to look at the grave.

The thing in the grave roared at the unicorn stallion standing over the rim. The stallion hummed powerfully. Whatever the unicorn said, Ami couldn't translate. A ball of light gathered around the unicorn's horn. The pressure was different. This made her insides vibrate uncomfortably.

"Close your eyes!" Ami shouted, turning away with her eye tightly closed. Despite this, light from a supernova erupted across her eyelid. The creature screamed its pain in numerous voices.

It took several minutes for the light to fade into darkness. When Ami opened her eye, her vision was unusual. Everything was in various shades of gray. It was as if all the color was sucked out. What made it even more strange was the unicorn. He was the only source of hue. His golden horn shined like the sun against the monotone scenery. Glowing emerald eyes stared at her without emotion.

"Thank you," Ami mumbled.

"Wraiths are not meant for this world," the stallion stated, his tone cold.

"That was a Wraith?" Ami asked.

"Yes. A witch was devoured and buried," he answered.

"Did it consume the villagers?" Ami asked.

The stallion shook his head. "Their souls are still in this world."

"Are they in the forest?" Ami asked.

"My duty is to deal with Wraiths," the stallion said icily. "Take care, odd one."

"Don't trip over your tail on your way out," Ami replied dryly.

The unicorn scoffed indignantly and trotted off. A shift

of the Person she was held against brought her attention to them. She lightly tapped the arms, holding her tightly.

"You can let me go now," she said deadpan.

"Sir, I can't see," a shaky deep voice answered.

Ami twisted around. "Flander?"

CHAPTER II

Uriah ran towards them, teeth bared at Flander. The Centaur was still holding Ami tightly and refused to release her. Ados and James arrived a moment later, shouting at Flander. Flander shouted back. Ami stared at Ados. The Elf was surrounded by gentle green flames. It wasn't like the eerie green magic Salvador's rings gave off, but more like melted emeralds. It was strangely comforting.

"Lads, let's calm down," Ami said, trying to stop the insults and threats. When the males didn't hear her or refused to listen, she let out a loud, short bark that silenced them. "Lakeshore, report."

The Werewolf looked at her weirdly. Ami stared back.

"Lakeshore, the captain gave you an order," Ados said nervously.

"What?" Uriah asked, confused.

"I thought she was humming," James said.

"I understood her," Ados stated, bewildered.

"What did she say?" Uriah asked.

"Report."

"I wasn't able to monitor the entire perimeter. However, I saw tracks leading to the Howling Forest in different areas.

They didn't look like animals, and whoever it was, they wore boots of unknown design. They didn't look recent, at least," Uriah reported.

"Atorra, Fallenleaf?" Ami asked.

"Our turn." Ados nodded to James.

"Right. I took the eastern side of the village. All the buildings are falling apart. There's nothing salvageable around here. We'll need to hunt soon to get fresh food," James reported.

"I took the western side. My observations are the same as Atorra's," Ados answered.

"Then Flander is next," Ami said, looking up at the Centaur. She tapped his arms with her fingers to get his attention.

"She wants to know why you're here, Centaur," Ados said, his tone cold.

Do they have some kind of history? Ami wondered.

"I am Flander of the Yellowtail tribe, a soldier from Putra Thyllisala. I was reassigned by General Rikardi to assist with Captain Rose's mission," Flander answered with a slight shake in his deep voice. "Captain, I still can't see," Flander whispered in her ear.

"Apparently, all I'm doing is humming," Ami answered deadpan.

"What was that light?" James asked.

"A unicorn banishing a Wraith," Ami answered. Ados translated for her.

"A Wraith? So, another witch was here?" Uriah asked.

"Another? How many witches are there?" Flander asked.

Ami sighed. A headache crept up her temples, and her chest started to throb.

"Let's go to camp. Flander, let go of me," Ami ordered. Ados translated again, his tone harsh towards Flander.

The group slowly made their way back. Flander kept his large hands on Ami's shoulders as she served as his eyes. Out of the corner of her eye, random shades of green flickered in and out of sight. Whatever magic the unicorn used seemed to finally be wearing off. The air was filled with tension. Ami observed Uriah and James giving Flander suspicious looks. Ados glared at him.

There were so many questions Ami wanted to ask Flander. She had answers for a few of them that she wanted to be confirmed. Why was it crucial for the general to assign a Centaur to her cover? Rikardi wasn't well-liked amongst the Centaurs, and several openly detested him. She couldn't see how using her would work in his favor. Even she didn't know where she stood in Centaur politics. Also, why Flander? He was good friends with Andrew La Fae, a perpetrator in the bleach incident, and had never tried to defend her when the other males pranked and humiliated her. He was two years younger than the other three and had been barely away from Talient for less than two years.

Are there family connections? Ami asked herself. *Are the Yellowtail and Roos tribes related or allies somehow? I would have thought he sent someone around the same age as the other three. Until I stop humming, I won't be able to ask.*

"Sir?" Ados interrupted her thoughts.

"Yes?" Ami answered.

"Now she's talking," Uriah said. He sounded relieved.

"What's our next move?" Ados asked nervously.

"Right now, we need fresh food," Ami said. The rest of the colors flooded back into her vision. She covered her eye with a hand. Taking deep breaths, she slowly reopened her eye. Everything was back in full color. Ados looked worried. James and Uriah tried to hide their worry with deep frowns. Flander was blinking rapidly. It seemed like his vision was returning as well.

"Uriah and James, go hunt and gather mushrooms. Ados, gather more wood for the fire. Flander and I will stay at camp and start a fire. Dismissed," Ami ordered.

"Um, sir?" James asked hesitantly, raising his hand like a student.

"Yes?" Ami asked in a dangerous tone.

"Why mushrooms?" James asked.

Ami pointed at Flander. "Centaurs don't eat meat."

James blushed in embarrassment. "Oh, um, my bad, sir."

"Go."

Uriah and James ran towards the dome opening. Ados seemed reluctant to leave, but did when Ami stared at him unblinkingly. Ami gathered the remaining sticks they had gathered before. Placing them in the fire pit, she murmured a spell. The tiny flame lit the sticks easily.

"Was-Was that magic?" Flander stammered. He stared at the growing fire.

"Yes," Ami stated.

"I wish I could learn," Flander said wistfully.

"Why can't you?" Ami asked.

"Males aren't allowed to learn magic," Flander pointed out.

"How will they know?" Ami inquired.

Flander opened his mouth to answer but shut it again, frowning. Ami turned her attention back to the fire. Her chest throbbed painfully on her right side. She rubbed the sensitive area, hoping to ease the pain.

"Are you all right?" Flander asked.

Ami let out a huff. "When trying to escape, I landed on my chest harder than I thought. I'll have bruises from the throbbing of it."

"Are there any balms you can use?" Flander asked.

Ami shook her head. "We only brought clothing and cooking utensils. We didn't expect to fight demons."

Flander shivered. "That was a nightmare come to life."

"If you hadn't pulled me, I would've been dragged in. Thank you, Flander," Ami said sincerely. The brunette Centaur blushed down to his neck.

The sound of someone clearing their throat filled the air. Ados had returned with an armful of thick sticks. The Elf placed his bundle where the last pile was. Then he purposely sat in between Ami and Flander.

Why is he being so childish? Ami wondered. It was starting to irritate her. Before she could question Ados, Uriah and James returned. Uriah had a small deer draped over his shoulder. James carried numerous mushrooms in the bottom of his shirt that he had made into a makeshift basket.

"Are these enough mushrooms, sir?" James asked.

"Bring them here." Ami pointed to her free side. James obeyed. Ami sorted the mushrooms, showing James how to identify good ones from bad ones and which ones were more flavorful.

Meanwhile, Uriah carefully skinned and gutted the deer. Ami glanced over. She hummed approvingly. Uriah paused, eyeing Ami warily.

"Not bad," Ami stated. She turned her attention to how to prepare their early dinner.

Soup was out of the question. Making different soups would take too long when they only had one soup pot. She wondered if there was a frying pan around. Grammy had one passed down several generations. An idea came to mind.

"I'll be right back," Ami said, standing up.

"Captain, I'll go with you—" Ados also started to get up.

"I'm more than capable of being alone," Ami said coldly.

"Yet you screamed when you were with a Wraith," Uriah sneered as he separated the deer's guts.

"I'll make sure not to scream next time I'm about to be dragged to the Pits," Ami snarked back.

She made herself walk calmly back into the village. Taking a deep breath, she refocused on her idea. It took over an hour, but she found a frying pan that somehow withstood time magic. Ami smiled at it fondly. It was almost exactly like the one Grammy used. Matte black and heavy, Ami remembered Grammy using it against one of the head servants when he refused to understand the word "no." No one went to his funeral. With a spring in her step, she went back to camp. Uriah was cleaning his blade, eyeing the three tense males. Ados glared at Flander as if he insulted his mother. James was gritting his teeth, and Flander stared at the fire, trying to ignore everyone.

"I'm back," Ami announced. All the males jumped.

"Did you find what you were looking for?" Ados asked.

"Yes," Ami answered. Getting close to the fire, she adjusted the burning pieces of coals. All the males started shouting.

"Captain!" Ados shrieked.

"What are you doing?" James shouted.

"Are you crazy?" Uriah bellowed.

"Stop!" Flander yelled. He reached over and yanked her hand out of the fire.

"What?" Ami asked innocently. She didn't understand why they were freaking out. She and Grammy used to do it all the time when they were baking. Gramps would shake his head and continue washing the dishes.

"Are you trying to add more burns to your body?" Flander shouted.

"What other burns do you speak of?" Ami asked, fighting down a smirk.

"The ones on your ..." Flander trailed off as he stared at her hand. Aside from black streaks from the burnt wood, her hand was normal. "How?"

"Dragon."

Yanking her hand out of his grip, she resumed her task. Making a flat area, she placed the frying pan on it. As it warmed, she started to separate the stems from the caps of the mushrooms. She cooked the caps first, using the ladle as a makeshift spatula. As they cooked, she instructed Uriah to season the meat with the remaining herbs in her bag. As he did, she scooped the cooked caps with the ladle and divided them into each individual bowl. She tore the stems into smaller pieces before putting them in the hot pan. As they sizzled, Ami hummed a tune. She gave Flander a larger portion of the torn stems when they were finished. Then she cooked a thin slab of meat for each male in the mushroom-flavored pan. She served Uriah first, James second, and Ados third. The smell of her portion was tantalizing.

"You don't have to wait for me," Ami stated when she noticed they weren't eating.

"We can wait," Uriah stated.

Ami let it go. There were some Rascal customs she didn't understand regarding food. She took a bite of her piece of meat, humming happily. The frying pan made it perfectly crispy. It was definitely coming with her from now on. She didn't know how she would put it in her bag, but she would make it work. She glanced at the males. Flander was gobbling his mushrooms as if he hadn't eaten in days. Ados was happily munching on his. James looked like he couldn't decide if he liked it or not. Uriah tried to look neutral, but his eyes lit up every time he took a bite. Ami ate her meal happily.

Egan winced, grinding his teeth together with each whiplash. Unlike Ryft, he refused to scream and beg for mercy. His master would only whip him longer.

"I'm disappointed," Emyr said as if commenting on the weather. "I thought I gave specific orders about bringing Amaranth home."

Egan panted. The sharp pain pulsed up and down his back. Sweat dripped down his face and onto the dry ground. The droplets dried instantly. Suddenly he was yanked upwards by his black hair. The Shadow King's face was emotionless. His eyes were like a shark's eyes. Egan preferred the little mistress' energetic eyes and bright expressions.

"Answer me, servant," Emyr hissed. "Why did you not bring Amaranth home?"

Egan licked his parched lips. "*Passhu* ..." He whispered. Emyr's eyes widened. "A *passhu* is guarding her."

"Do they know what she is?" Emyr asked, his tone oddly sounding worried.

Egan blinked rapidly as sweat threatened to drip into his eyes. "I don't know. They guard her well."

Emyr released him. Egan crumbled to the floor. The chains that bound his arms back rattled as if irritated. Egan dared look up from his prone position. Emyr had a thoughtful look on his face.

"Have any of the other Shadows approached her?" Emyr asked.

"No, she has banished those who speak to her," Egan answered. He hated how his voice quivered.

Emyr sighed. "Very well." With a wave of his hand, the chains holding Egan disappeared. The Shadow nearly laughed hysterically at the relief. "Continue watching her, Egan. When the *passhu* isn't looking, grab her immediately," Emyr ordered coldly.

"Yes, master," Egan whispered. In a swirl of shadow, he disappeared.

The past two days had been interesting. Since Flander had joined the cover, the males had engaged in what Ami could only suspect was male posturing. Ami didn't understand it. Before, Uriah had held some contempt for her, and James hadn't seemed interested in doing anything to impress her, while Ados used to be terrified of her. Now they were trying to outdo each other to impress or gain compliments from her. Ami shook her head at their antics. It had to be a weird Rascal thing.

Ami and Uriah spent the past two days inspecting the footprints the Werewolf found during his patrol. At first, Ami thought they were left over from when she killed the witch. Soldiers and priests were all over the area. However, upon further inspection, they noticed that the footprints originated from the east. It was there they discovered a magically made door in the dome.

"What are your thoughts?" Ami asked, staring at the strange door. It was shorter than a standard door and oval-shaped.

"I don't know much about magical theory, but this screams sabotage and infiltration," Uriah said, crossing his arms.

"How so?" Ami asked.

"Huh?" Uriah blinked.

"How does this magical door result in sabotage and infiltration?" Ami clarified.

Uriah stared at her as if she asked him to solve a complex riddle with a ridiculous answer. Turning thoughtful, he gazed at the magical door.

"It's not Rascal," Uriah stated. Ami looked at him, nodding for him to continue. Uriah took a nervous breath and continued, "Very few Rascal males know magic. Even if they tried to learn secretly, they couldn't obtain this level without someone in their family knowing. The family Bond would've notified them."

"Why and how?" Ami asked curiously.

"I know that females have a larger capacity for magic than males. It allows females to exert control over them. If a male's magical core becomes equal to or greater than the female's, the Bond will notify the matriarch of the potential threat," Uriah explained.

"Are family Bonds somehow sentient?" Ami asked.

Uriah moved his head from left to right. "I think it's more of providing security for the family. In Rascu, females are heads because they prioritize family over everything else. From stories my mother told me, males wouldn't do that."

"You don't agree."

Uriah looked uneasy. "That's not my place to say."

"Very well," Ami said. She changed the subject. "This type of magic is very delicate and requires a lot of concentration and knowledge. You see where the door curves?" She pointed to the arch. Uriah nodded. "Most would cast a square shape to help hold its shape. Just like a house, the dome is pushing pressure on the doorway. By creating an arch, not only is it stable, it actually has less pressure and thus will last longer than a normal doorway."

"Whoa," Uriah commented. Ami felt proud that the Werewolf sounded impressed. "Who would know that?"

"Magic users of another nation," Ami replied.

"Goya," Uriah whispered in horror.

Ami nodded. "It seems their abrupt pause was only a ruse."

"Are they responsible for the time magic as well?" Uriah asked.

Ami stared in the direction of the Howling Forest. "I haven't investigated it to determine that."

"But you suspect it," Uriah stated confidently.

"Suspect, yes. I'd rather be certain than assume."

"Why do more work when you already know who did it?" Uriah asked, his tone painfully naïve.

"Assumptions will get you killed," Ami said in a hard tone. She glanced at the sky and added, "Let's return to camp and eat."

Her chest throbbed painfully, this time on her left side. Sucking in a sharp breath, she slowly let out a breath.

"You're still hurting?" Uriah asked gently.

"Yeah. It's the other side now. Just bruises making themselves known," Ami said, trying to sound casual. By Uriah's skeptical look, she wasn't successful.

The other three males were already at camp. The fire was starting to warm the frying pan. The air wasn't as tense as in the past two days. Flander and Ados appeared to be ignoring each other. James jumped to his feet when he noticed them.

"Sir, we have only enough mushrooms for one more meal," James informed her.

"Flander will have the rest of them. We'll get more this evening," Ami replied.

She put the frying pan on the fire. Glancing at the remaining meat, she started calculating how long it would last.

If the lads weren't so squeamish, we could've eaten the organs while fresh. Ami thought with a huff. *We have enough for the rest of today and breakfast tomorrow. One of us will need to hunt after we eat.*

After cooking and eating, Ami assigned Flander to mushroom foraging and James hunting. Uriah and Ados were assigned guard duty. Meanwhile, Ami sat in her tent, writing her daily report for Mason. Finishing a few hours later, all the males were around the fire when she exited her tent.

"Sir, what will we do tomorrow?" Uriah asked.

Ami pondered the thought as she prepared dinner, teaching Ados how to separate the stems from the caps and season them properly. As the mushrooms cooked, she went over what they'd already accomplished. Each male had examined the magical dome's western, southern, and eastern parts. The northern part of the village contained the cemetery and the Howling Forest.

"We will see how much we can investigate the forest," Ami finally answered, placing all the mushrooms into Flander's bowl. James handed her several pieces of meat. They sizzled pleasantly.

"Is that safe with that Wraith thing still there?" Flander asked nervously.

"The unicorn got rid of it, right?" Ados asked.

"I believe so. I'm unsure how much investigating we will

accomplish, but we will do as much as possible," Ami said encouragingly.

They ate in comfortable silence. Ami stared at the fire until she heard someone call for her.

"Pardon?" Ami asked when she realized the males were looking at her.

"Um," Flander said anxiously, "I heard you knew stories of different versions."

"The last time I told you a story, you stated that no Centaur would believe such lunacy or something of that sort," Ami stated blandly. Flander flinched.

"What story was that?" Ados asked curiously.

"Mary the War Mage."

"That's one everyone basically knows. What about one someone hasn't heard?" James suggested.

"Like what?" Ami inquired.

Each male looked deep in thought. Then Ados had an "Aha!" moment.

"Do you know any good stories about constellations?" the Elf asked eagerly.

"I know many." Ami smiled.

"We're going to stargaze?" Uriah asked in disbelief.

"What's wrong with that?" Ados asked defensively.

The Werewolf shrugged. "Seems childish."

"How so?" Ami asked.

Uriah looked uncomfortable. "I don't know," he mumbled under his breath.

"I think it's interesting how our ancestors looked at these tiny balls of light in the sky and decided to tell stories that lasted for generations," Ami commented softly. "Let's find a spot."

It was still early evening. The five wandered through the open grassland to find a spot to lie down. Ados and James wrestled for what they considered "the best spot." Ami carefully found the softest feeling grass and lay there. Flander lowered his horse body down first, facing her, and laid down sideways before carefully twisting his Elven torso to face the sky next to her. Seeing the Centaur's close proximity to her, Ados abandoned his wrestling match and slid onto the grass beside her. James chuckled, lying on Ados' other side. Ami saw Uriah reluctantly join them on Flander's other side.

For a while, they lay there chatting about random, inconsequential things. Soon the evening sunset of oranges and dark purples eased into navy blue. The stars started their nightly competition on who could shine the brightest that night. Ami began with the most common constellation, Big Ladle and Small Bowl. A story of how a giant, irritated about his larger brothers getting bigger portions than himself, threw his mother's soup ladle into the sky in anger. His mother was angered that he threw her only ladle, took his bowl, and threw it into the sky. The males chuckled at the story.

Ados was next, pointing to a constellation next to the Small Bowl called Butterfly Wing. A young Faerie female was in love with an Elf from an opposing clan. She cut off her wings for her beloved, only to find him with another female. In her despair, the Faerie female cried to the stars. The stars heard her wailing and lifted her to be with them in the form of the wings she cut.

The mood was somber. After a moment, James told a tale. His constellation, Lonely Wolf, was about a Werewolf without a pack. He roamed the lands, howling his loneliness and sorrow. He continued, never befriending another Were or Person until he couldn't take his loneliness anymore and climbed a mountain. There he met a female Dragon.

The female was in hiding from her clan. They wanted her to marry and lay eggs for the clan, but she refused. Somehow the two started talking. Soon the Lonely Wolf forgot why he went to the mountain in the first place. One day, he returned from hunting to find the Dragon gone. Finding drag marks and numerous footprints, he followed the Dragon's scent. He found her bound with numerous males surrounding her. In a rage, he attacked the male Dragons. The male Dragons outnumbered him and beat him nearly to death. Desperate to save her friend, the female Dragon cut the Bonds she held with her clan, killing herself instantly. Seeing his only friend sacrifice herself for him, the Lonely Wolf let out one last howl of sorrow. On summer nights, the Lonely Wolf can be seen with a flickering series of stars representing his Dragon friend.

When James finished his story, Ados was openly bawling. Flander was wiping his eyes. Uriah was sniffing noisily. Ami felt several tears fall down her cheek.

"*Ta-bo*, Atorra. You know how to break a heart," Ami commented, wiping her wet cheek.

"Sorry, sir," James muttered.

"It's all right. I wasn't expecting to cry over friendship," Ami said light-heartedly.

They took a few minutes to gather themselves. Then it was Flander's turn. His constellation, The Archer, was about a proud Centaur who could shoot an arrow so accurately that he didn't even have to know what his target looked like to hit it. Several of his peers grew suspicious of his skill, given he had lacked talent when they were younger. The Archer habitually went into the woods every two months by himself. The suspicious Centaurs followed him one day.

The Archer came to a pond. When he touched the water, a large fish rose from its depths. The Archer placed his bow in the fish's mouth. The fish closed its mouth and appeared to suck on the bow like candy. This repeated three times. After the third time, the fish spat the bow into the shallow water. The Archer retrieved it, bowed at the fish, and left. The Centaurs who witnessed this decided to expose the Archer as a fraud. At the next competition, they had a bow that looked precisely like the Archer's and switched them out. To their surprise, the Archer continued to shoot like he always had. They were confused. Didn't the Archer gain his talent from the fish or the bow?

They confronted him and demanded how he became so good at archery when he didn't use to. The Archer explained that he realized he wasn't good at archery but wanted to do better. He practiced until he excelled at it. Then they demanded to know about the fish in the woods. The Archer explained that he accidentally dropped his bow in the water while walking, and the fish almost swallowed his bow. The two started to talk and became friends who met every two months.

"But then what about the bow being in the fish's mouth three times, the Centaurs demanded. Oh, that? The fish likes the taste," Flander finished.

Ami and the males laughed at the strange ending. They calmed down after several minutes. The atmosphere was calm and relaxing. Ami couldn't remember the last time she felt so relaxed with other People. The night air was cool. Ami waited for Uriah to start on his constellation story. She looked at the night sky, trying to see any other familiar constellations. The ground underneath her started to grow cold. Ami frowned. That was unusual. She turned her head. A long black shadow covered the grass. Multiple red eyes stared at her. Ami gasped.

Multiple hands grabbed her arms and legs. Ami struggled with a shout against the strange hands. Flander yelped. Ados yelled, grabbing Ami's right wrist and pulling her towards him. The Shadows shrieked in frustration. Ami gathered her magic into her left palm and banished the Shadows with a light spell. The Shadows screamed in pain before disappearing into the earth like evaporating ink.

Ami glanced at the males. They were on their feet. James glanced around, expecting the Shadows to return. Ados held her wrist in a vice grip, his whole body quivering in fear. Flander and Uriah looked terrified.

"Were those witches too?" Flander asked, his voice childlike and shaking.

"No. Shadows," Ami stated.

"Sir, can we please leave?" Uriah begged. Ami was shocked by the unshed tears in the Werewolf's eyes.

She thought about her options. They needed to investigate the Howling Forest or see how close she could reach it. Seeing the males' terrified expressions, she knew they didn't have enough experience to deal with this type of danger.

"We will head for Putra Hallas tomorrow afternoon. In the morning, we will investigate the forest as much as possible and then leave," Ami said.

"Will we get in trouble for returning so soon?" James asked fearfully.

"I will talk to General Mason," Ami replied.

"Do-do we have to-to stay in the d-dome?" Ados stammered. Realizing he was still holding her wrist, he released it suddenly as if burned. "I'm sorry, Captain."

"I will keep watch for the remainder of the night," Ami said.

"Why you?" Uriah sniffed noisily. Ami watched him wipe his face with his hands.

"The Shadows want me for some reason, and I'm the only one who can perform the spell that banishes them," Ami explained. "Let's return to camp."

The males trailed behind her. Ami relit the fire while the males readied themselves for bed. She heard each male settle down and slowly fall asleep one by one. All except Uriah. The Werewolf laid still as a stone. When the others were asleep, Uriah moved and exited his tent.

"Couldn't sleep?" Ami asked softly. Uriah merely shook his head. He sat next to her.

Both stared at the fire in silence for a long while.

"I liked the stories," Uriah's voice rumbled in the air.

Ami smiled, watching a piece of coal fall. "They were enjoyable. I was surprised by Flander's. That ending was a twist."

Uriah hummed in agreement. "James' was good too."

"He's a good storyteller," Ami commented.

"What are giants like?" Uriah asked.

"Which ones?" Ami asked.

"How many types are there?" he asked curiously.

"In Vinci, there are mainly ice giants. Goya has ones that occupy one of their large lakes. It wouldn't surprise me if others were in the Unknown Lands beyond the Wilds," Ami explained.

"What are ice giants, exactly?" Uriah asked.

"They're a type of People who are taller and stronger than Centaurs. They average eight feet tall and have light blue skin that blends in with the snow. Their hair is coarse and varies in color, much like Elves. Many braid their hair to keep it out of their faces. That's ice giants in a nutshell," Ami said with a shrug.

"Are they hostile?" Uriah asked.

"Only when provoked, as anyone would be," Ami replied vaguely.

Uriah hummed as if deep in thought. They stayed in silence. Ami fed the fire to keep Uriah warm. Looking at him, she saw him nodding off.

"Lay down and sleep. I'll keep watch," Ami said gently.

Uriah obeyed without comment. He laid down, facing the fire. His head brushed against Ami's right leg. Unknowingly, Ami started to hum a melody. Uriah quickly fell asleep. Ami continued to hum, her magic ready to be released in her chest.

From the village, she never noticed the pair of red eyes watching her sadly and in pain.

CHAPTER 12

The Howling Forest seemed far more imposing than when they had first arrived. The five avoided the cemetery, keeping an eye out for anything suspicious. The only thing Ami noticed was how several older graves looked disturbed. Knowing she couldn't investigate, she focused on the forest.

"Sir ..." Uriah panted heavily.

Ami looked over her shoulder. The males were at the edge of the village. Flander had his hands on his chest, sweat dripping down his face and horse body. Both ribcages heaved with exertion. James and Ados looked like they were struggling to stand with a giant invisible boulder on their shoulders. Uriah was only a few steps ahead of them, trying to follow Ami. He was down on one knee, the pressure preventing him from moving further. Ami stood several feet ahead of them.

"Stay where you are. Don't move," Ami ordered.

She closed her eye. Her magic pulsed outwards, testing the time magic. The pressure didn't change. That was a good sign. It meant the time magic was stable for now. Pulling her magic back in, Ami contemplated what to do next. Taking in a deep breath, she slowly released her magic. She was curious about how the time magic would react to her passive magic. After a few minutes, she noticed something remarkable.

When she released her magic, the light was bright enough to be seen by Ami. Now, it was shining more brilliantly. Ami sunk into her mind to look at her core. She was shocked to see it twice as big as it was before.

What's going on? Ami asked herself. Her passive magic continued to grow brighter and more robust. In addition, the pressure around her was lessening.

"Sir?" Uriah's voice made her jump, breaking her concentration. Her magic sucked back into her body like a vacuum.

She turned around. All four males walked up to her, no longer sweating or fighting against the pressure.

"The pressure went away," Flander said.

"Did you do something, sir?" James asked.

"I'm ... not sure," Ami admitted. "I was trying to determine what was stabilizing the time magic, but found nothing."

"Are we going further towards the forest?" Ados asked nervously.

"Yes, we need more information," Ami said firmly.

They slowly edged their way toward the looming forest. The pressure didn't reappear until they neared the tree line.

"See if there's anything close to the tree line. One of the villagers may have left something," Ami instructed.

They spread out into a sparse line. The males could barely get to the tree line. Ami managed to venture a foot or so into the Howling Forest. Ami frowned as she searched. There weren't any footprints or noticeable disturbances in the brush or low tree branches. Small branches should've been broken and the earth disturbed with so many villagers being dragged or forced to walk into the Howling Forest.

Has the time magic progressed so quickly that it erased traces of their existence? Ami wondered in horror.

"Captain!" James yelled from a distance to her right.

She rushed to the Elf. He was pointing to a bush. Sticking out was a worn, red knapsack. When she picked it up, she could tell it held small items that clinked together. From what she could tell, it appeared half-full. They regrouped away from the forest. Ami felt terrible for the males. They looked utterly exhausted from fighting the pressure.

"Do you think one of the villagers left it?" Ados asked.

"We're about to find out," Ami said.

The males crowded around her, excitement and hope vibrating out of them. Ami opened the top of the knapsack. Inside were numerous metal squares. She pulled one of them out. Once she did, she knew what it was.

"What is it?" James asked, looking at it in confusion.

"A memory disc," Ami said.

"What's that?" Flander asked.

"It's an item that records information. What makes me curious is how and why remote villagers came upon them," Ami said. Numerous suspicions began to swirl in her mind.

"Isn't that something the Dali family would know about?" Uriah asked. When Ami gave him a questioning look, he added, "They specialize in security cameras. Wouldn't they have some of the disc things?"

"We may have to request their assistance to see what is on them. Let's go and pack up. We must go to Putra Hallas and tell them what we found," Ami said.

The males were relieved to be leaving the village. Ami was worried. Why were these left at the edge of the forest to be found? Did someone know she was coming on this mission? Did the Goyans have something to do with this? Her gut was telling her this was a trap. However, she didn't know what kind.

They packed up the camp quickly. After ensuring the fire pit was cold, they left the magical dome. As soon as she stepped out, her shirt ripped, and it felt like it had shrunk three sizes. She gasped in surprise. She looked down to see what was going on. Two large lumps of squeezed breasts greeted her from her ripped shirt collar.

"Sir?" Uriah asked.

"Atorra or Fallenleaf, do you have a spare shirt?" Ami barely managed to ask. The shirt was feeling more like a corset.

"I do, sir," Ados said.

Ami could feel herself get lightheaded. Frantically, she ripped her shirt off, freeing her chest. The feeling of sweet freedom was ruined when Ados' shirt was shoved in her face abruptly.

"Divert your eyes, Fallenleaf! Atorra!" Uriah snarled.

Ami took a few liberating breaths of fresh air. Then she looked at her chest. It was fascinating to her. She heard of females going through chest pains and their breasts developing naturally, but she never thought she would experience it.

Maybe the pains in my chest weren't entirely from trying to escape the Wraith. Ami thought. Realizing she was surrounded by males, she put on Ado's shirt. "I'm dressed, lads," Ami confirmed.

All the males were blushing dark red and refused to look her in the eye. She examined each male. Were they taller than before? The Elves' hair was longer than usual.

Nodding at James and Ados, she said, "Your hair is much longer than before."

"So is yours, Captain," Uriah pointed out, glancing at her for a split second.

Ami felt her hair. It was true. Her hair had grown several inches. It reached her eyebrow.

"Is it strange that I didn't notice?" Ami asked.

"No, my fur is longer and thicker," Uriah said, holding his arm out. It was thicker, making it seem like he gained muscle.

"My hooves are longer," Flander said, staring at his feet in shock.

"But why didn't we notice in the dome?" James asked, looking at the dome.

"Time magic is an obscure branch that doesn't make logical sense. Perhaps because we were not present when the dome was created, the magic did not affect us the same way it affected the buildings or the villagers who were present when the magic was performed," Ami suggested.

"That kind of makes sense," Ados said slowly. "Also, our magic may have resisted it to a point."

Ami blinked. She didn't think of that. "Very good observation, Fallenleaf."

Ados blushed darker. "Thank you, sir."

"But why didn't we age while in the dome?" Uriah asked.

"Is the dome some kind of time capsule?" Flander asked. They looked at him with confused looks. "W-well, the dome was created to contain it, correct? Maybe time flows differently in there."

Ice went down Ami's spine. "Just like last time," she whispered.

"Last time?" Uriah asked.

"When I first came to the village, I wasn't aware of the dome. I'm still not sure how I got here. I stayed in the village for two days. But when I returned to Putra Hallas, they told me I was missing for seven days," Ami explained.

"So, how long has passed this time?" Uriah asked.

Ami whipped to face Flander. "When did you receive your order from General Rikardi?"

"On the fourth day of Thetis," Flander answered.

That was the day we left. He didn't waste any time. Ami thought bitterly. Then she asked, "How long did it take you to arrive from Putra Thyllisala?"

"About a day and a half," Flander replied.

"That adds up about right," James said thoughtfully. "We arrived at the dome about early afternoon, and you went to the cemetery the next day, sir."

"True. Let's head to Putra Hallas and see how long we've been missing," Ami said. She shifted the red knapsack she had over her left shoulder. Her yellow one was under it.

The walk to the fort felt strange. It made Ami tense. Something was going to happen, but she couldn't predict what. After walking for thirty minutes, the ground turned sideways suddenly. Ami tried to follow its trail to make it right-side up. Ami stumbled further away into the heart of a grassy field. Her vision was doing something weird. All color faded until she saw shades of purples and grays.

Then she remembered nothing.

Damp soil filled her nose. Ami looked around. Her surroundings looked like a large cellar or underground storehouse. She couldn't shake the feeling that she had been here before. It was on the tip of her tongue.

"Still having difficulty remembering?" a familiar voice asked.

Ami swirled around. A redhead Elf with a bobbed cut stood with her arms crossed. She wore worn trousers and a tunic similar to Vincians.

"Felicia?" Ami whispered.

Felicia smiled softly, an odd feature on the usually aggressive voice. "Hello, Logic."

They rushed at each other, hugging each other fiercely. After a moment, they released each other.

"Is Emotion in the northern mines?" Ami blurted.

Felicia blinked her dark eyes at her. "You figured that out quick."

"And we are?" Ami asked, looking around the room.

"You don't remember?" Felicia asked mysteriously.

Ami studied the room. There were numerous shelves with clay jugs lining the walls of the carved-out earth. She inhaled slowly, trying to identify the familiar scent. Whatever memory she had of this place still wasn't making an appearance.

She walked closer to the clay jugs. When she saw the identi-fier, she knew.

"The royal wine cellar?" Ami gasped.

"All in one," Felicia confirmed.

"Why are you in Goya?" Ami demanded.

Felicia shrugged. "I don't know."

"Are you being held prisoner?" Ami asked. The wine cellar was starting to fade.

"I'm not sure why I'm here. All I know is that I'm here," Felicia said, her voice fading into darkness.

Several pulses from different Bonds tore her attention away from Felicia. They were insistent and loud. Ami pulsed back, asking why they were bothering her. One Bond sent images of Rikardi collapsing, holding his chest as if having a heart attack. Another Bond was frantic, as if the Person on the other side was about to have their own heart attack. Ami pulsed calmness through all her Bonds. One remained firm, insisting on knowing what happened. Ami pulsed that she didn't know. The Bond wasn't satisfied and wanted her to wake up to find out.

So bossy.

Ami slowly woke up to reality. The smell of burnt flesh filled her nose. Her entire body felt like it was smoking. Her muscles felt crispy. Random spasms vibrated her arms and thighs. It was then she realized two different People were hold-ing her hands. Holding her left hand was Ados. The Elf was asleep with his arms serving as a pillow. His right hand curled around her left one. Holding her right hand was Flander. The Centaur sat upright, his head leaned back, his mouth agape. Drool went down his chin. Uriah and James were asleep in hard chairs at the foot of her bed. Their bodies were contorted, and Ami knew their backs and necks would be stiff.

Looking around, she recognized the healing room at Putra Hallas. She painfully moved her left hand out of Ados' grip without waking him. Her entire arm felt like it was engulfed in magical fire. Tears fell from her lone eye as the nerves over-whelmed her senses. When she could focus, her eye stared at the dark purple raised veins throbbing against her pale skin. The purple veins continued all around her body.

What happened? she wondered.

"Lads?" Ami's voice croaked. She sounded like an old wise Person who was too fond of tobacco. Her odd voice jolted the males awake.

"Captain!" they cried.

"What ..." Ami tried to ask.

"We were so worried," Ados said. He had dried tear tracks on his face.

"You weren't breathing at all," James added. Tears filled up his eyes. He looked away, trying to hide them.

"What happened?" Ami croaked louder this time.

The males glanced at each other.

"You were struck by lightning," Uriah replied quietly.

"There wasn't a storm," Ami pointed out. A tickle formed in her throat, causing her to cough.

James tried to get up, but collapsed back into his chair. Ados got up instead. Less than a minute later, he returned with a glass of water. Ami thanked him and sipped on the water.

"It was weird," Flander admitted, wiping the drool off his chin. "We felt some kind of powerful presence."

"Then we realized you were in the middle of the field and walking oddly," James added.

"I had a very bad dizzy spell," Ami said.

"From what?" Ados asked.

"When I was hit with demon fire, I lost my left horn. My balance has been off ever since," Ami explained.

"Looks like it's back," Uriah said, nodding at her.

"What?" Ami gasped. Without thinking, she tried to move her arm, but her muscles clenched tightly, refusing to move. The pain made her gasp. More tears gathered in her eye. "How did I get struck by lightning?" she asked, struggling to keep her voice steady.

"Sir, are you okay—" Ados started to ask.

"What's going on here?" Theo's demanding voice filled the room. The Werefox stormed in, looking furious. Ami hadn't seen that look since she snuck out to the café. "Why didn't you alert me when my patient awakened?"

"We need to ask what happened—" Uriah started, standing up intimidatingly.

"That isn't your call, soldier," Theo interrupted coldly. "The patient's health is my highest priority, which ranks higher than your need for information. Visitation hours are over. You need to leave so I can check on my patient." The black Werefox stood firmly despite Uriah being almost a head taller.

"I'll see you later, lads," Ami stated, dismissing them.

Begrudgingly, the four males obeyed. Theo watched them leave. He huffed. "I swear, I don't get any respect."

"It's because of your accent," Ami said.

"Well," Theo snootily said as he came to her side, "it doesn't excuse their negligence."

"Rascal males worry in different ways," Ami said diplomatically. "Why are you here? I thought you would still be in Talient."

Theo blinked at her. "You don't know how long you've been missing, do you?"

"Missing? How can we be missing on a mission?" Ami asked incredulously. This prompted another coughing fit.

Theo grabbed his stethoscope and listened to her chest as she coughed. The cold instrument moved to her shoulders and back.

"I'm going to put you on some antibiotics. Coughing is probably due to the tears in your lungs," Theo murmured.

"How long were we gone?" Ami demanded hoarsely.

"Six months."

How did it get that bad? Ami had never encountered time magic so out of control. Even in Vinci, the most time lost was a few hours.

"Then why are you here?" Ami asked, drinking the rest of the water.

"The Centaur general ordered me to come here in case there were any injuries shortly after you left," Theo answered as he took her empty glass. He walked over to a nearby sink and refilled it.

"But you finished your internship already, correct?" Ami asked. She accepted the fresh water.

Theo grinned. "Dr. Elderflower offered me a permanent position, and I accepted."

"What about your family in Roy?" Ami asked.

"They came about a week ago. They were planning on relocating here for a long time and finally made a decision," Theo said.

Something in Theo's tone made Ami suspicious. Feeling a headache and the pain in her muscles, she shelved the suspicion for now. She had to figure out what happened.

"I was told I was struck by lightning," Ami stated.

"Yes, a bizarre occurrence. From what I heard from the soldiers, you weren't the only one," Theo replied.

"What was it exactly?"

"Honestly, no one really knows," Theo admitted. "I've never heard of lightning striking without rain clouds, and the fact it was purple was even stranger."

"Purple?" Ami asked.

"Is there another color of lightning?" Theo teased.

"Yes. Red and blue," Ami said.

Theo's ears jerked up. "You know of this?"

"There are numerous tales and legends about colored lightning. Red often occurs when People pray to the Almighty One to destroy witches. Blue lightning happens in Vinci after *Bla'ju da Veris*. I've never heard of purple, though," Ami explained.

"What's Blah, uh, thingy?" Theo asked.

Ami paused to translate. "It means 'Sheet of Whiteness' to describe the massive blizzards that blow every ten years."

"Why is it called Sheet of Whiteness?" Theo inquired.

"Because everything is buried in snow; even half the royal castle is buried when it happens. All you can see is a sheet of whiteness," Ami explained.

"That's a lot of snow," Theo commented. His gaze turned far away, as if trying to imagine what that looked like. "You said you know about different lightning colors but were surprised there weren't rain clouds when the purple struck you. Why is that?"

"Usually, odd lightning colors occur during a major event or weather phenomenon. The fact that this purple lightning occurred without any prompting is concerning," Ami explained.

"It means it can't be predicted," Theo surmised.

Ami nodded. "Exactly."

"Well, that sucks," Theo said. "I'm going to get your medicine. Do you need any more water?"

"No, thank you."

"I'll be back." Theo smiled.

Ami relaxed as much as her burnt muscles would allow her when he left. She remembered her dream. Was it a dream? Why is Felicia in Goya? How did her body get there? Was she safe? Was she okay? Can she escape? So many questions swirled in her mind without answers.

She forced her left arm up. The pain was incredible. With tears flowing down her cheek, she reached for her left temple. Her body jumped when she touched the horn. It felt different from her other horn. This one was unnaturally smooth, almost like marble. Then she looked at her arms.

I just keep getting uglier and uglier. She thought bitterly. Out of the corner of her right eye, she saw a pair of red eyes watching her.

"Egan?" Ami called out.

The horse Shadow staggered out of the inky pool and collapsed beside her bed. Silver blood gushed out of gray wounds. Adrenaline filled her abnormal veins, numbing her muscles as she jumped out of bed and to Egan's side.

"What happened?" she demanded.

Egan panted heavily. She could smell the rusty metal of chains and old blood. "My master ... was not pleased with ... me," Egan wheezed.

"Because of me," Ami said softly.

"He ... He grows impatient," Egan added. He groaned in pain.

"If I heal you, will you promise not to drag me to his realm?" Ami asked.

Egan stared at her, his panting becoming more labored. "Yes."

Drawing on her memories, Ami gently touched the most extensive wound on Egan's ribs. Soft white light emitted from her palms. She directed her magic to heal the wound. She half expected Egan's magic to resist since he was a Shadow. Surprisingly, it went smoothly. Before she knew it, the wound was healed. Removing her hands, she turned her attention to the others and halted.

All the wounds were gone. Only remnants of dried silver blood remained.

"Thank you for healing me, little mistress," Egan said, his horse mouth not moving, yet his voice sounded beside her. His voice sounded tired.

"I'm not sure what I did," Ami admitted.

"You are a powerful Healer, little mistress," Egan claimed confidently. The Shadow horse moved to a more comfortable position on the floor. Then he looked at her. "Why are you here, little mistress?"

"I thought Emyr had his little Shadows watching my every move?" Ami answered.

"Not since you banished the last desperate bunch," Egan answered bitterly.

"I don't appreciate being grabbed like that," Ami said.

Without warning, Egan's form morphed into an Elf's body. Shadows covered him in the shape of black robes. Shaggy black hair, pale skin, dark eyes, a thin nose, and thin lips that looked too wide to be normal stared at her exposed arms.

"What's this?" Egan asked dangerously.

Is it strange that I think it's weird that his mouth moves when he speaks? Ami thought. Unlike his horse form, his voice was nasal, as if he had a sinus infection. Shaking out of her thoughts, she replied, "I was struck by lightning."

Egan stared at her. "That's not lightning."

"Then what is it?"

"That's from a phoenix," Egan growled.

"A phoenix?" Ami scoffed. That was absurd. Phoenixes were a myth, not something real. Also, phoenixes were said to be made out of sacred fire, not lightning.

"Why you, little mistress?" Egan murmured.

"Do you know this phoenix?" Ami asked.

"Who are you?" a booming voice demanded.

Second-Commander Douglas, four other soldiers, and Theo were at the room's entrance. Douglas and the soldiers glared at Egan as Theo looked at Ami worriedly.

"Next time, little mistress," Egan said, his grin morbidly wide. With a bow, shadows engulfed him, and he disappeared.

"Captain, are you all right?" Douglas asked, walking quickly over to her.

"Yes, I'm fine," Ami said.

Douglas and Theo helped her back onto the bed. She hated how weak her muscles felt. It reminded her of when she woke up from the coma.

"Who and what was that?" Douglas ordered.

"An acquaintance," Ami replied. She closed her eye. The headache was getting worse.

"Excuse me, I need to administer medicine to my patient," Theo said, gently pushing through the soldiers and past Douglas.

"We will discuss this later, Captain Rose," Douglas warned.

"Yes, Commander Douglas," Ami retorted tiredly.

Douglas and the soldiers left. Theo gave her numerous pills to swallow. Each one felt like a lead weight in her stomach. She only had one thought before the medicine knocked her out:

Where was Salvador?

His head felt like it was filled with water. His ears couldn't quite distinguish what the People around him were saying. Wherever he was, it hurt his eyes. It was too bright. His body was moving, but he wasn't aware of it. He could feel his mouth move. The words he was saying were muted. He didn't know who he was talking to.

Where am I? What happened? Blaine asked himself. All he remembered was leaving the police station after a failed negotiation with the police chief in the Winter District, and then someone grabbed him. He felt the sensation of being whisked away, and that's when he knew his father had found him. His memory was fuzzy after that. Actually, all his memories after that were cloudy and unclear.

He looked around. Something like a bubble surrounded him. Thick, root-like magical threads covered the outside. He stared at it, trying to understand what he was seeing.

Am I being controlled? Blaine wondered. Ice-cold realization shot down his spine. The magical roots vibrated and constricted more around the bubble. *I am being possessed.* Blaine thought, his mind racing. Who's trying to control him? Was it his father?

That made Blaine furious. His magic reacted to his anger, whipping up a small windstorm inside the bubble. The magic shook the bubble's walls. The more he thought about his father controlling him, the hotter his anger burned.

How dare he! After everything he did to me, he still wants to control my life! I won't have it! Blaine roared.

The windstorm he conjured grew stronger and stronger until it became a tornado. It tore at the bubble, shattering it like glass. The magical roots shrieked. They came straight for Blaine. The blond Werewolf felt his body heat up. Red and white flames covered him like a shield. The root threads screamed when they made contact with the magical fire. Those that touched the fire remained on fire until they blackened and turned to ash. He focused on his magic, burning hotter and hotter. Sweat dripped through his fur, sizzling into steam when it made contact with the now blue flames. Then he released it. Like a volcano erupting, it burned everything in its path into ash. For the first time since he had been captured, all his senses returned. He didn't even register where he was. His magic instinctually teleported away to somewhere safe. He collapsed in the familiar, dusty warehouse. His body shook from magical exertion. His stomach revolted. He vomited onto the floor.

"Well, well, well. What do we have here?" a familiar voice said snidely. Blaine gazed up at the source.

"S-Shayne ..." Blaine whispered, his body shaking violently.

"Are you declaring war, Blaine?" Shayne asked with a dangerous glint in his eyes.

"Sigrid ... I need to ..." Blaine tried to say, but his brain was blacking out.

"What? To court her again? You lost that chance, Blaine," Shayne said with his lips curled back to show teeth.

What? Our courtship ended? When? Blaine went into what memories he could recall. Only one was clear. He was trying to get the three remaining gang members to obey him. He couldn't remember why he was yelling at them. Rune came in with someone else. Then Blaine realized who it was.

Sigrid. He could see the deep scars from demon fire. Her beautiful hair was gone. Her left horn and eye were gone. Her remaining eye shined bright with fury. Even though she was angry at him, he still found her beautiful. Her words dug into him.

But I was already under my father's control, Blaine remembered.

More ice dumped down his back, making his stomach revolt again. Unable to control it, he vomited again. This time was far worse. It felt like chunks of his stomach came up. When he gazed back at Shayne, the Werewolf actually looked concerned.

"Please ... find Sigrid ..." Blaine begged pitifully.

"Rune, prepare a bed. Philip, help get him on the bed. Benton, fetch water for him," Shayne ordered sharply.

Blaine's vision blurred into darkness.

Putra Hallas would never be a place Ami could ever feel safe in. Even though Hector, Bru and the witch were dead, unease followed Ami within its walls. She barely ate the food, not trusting the cooking staff. In addition to her anxiety, she was worried about Salvador. The Dali heir was on suspension for attacking a fellow soldier. The incident happened several days after Ami and Lee left for Talient. Salvador apparently had a nightmare, and one of his dormmates had tried to wake him. When he had woken up, Salvador grabbed his dormmate by the throat and proceeded to pound his head into the bedpost. The other three dormmates and four patrolling soldiers who heard the commotion had separated the two. The injured dormmate suffered several head wounds that left scars, and his family called for the removal of Salvador from the military.

Lord Dali was notified of the attack and took Salvador home until cooler heads could make a decision. It appeared Conri was forcing the curse too early.

Conri, why are you doing this? Ami thought sadly. What was making the ancient wolf so anxious? Was there another witch in the vicinity? Why didn't he alert Salvador so he could tell Ami?

This made Ami ponder her earlier revelations. Was there really a curse? Ami was convinced it wasn't a curse. For one, the witch who cast the curse would've stayed nearby to torment the Dalis for generations out of pure pleasure. The fact that no witch remained nearby for the curse to come to fruition was suspect. Witches were anxious as well as ruthless when it came to their own curses. Then another thought came to mind. Why Salvador and not his father, Lord Dali? The curse story clearly stated firstborn heir. Lord Dali was the firstborn male in the Dali family and hadn't acquired the curse. Were there other requirements that Salvador wasn't aware of in the story?

There has to be documentation about this so-called curse. I'll write to Lord Dali about his family library. I need to get to the bottom of this to save Salvador, Ami thought to herself.

"Sir, are you ready?" Uriah asked.

All four soldiers were waiting outside her room, peering in worriedly. Each had their own large knapsack over their shoulders. They were leaving for Talient today.

"I am," Ami replied. She grabbed her patched-up yellow knapsack. It had only suffered several rips from the lightning strike. Miraculously, the cast iron pan was unharmed. Strangely, the red knapsack had disappeared. While she recovered, the males had taken several soldiers to show them where she had been struck, and they had searched for the mysterious knapsack to no avail. She managed to crudely sew her knapsack back together using her magic. She would have to ask the

Dragons to resew it properly.

Her muscles felt stretched as she walked. Thankfully, Theo's healing magic sped up her healing progress. They walked to the entrance of the fort. Commander Douglas and a few soldiers were waiting for them. Theo had already returned to Talient a few days ago.

"While it is always a pleasure to see you, Captain, hopefully, you can visit my fort for a friendly visit next time," Douglas said warmly.

Ami smiled. "Hopefully, next time will be just that."

Douglas nodded. "Safe travels, Captain."

Ami saluted. All soldiers in the vicinity copied her. Douglas saluted back. They left the fort with the sun high in the sky.

"Was that the fort where the previous commander was found dead?" James asked randomly.

Uriah and Ados hissed at him for his rudeness.

"It is. He was a sacrifice to a witch," Ami answered, her tone deadpan.

"What?" Flander gasped.

"I wasn't there, but General Lee and several soldiers found what was left of him in a secret chamber under the fort," Ami added.

"What were you doing?" Ados asked curiously.

"I was chasing the witch."

Flander walked up beside her. "How do you identify a witch?"

Ami thought about it. "One is the smell. Witches give off a perfume of sickly-sweet poppy juice. Under that perfume is the smell of death. Another is behavior. Witches are highly ambitious and ruthless. However, they are excellent actors, so you must be careful."

"How did you identify the witch at the fort?" Flander asked.

"I didn't. While I knew there was a witch, I didn't know who it was. All I knew was a strange female was talking to a soldier, now dead, and I was sensing dark magic somewhere in the fort. The dark magic was in the basement where Hector was found," Ami explained.

"How did you find the witch?" Uriah asked, coming to her other side. Ados and James walked closely behind her.

"When General Lee and the soldiers descended into the basement, I saw someone sneaking out. I exposed them, and it was a soldier under suspicion. When he spoke, it sounded like two People were talking at the same time. Then when we got to the village, the soldier's skin fell off, revealing the witch," Ami continued.

"Wait, she was wearing his skin?" Flander nearly shrieked.

"That's brutal," James muttered.

"You didn't mention this when we went to the village," Uriah pointed out.

"What happened in the fort wasn't vital to our mission in the village," Ami said coolly. "Our mission was to find out where the villagers could have possibly been moved or if they had been killed. If they had been killed, then by who and why."

"She's got you there," Ados said.

"Shut it," Uriah snapped.

Ami shared more information about witches, including several stories from Vinci until they made camp. The soldiers had provided them food for their journey. Ami was still suspicious. To her, it smelled odd.

"Captain, is there something wrong?" Flander asked as she made a face at the food in her bag.

"It doesn't smell right," she said.

Uriah smelled his food. He also made a face. "She's right. It does smell weird."

"Weird, how? Like different herbs or food went bad?" Ados asked, sniffing his as well. He made a face. Then sneezed.

"I don't know what it is, but my gut is saying don't eat it," Ami stated.

"I'll go hunt," James offered. Ami nodded. The Elf left.

"Come, Flander. I think I know where we may find some wild onions and roots," Ami said, standing up. "Lakeshore and

Fallenleaf, build a fire and the tents. We'll be back soon."

Ami and Flander searched the nearby field until they came to a clump of wild potatoes. They dug the roots out, happy with the finding. The potatoes were small but firm. With the number they found, it would be a filling meal. Ami spotted a creek nearby. They used the stream to clean most of the dirt off the small potatoes. They carried their load back to camp. James hadn't returned. Uriah was tending the fire, carefully placing pieces of wood on the growing fire. Ados was double-checking the tents. He grinned when he saw Ami.

"Welcome back, Captain," Ados greeted.

"Greetings," Ami replied. "We found potatoes."

"Really?" Uriah asked. His ears perked up.

"Yeah, Captain Rose is skilled in spotting wild vegetables," Flander praised.

"You flatter me, Flander," Ami smirked.

Uriah continued to tend the fire. Ados insisted on helping Ami prepare the potatoes. Halfway through, Ami began to grow concerned. James hadn't returned yet. She instantly spotted several rabbits and deer when she and Flander were in the field.

"Fallenleaf, finish the potatoes. I'm going to see if Atorra needs assistance," Ami ordered.

"Yes, sir."

Ami walked in the direction James had taken off in. She followed his tracks to a small grove of trees. Then she heard faint grunting. Curious, she slowed her pace. Unknowingly, she crouched in a defensive position. The grunting grew louder as she entered the grove. After walking a few feet, she found the source. A giant boar with dark yellow tusks and matted black-brown fur excitedly grunted as it circled a tree trunk.

Ami silently moved closer. The boar was drooling, its dark eyes hyper-focused on its target in the tree's branches. Ami gazed up. A terrified James clung to the tree trunk, barely supported in the tree's lower thin branches. Ami knew little about boars except they were detested and killed without question. She took in the deepest breath she could muster.

Rrroooooaaaaarrrr!

Her Dragon roar scared the boar, making it soil itself as it ran away, its squealing high-pitched. As the boar ran away, James unceremoniously slid down the tree trunk. The Elf had his eyes closed tightly, waiting for the predator to attack him. Ami gently reached out and touched his arm. Her touch made him gasp. He opened his eyes and stared at her.

"C-Captain?" James whispered.

"I'm here, Atorra," Ami said softly. She crouched down to his eye level.

James was still holding the tree trunk like a lifeline. Then he began to sob. Ami rubbed his back soothingly with one hand. After a few minutes, his tears cleared up. Hiccups squeaked out of his lips.

"I was so scared," James murmured.

"I know," Ami said, her voice still soft. "It's over now. Can you stand?"

"Yeah." James stood up shakily. His hands trembled.

"What happened?" Ami asked.

"I was tracking this deer into the grove. Then I noticed behind me something following me. That's when it charged out of the grass and chased me up the tree," James explained. "I'm sorry, sir."

"What for?"

"I haven't done my share of the hunting. I failed," James said, hanging his head.

"You didn't fail," Ami stated. James' head shot up, confused eyes staring at her. "There is still daylight left. Let's find some dinner."

James nodded. They found some rabbit tracks and pursued them. Before sunset, they made it back to camp with four rabbits.

"What took so long?" Uriah growled.

"James encountered a large boar that trapped him in a tree," Ami explained.

The other three males started laughing. James blushed dark red. Ami stared at them deadpan.

"I don't find this funny," Ami said.

"It is a little, sir," Ados chuckled.

"I've seen numerous People get gored and eaten alive by boars," Ami snarled. That stopped the laughter. "Uriah, since you're so hungry, prepare the meat."

The atmosphere was tense. James glared at the other males. Ados and Flander refused to look anyone, particularly Ami, in the eye. Uriah remained focused on his task. Soon, Ami placed her cast iron pan on the fire to warm it. Ami cooked the potatoes first. Then Uriah handed her slices of meat. Ami divided up the meals in each bowl. They didn't speak as they ate. Ami lamented that she was out of herbs. At least she knew the food wasn't poisoned.

"Captain?" Ados broke the silence.

"Yes?" Ami answered.

"I'm sorry."

"You're apologizing to the wrong Person," Ami said firmly. She glanced at James.

Ados realized this. "James?"

"Yeah?" The Elf had half of a potato in his mouth.

"I'm sorry for laughing at you," Ados said sincerely.

James stopped chewing. He stared at the other Elf intently. "We're good," he finally said.

"I'm sorry too, James," Flander said, his voice a low murmur.

"Sorry, James," Uriah grunted.

James swallowed. "We're all good."

The tense air ebbed away. Soon the males were chatting like nothing happened. Ami was glad the air was cleared.

"Um, captain?" Ados asked hesitantly.

"Yes?"

"Are-Are we good?" Ados stammered.

Ami glanced at the males peering at her apprehensively.

"Yeah. We're good. Good night, lads," Ami said. She picked up her bowl and went inside her tent.

The low tones from the males drowned into white noise as Ami lay in her bed cot, thinking about how to break the Dali curse.

CHAPTER 13

They entered the northern gate into the Winter District. Ami sighed as her mind swirled with thoughts about how to deal with the Dali curse.

"Captain, are you okay?" Ados asked softly. The Elf was a worrywart today. She couldn't go one minute without him asking if she was okay.

"Yes. Why do you ask?" Ami replied.

"You've been sighing a lot since we entered the capital," Uriah commented.

Out of an alleyway, Shayne walked briskly towards Ami. He had had a growth spurt. Now a few inches taller than Ami, his long legs reached Ami and company quickly.

"Who are you?" Uriah demanded, coming almost flush to Ami's back.

Shayne ignored him, his deep eyes on Ami.

"What's wrong?" Ami asked.

"We have a problem, sir," Shayne stated. He glanced at the males with her and added, "It's Blaine. There's something wrong."

Ami knew it had to be bad if Shayne was worried about Blaine.

"Lead the way," Ami ordered.

Shayne guided them in and out of various alleyways. He brought them to the warehouse. Entering, Ami could smell the rancid smell of dark magical residue. A large splatter of vomit was near the middle of the warehouse. Chunks of potion ingredients mixed in the vomit made Ami curious. Had Blaine been force-fed potions?

"Boss, he's over here," Shayne said.

Against a wall on a makeshift cot laid a shivering Blaine. The blond Werewolf's eyes were bright neon blue. Ami faintly recalled they were fainter the last time they met. When he saw her, he started blubbering.

"Sigrid, I-I'm s-s-sorry. I-I believe you. I-I believe you. Please-please, f-forgive me," Blaine stammered through his shivering.

"I know, Blaine. I know," Ami replied softly. She grabbed his shaking hand. Blaine squeezed it tightly. Guilt filled Ami's chest. Turning to the males behind her, she barked, "Shayne, find more blankets for him. One of you find a Healer—"

"On it, boss," Rune answered before running off.

"And bring me water for him to drink," Ami finished.

"I've tried getting him to drink, boss, but all he did was throw it back up," Philip replied, his tone sad.

Ami racked her brain for another solution. An idea popped into her mind. "Hand me the water," she ordered.

Philip handed her the bucket of fresh water with a ladle in it. Ami took the ladle out and set it on her lap. With her free hand, she searched her memory for the spell she sought.

The air was freezing. Snow crunched under her feet as she walked through the forests of Vinci. With her was a young ice giant. She knew him well. His name was Fannar. His bright blue skin stood out against the white fur coat of a skell his older brother killed for him last winter. They came to a wide creek. They needed to get to the other side for some reason. Most of the stream wasn't frozen.

Ami watched as Fannar crouched down on the creek bed. He placed a blue finger barely on the surface of the moving water. With a murmured word, ice spread from his finger to the other side.

Ami placed her finger on the water's surface and repeated what Fannar did.

"Sir, what are you doing?" James asked.

She felt the chill from the bucket as the water became solid ice. Grabbing the ladle, Ami used it to smash the new solid ice into chunks. Holding a piece, she opened Blaine's mouth and forced it in.

"Suck on this. Do not chew," Ami ordered in a no-nonsense tone.

Blaine nodded, obeying without question. Turning to the males, she noticed Rune hadn't returned yet.

"Benton, please show the lads where the deli is. Ask Patsy for some soup," Ami said.

"Where are you going to be, sir?" Ados asked anxiously.

"I'm going to be here with Blaine and explain to the Healer what's happening," Ami replied.

"Who is he?" Uriah asked, eyeing the shivering Blaine with suspicion.

"I'll explain later. Please go get food," Ami urged.

"Try to keep up," Benton said gruffly. He walked out of the warehouse without waiting. The four soldiers hesitated before reluctantly following the Centaur.

Shayne returned with a large pile of blankets. Ami carefully wrapped them around Blaine. He opened his mouth to show the ice was gone. Ami replaced it, repeating her instructions softer this time. Blaine continued to shiver uncontrollably.

"Boss, I brought a Healer," Rune announced as he entered. Behind him was Dr. Elderflower.

"Captain, what's going on?" Dr. Elderflower asked. He then noticed the vomit. "Is that what I think it is?"

"If it's what I suspect as well, then yes," Ami answered. "He's over here."

Dr. Elderflower came over swiftly. Ami saw that he carried a Healer's potion kit with him. Ami moved to let the doctor examine Blaine. As he did, Ami stood with Philip and Shayne.

"What happened exactly?" Ami asked, her voice low.

"We're not sure, sir," Philip replied, his voice matching hers. "We were in the warehouse looking for a crate when he came in as if by magic."

Teleportation, Ami thought. Given Blaine's affinity for magic, she wasn't surprised. "What else happened?" she asked.

"He was shivering uncontrollably. He kept vomiting that stuff over there," Shayne murmured, nodding to the smelly puddle on the floor. "He looked like he woke up from his worst nightmare."

"He probably did," Ami muttered.

"Captain, can you come over here, please?" Dr. Elderflower called out.

Ami came to the doctor's side. Blaine's hand immediately reached out to her. Ami grabbed it, noticing how relaxed Blaine became.

"He's suffering from a heavy dose of poppy juice and *pow-wow.* It appears he's been taking it for at least a year," Dr. Elderflower explained.

"That's an interesting combination," Ami commented. It at least confirmed one of her suspicions.

"Sadly, it's commonly sold on the streets in poor city districts. He's going through major withdraws as his body rejected the potions," Dr. Elderflower said.

"What if he was force-fed these potions?" Ami asked.

Dr. Elderflower looked at her sharply. "What are you implying?"

"You're a doctor and a Healer. What is poppy juice used for?" Ami asked.

"It is medicinally used to relax patients who are having panic attacks and insomniacs. However, it is always in small doses," Dr. Elderflower answered.

"What is *pow-wow* used for?" Ami asked.

"Where are you going with this?" Dr. Elderflower asked.

"Please answer the question, Doctor."

Dr. Elderflower frowned. "It is a drug to boost testosterone."

"What are the main side effects?" Ami asked.

"Insomnia, jittery nerves ... No."

"Yes. Combine poppy juice and *pow-wow*; you have the perfect drug to control someone," Ami answered.

"You've seen this before?" Dr. Elderflower asked incredulously.

Ami nodded. "Unfortunately, in Vinci. There are always ladies desperate to snag a rich husband to elevate their social standings."

"Hmmmm. People never learn, do they?" Dr. Elderflower murmured to himself. He opened his potions kit. Pulling out several potions, he instructed, "He will need something on his stomach for all these potions. Only feed him broth, no solids, for at least a week. After that, small portions only and no meat. Once the worst withdrawals subside, he can start eating normal food. These three need to be taken right after he eats today." He handed her three vials that contained bluish liquids.

The doctor continued, "They'll help stabilize his immune system and flush out any remaining residue from the potions. Come to me tomorrow for the next dose. I'll be brewing more tonight. If anything changes, let me know immediately. I'm going to collect samples from the vomit and then return to the hospital. Any questions?"

"No. Thank you for coming, Doctor," Ami said gratefully.

Dr. Elderflower nodded. "I'm doing my job."

The older Werewolf collected numerous samples from the vomit and left. A few minutes later, Benton and the four soldiers returned with arms full of takeout boxes.

"Did you raid the place?" Ami asked.

"Patsy and Howard send their regards," Benton replied. He glanced around. "Where are we eating?"

"Did you get soup?" Ami asked.

Benton nodded. "Give me a sec."

After sifting through the boxes, Benton handed the soup container to Ami. She went to Blaine's side. Blaine was still shivering, although they weren't as violent as before.

"Blaine, you need to sit up for a bit," Ami said softly. She helped him sit up. He slumped against the wall. He struggled to keep his eyes open. Ami took the lid off the container. The smell of chicken broth woke Blaine up. His stomach rumbled loudly. She carefully spoon-fed Blaine, who greedily slurped the broth quickly. Some strength returned to him. He whined impatiently, wanting more broth.

"You don't want to throw up again, do you?" Ami asked, her tone soothing. Blaine grimaced. His ears went flat on his head. He managed to drink half of the soup container. His eyes began to droop sleepily. "Take these before you go to sleep," Ami urged, popping off the top of the first vial.

"No more potions," Blaine slurred.

"Blaine, you can trust me," Ami reassured him.

Blaine looked at her with genuine emotion. "I know."

Making a face with each downed potion, Blaine snuggled deep into the blankets and passed out. Ami almost slumped over in exhaustion.

This is why I never went into the medical field. She thought. Recapping the broth container, she stood on aching legs.

The males sat towards the back of the warehouse. The gang members sat on the left side, and the soldiers on the right. Each group eyed the other with suspicion. Ami made her way to them.

"Here's your food, sir." Rune handed her a takeout container.

Ami glanced around. "Why haven't you eaten?"

The soldiers looked embarrassed. The gang members were unfazed.

"It's not proper for a male to eat before a female," Flander remarked sheepishly.

Ami opened her mouth but shut it. She was too hungry to argue. Opening the container, she was greeted with a roast beef sandwich with white cheddar on homemade bread. The two sides were coleslaw and cheesy macaroni. Ami dug into her meal. The various pops of containers being opened echoed softly in the warehouse as the males ate their meal with her.

Ami swallowed a bite. "Rune, what did you get?"

"It's called a club sandwich. Howard had us test it a few weeks back, and it's becoming really popular. It's got turkey, chicken, two different cheeses, lettuce, and tomato. You want a bite?" Rune explained.

Ami shook her head. "No, I'll ask for it when I see them next. I was just curious." Looking at the soldiers, she asked, "How are your meals?"

"Very good, sir," they murmured, their mouths full.

Ami hummed in pleasure. She missed Patsy and Howard's cooking. She briefly wondered if Patsy was still making her tomato soup. The elderly Elf made it almost exactly like Gramps did, and Ami wanted to know how to make it.

"Who is he?" Uriah asked, glancing at where Blaine lay.

Ami chewed her food thoughtfully. When she thought of an answer, she swallowed. "He's my ex."

"Your what?" Ados asked.

"My ex. We courted for over a year," Ami replied, her tone short. She hoped her tone would tell them that she did not want to talk about it.

"How did he become your ex?" Flander asked curiously.

"I died," Ami answered.

All the males flinched. Ami took a large bite of her sandwich, hoping it would dissuade any additional questions. The problem was now the food tasted bitter. She forced herself to finish her meal. The taste improved when she ate the cheesy macaroni. After everyone finished eating, Philip and

Ados gathered the empty containers and left the warehouse to dispose of them. Shayne subtly signaled Ami over to a private corner. The Werewolf glanced over at where the sleeping Blaine lay.

"What's the plan with Blaine?" Shayne asked quietly.

Ami stared at the wall, thinking. Blaine wouldn't be welcomed back in the Winter and Spring districts, especially since the gang members vehemently opposed his presence. However, Blaine needed to recover his strength to deal with whatever his possessed self did over in the Summer and Autumn districts. She didn't want him to relive such an ordeal. No one deserved that.

"He will stay here until he recovers," Ami replied finally. She raised a hand when Shayne opened his mouth. "He is not becoming your boss or mine. Once he recovers, he will be returned to his side of the city."

"What if he wants to court you again?" Shayne asked.

"It won't come to that," Ami reassured him. Shayne didn't look convinced. "Why don't you believe me?" she asked.

Shayne looked away. "Blaine can be very charming."

"Charm doesn't equal trust, and he has much to acquire for me to consider him my acquaintance again," Ami said bitterly. Just the thought of Blaine being her friend made her heart ache and a small fire light up in her stomach. "I don't feel the same way about him anymore. I'm not the same silly female I was two and half years ago."

"You were never silly," Shayne said quickly.

"I was with my heart," Ami said, giving him a sad smile. "If I do court someone, it won't be Blaine."

Shayne seemed appeased by her words. "Are you going to the Inner City?"

Ami nodded. "I must hand in my reports to General Mason and explain what happened."

"Are you able to tell us?" Shayne asked.

"I don't see why not. I'll try to come for dinner," Ami said.

Shayne grinned. *He's getting quite handsome,* she thought. All her lads were getting good-looking as puberty hit them like a barreling skell. *I'm going to have to shove the females off of them soon.*

"Sir?" Shayne asked.

"Hmm?"

"Are you okay?" Shayne asked. "You seem troubled."

"I just realized how handsome you lads are," Ami stated. She saw Shayne's blush and felt the others through the Bond. "I will have to shove the females away from you if I don't keep watch."

"You ... think I'm handsome?" Shayne asked, still blushing.

"Yes," Ami answered. Realizing the time, she said, "We have to go."

The gang members said their goodbyes. The four soldiers quietly followed her out of the warehouse. It wasn't until they were back on the main road that they barraged her with questions.

"Who are they really, sir?" Uriah asked.

"Why are they so casual with you?" Flander asked.

"What do they want from you?" James demanded.

"How do you tolerate them?" Ados complained.

"*Ta-bo,* you are nosy," Ami commented teasingly. Glancing over her shoulder, the males were giving her unconvinced looks. "I met them when I roamed the streets at night. I taught them how to get food and asked some locals to let them work for them," Ami said carefully.

"What do you get from them?" James asked.

Ami paused at the question. The way James asked seemed like it was normal. "I get their friendship, and they get mine. What else would I get?" Ami asked.

"No, that's not what I meant," James clarified. "What deal did they make with you in exchange for you teaching them Rascal ways?"

Ami shrugged. "Nothing."

"What do you mean nothing?" James asked incredulously.

Ami chuckled. "Just because I'm female doesn't mean every male that comes in contact with me has to have some kind of political clout or that I intend to use them for whatever I deem necessary. They are my friends, not my servants nor indebted to me."

That appeared to suck the argumentative winds out of James' sails. The Elf looked troubled as he processed Ami's words.

"Is that why they're so casual with you?" Flander asked.

"I suppose so."

Ados and Uriah remained silent. What she really wanted was to get in her bed and not leave it for three days. That idea had her picking up her pace. If the males noticed it, they didn't comment. When they reached the Inner City, the passing Knights greeted Ami warmly. Ami greeted them back.

"Sir, how are you on such friendly terms with the Knights?" Uriah asked nervously.

"I was their training master," Ami answered.

Unbeknownst to her, the males visibly gulped. The Werewolf guards at the Iron Gate smiled at her as they approached. One whistled the gates open. Ami nodded at them as they entered the Common Grounds. Stan, Michael, and a large group of Knights greeted her halfway to the mansion.

"Captain, are you well? We heard you were injured," Stan asked worriedly.

"I'm fine. As much time as I spend in the hospital wing, I should start learning how to heal while I'm there," Ami said jokingly.

The Knights chuckled.

"General Mason is waiting for your briefing. We'll see you later, Captain," Michael said.

"Thank you. I'll see you later," Ami smiled.

They entered the mansion. Three Dragons were cleaning the foyer. They started to greet Ami, but stared at her in shock.

Reshmi was right about Dragons not typically having breasts. Mom's clan must be the exception. Ami thought.

They went up the stairs to Mason's office. His door was open. The Werewolf was reading several documents. Ami knocked on the door. Mason's head shot up.

"Captain, welcome back," Mason greeted her somewhat warmly. Ami hoped he was warming up to her.

"Greetings, General Mason," Ami returned the greeting. When all five entered, they saluted.

Mason gave Flander a narrowed look. "I don't remember signing off a Centaur as part of your cover." Seeing them still saluting, he ordered, "At ease, all of you."

"Soldier Flander told me that he was assigned to my cover by General Rikardi," Ami stated.

Mason's narrowed look turned into a glare. "Did you ask him to give you a Centaur as part of your cover?"

"No, sir," Ami answered honestly.

Mason stared at her as if determining her truthfulness. With a sigh, he leaned back into his chair. "What happened in the village, and why did it take six months to investigate?"

Ami explained everything she and the males discovered, including the Wraith. Mason listened intently, his ears going up and down with his emotions. When she finished, she reached into her yellow knapsack for her reports. She handed Mason a large stack of paper. Mason took it.

"If I read as many fiction novels as I did your writing, I'd be more culturally literate," Mason said with a smirk.

Ami gave a small smile. "I know of several, if you're interested."

Mason shook his head. "No, thanks. You give me plenty to read. I'll call you when I get done. Dismissed."

They saluted and left the mansion. Ami noticed how the Dragons avoided them. She wondered what was going on.

I'll ask later. I'm too tired right now, she thought tiredly.

"Where are we staying?" James asked. They were walking through the gardens.

"With the Knights," Ami answered.

"What about you, sir?" Flander asked.

"I have a room there."

"Why?"

"Because some males thought it was a good idea to dis-obey and harm their superior officer," Stan said, sneaking up beside them.

All four males jumped. Ami smiled.

"How are your sons, Stan?" Ami asked.

"Oh, rowdy as always," Stan said proudly. He walked beside her. "They drive my wife nuts, but she wouldn't have it any other way."

"How old are they again?" Ami asked.

"Jola is almost eight, and Piers is six," Stan replied.

Ami was amazed. How are they growing up so fast? Granted, she had never met them, but Stan had told her numerous stories about when he had gone home on leave. The two chatted all the way to the Knights' Quarters. Once there, the other Knights swarmed Ami and her soldiers, dragging them into several literature debates. Ami watched in amusement as Uriah defended an unpopular poet named Pilot Highland. The poet was notorious for writing sappy, sometimes obsessive love poems with dark tones.

Uriah apparently enjoyed the poet's works and didn't like how Black called Highland "a pathetic excuse of a male that couldn't talk to a brass knob because even it would be repulsed." When that debate died down, Ami discussed with a Knight and Flander about Timmon's first play, *The Bard That Couldn't Sing*. They discussed their favorite characters and favorite scenes.

Before she knew it, the Knights were getting ready to switch to the night shift. She coordinated with the Knights and helped set up temporary cots for the four males. Their cots were near the back of the quarters, several rows from Ami's room. Telling everyone good night, Ami went into her room. Without changing clothes, she plopped on the covers and slept.

Blejan hummed as she carried a tray filled with pastries and tea for the Centaur general. Ever since Angel left the capital on her mission, Rikardi had been working non-stop on the never-ending pile of reports and letters, rarely leaving his office before midnight and in it before dawn. She had a feeling Angel was the general's only true friend. She never heard Lee or Mason express concern over Rikardi. Tso's office was heavily warded against the Dragons, not trusting them with whatever secrets they might uncover and tell their master. Blejan continued to hum as she entered the general's office. His desk was a papered mess. Dark circles were forming under the Centaur's green eyes. He looked like he had aged a decade in the past six months.

Angel's absence is weighing heavily on him. Blejan thought sadly. *Good thing I have news to cheer him up.*

"Sir?" Blejan called out.

Rikardi looked up at her with a tired glare. Before, the young Dragon would have recoiled at the look. After interacting with him more with Angel, she wasn't scared of him anymore. She set the tray on the stand next to the desk.

"What?" Rikardi grunted.

Blejan smiled. "Angel has returned."

Rikardi's eyes widened. A light she could only describe as joy entered his green eyes, almost making them glow.

"When?" Rikardi asked, his tone more civil.

"Two days ago. Have you heard about her condition?" Blejan asked carefully.

"What condition?" Rikardi demanded, his tone hard.

"She was struck by purple lightning," Blejan said.

Rikardi was on his feet in a flash, storming out of his office. Blejan ran after him, calling for him to stop. The Centaur was faster than she anticipated. She was out of breath when she reached the Knight's Quarters. Rikardi was already inside.

"What is this I hear of you being struck by lightning?" Rikardi's voice was oddly soft when Blejan approached Angel's room.

Blejan barely stopped a gasp from leaving her lips. Angel's left horn had somehow regrown during her mission. It was black onyx and glowed amethyst in the barn-like structure. Her pale skin was beautifully paired with her protruding purple veins. As Angel shook her head, Blejan noticed beautiful white scales encompassing her hairline. It was unnoticeable to other People but apparent to Dragons.

Then there were her breasts. They were evident underneath the tight purple tunic Angel wore. While it was typical for Dragons not to have them, it wasn't unheard of. Blejan remembered stories her parents told her of Dragons with milk glands. They were highly prized and sought after by the royal family. She knew there was a reason, but the answer wouldn't come to her. She was too busy staring at Angel. In conclusion, Angel was the personification of beauty for Dragons. Tears gathered in her eyes as she gazed at her friend with admiration. Angel seemed to take her tears for something else.

"Blejan, I know it's shocking ..." Angel trailed off.

"You're so beautiful," Blejan gushed.

Angel did not expect that kind of reaction. Her gaping mouth was proof. Shaking her head, she turned her attention to Rikardi. "It happened when we left the dome. I had a severe dizzy spell, and then I was struck," Angel explained.

"Do you remember being struck?" Rikardi asked.

Angel shook her head. "No. All I remember was my color vision going purple and gray before blacking out."

Purple and gray? Blejan thought in alarm. *That would mean ... That's interesting. I wonder if the Eldest is aware.*

"That is odd," Rikardi said with a deep frown.

Angel stared at Rikardi. "You're not sleeping in your office again, are you?"

"We're talking about you, not me," Rikardi said defensively.

"I hate talking about me," Angel retorted. To Blejan, she asked, "Has he been sleeping in his office again?"

"No, Angel," Blejan confirmed. Rikardi smirked. Mischievously, she added, "But he has been working until midnight and coming in before dawn. The only reason he isn't bone and skin is because I've been forcing him to eat pastries and drink tea."

Angel gave the Centaur a disappointed look. Rikardi blushed in embarrassment. He glared at Blejan for her betrayal. Blejan smiled innocently at him.

"Sir, I believe you've earned a well-deserved nap," Angel said in a tone that sounded like an order.

"I believe I am of higher rank here," Rikardi pointed out.

"I'm not ordering in a military sense," Angel replied smoothly. "I'm ordering as a concerned friend."

That left the Centaur gobsmacked. Blejan felt warmth as she watched the Centaur stumble over his words of thanks. The two females watched the Centaur leave the Knight's Quarters. When Rikardi was out of sight, Angel slumped against the doorframe of her room.

"Angel?" Blejan asked. The white-haired Dragon looked defeated.

Angel huffed. "You probably shouldn't talk to me. Reshmi won't like that."

"What did that worthless bag of sewing material say or do this time?" Blejan hissed.

Her opinion of the elder had plummeted due to the rumors rotating in the kitchens over the past year. Blejan couldn't help but listen to the ridiculous rules the elder was trying to impose on them. Blejan stopped paying attention after the tenth stupid rule, which forbade them from talking to non-Dragons. There was no way she was obeying that rule. Angel gave her a lopsided grin. Blejan loved that smile. It meant Angel was trying not to laugh boisterously.

"Come inside," Angel offered.

Blejan entered the room, looking around curiously. It was her first time in this room since Angel moved in. She wondered who was assigned to clean it.

Angel shut the door. "You may want to sit down for this."

Blejan sat on the bed. "What happened?"

"Well, you noticed these, right?" Angel asked, pointing to her chest.

"Yes. What about them?" Blejan asked, not sure where this was going.

"Reshmi declared that because I have breasts, I am a halfling—" Angel started.

"That ignorant, useless assortment of scales!" Blejan bellowed, rising to her feet.

Angel looked surprised. "I've been called many cruel things, Blejan. This isn't the first nor the last," Angel said in a dark tone.

"No, you don't get it, Angel," Blejan insisted. She took a few heated breaths and explained, "To be called a halfling by an elder is a declaration of exile. That she exiled you because you have milk glands is the stupidest thing I've ever heard in Dragon history."

Angel grew interested. "So, have there been Dragons with breasts before?"

"Of course there have," Blejan huffed. "They are highly sought after by the royal family for some reason. I can't remember why, but it is not completely unusual."

Angel significantly relaxed when she said this. Blejan couldn't imagine what mental anguish Reshmi's comments put Angel under.

When I get my claws into her throat ... Blejan thought darkly.

"What else did she say?"

Angel grimaced. "All the Dragons in the capital are ordered not to serve me either food or clothing."

Fury lit up in Blejan's blood. A deep growl emerged from her chest. It took all her willpower not to march to the sewing room at that moment to challenge Reshmi to an honor duel.

This is how we treat a free Dragon? Blejan asked herself angrily. *No, I refuse to obey such an order. Reshmi can try all she likes, but I refuse to obey a scale-turner like her.*

With that conviction, her anger slowly calmed. It didn't completely go away. It slowed to low-burning coals, waiting for more fuel to heat up again.

"I'm sorry you had to go through that, Angel," Blejan said sincerely. "You don't deserve to be treated like that by them."

Angel shrugged like it was normal. "Sadly, I'm used to it."

"Can you do me a favor?" Blejan asked.

"Possibly."

"Please don't let this color your view on the other Dragons," Blejan pleaded. At Angel's frown, she continued, "Reshmi only has control and influence over the Dragons in the capital, not anywhere else."

"And you," Angel pointed out with a sad smile.

Blejan scoffed. "I'd like to see her try to control me."

Angel chuckled at Blejan's defiance. "I'm glad you know the meaning of loyalty, Blejan. It's a rare commodity these days," Angel said.

"You also have your Knights and the Centaur general," Blejan pointed out.

Angel gave her a genuine smile this time. "You're an awesome friend, Blejan."

Blejan felt warmth fill her chest at the declaration. It buckled her knees, making her sit on the bed again. Tears filled her eyes and soon fell down her cheeks. No one had ever called her a friend before, much less an awesome one. She was always Bleddyn's little sister or someone who helped in the kitchens.

The feeling was overwhelming. Angel came to her side and rubbed her back as Blejan fruitlessly tried to wipe her tears.

"I'm sorry," Blejan said wetly.

"It's okay. I didn't mean to make you cry," Angel said with humor. Blejan was glad Angel wasn't offended.

A knock interrupted the moment. Angel got up and answered. Blejan wiped her face with the bottom of her shirt.

"Who's the male with you?" asked a burly Werewolf.

"Her name is Blejan, and she's a Dragon," Angel replied coldly. "And why is it any of your business?" Blejan couldn't see it, but she imagined the Werewolf was blushing. Angel had that effect on People. "Why are you here?" Angel asked.

"We were ... We were wondering if you could show us around Talient," the Werewolf asked shyly.

"And you can't explore on your own why?" Angel asked, unamused.

"*Ta-bo*, Uriah, you suck at this," another male voice murmured in frustration. "Sir, we wish to spend time with you outside the Inner City."

Angel seemed speechless. Blejan couldn't blame her. Not even the Knights spent time with her in a non-professional manner. Blejan concluded it could be because most of them were married, and it wouldn't be proper for a married male to hang out with a single female outside of business.

"All right. I'm in the mood for coffee anyway," Angel said. Turning to Blejan, she said, "Are you okay?"

Blejan smiled. "Yes, Angel. I am." Ideas began to swirl in her head. Saying goodbye, Angel left with the males outside. Blejan had to stop herself from cackling madly. Getting up, she struggled to keep a calm face as she went back to the mansion.

CHAPTER 14

The café was busy when they arrived. Ami and her soldiers stared in amazement at the line that exited the glass door and continued along the side of the building.

"I didn't realize it would be so swamped," Ami said in awe.

"Is it usually?" Ados asked.

Ami shook her head. "No, while it gets a good amount of business, I've never seen anything like this."

She then noticed that the line seemed to be specifically for the bar. She broke out of the line and used the other glass door to enter. Chastity was writing down orders on cups the customers at the bar brought, placing them in the back two at a time, picking up two more while announcing the order was done, and then returning to the bar to take more orders. The overwhelmed Elf barely greeted Ami as she continued her never-ending task. Ami glanced around and noticed that the booths were entirely filled, but no one was taking their order. The couch and loveseat area was a mess. Where were Logan and Shayne?

"Ma'am, can you see what the holdup is? We've been waiting for over ten minutes for someone to take our drink order," one of the patrons in the booths asked in slight irritation.

"I will. Please give me a moment." Ami nodded.

She went to the hallway next to the bar and glanced in from the alternate kitchen entrance. Logan and Shayne were desperately trying to keep up with the coffee. Shayne was making three pots at once while Logan did his magic. The dishes were piled, and Logan was about to run out of measuring utensils. Coming up with a game plan, she grabbed Leandra's waitress apron, put it on, and took a spare notepad and pen.

"Lakeshore, Fallenleaf, get over here," Ami barked. She barked out more orders when they appeared, "Lakeshore, assist Logan in making coffee. Fallenleaf, get on those dishes. Tell Shayne that I said to fire up the grill. Go through here." She pointed to the alternate kitchen door.

She continued to give orders as Uriah and Ados entered the kitchens. "Atorra, assist Chastity in gathering orders behind the bar. Flander, start cleaning the couch and loveseat area. Cleaning stuff is in the hallway."

"What are you going to do, Captain?" James asked.

"I'll be waitressing." Ami grinned.

The next three hours were a mindless rush. When Ami's side was slow, she went into the back to help dry and stack dishes. Flander soon minded the bar and took orders from the barstool patrons while Ami managed the booths and the hangout area. Finally, everyone left. The café felt oddly empty. Before Ami could say anything, Chastity hugged her tightly.

"You are truly a blessing, little flower," Chastity said gratefully.

"It's no problem," Ami said tiredly.

They took their time cleaning up, no longer pressured by patrons. Chastity took over the grill and Logan started to make coffee for everyone. Uriah, Ados, and James finished the remaining dirty dishes quickly. Flander put the hangout area back together while Ami finished up the booths. They all convened at the bar. Chastity and Shayne came out with steaming plates of food. Shayne handed Ami hers first. It was hamburger steak with white gravy, mashed potatoes, green beans, cheesy broccoli, and garlic bread.

"Thank you, handsome," Ami smirked.

Shayne blushed. "You're welcome," he shyly whispered.

Shayne is really cute when he blushes, Ami thought. It made her heart beat a little faster.

"Hey, aren't I handsome?" Logan protested, hands on his hips dramatically.

"Yes, you are," Ami said.

Logan blushed darkly. He quickly excused himself to the back. The soldiers received the same, except Flander. Instead of hamburger steak, he had larger servings of each side. Ami dug into her food. When they finished, Shayne gathered their plates as Logan gave them fresh coffee. Ami sipped on hers, savoring the raspberry and chocolate flavor. The soldiers appeared surprised and delighted by the flavors Logan created.

"Who makes the coffee?" Uriah asked.

"Logan does," Ami answered.

"He's good," Uriah commented. Ami was surprised. Uriah didn't give out compliments.

They sat and chatted for about an hour. Before they left, Shayne pulled Ami into the hallway, looking severe.

"What's going on?" she asked.

Shayne pulled a black envelope from his back pocket. Ami recognized it.

"The Blackhill messenger insisted you received this invitation when I told him you were back in town. The party is tonight," Shayne whispered.

"Thank you." Ami placed the envelope in her pocket. "How's Blaine?"

Shayne grimaced. "Still shivering and throwing up. It's gotten better today. Rune is watching him. He keeps asking for you."

Ami shrugged. "I'll try to see him tomorrow."

Shayne didn't seem happy about that. "Sir, when can he leave?"

"Shayne," Ami said strictly, "he has to recover first. If we drop him off on the other side of the city, the same thing will happen, and it'll be much worse. Do you want him to randomly pop in and vomit everywhere?"

The young Werewolf looked ashamed. "I see your point."

Ami placed a hand on his shoulder. "I know it's hard. I'll see if Dr. Elderflower has any potions to speed up the process, okay?"

That perked Shayne up. "That would be great."

"We're going to head out. Let me know if you need anything," Ami said.

"Will do, boss."

The soldiers chatted amicably on their way back to the Common Grounds. Ami's mind returned to the Blackhill envelope, metaphorically burning in her pocket. She wondered if Sable, Mark, and Priscilla would be there. Even though they were annoying for the most part, they were entertaining. Ami's heart pumped faster when she thought of Viovel.

How will he react to seeing me after six months? Will he greet me as a friend or a guest at his mother's party? Ami thought. He was handsome, and she enjoyed seeing his reactions when she did something out of the Rascal norm.

"Captain?" Ados interrupted her thoughts.

"Yes?" Ami answered. Glancing around, they were in the Common Grounds near the gardens.

"What are you thinking about?" Flander asked boldly.

"About the party I'm going to tonight," Ami replied.

"Oh? What are we wearing?" Ados asked excitedly.

"Is there a theme?" Uriah asked.

"That'll depend on the family—" James answered.

"And their social circles," Flander added.

"No." The word silenced the males and stopped them in their tracks. Ami faced them with a stern look.

"Captain?" Ados asked uncertainly.

"I'm going to a party. This is not a group assignment. This

is politics," Ami stated. "You will stay at the Knight's Quarters."

"What will we do while you're gone?" James asked. The males were looking at her with lost expressions.

"You can talk and debate with the Knights about various pieces of literature. You can run laps around the Common Grounds if you're feeling energetic. Or you can lay in your cots and gossip like females. I don't care," Ami listed off. She resumed walking.

Uneasiness radiated off the males as they followed her to the Knight's Quarters. Ami greeted the Knights in the large dorm. She went to her room and closed the door.

Now, what to wear ... Ami pondered as she looked at her meager wardrobe. All she had was the black and pink suit and the black and purple suit. She chose the purple one since she wore the pink one last time. *I'll need to get with Shayne to see if more hidden crates exist.* The clothing magically fit her perfectly, even with her new breasts.

Unfortunately, her eye patch had that pink piece of fabric. Using her claws carefully, she tediously unsewed the threads holding the pink fabric in. Thankfully, it was an added piece and not the main fabric of the patch. Pleased to see the remaining material was black, she finished her outfit. Summoning a mirror, she admired how the clothing cleverly hid her female figure. She then fixed her hair with the gel Perry gave her. She liked how fast her hair was growing. She couldn't wait until it was to her chin again.

Several firm knocks came from her door. Ami checked her internal clock. She still had time before making her way to the Blackhill party. Waving the mirror gone, she opened the door. Her four soldiers stared at her in astonishment. Ami inwardly sighed. When are they going to leave her alone?

"Sir?" James asked.

"Yes?" Ami answered sarcastically.

"Why are you dressed like that?" Uriah asked, eyeing her critically.

"Do you enjoy corsets?" Ami asked.

The males looked at each other.

"Um, no?" Ados answered.

"Neither do I. What do you want?" Ami demanded.

They started to act nervous. Frustration began to creep up Ami's back and into her shoulders.

"What are you four doing?" Michael barked. They backed away. The older Werewolf saw Ami. "Hello, Captain. Another party?"

"Yes, I need to get going." Ami nodded.

"Do they obey orders?" Michael asked, side glaring at the four males.

"So far, they have," Ami said. "They have diverse tastes in literature. The debates tonight should be interesting."

Michael grinned. "We'll be sure to include them, Captain. Have fun."

"Like swimming in a pool of bloodthirsty sharks is fun." Ami made a face. Michael chuckled.

Saying her farewell, she left the Inner City. The Blackhill party was at the same house. Strangely, the house didn't appear intimidating like last time. Instead, it projected strictness like a prison.

I wonder if that's why Viovel is in the military, Ami thought as she showed her envelope to the entrance guards. After a flash of magic, she was granted entry. She entered the main hall and waited in line to be announced.

"Please welcome Lord Sieghild." The announcer's voice traveled through the hall effortlessly.

Unlike last time, she was immediately swarmed by Sable, Priscilla, and Mark.

"My lord, we have missed you," Sable said with a wide grin, swiftly latching onto Ami's left arm. Ami was pleased to see both females had toned down their makeup.

"Indeed, we have missed your presence. The dancing hasn't been the same," Priscilla added, latching onto Ami's other arm.

"My apologies, Lord Tremors. I seemed to have collected the ladies on each arm," Ami said with a half-smile.

Mark gave him a grin. "I am glad they are there to deter others who have been eyeing you from afar."

"Oh?" Ami wasn't used to that type of attention, especially from females. Females tended to scorn or make disgusted faces whenever they were in her presence on such occasions.

"Where have you been, my lord?" Sable asked.

"I've been out of town on business," Ami replied.

"Oh, my ... What happened to your hand?" Priscilla cried, staring at the purple veins visible on the top of Ami's hand.

"It's on your neck too. That wasn't there before," Sable pointed out.

"Did something happen on your trip, my lord?" Mark asked.

Ami glanced at each of them. They each had a genuine look of concern on their faces. But she knew how good actors and actresses Nobles were. However, honesty was the best policy in this instance.

"I was struck by purple lightning on my journey back," Ami said truthfully. Luckily, or unluckily, there were eight other purple lightning strikes around Rascu. She didn't know if anyone else survived like she did.

The three gasped in horror.

"And these ..." Sable trailed off, staring at her left hand.

"Are the results of the strike. I was lucky to survive," Ami admitted.

"That had to be terrifying," Sable said with sympathetic eyes.

"And painful." Priscilla winced.

A savory aroma filled the air. Ami's stomach growled.

"It appears they opened the food bar at a decent time. Let's get something to eat," Ami suggested.

The two females didn't release her arms until they reached the food bar. The food presented was more like a buffet meal instead of finger foods. Servers, a mixer of male and female

Elves, expertly served them portions of their requests. Ami gathered a full plate, while Sable and Priscilla had only two items.

"Ladies, there is no reason to starve yourself. I urge you to get another two servings," Ami said.

The two frowned.

"It is unsightly for a female to gorge herself on food," Sable muttered. Ami heard her anyway.

"Think about it this way: you're gathering energy for tonight's dancing. You'll easily burn whatever calories you consume. Also, you should enjoy the food. That's what it's there for," Ami argued.

The two females looked uncertain for a moment before taking Ami's advice. Ami was pleased they added meat to their plates. The four found a table to sit near the middle of the hall. Mark and Ami gathered drinks for the ladies and themselves. As they ate, the three young Nobles shared the latest gossip. Ami listened attentively for anything about the forts or what the Nobles thought about the bandit situation.

A musical laugh distracted Ami for a moment. She turned her head slightly, listening for it again. It was familiar, but she didn't know how. When she didn't hear it again, she shrugged it off. After eating, the two females excused themselves to use the bathroom.

"How is traversing the blood-soaked waters of the nobility, Mark?" Ami asked. During dinner, Ami noticed how tense the young lord was as he ate.

Mark shivered. "Far worse than I imagined."

Ami tilted her head. "Not all riches and power?"

"My mother seems to fall under that delusion," Mark grumbled. "She sends me to these parties thinking I have a chance of a higher ranking Noble to notice me and welcome me into the family."

"What does your family do?" Ami asked.

"Currently, my mother runs a little boutique in the Winter

District. It doesn't get a lot of business or interest from any Nobles. Most of the time, she is discouraging riffraff from throwing trash in front of her shop," Mark explained sadly.

Ami made a note to visit the shop.

"Hopefully, something will come out of this party to help you and your family," Ami said encouragingly.

"The only good thing here is you, my lord." Mark chuckled darkly.

"Don't let your hostess hear that," Ami warned.

Mark seemed to realize what he had said and hung his head. "My apologies."

"You have to be careful about what you say, especially when you're in the den of vipers," Ami advised.

"Thank you for your advice, my lord," Mark said gratefully.

The musical laugh reached Ami's ears again. She glanced around, trying to identify the source.

"Is something wrong?" Mark asked.

"I keep hearing a familiar voice, but I can't figure out who—" Ami started and stopped when she saw the source.

The image of wildflowers and sunshine on a warm spring afternoon filled her mind as she watched the one Person she had thought she would never see again. In the middle of a crowd of flirting males was Leila. She wore a navy blue fitted dress that outlined her full hourglass shape. Her navy-colored hair was pulled back in a loose ponytail full of playful curls. Ami was still over a head taller than the Werecat. Even with her heels, the top of her head reached Ami's shoulders. Mark was saying something, but she couldn't hear as she stood in shock at the sight of her first friend. Reality brought her back. She walked up to the group.

"Leila?" Ami called out.

Leila turned, her deep blue eyes confused when they met Ami's single amethyst. Despair began to fill Ami's chest. Then a light of realization hit Leila, making her gasp.

"Bestie?!" Leila exclaimed. Realizing where she was, she quickly excused herself and dragged Ami to the other side of the hall.

Ami let her, still shocked that Leila remembered her. Leila glanced around, trying to find some privacy. Their spot was good as it gave them a view of the hall without being snuck upon. Ami waved a hand. A light purple dome surrounded them.

"Privacy spell," Ami clarified when she saw Leila's confused face. The next thing she knew, the two females hugged each other fiercely. She wasn't sure who started crying, but soon they both were.

"Leila, I've missed you," Ami sobbed on the Werecat's shoulder.

"I've missed you too, bestie." Leila's reply was muffled in her shoulder.

When Ami pulled away, a stream of questions babbled out of her mouth. "How are you here? Where are your parents? Did you get my letters? Why are you here? What happened?"

"Whoa, bestie. One question at a time." Leila wiped her eyes and cheeks. "Okay, um, there have been a lot of things happening in Roy that I couldn't tell you about. Remember when we first met? I said my parents were there on business?"

"Yes." Ami nodded.

"Well, I didn't know this at the time, but my parents were scouting for a new house. So, back in Roy, before we visited Rascu, my parents were put under government surveillance. For some reason, they thought my dad was involved in this radical political group that opposed the government. He wasn't, but they still watched us. Which is really creepy when I think about it," Leila explained.

"When did you come here?" Ami asked.

"Let's see ..." Leila thought for a bit. Her eyes were distant as she went through her memories. "We got here about three weeks ago. I kinda became aware a little after we got back from Rascu. I started to notice certain People watching us. My parents had been slowly saving up money and sending over possessions so we wouldn't raise suspicions. They were strict about me telling anyone, and that's why I couldn't say it in my letters. Came to find out that the government was reading our letters too.

"About four months ago, my parents decided it was time to leave for good. We had to travel south to Port Hynio, where my uncle owned a shipping business. My uncle snuck us in his ship, and we arrived over a week later. We just got settled in when my parents felt safe enough for me to come to this party," Leila finished.

"Wow, that's ... terrifying," Ami managed to say.

"Yeah, tell me about it," Leila said with a shiver. "It's a good thing we left when we did because after we came here, we learned that a military coup happened and took over the government."

"Was it part of that political organization?" Ami asked.

Leila shook her head. "It came out of left field. No one suspected the military would take over like it did. I'm surprised Lakola is now the leader."

"Lakola?"

"Oh, he was a prominent war hero during the Jungle Wars several years ago. He was a colonel, I think, until he led the coup," Leila explained.

"Did you know him?" Ami asked.

"Not personally. I only met him a few times at different parties my parents hosted whenever they completed a historical restoration. He was decent, nice to me at least, but stiff," Leila said.

"Huh." Ami tried to absorb all the information Leila shared just now. That was a lot to deal with. No wonder their letters were scattered.

"Now to you," Leila stated, giving her a stern face. "Why are you wearing an eye patch? What's with the purple veins? Why is your hair so short? Did those cadet guys do something to you? Cuz if they did, I'm gonna go beat them up. Do you have a boyfriend yet? Is the café still around?"

Ami chuckled. "A lot has happened since our last letters."

She explained everything, from her promotion to Warehouse Guardian to the illegal mage. She spared the details of the Shadow Realm. She lifted her eye patch, showing the burn scar stretching over her face's left side. She told brief descriptions about Putra Hallas and the witch. The names of the People involved were excluded. Ami only gave their titles. She told her of being struck by lightning. Leila started to cry again.

"I'm never leaving you again," Leila sobbed.

"It's not your fault, Leila," Ami tried to console the Werecat.

Leila wiped her cheeks and eyes again. "Great, now my makeup is ruined."

"Do you have any to reapply?" Ami asked.

"Yeah, but I don't think it'll do anything different." Leila sniffed. "Do you know where a mirror is?"

Ami waved her hand. A full-length mirror appeared. Leila jumped, hissing.

"Warn me next time," Leila huffed. She immediately started to reapply her makeup from a bag. Ami had no idea where it came from. Maybe it was a form of Leila's magic?

"Thanks, bestie," Leila said, putting the last makeup in her bag. She hid it behind her back. When her hand reappeared, the bag was gone. Ami was convinced. With a wave, the mirror disappeared.

"I think I need a drink," Ami said.

"Me too. I feel like we both talked forever," Leila agreed.

The privacy dome went away as soon as they exited it. Leila was at Ami's side, hugging her arm as she used to when they walked Talient together before. Warmth flooded Ami's heart. The hole in her heart began to heal.

"My lord!" Several voices called out.

Sable, Priscilla, and Mark walked up to her. Sable and Priscilla glanced at Leila before turning pleading eyes to Ami.

"My lord, we wish to dance with you, but the conductor doesn't know the song you played before," Sable said, batting her eyelashes.

"My lord?" Leila asked, looking at Ami with a raised eyebrow.

"You don't know who this is?" Priscilla asked, scandalized.

"This is Lord Sieghild. He is well-known amongst the Nobles for his dancing," Mark explained.

"Really?" Leila asked, getting a sly look. "I may have to test you on that, my lord."

Ami grinned back. "I look forward to the challenge."

"Lord Sieghild," a familiar voice said from behind her. Viovel walked up to her. Ami's heart started to race. Viovel was dressed in black and silver. An amethyst brooch adorned his left breast. The feral thought of ripping his shirt open while kissing him flashed through Ami's mind. She forced the thought away. Now was not the time.

"Viovel, thank you for the invite," Ami said, disconnecting herself from Leila. They shook hands.

Viovel stared deep into her eye. "I'm glad you're here. How's business?"

"Busy and painful," Ami said.

Viovel's eyes widened when he noticed her veins. "Will you share the story later?"

"I will."

"Thank you," Viovel nodded. Looking to his left, he said, "This is Doran Flagstaff."

A tall orange Werefox stood beside the Blackhill heir. He was dressed in a gray suit with blue accents. It wasn't made of delicate material like Viovel's suit, but it wasn't cheap either.

"Well met, Lord Flagstaff." Ami extended her left hand. Doran took it. His grip was firm. When her hand was released, she gestured to Leila. "This is Leila Moonbeam."

Leila curtseyed perfectly. "Greetings, gentlemen."

The two males awkwardly greeted her back, not used to such courtesy.

"Viovel has told me about this dance you invented on the spot at the last party," Doran spoke, his voice curious.

Ami chuckled. "I think a few party attendees are eager to start dancing as well." She turned to Leila. "Leila, will you accompany me?"

"Gladly, bestie," Leila said a little too eagerly. Grabbing her arm and at her side closely, the two walked towards the orchestra. "Girl, that chocolate Pulutra has his eyes on you," Leila said in a conspiratorial whisper.

"Pulutra?" Ami asked.

"He's an ancient god in Royian mythology renowned for his beauty. He also was the god of sex and the arts," Leila explained.

"And Viovel resembles him?" Ami asked.

"Using his name as I did is saying something for one's looks," Leila said. "You're more like Pulutressa, his twin sister."

"One moment," Ami said.

The conductor this evening was a female Werefox. Her coloring was like Theo's: Black with tuffs of reddish-blond fur around her ears and hands. Leila squealed when she saw her.

"Mrs. Van Gogh!" Leila called out.

"Leila, my goodness! I'm so glad you made it out safe," Mrs. Van Gogh replied. The two females hugged each other.

"Any relation to Theo van Gogh?" Ami asked when they parted.

"Yes, he's my son," Mrs. Van Gogh replied proudly.

"He's an excellent Healer," Ami commented.

"Oh, good. I'm glad Theo finally found his niche. Has he made friends?" Mrs. Van Gogh asked.

"I am not sure. I've only seen him in a professional setting," Ami said carefully.

"Please be his friend," Mrs. Van Gogh pleaded. "He's been a loner for a long time and needs friends."

"We'll see," Ami said. "I was wondering if you could play a song for us?"

Mrs. Van Gogh frowned. "I can't play any music until the lady of the house makes her announcement."

"I understand. Thank you," Ami said.

"I'm going to stay and catch up," Leila said. The two immediately started conversing in Roy.

Ami felt a little disconnected but shrugged it off. She returned to Viovel, Doran, and the three Nobles. Sable and Priscilla attached themselves to her sides like hungry leeches. Mark looked left out.

"You can hold on to my tail, Mark," Ami offered with a teasing smile.

Mark blushed. "No, thank you, my lord."

"If the offer is still open, I'll hold it," Viovel said.

Ami choked down a laugh. She wasn't serious, but she played along. Her white tail elongated to reach Viovel. Carefully, she wrapped it around Viovel's wrist. The Werewolf seemed pleased. Doran glanced between the two with a worried look. A loud horn broke the air. The sound surprised Ami, making her release Viovel's wrist. Her tail retreated back to her. Sable and Priscilla barely covered their surprised shrieks. Lady Blackhill came on her platform. She wore a crimson silk dress. Rubies adorned her loosely curled hair.

She's wearing more expensive items this time. Is she trying to impress or show off? Ami asked herself. She glanced around at the other guests, trying to see if someone of higher rank was in the long hall. Due to this, she missed Lady Blackhill's speech. Everyone politely clapped as Lady Blackhill stepped down. The orchestra began to play "In the Garden with a Lady," a familiar song used for the waltz.

"My lord, may I have this dance?" Sable and Priscilla tried to say at the same time. Sable managed to finish asking first.

"I will dance with Sable first. The next song is yours, Priscilla," Ami said.

"I'll hold you to that," Priscilla said snootily.

The waltz with Sable was pleasant. She was a good dancer.

They chatted about minor things like what other guests were wearing and who their dance partners were. When it ended, another song started to play a moment after.

"Shall we?" Ami asked Priscilla.

The female Elf tried to act haughty but was happy with the invitation. It was another waltz. Priscilla started to act nervous and stepped on Ami's foot.

"I'm sorry," the Elf muttered. Her face was pink.

"It's all right." Ami shrugged it off. Priscilla started to look at her feet and stepped on Ami's other foot. "Priscilla, look at me."

"Yes?" Priscilla answered. The female looked like she was ready to burst into tears.

"Take a few deep breaths," Ami instructed gently. Priscilla obeyed. Their movements slowed. "As we dance, I need you to look at me and let me lead."

"But females—" Priscilla hiccupped. "Females are supposed to lead."

"You're not ready yet, but you can learn from me," Ami assured, her tone soothing. "Ready? Follow my lead."

They went through the dance steps slower than the other guests. Ami tutted when Priscilla tried to look at their feet.

"The waltz steps are a box. When you think of a box, it's four easy steps," Ami instructed. "One, two, three, four. One, two, three, four."

Once Priscilla relaxed and let Ami lead, she stopped stepping on Ami's feet. The Elf seemed to be enjoying herself by the time the song ended. Ami escorted her back to Sable and Mark. Sable seemed ecstatic while Mark was smiling. Viovel and Doran were gone. Leila hadn't returned.

"My lord, will you assist me in getting the ladies a drink?" Mark asked.

"Of course." Ami nodded.

"That was a kind thing you did for Priscilla," Mark commented as they retrieved champagne flutes in both hands.

"How so?" Ami asked.

"She struggled with finding adequate tutors due to her Noble status. The ones that taught her were overly strict and damaged her self-esteem," Mark explained.

"She just needed to relax. She had the basics down," Ami pointed out.

They grabbed a flute of champagne in each hand. Mark handed one to Sable, and Ami gave one to Priscilla. The female Elf blushed with a whispered thanks. They chatted amicably. Priscilla couldn't look at Ami without blushing a darker hue.

"Bestie!" Leila came up to them.

"Hello. How did your talk with Mrs. Van Gogh go?" Ami asked. Out of her sight, Sable and Priscilla gave Leila the stink-eye, and Mark was frowning.

"It took longer than I thought. I'm sorry if I seemed rude before. The van Goghs are family friends, and we didn't know if they were able to make it out in time," Leila explained, ignoring the three Nobles.

"Are you and Theo friends?" Ami asked, a bit confused.

Leila shook her head. "Theo was always one to prefer books to People. Whenever I tried to talk to him, he was rude and told me to leave him alone."

That explains why he's socially awkward and always talks about medical books. Ami thought. "He seems to be coming out of his shell in Rascu," she said encouragingly.

"Where is he, anyway?" Leila asked.

"He's an apprentice Healer at the Common Grounds," Ami said.

"Oh, is that where—" Leila started. Ami cleared her throat loudly, giving Leila a pointed look. "He healed your muscles," Leila finished quickly.

"Yes." Ami took a long sip of champagne.

"Why were you taken to the Common Grounds and not the city hospital?" Mark asked.

"When I was struck, I was knocked unconscious. After I woke up, I was told some soldiers who went to investigate found me and took me to the Common Grounds," Ami said smoothly.

"That's understandable," Sable said. "I'm sure the soldiers trust their Healers and would think of their hospital before thinking of the city's."

"My lord, can we do line dancing again?" Priscilla asked randomly.

"Oh, yes. Let me talk to the conductor," Ami said, giving Mark her champagne flute.

"I'll come with—" Leila started.

"Actually," Viovel appeared out of nowhere, "I need to speak to Lord Sieghild, please."

Ami mouthed, "I'm sorry," to Leila before following Viovel to the opposite side of the long hall. One particular area was shadowed and out of sight. Viovel swirled to face Ami.

"I feared I wouldn't have a chance to be with you tonight," Viovel said sadly.

"There's always after the party," Ami suggested, fighting against a wide grin.

Viovel snorted. "You'll probably be asked to escort your lady home."

Ami frowned. "She's my best friend, not my courted."

Viovel stared at her as if processing her words. "Huh?"

Ami failed to stifle a laugh. It was strange how People assumed they were courting because they were friendly with each other.

"She's my best friend," Ami reiterated.

Something uncurled and loosened in Viovel's posture. The Werewolf looked like a significant weight had been lifted off of his shoulders.

"I see," Viovel muttered.

"Do you?" Ami asked, her voice lowering. She stepped closer to Viovel, almost flush. The Werewolf watched her with interest. "I still say we will have time after the party," Ami murmured, looking at the intricate embroidery of his silk vest.

She resisted the urge to trace the needlework with her fingers.

"The side alley," Viovel said quickly. Clearing his throat, he said slower, "Come down the side alley. I'll be waiting for you."

"Sounds like a date," Ami said.

She turned and went to the orchestra, not waiting for Viovel's reply. Speaking to Mrs. Van Gogh, she convinced the conductor that the song was appropriate and not offensive. When the song began to play, those who had attended before recognized the tune and cheered. Ami gathered the males and females into lines and refreshed their memories. At one point, Ami and Leila danced together. Leila looked like she was having fun. Viovel was far more relaxed and danced more than last time. The line dancing moved to other dances as different songs played. Before Ami knew it, the party was over.

"Bestie," Leila panted, her ears dark pink, "can you walk me home?"

"Of course. Sable, Priscilla, do you have escorts?" Ami asked.

"I'll be walking them home. We live close together," Mark replied.

"I'm trusting you with them," Ami said in playful sternness.

Mark seemed to take it to heart. "I'll protect them with my life, my lord."

"Will you be at the next party?" Priscilla asked.

"I certainly hope so. I'll see you later," Ami said with a wave of goodbye.

The two females exited the Blackhill residence in high spirits. Leila led Ami further down the street to a crossway. They turned left.

"What's the deal with everyone thinking you're a guy?" Leila asked bluntly.

"My alliance with Jasmine isn't going how I thought it would," Ami admitted.

"How so?"

"Since I woke up, she has been distant, leaving me in the dark about the discussions in Old Congress. I only hear what the Knights and Nobles gossip about, but that doesn't help me if she decides to terminate our alliance," Ami explained bitterly.

"What happens if it comes to that?" Leila asked quietly.

"I will be deported," Ami stated.

"Wait, what?" Leila looked at her incredulously. "Even though you're part of the military and have a high rank?"

"I am still Vincian," Ami pointed out.

"That's stupid," Leila grumbled. After a moment, she said, "As Lord Sieghild, you're networking and forming more allies."

"Correct."

"How will that help you as Amaranth if everyone assumes you're a male? Aren't males looked down upon here?" Leila asked.

"As an outsider, People tend to let out more than native Rascals," Ami stated. Seeing Leila's confused look, she added, "Rascals have extensive networks within their families that go back generations. They must be careful of who they associate with and what information to give out. As a foreigner, I don't have those limitations."

"But you will once you officially form alliances," Leila pointed out.

Ami shook her head. "Not necessarily. The alliances with families Bond them to various members of society, thus invoking sacred Oaths and Vows unique to their families. They only activate with Bonded allies and those of Rascal blood. Since I don't have those—"

"Those Oaths and Vows don't apply to you," Leila concluded. "Huh."

"Exactly. You can use that to your family's advantage as well," Ami suggested.

"Because I'm female?" Leila asked.

"Are you the only daughter?" Ami asked.

"I am."

"Then, besides your mother, you have the most power in Rascu," Ami replied.

"Wow, this is an eye-opener," Leila said in wonder.

"It's a lot to take in, and we haven't even scratched the surface," Ami sighed.

"Ah, here I am," Leila said, pointing to a townhouse. It was part of a long line of older brick townhouses in a decent section of the Spring District. Ami patrolled this area at night before the fire. She liked the smell of tulips and azaleas when they were in bloom. Leila's townhouse had light blue shutters, making it stand out against the traditional red or orange.

"I'm glad you're safe, Leila," Ami said sincerely.

"I can't believe I get to see you more often," Leila said, tearing up.

They hugged tightly. At that moment, their Bond reunited. It brought tears to Ami's eye.

"Leila?" Charlotte called from the front door.

With a mischievous smile, Leila shouted, "Thank you for escorting me, Lord Sieghild."

Playing along, Ami replied, "It was my pleasure, my lady." To Charlotte, she said, "Lady Moonbeam, good evening to you."

"Thank you, sir," Charlotte answered uncertainly. "Leila, come inside."

"Bye, bestie," Leila whispered before running to her mother.

Nodding at both females, Ami hurried back to Blackhill mansion.

CHAPTER 15

"I don't understand what you see in him," Gemma said casually. She watched the clean-up crew with a careful eye.

"Who, Mother?" Viovel asked innocently.

Gemma gave her son a flat look. "That foreign lord, Sieghild. He is uncouth and lacks dignity."

"He makes your boring parties interesting," Viovel said boldly.

"My parties are not boring," Gemma hissed.

"You sure about that?" Viovel asked knowingly. He could tell this party had twice as many attendants as the previous due to Lord Sieghild's known attendance. The party that the lord had missed had not even a third of the invitees come when they learned he couldn't attend.

Gemma gritted her teeth. Viovel hated the sound. It made his ears tingle like an enemy sneaking up behind him. He wondered if she did it on purpose or out of habit.

"The Blackhills have always strived for connections. That is our industry," Gemma said, as if she was trying to convince both of them.

"I'm following that tradition to the letter," Viovel said. A servant came over to ask a question about the tables. Viovel answered the question.

Gemma waited until the servant left. "You know how Vincians are."

"Are they really like the stories told?" Viovel challenged. "Lord Sieghild has taught us dancing. Oh, how the earth trembled when we learned that!" he added dramatically.

"Viovel, take this seriously," Gemma growled.

"I am taking this seriously. You're the one who is so old-fashioned that you don't see what Lord Sieghild is doing," Viovel said, his tone suddenly solemn.

"What is he doing?" Gemma asked, her voice almost small.

"He's fusing the lines between males and females. Can't you see how much more relaxed People were when dancing? How happy they were when they didn't have to worry about tiptoeing around each other?"

"Those etiquette and social lines are there for a reason," Gemma said haughtily.

"To divide us," Viovel retorted.

"To unite our society," Gemma argued vehemently.

"Where is the unity when males can't even decide who to marry or choose a different career? Where is this perfect society where males can't even look at a female for fear she feels offended such that he's punished by her family and his so badly that he commits suicide? What unity do you speak of, Mother, because that world doesn't exist?" Viovel went off, huffing at the end of his rant.

"That is an exaggerated story told by males—" Gemma said dismissively.

"Great Almighty One!" Viovel cried out, walking away. Frustration and anger boiled under his skin and in his chest.

"Viovel!" Gemma called after him. Her stomps told him she was following him.

Viovel's feet led him to the side gardens. His heart lifted and then fell. He was supposed to meet the mysterious lord at the side alley. Glancing at the warded gates, all he saw was an empty street.

"Viovel, what I do is for the benefit of the family—" Gemma started as she descended the steps.

"That's a lie!" Viovel snarled, swirling around to face her. Her startled face gave him cold satisfaction. "Everything you do is for your benefit and your vanity. Nothing you have ever done was for my benefit."

Gemma's eyes turned stone cold. "I allowed you to join the military. I allowed you to have friends. I allow you to attend these parties in hopes of earning connections."

"Allowed? Allowed?!" Viovel cried in an almost hysterical howl. "After how much begging and pleading did I have to do? How many times did I have to get on my knees and humiliate myself until you were satisfied? How often did I have to do something shameful to earn your approval for every little thing? For once in your pitiful life, leave me alone!" Viovel roared.

He turned and walked to the gates. Grabbing the iron bars representing his personal prison, he rested his forehead against them. His body shook as he fought against the tears that went down his furry cheeks anyway. All his anger, frustration, hopelessness, and a darker emotion he couldn't name engulfed his being. Gentle hands from the other side of the gate softly wrapped around his. Viovel looked up. Lord Sieghild stood there. What shocked Viovel was the lord wasn't looking at him with pity. It was like he knew what Viovel was going through.

Someone understood.

Lord Sieghild didn't say anything. His thumbs rubbed the dark brown Werewolf's wrists soothingly. Hiccups came from Viovel's lips as his tears rained down harder. The two stood there in the quiet side alley. Eventually, their foreheads were pressed together, still silent. No words were spoken between the two. It took a while for Viovel to register what he was hearing. The tune was low and didn't upset the atmosphere they created. It hit him like smashing a rock against flint and making a spark. Lord Sieghild was singing. He didn't know the song or the words. It was more than likely Vin. But the music calmed the darker emotion that welled alongside the anger, frustration, and hopelessness.

For the first time, Viovel felt peace.

Ados would honestly admit that he was restless. His mother always said he couldn't sit still as a child. That boundless energy helped him in the military. Now, it was driving him insane. Ami—he only called the captain by her nickname in his head—was away at a party. Dressed as a male. A disguise.

Why would a female need to be in disguise? Who is Ami hoping to meet and gain an alliance with? Why didn't she want to bring her trusted soldiers with her? Was she ashamed of them?

Ados shook his head at the last thought. *No, Ami isn't ashamed of us.*

The Knights' explicit acceptance of them was evidence of that. If Ami was ashamed, she would've ordered them to sleep elsewhere and away from her. Ados' leg started to shake up and down without him realizing it. Ami was a mystery. One that Ados wanted to put the pieces of the puzzle together. He had hoped his comrades would help, but they seemed to be putting together pieces themselves.

But why did this party make Ami excited? Ados wondered. There had to be someone at the party that Ami was eager to meet. A sudden bolt of uneasiness went down his spine. What if Ami met a male she wanted to court?

Ados struggled to get his breathing under control. A weight settled beside him, and an arm wrapped around his shoulders. The smell of leather and hay filled his nose.

"Calm down," a deep soothing voice ordered. Slowly, Ados did. He looked at his comforter. Clarence looked at him with concerned eyes.

"Thank you," Ados muttered.

"She's going to be all right," Clarence stated confidently.

Ados flinched. "Why do you say that?"

"Rose is tougher than she appears and sharper than any sword crafted by the blacksmith," Clarence said, his confidence never wavering. "If she can calm the dictator during a rampage, then a party is nothing."

"Wait, what?" Ados gaped at him.

Clarence removed his arm from Ados' shoulders. "Yeah, the dictator found out about an incident involving the captain. The dictator was storming her way to the warehouse to magic the truth out of every male when Rose managed to intersect and calm her down."

Ados stared at the Centaur to determine if he was telling the truth. A few Knights nearby confirmed Clarence's story. A new appreciation for Ami formed in Ados' mind.

Maybe Ami could help with his situation.

James eyed the Knights around him warily. They were relaxing in the common area, talking and chatting as if nothing unusual happened. James couldn't believe he was surrounded by the best of the best in the Rascal military. To become a

Knight was to go through the Pits several times before being accepted. Then, he came to find out that his captain used to be their training master! The moment felt surreal.

He leaned against one of the couches. His eyes were fixed on the soldiers guarding the captain's room. Four soldiers went in there with tools and pieces of wood when a slave told them something. Whatever it was, it got the Knights excited. James tried to see what was happening, but the two burly Werewolves guards stopped him before getting there. He couldn't even hear what was going on with the constant laughing and loud conversations.

James sighed. When was the captain coming back? What was so important about a party? Shouldn't she be more concerned about her soldiers than politics?

It was going to be a long night.

Flander felt uneasy being surrounded by stronger Centaurs. He knew most of them distantly by their clans. It wouldn't surprise him if they were third or fourth cousins. Amongst his siblings and first cousins, Flander was the weakest. He was the slowest Centaur in his age group in his clan and, according to female Centaurs, not attractive. It was a relief to enter the military, where he had tested his brain and realized he understood things his clan peers never did. Remembering classes reminded him of his treatment of Captain Rose.

He flushed in embarrassment at the memories. Why had he been so stupid back then? Shame swarmed his chest and heart when the recollections came at him fast and furious. Inwardly, he knew he had done it to be liked. He had been tired of being the outsider, and Andy was the first Person who greeted him like a friend. Only during the bleach incident had Flander realized how deep Andy's hatred for Captain Rose went, and then he started to distance himself from the Faerie. They hadn't spoken or written to each other since they each left for their own forts. Flander wondered if Andy was stationed with Milan or Julius.

Then his memory of being assigned to Captain Rose's cover came to mind. He was thrilled to have been selected. As he had run to join them, thoughts popped up in his head. Did she forgive him? Did he have potential? How did she view him now? When he had heard her screams, his blood had gone cold. He hadn't even thought. He just reacted. Rose never screamed, not even when the males put buckets of worms in her bed.

Once he was part of the cover, Flander realized he was again at the bottom of the hierarchy. But it was okay this time. Captain Rose didn't act like she held any ill will against him and was a fantastic cook. It surprised him since males were often taught how to cook for females. Then she taught him how to find wild vegetables as if it was the world's most normal thing. His fascination and curiosity grew each time he interacted with her. Was this what she had been trying to tell them while they were cadets? Why had he acted like a moron then? Oh, yeah. Peer pressure and insecurity.

Discovering that the magical dome was a time capsule was one of the best and most personal memories Flander held. Not only did Flander help contribute to the theories they spoke of, but Flander also managed to glimpse at a female in her glory. That was until Uriah forced his head in the opposite direction. Flander didn't mind. He saw enough to appreciate Dragons more.

Uriah was very uncomfortable. One of the Knights, a dark brown Werefox, was passionately telling him how some writer of a play he had never heard of was one of the greatest bards in Rascal literature history. Fortunately, a different Knight sat next to Uriah and interrupted.

"Rhys, no one cares about Plusso," the Knight, an Elf with short brown hair, stated with boredom in his voice.

"But even Rose—" Rhys tried to argue.

"Agreed that even though he is a good writer, he is not the best. He basically wrote a fanfic on Thumes's works. Even you have to admit that," the Elf Knight retorted.

Rhys sighed. "Fine. I'm going to get something to eat."

"Get me something, too," the Elf added.

"Whatcha want?" Rhys asked.

The Elf shrugged. "Something salty."

Rhys waved and left. The Elf turned to Uriah. "So, how's it going?"

Uriah stared at him, speechless. After finding his tongue, he said, "It's f-fine."

The Elf hummed, not convinced. "You know, Rose doesn't like males who act like leeches."

Anger flared in Uriah's chest. "Who are you calling leeches?"

"You four," the Elf said bluntly. "I'm Perry, by the way."

"Uriah," the Werewolf answered after a moment, feeling odd. "What do you mean, though?"

"What I mean is that Rose like males who have confidence and can follow orders without her having to babysit them," Perry said, his tone serious.

"How do you know this?" Uriah asked.

"Because she was our training master, and that's how she treated us," Perry said confidently. "Not once did she question our patrols and routines or even ask us about our Oaths. She trusted we knew what we were doing and made us better."

Uriah stared at his hands, trying to absorb what the Knight told him.

"Don't you worry?" Uriah blurted.

Perry blinked at him. "About what?"

"That ... that if she starts hanging around Nobles, she'll start acting like them?" Uriah asked, leaving out "towards males."

Perry smirked. "No."

The answer surprised Uriah. "Why?"

"Because she's Vincian."

Confusion replaced the previous worry. "What does that have to do with anything?" Uriah asked.

Perry continued to smirk before getting up to talk to another group of Knights on the other side of the room. Uriah didn't understand what Perry was trying to say. Why was he being mysterious about it? Was it an open secret, and Uriah didn't know it? Glancing around, he saw Rose enter.

His heart started to beat faster. Without realizing it, he moved to be at her side. Rose didn't appear to notice him at first. Her expression was of deep thought. In a blink, the look was gone.

"Lakeshore, why are you still up?" Rose asked.

"I couldn't sleep," Uriah mumbled clumsily. That part was genuine.

"Well, I'm back, so go to sleep," Rose ordered.

"Captain, the Knights are doing something to your room," James said eagerly, appearing beside Uriah.

Rose frowned a little. "Thank you, Atorra. I'll see what's going on."

"Can we come?" James asked. Uriah wanted to smack him.

Rose ignored him and went to her room. The two Knights guarding it greeted her warmly.

"What's going on?" Rose asked.

"Well, apparently—Oh, here she comes," one of the Knights said, looking over Rose's shoulder.

Uriah followed their eyes. The slave from before walked up to Rose with a knapsack over her shoulder and her arms filled with a large pillow and blankets.

"Blejan, what happened?" Rose asked.

"I spoke to the master and told her that I will be your personal Dragon from now on," Blejan told her.

"You told her?" Rose asked slowly in amusement.

"Yes. The master had no argument against it, and I wouldn't have accepted any," Blejan answered, her head held high.

"What if she tries to do something through the Bond?" Rose asked.

"Then she will feel my wrath," Blejan growled. It reminded Uriah that Dragons were known as the most dangerous People before the enslavement.

That made Rose smile. "What does this have to do with the Knights in my room?"

"Oh, I asked them to fix something up for both of us," Blejan said with a smile, her dangerous look vanishing.

"Is it finished?" Rose asked.

"Captain?" a Knight, an Elf, poked his head out from her door. Uriah couldn't see much of the room.

"Can I come in and sleep finally?" Rose asked.

"Give us a minute to clean up," the Elf said before closing the door.

After several minutes of listening to noises that sounded like banging and sheets being moved, the four Knights exited the room. They eagerly nodded for Rose to enter. Rose did so cautiously. Then she stood in the doorway, staring at their work. Uriah peeked over her shoulder. The Knights had created a bunk bed and an extra dresser for Blejan on the other side. Uriah was grudgingly impressed at their carpentry skills.

Was that a skill required for a Knight or a side hobby? he wondered. He could feel the Knights' anticipation as they awaited Rose's verdict.

"Thank you, lads," Rose said. Strangely, it sounded hollow.

"Captain, are you not pleased?" Stan asked. Uriah remembered him.

Rose shook her head. "I have a lot on my mind right now. I'll talk more in the morning."

To Blejan, she asked, "You want top or bottom?"

Blejan smiled, despite her eyes being worried. "I'll take the bottom bunk, Angel."

Turning to face them, Uriah saw how aged Rose looked. She said, "Good night, lads."

Each Knight murmured a good night as Rose closed the door behind her and Blejan. Uriah walked back to his cot. The other three gathered near him.

"What happened?" Ados asked.

"Not sure. The captain wasn't happy, though," James answered.

"Do you think the party didn't go as planned?" Flander asked.

They shrugged. Uriah remained quiet. His thoughts went deeper. Was it because the Knights transformed her room without permission? It would explain her hollow thanks. Then again, she had been deep in thought when she entered. What was she thinking about so hard? He had only witnessed that expression before when they were investigating the cursed forest.

Something was profoundly worrying his captain.

The view from the high platform was torture. The stadium itself was a work of art in modern architecture, but Lord Dali couldn't admire it. His eyes were on the stadium grounds. A lone figure on his knees, arms bound by iron chains that glowed green, was surrounded by six priests, chanting in what was considered the "holy language." With their chanting and rituals to "dispel" the demon Conri, they made Lord Dali grind his teeth as Salvador tried not to scream in pain. Lord Dali didn't buy into the demon business, but didn't express his displeasure. The priests could harm Salvador even more. He felt his son's pain whenever Salvador's tight grip on their Bond faltered. He didn't know who had taught him to hide his emotions through the Bond, but Lord Dali admired and hated it.

He had known about Conri before Salvador was born. The Wolf King of the Forests was famous in Roy, and numerous tales of his adventures and quests varied from town to town. Lord Dali's beloved wife loved the stories and wanted to spend their honeymoon searching for the places where Conri supposedly roamed or visited.

If we hadn't found that cave ... Lord Dali thought bitterly.

"Caleb, how much longer will the priests be here?" Luther asked. A gray Werefox and Lord Dali's best friend, he looked like he felt Salvador's pain. He probably did to an extent, as Luther was Salvador's godfather.

Lord Dali rubbed his face with his hands in frustration. "I can't get them to leave without harming Sal further. They can set up a ritual to repeatedly torture him, claiming it will drive demons out. I have no control over this." Tears threatened to spill, but he forced them back. He had to be strong for his son.

"And Deena? She's allowing this to happen to her brother?" Luther growled. He wasn't close to the heiress, since the clan's females often occupied her time and attention.

Lord Dali sighed heavily. "She thinks this is the best solution."

"For her brother to be tortured?" Luther exclaimed. "Does she believe those lies those so-called priests tell her without question? Does she not value her family?"

"I don't know anymore," Lord Dali whispered. Luther's voice faded as he sunk deep into hopelessness. All Lord Dali could see before him was his world falling apart. His son was tormented by religious priests, with his daughter supporting them, while he was helpless to stop any of it.

Sometimes I hate being a male in this nation, Lord Dali growled mentally. When his wife had passed in childbirth, Lord Dali lost any influence over his children to his wife's family. He had barely recovered Salvador from their bloody claws, but couldn't save Deena. His wife's family was deeply religious and believed every word the priests said without question. Fortunately, his wife had been sensible and had a mind of her own. Then a thought hit him.

A female who is sensible and doesn't blindly follow the priests. He tried to recall what Salvador had told him before the priests were summoned. Salvador was speaking about someone fondly. *Who is Salvador in love with?* Luther's voice broke his thoughts.

"Well, what do you think?" Luther asked with an eager face.

Lord Dali blinked. "Of what?"

Luther stared at him. "I just told you of my plan to get rid of the priests, and you didn't hear a word?"

"No, I didn't," Lord Dali said sheepishly.

"Caleb, I had a brilliant idea and everything!" Luther whined.

"Summarize it," Lord Dali stated, almost like an order.

Luther huffed. "Basically, we slaughter the priests, hang their corpses outside the city, and declare war on the temple." At Lord Dali's incredulous stare, Luther added, "Oh, and hook up Sal with his female."

"His female?" Lord Dali asked, still trying to wrap his head around Luther's obnoxious plan.

"Don't you listen to your child when he's home? All he talks about is this Rose female. He practically swoons whenever he thinks of her," Luther explained.

Amaranth Rose. That was her name. Lord Dali remembered now. Salvador had been telling him what happened in the village when the priests came. Rose didn't trust them and challenged them directly.

"I think I have a solution to our problem," Lord Dali said, his voice in awe realization.

"What is it? Please tell me I can kill something," Luther asked.

"Only when she's done with them," Lord Dali replied.

"Who?"

"Amaranth Rose. She isn't influenced by the priests and even challenged them at the village near Sal's fort," Lord Dali said. Hope grew in his chest for the first time in a long time.

"Will she come here?" Luther asked. He glanced at the lone figure below.

"She will once she hears what's happening," Lord Dali said, a sadistic pleasure flaring in his chest at the thought of what Rose will do to the priests. "Get me a carriage."

"On it." Luther nodded. He left quickly.

Lord Dali pulsed his plan to his son. Pain shocked up the Bond from whatever the priests were doing. But Lord Dali managed to receive his son's message.

Relief.

"Caleb, the carriage is ready," Luther announced.

"Let's go to Talient," Lord Dali ordered.

Luther rode with him in tense silence. The horses raced down the roads to the capital as if a pack of wolves from the Pits chased them. The Werewolf lord wondered if they could sense his urgency. While it usually took three days to get to Talient from Pluth, the carriage horses were bred for speed, and the carriage was designed to withstand abuse from the dirt roads. They arrived at the outskirts of Talient in the late evening. The driver started to slow the horses down so they wouldn't get pierced with arrows. He stopped them just in time.

"Halt! What is your urgency?" a Centaur Knight demanded at the western entrance. Several Knights watched from above with prepared their bows.

"Lord Dali needs to speak with Lady Rose immediately!" the driver, a gray Werewolf, answered.

"Escort!" The Centaur Knight ordered. Immediately, two Centaurs and two Werewolves appeared on the sides of the carriage. They trotted with the horses to the Inner City. When they reached the Iron Gates, they ordered the driver to stop. The driver obeyed. Then he stepped down and opened the carriage door.

"My lord, we have arrived," the driver said with a bowed head.

Luther and Lord Dali stepped out of the carriage.

"Thank you, Damius," Lord Dali answered the driver. To the Knights, he said, "I will return shortly with Lady Rose."

"The captain isn't in the Inner City at the moment," one of the Werewolves guarding the Iron Gates informed him.

Lord Dali frowned. "Where is she?"

"She is at a local café with her soldiers," a different soldier replied. "I can guide you, sir."

"Please do," Lord Dali said quickly.

The soldier barked orders and motioned for Lord Dali and Luther to follow him. The soldier weaved in and out of the passing crowds towards one of the towers. They came to the main street. Lord Dali wasn't sure where they were, but he knew they were in the Spring District. Thankfully, Rose was leaving a building with four male soldiers.

"Lady Rose!" Lord Dali called out, running towards her. He ignored Luther's shout.

Rose blinked at him. "Lord Dali?"

"I know we haven't met formally, but yes, I am Lord Dali," he greeted her somewhat breathlessly. He stopped a short distance from her. Luther caught up behind him.

Rose nodded. "I am Captain Amaranth Rose. Salvador has your build."

Lord Dali felt touched. Then the reason why he was there

snapped him back to reality. "Lady Rose, you are needed in the city of Pluth."

"What's wrong with Sal?" Rose asked immediately.

Does she feel the same way? Lord Dali wondered. He glanced at the male soldiers. They hovered around her protectively. "I will explain on the way. I have a carriage to take us," Lord Dali stated.

Rose frowned. "My lord, the night is upon us, and I must alert my superiors."

"Our horses can make the trip in several hours," Lord Dali insisted, some desperation slipping into his voice.

Rose walked over to Lord Dali. She placed her hand on his shoulder in a comforting manner. Her purple eye was intense.

"I understand your urgency. However, I cannot leave without notification of my military superiors. Also, if your horses ran here without stopping, they will need to rest unless you're willing to change out your horses with a fresh set," Rose explained calmly.

Lord Dali let out a deep breath. What she said was logical. It didn't mean he liked it. All he could think of was how Salvador was suffering.

"Come. You may stay at the mansion." Rose gently guided him to walk next to her.

Lord Dali was stunned. Was a female allowing a male to walk with her as an equal? Now he was intrigued. He ignored the gawking Luther and the soldiers. Ordinary citizens did a double-take when they noticed the two.

"What's going on with Sal?" Rose asked.

"The priests are there," Lord Dali stated.

Rose hissed under her breath. The hiss evolved into a growl. Lord Dali started to feel better about his decision.

"What are they doing to him?" Rose asked, her tone quiet. It made the fur on his neck and shoulders stand up.

"They've been performing numerous rituals and chantings," Lord Dali replied.

"What kind of rituals?" Rose inquired.

"I'm not completely sure," Lord Dali answered shamefully. "They won't let me get close to Sal or see what they were doing."

"What about Deena?" Rose asked.

"What about her?"

"Does she tell you what they're doing or what kind of rituals they perform?" Rose asked.

Lord Dali frowned. "No. She and the rest of the clan believe the priests are doing the right thing. I'm the only one who can feel his pain."

"And me," Luther added.

Rose paused in her walking. Lord Dali, Luther, and the four soldiers copied her. She looked at Luther. "Who are you?" she asked politely.

Luther puffed out his chest. "I'm sure Sal has mentioned his amazing godfather and favorite uncle."

"He hasn't," Rose said in a deadpan tone.

Lord Dali wasn't sure if she was joking or not. When she didn't laugh or smile, Luther deflated.

"Really? He hasn't mentioned me at all?" Luther asked, his voice sad.

"There's a lot about Salvador that I don't know," Rose pointed out, resuming her walk. This time Lord Dali and Luther walked behind her, side by side.

While Luther was disappointed and shocked, Lord Dali reassessed what Salvador had told him. As a father, he kept a close ear on any female potentially interested in his son, and vice versa. While it appeared that Salvador was infatuated with Rose, it was clear that he hadn't been entirely open with her about his family. Was he ashamed of them? Did he fear her rejection?

Rose led them to the Inner City and gained them entrance into the Common Grounds. Just as they came to the mansion, Lady Jasmine exited with Tso. The two females stopped, staring at each other. Their magic made the air crack as if filled with electricity. Tso was barely able to conceal his sneer at Rose. The white-haired female ignored him, her full attention on the dictator. Then without saying a word, Jasmine left, going towards the gardens. Tso seemed surprised. In something entirely out of character with the Werefox, he ran after Jasmine.

Lord Dali narrowed his eyes. Something was wrong here. Tso never ran after a female, especially Lady Jasmine. While he didn't like the female, Tso was politically wise not to show it so blatantly. The fact he showed so much emotion now was unnerving. Lord Dali missed the calculating look on Rose's face. It was gone when she broke the silence.

"Lord Dali and Sir Luther, please follow me," Rose said genially.

When they entered the main lobby, they were greeted by a slave. Lord Dali thought it was a female due to the dress it wore. Rose seemed to know them well.

"Blejan, please prepare a room for our guests," Rose said.

The slave bowed with a smile. "Of course, Angel."

"Angel?" Luther asked when the slave left.

Rose smiled mysteriously. "It's their name for me."

"What does Sal call you?" Luther asked.

Rose's smile disappeared. "Ami. What does he call you?"

"Uncle Luther, or Uncle Lu if he's in a hurry," Luther replied.

Rose hummed. Silence filled the room. The four soldiers shifted from foot to foot nervously. Lord Dali wasn't sure how long they had waited in silence when Blejan returned.

"Angel, their room is ready," Blejan announced.

"Thank you. My lords, please follow Blejan to your room. I will see you at dawn," Rose said with a short bow. Stunned by the courtesy, Rose left before Lord Dali could say anything else. The four soldiers followed her.

"My lords, please follow me," Blejan offered with a motion of her hand.

"Lead the way," Luther grunted.

Their room was on the third floor. Blejan opened the third door on the left.

"The bathroom is on the left. I will bring dinner shortly. If there's anything else you require, please ask for Blejan," Blejan explained, her head bowed respectfully.

"Thank you." Lord Dali nodded. They entered the room and shut the door. Inside were twin beds. Lord Dali was relieved. Luther sprawled when he slept and kicked like a horse.

"What are your thoughts?" Luther asked, sitting on a twin bed.

"I think she'll assist in dealing with the priests," Lord Dali said, sitting on the other twin bed.

"What about Sal and this female?" Luther asked.

Lord Dali thought over it carefully. He answered, "I think Sal is more taken by Rose than Rose is by him."

"I agree." Luther nodded. "She seems to only see him as a friend or a brother in arms."

"Agreed."

Two short knocks before the door opened. Blejan came in with two trays filled with piping-hot food. She handed a tray to each of them, bowed, and left again. Lord Dali's mouth watered. The meal smelled delicious.

"Man, if this is what the cadets eat daily, I can see why they complain when they get to the forts," Luther moaned with food in his mouth.

Lord Dali agreed. The meals consisted of fried steak with white gravy, creamy corn, cheesy broccoli, and mashed potatoes with brown gravy. A slice of cheesecake and a large glass of milk each finished the meal. The two males ate in silence. Each was lost in their own thoughts. After they ate, they took separate showers. Exhaustion hit Lord Dali like a kick in the chest from a horse when he lay in bed.

"Caleb?" Luther asked in the darkness.

"Yes?" Lord Dali answered.

"Are you sure we can't kill the priests?" Luther asked.

"Go to sleep," Lord Dali ordered.

Ami waited outside of Dr. Elderflower's office with a frown. She hadn't expected the priests to make a move so soon. When Dr. Elderflower opened his office door, she smoothed her face to a neutral expression. The Werewolf had several vials of potions in his hands.

"These two need to be taken with food." Dr. Elderflower motioned to the two colored dark brown. "These," he said as he pointed to a purple vial and a dark green vial, "need to be taken at night. They should alleviate most of his symptoms by now. How is he faring?"

"He appears to be doing better. He's not shivering anymore, but his body temperature is still low compared to before. He managed to eat a piece of toast and not vomit the other day," Ami reported.

"That's fantastic news," Dr. Elderflower said glowingly. "He's making fast progress. This should be the last large dose of potions he needs. He should be able to handle solid foods from now on."

"Thank you, Dr. Elderflower," Ami said sincerely.

"Always happy to help."

Ami left with the potions. It was almost dark. Shayne and the others would be eating dinner soon. Ami went to the warehouse. Inside, Blaine sat on the cot wrapped in a blanket. He perked up when he saw her.

"Sigrid," he greeted her warmly.

"Blaine," Ami greeted back, her tone lukewarm. "Dr. Elderflower said this is the last dose you must take."

"Then, no more potions?" Blaine asked warily.

"No more potions."

"Finally," Blaine said dramatically.

"Have you eaten?" Ami asked.

"Yeah, Shayne got me a sandwich a little while ago," Blaine said.

"Then take these two," Ami said, handing him the two dark brown vials.

With a grimace, Blaine gulped them down, complete with a full-body shiver with each gulp. "That is disgusting." The blond Werewolf gagged.

"These two will need to be taken before you go to sleep. I have to go," Ami said quickly.

Blaine grabbed her wrist before she could make her escape.

"Sigrid, I'm sorry," Blaine whispered.

"I know," Ami said, not looking at him. Her heart throbbed from pain.

"Then what can I do to fix this? Fix us?" Blaine asked. She hated how pathetic and genuine he sounded.

"I don't have time for a relationship, Blaine," Ami said, glaring at him coldly.

"You did before," Blaine pointed out stubbornly.

"Before, I wasn't aware of the evil hiding in the background. Bigger things are happening, and I don't have time to spare," Ami snarled. She yanked her wrist out of his grip and left the warehouse. As she walked to the Common Grounds, all she could think about was saving Salvador.

CHAPTER 16

The city of Pluth was bustling with tension and worry. Even from inside the cramped carriage, Ami could feel it. Ami was almost in Uriah's and Ados' laps while James was squished against the wall with Luther and Lord Dali, who insisted Ami call him Caleb. She looked through the small, tinted window behind Uriah's furry head. Unlike Talient, Pluth was a modern city without any external connection to Rascal architecture. Ami hyper-focused on this detail as waves of nausea threatened to empty her stomach. The carriage ride was on Ami's top ten list of unpleasant experiences. As the carriage hurried down the street, Ami barely caught a glimpse of a Person here and a Person there. The lack of People piqued her curiosity.

What was so scary about Pluth in the daytime that the People didn't want to venture out? She thought.

The carriage finally stopped in front of one of the many towers. Ami nearly vomited in relief. Ados looked as bad as she felt. Ami stumbled out of the carriage, leaning against it for support. Ados joined her. Uriah and James stood nearby, looking concerned.

"C-Captain," Ados stammered.

"Don't speak," Ami ordered. Once the nausea faded, she

took in her surroundings. The building in front of them was a plain, square, concrete skyscraper with a large sign in brass stating *Dali Security, Inc.* Looking up, she couldn't see the top.

Flander wheezed heavily from the other side of the carriage. The Centaur had been forced to run behind the carriage. Ami was impressed that he had managed to keep up. Seeing how he was about to collapse, she mentally noted to improve the cover's stamina when they trained. A male Werewolf dressed like a bodyguard came out to greet Caleb. The Werewolf lord muttered something to the male. He went back inside the building. A few moments later, the bodyguard returned with a large water bottle. He gave the bottle to Flander, who thanked him breathlessly.

"Caleb?" Ami asked.

"Yes?" Caleb turned to face her.

"Where's Sal?" she asked.

Caleb's face fell. "He's in the stadium. The priests have it surrounded with their own security." When Ami continued to stare at him, he asked, "What is it?"

"Aren't you going to take me to him?" Ami asked. Isn't that why she was here in the first place?

"The priests aren't going to let you through. We need to come up with a plan," Luther argued.

A small knot of frustration curled in Ami's chest. Then she remembered something Salvador said. *Conri said I was an ally. Do I have a Bond with him?* Ami thought.

She closed her eye and went to her Bonds. She examined her Bonds closely. The type of Bond Conri referred to was an ancient one, one that even the Vincians rarely used. Its string would be utterly different from the others. Using her magic, she pulsed a small amount in all directions. A reaction similar to a muscle jerk caught her attention. She eagerly followed it. The Bond was dangling loosely, as if about to be cut loose. Ami stared at it.

While she could see the string, it had no color. Glancing

at her other Bonds, this one looked dead. She wasn't sure if she was doing the right thing or what would happen, but she needed to get to Salvador. She reached up and grabbed it. The string erupted into swirls of browns and greens as soon as she did. It felt far different than her other Bonds. She surmised it was because it was with Conri. Focusing on the Bond, she opened her eye. The image of a string appeared before her like a guide. She started to walk. Her males quickly followed behind her. She ignored Caleb's and Luther's shouts.

Ami learned rather quickly that Bonds don't care about buildings or other obstructions that may hinder its path. More than several times, she ran into a wall of a random building by focusing on the Bond string too much. Ami ignored the males' stifled chuckles. Eventually, with a smarting lip and bruised ego, she found the stadium. She and her cover stood watching from an alleyway across the street from the stadium. Two white-gowned guards guarded one entrance, looking bored. Ami sensed magic around the entrance but couldn't determine its exact purpose from where she stood. From their viewpoint, she couldn't see any other entry or exit. There also didn't seem to be any other guards.

That's odd. If the priests were so secretive, you'd think they would have heavier security, Ami thought as she tried to formulate a plan. *Even the magic around the entrance isn't strong or warded against intruders. Are they that arrogant or lax?*

"Captain, what's the plan?" Uriah murmured.

Ami glanced around. The building was newer than anything she'd seen in a long time. The sides were smooth and made of concrete. Getting a good grip while climbing up the wall would be difficult. The windows also didn't have ledges, created to be flush with the concrete walls. Another difficulty.

"We're going to need a distraction. Volunteers?" Ami asked.

"What kind of distraction?" Flander asked.

"I have one volunteer. I need another," Ami stated, not looking at the paling Centaur.

James sighed. "I'll do it."

"Thank you," Ami said. "Lure the guards away from the entrance. We will need to be able to get through the front door."

"How?" James asked.

Ami shrugged. "Start wrestling."

"Centaurs don't wrestle," Flander pointed out.

"You're about to learn how," Ami retorted. "Go."

As reluctant as they seemed about their task, James and Flander put on a believable show. Pride swelled in Ami's chest at the display. Their "wrestling" instantly grabbed the guards' attention. They abandoned their posts to yell at and try to separate them. Ami, Uriah, and Ados quickly snuck inside. Ami was surprised that she didn't feel the normal tingle of passing through magic. They entered a large lobby area. In front of Ami were stairs that led to seating in the upper tiers. She spotted a set of stairs that led down to her right. Against the walls were empty kiosks that would serve snacks and drinks during events. That was when they noticed the chanting.

It echoed eerily through the massive empty halls. The hairs on Ami's neck and arms went straight up. Glancing at Uriah and Ados, they were also disturbed. Carefully they walked the set of stairs that went down. The chanting grew louder the closer they got to the main arena floor. What she saw made her gasp in awe.

The main arena was transformed entirely from the regular immaculate cut grass used for sports. The grass was three feet high, and the dirt looked like mulch. Random trees and shrubs sprouted around the field. The air smelled like ozone. Even though it was daytime and the stadium had an open ceiling, it was dark, like twilight. It was as if they had entered a haunted wood.

Then she saw the chanters. The cover crouched down slightly to sneak up behind the chanters. Dressed in the traditional white and gold robes, they were all Elves. Ami counted four males and two females. Then she noticed what they were standing on. At their feet were large, dark yellowish, glowing runes carved into the ground. A pained gasp stole her attention. Salvador was in the middle of the chanters. His arms were bound by numerous iron chains that glowed green against his fur. He was on his knees and about to collapse. Minor bloody cuts covered his entire body. Ami wouldn't be surprised if more were hidden under his dirty pants. Salvador let out a pained whimper.

That sound, that specific noise, snapped something in Ami. Her magic roared. Her anger made her cold. Standing straight up, she walked between two chanters. As she did, her magic erased the runes etched in the ground. The ritual the chanting priests were performing disappeared. The priests cried out in surprise. Ami ignored them. Her only focus was Salvador. The Werewolf had collapsed onto his face. He panted heavily into the ground, as if relishing the feel of the earth. He had lost too much weight in Ami's eyes. The pair of pants he wore threatened to fall off. His bulky figure was gone. His fur didn't shine and was filthy.

"What do you think you're doing?" a female Elf shrieked, stomping her way toward Ami.

Ami didn't answer her. She examined the chains, looking for a way to break them. A small hand gripped her shoulder roughly. In one smooth motion, Ami turned. The female Elf sneered at her.

"You are not authorized—" she started to say until Ami backhanded her. The Elf landed on the ground with a solid thud. A second later, loud snoring was heard from the knocked-out Elf. Ami looked around at the shocked priests. Without a word, she hit each priest with a small ball of magic. Each priest fell to the ground asleep.

"Lakeshore, Fallenleaf," Ami spoke, her voice echoing in the still air. The two flinched, straightening their postures at her voice. "Take out the trash."

As the two followed orders, Ami returned to the chains. Each chain had a rune etched into it. Most of them were for "fire" and "containment." The one she was looking for was "freedom." It was difficult because its shape was almost identical to the "sky" and "wind" runes. It took well past Uriah and Ados throwing the unconscious priests out of the stadium before she stumbled upon the correct one. She pressed her finger against the chain link near Salvador's torso. Her magic replied instinctively.

Chink, chink, chink!

The chains fell away loose from Salvador. Ami caught him before he fell entirely to the ground. Holding him made her realize how much weight Salvador had lost since she last saw him. She quickly picked him up, bridal style. Salvador didn't wake. He hung limp in her arms like a rag doll.

"Sir?" Ados asked.

"Let's return to Lord Dali," Ami replied, her voice monotone. Cold anger drummed through her veins. Her other emotions were on mute. Her magic swirled dangerously, waiting for approval to create a hurricane. The feel of Salvador in her arms was the only thing rooting her to reality and holding back the raging monster clawing in her mind.

They walked out of the stadium. As they reached the top of the stairs, Ami swore she heard a whisper from the arena. She paused, looking over her right shoulder. Strangely, the stadium looked more haunted than before. It was as if it was a hidden graveyard. Shivers went down Ami's spine. If she walked faster to leave the stadium, it was for Salvador. When they reached the exit, they saw Flander and James sitting on the guards like makeshift cushions.

"Captain." They stood up. The guards didn't move or make a sound. Behind the downed guards were the still-sleeping bodies of the tossed priests.

"Let's go, lads," Ami said. The warm sun thawed some of her anger and her monotone voice. She didn't know how she knew the way back, but somehow she led them back to the tower.

Caleb was pacing in front of his building. Luther was talking with his arms waving dramatically. The carriage and horses were gone. When Caleb noticed Ami and her cover, he nearly tripped over his feet mid-turn. Stumbling a few steps, Caleb gathered his footing and raced to them. Luther followed.

"Salvador, my son, are you all right?" Caleb asked frantically. He started lightly patting his son's face, trying to wake him.

"He passed out from the pain. I destroyed the ritual runes. The priests are unconscious. The chains are useless now," Ami reported in a monotone voice. The raging monster was growling and pacing like a caged animal.

Caleb nodded, still looking at his son with a torn look of relief and pain. "Come inside. Let's get him settled."

Luther went ahead to call a Healer. Caleb ushered them in. The guards at the front lobby gate became alarmed when they saw their boss's son in such a state. The guards got them through their security protocols quickly and without hassle. Caleb led them to the elevators. Ami was surprised at how roomy they were. All of them were able to enter without being squished. The rage ebbed away as Ami's memories went nostalgic. As the elevator went up, all Ami could think was how the voices would have loved this feeling. Felicia would've loved it the most, despite the aggressive voice's objections. Emotion would've squealed like a child on a swing set. Blessing would absorb the excitement in her own motherly way. Serene would hum a song in happiness.

Great Almighty One, I miss them, Ami thought sadly.

The elevator stopped at the twelfth floor. When the doors opened, they saw Luther standing about halfway down the hall. He motioned for them to come. Entering the room he motioned to, Ami was surprised to find a makeshift hospital room. What really surprised her was seeing Theo.

"Amaranth, it's good to see you again," Theo greeted her.

Ami carefully set Salvador on the bed. He didn't even stir. "We'll catch up later. Please tend to your patient," Ami said, her voice still monotone. "Caleb, does your building have a fitness center?"

"It does. Why?" Caleb asked, barely glancing away from Salvador.

"What floor?" Ami asked. The raging monster was starting to pace again. She needed to release her emotional energy in a non-murderous way.

"The third floor. Why—"

"Excuse me." Ami abruptly left the room. She bypassed the elevators and took the stairs. Ignoring the males calling after her, she reached the third floor. The entire floor was the fitness center. That was fine with Ami. Taking off her sandals, she went to the closest treadmill. She set the speed to her running pace and ran.

Her magic and emotions were all over the place now that Salvador wasn't grounding her. Anger, frustration, and confusion clouded her mind. She ran despite the raging monster pacing more and more impatiently in her head. Ami knew this monster. This creature she created in her mind did awful things when it took control. She swore a long time ago to never let it go that far again. The only way to calm it down was to exhaust herself. It didn't help that the males were trying to talk to her. It egged the raging monster closer to the surface. Can't they tell that she doesn't want to talk? Can't they see that she's angry?

They. Would. Not. Shut. Up.

Ami punched the stop button, her fist making a sizeable dent in the control panel. The treadmill stopped working. She swirled to face the males. They each took several steps back. She imagined she looked deranged.

Panting like a diseased animal, she snarled, "What in your clueless brains makes you think that I want to TALK? GET OUT

OF MY SIGHT!" Her roar shook the mirrors in the center. The four scrambled out of the center as if she had summoned Egan in his horse form to chase them.

Still feeling frustrated and angry, she went to the weights. Time was meaningless to her as she underwent numerous dumbbell exercises. When her arms gave out, she put the dumbbells away and went to the machines, focusing on her legs. When her legs gave out, she finally stopped. The monster was gone. Her anger had cooled. She was in control again. She was drenched in sweat. She looked outside through the glass windows and realized it was nighttime. All she wanted to do was shower and sleep.

She went to the female locker room. On one of the benches was a pile of clothes. Curious, Ami walked over to look. On top of the clothes was a note.

Lady Rose, here are fresh clothes for your post-workout. Towels are in the main cabinet. Body wash is in the shower. Come to the elevator area after your shower.
    Luther

Ami found the towels and body wash. She cranked the shower all the way to its hottest. Ami could only think about the priests and their rituals as she stood there. She knew for certain that the Dali curse was no longer a curse. Where had the idea of Conri being a demon come from? As far as Ami knew, Conri wasn't even in Rascal folklore. If Salvador hadn't mentioned him, she wouldn't have found out that Conri was actually a Royian folk hero from her research in the library. So where had the Dali curse story come from? Was it made up? If so, who had made it up, and why? Did Caleb, Luther, or perhaps both know more than what they were letting on? Why did the priests think Conri was a demon? What did they get out of this? Why was Deena allowing this to happen to her brother? All these questions slowly disappeared as the scalding hot water and steam eased Ami's sore muscles.

After using the body wash, she rinsed off quickly. Exiting the shower, she dried and changed into the clothes gifted to her. They were a purple tunic and white leggings. Oddly she found a strange item. Looking at it for a long while, it finally clicked that it was some type of bra. The material was stretchy, yet firm. Several tries later, she figured out how it went. It felt odd, but she did like having her breasts not bouncing all over the place.

I'll have to ask where to get more of these, Ami thought.

She carried her dirty clothes in one hand. She tossed her used towel in a nearby bin labeled with a sign for dirty towels. She found her sandals and slipped them on. The elevator area was on the opposite side of the showers and the treadmills. Near the elevators was a type of bar. At first, Ami thought it was a check-in area. As she drew closer, she saw Luther piddling around.

"Ah, Lady Rose. How was your workout?" Luther asked casually.

"Much needed," Ami replied.

"Quick question: Are you allergic to anything?" Luther asked.

"Melons, silk, and satin," Ami answered.

"All melons?" Luther asked. Ami nodded. "All righty then. One moment."

Ami watched Luther place chunks of pineapple, strawberries, blueberries, a scoop of brown powder—Ami hoped it was cocoa because that sounded delicious right now—and milk in a strange clear container. He placed a lid on it. Then he put the unknown container on a stand. Luther turned it on and pressed a button. A loud swirling sound made Ami jump. The contents were being shredded and mixed at a fast speed. The colors changed from yellowish pink to brown. Once finished, Luther removed the container, popped the lid, and poured the smooth liquid into a tall glass. Placing a straw in it, he handed it to Ami.

"Protein shake. You missed dinner," Luther explained.

Ami took the drink. The liquid was thicker than she expected. It took a moment for her to suck it up in the straw. Once she did, she was pleased with the taste.

"Thank you," Ami said quietly, sucking on her straw eagerly.

"No problem. Anything for the lass who helped my godson," Luther said with a forced smile.

"Are you upset with Sal or me?" Ami asked.

Luther looked startled at the question. Then he sighed. "More with Sal. Like, how could he not talk about me? Did I do something to embarrass him?"

"I didn't learn about his mother until I saw a picture of her in his room, and I had known him for almost three years then," Ami pointed out.

Luther blinked. "Hmmm. I'm overreacting, aren't I?"

"Salvador is a very private Person," Ami said carefully.

"Takes one to know one?" Luther asked knowingly.

Ami merely smiled around her straw. After drinking the shake, she handed the empty glass to Luther. "Thank you for the drink. Where are we staying?" she asked.

"I'll show you," Luther offered. He walked around the bar to the elevators.

They entered. Luther pushed the number fourteen. As the elevator moved, Luther said, "Your lads haven't been around females much, huh?"

"I apologize for the machine. I'll work to repay you," Ami said sincerely. She felt terrible about that now that her emotions were calm.

Luther waved her off. "Don't worry about it. Caleb will understand."

"How's Sal?" Ami asked.

"That Healer is wonderful," Luther commented, sounding surprised. "He healed Sal up in no time. Do you know him?"

"I do. Nurse van Gogh was my therapist when I woke up from my coma. He and Sal met a few times," Ami answered.

"That's good," Luther said as the elevator stopped at its floor.

Ami followed the Werefox down the hall until they stopped at the fourth door on the right. Luther pointed to the two doors on the opposite side. "Your lads are in those two rooms. Sleep well, Lady Rose," Luther said.

"Thank you, Sir Luther," Ami said with a small smile.

"Just Luther is fine."

"Ami is fine with me."

Luther left. Ami entered her room. She collapsed on the queen-size bed and fell asleep immediately.

Jasmine's arms shook. The last blood drawing took more out of her than she had realized. Even the Dragons were looking at her with concern. She scoffed. She could feel their hope that she would pass away in her sleep and free them. But with her sister so close and Belladonna's minion playing general, it would be worse for the Dragons if she died. Jasmine knew Belladonna planned to kill her just to take over the slave Bond. Unfortunately for Belladonna, Jasmine had backup plans upon backup plans to prevent that.

How can I eliminate this fake Tso without raising Belladonna's suspicions? Jasmine thought as she paced with a trembling cold cup of tea.

She would also have to locate the real Tso to rescue him and cure him of any poison Belladonna had experimented on him with. As much as she didn't like the Werefox, he was competent in his position. A small amount of trust was better than always being on pins and needles with the fake Tso. The other generals were getting suspicious of the fake Tso. That was helpful.

This could be my opportunity to gain the other generals as allies. If I can help with their suspicions and give them enough evidence that this is not Tso, they could help me locate the real one, Jasmine thought, trying to be positive.

It was hard to be optimistic right now. Amaranth was away from Talient. Jasmine's heart panged painfully. She missed her friend. A lot of unspoken tension was between them. Jasmine knew it was because of her sister's scheme. She couldn't tell Amaranth straight off the bat about Belladonna. Her sister has spies everywhere. Jasmine feared Amaranth was the pest Belladonna referenced. If Amaranth was, then perhaps Jasmine had a chance at defeating her sister for once.

Amaranth is my only hope right now.

The following day, Ami woke up feeling like she had been run over by several horses and the carriage the horses had been attached to and then sat on by all three of her cousins. Forcing her body to move, she took a long, hot shower. A sinking feeling gnawed at her stomach. Something was going to happen, and she wouldn't like it. She wondered if the priests would make an appearance and try to blame Caleb for rescuing Salvador. Hot anger surged in her chest.

I won't allow that to happen, Ami vowed.

Exiting the shower, she dried and changed into dry clothes. She chose a summer dress with short sleeves and reached her knees. The pattern was a mixture of different purples. It looked like a painter put a blindfold on and dipped the paintbrush in the closest shade. Ami liked it. Forgoing shoes, she exited her room. Waiting outside was her cover. Irritation and annoyance made Ami's only eyebrow twitch.

"Why are you waiting outside my room like beggars?" Ami demanded in an icy tone.

"W-We didn't know when you would come o-out," Ados stammered.

"It is highly improper for a male to wait outside his commanding officer's room like this," Ami stated, gesturing to their positions.

"We didn't know," Uriah murmured.

"Obviously," Ami nearly sneered. "Once this mission is over, we will be going over military etiquette, and I'll make sure to let the generals know that we will not be leaving for a mission until you four are up to *my* standards. Now get up."

She started down the hall, not waiting for them to stand. The smell of freshly made food led her to the stairs. Going down to the twelfth floor, the scent was more potent. Entering the floor, she briefly saw Caleb and Luther entering Salvador's room. Following them were Werewolves with pushing carts and covered dishes. Ami's stomach growled loudly. Hurrying down the hall, she peered inside Salvador's room.

"Ami!" Salvador called out as soon as he noticed her.

"Sal," Ami greeted back, entering the room gingerly. It was already crowded.

"Amaranth, we didn't realize you were up already," Caleb said apologetically.

Luther looked confused. "I told your males how to order food and have it sent to your rooms. Did they not inform you?"

Ami gave a forced smile. "It must've slipped their minds."

Luther frowned. Before he could say anything, Salvador said, "Dad, I would like Ami to stay and eat with us."

Caleb and Luther looked alarmed. Ami felt awkward. Caleb and Luther more than likely wanted to update Salvador on what had been happening since his imprisonment with the priests and the family situation.

"Salvador," Ami spoke, "your father and uncle have been worried about you. I'll catch up with you at dinner."

"Are you sure?" Salvador asked.

Ami nodded. "Yes. Enjoy your time with them."

Salvador seemed suspicious. "Okay. I'm going to hold you to that."

"See you later, good sirs," Ami said, dramatically bowing at them. Salvador laughed at Caleb and Luther's gaping faces. Ami smirked as she left. It disappeared when she saw the males hovering outside the room. Irritation flared in her chest. She said nothing as she left the room and headed to the elevators.

"Sir, where are we going?" James asked anxiously.

"What haven't we done this morning?" Ami asked instead as they waited for the elevator doors to open.

The males glanced at each other, not wanting to answer. Ados, the brave fool, did. "Eat?"

"Exactly," Ami snapped.

"Why didn't you tell us?" Uriah asked.

"Because I thought it was obvious, and there's no point in telling you where I want to go since you four seem to be impersonating leeches and following me everywhere," Ami snarled.

A dark cloud hung over the group as they awkwardly rode the elevator down to the main floor. Ami ignored the startled looks of the security guards. Being outside lifted the tension in Ami's chest. The males remained quiet, not wanting to stir her ire again. Ami looked around. The street was filled with fog. Taking a deep breath, she examined the smells around her. Horses, various People, moisture, smoke, fresh pancakes— She zoned in on the pancakes. Her nose led them to a hole-in-the-wall restaurant.

The restaurant was old but well-kept. Numerous worn red leather booths lined the walls. The middle was divided into more stalls clothed in the same worn leather. A counter separating the kitchens was moderately busy with the current orders. Only a few booths were occupied.

"How many, sweetie?" the Werewolf waitress asked warmly.

"Five, please," Ami answered.

"All right, please follow me," the waitress said, grabbing a handful of menus. She led them to the back wall where several Centaur-friendly booths were empty. Ami took her seat inside the booth. Flander carefully set himself down while the others cautiously got into the booth. Uriah sat next to Ami at a respectful distance. She was ready to kick him if he got any closer.

"What can I get you to drink?" the waitress asked, addressing the entire group.

"Coffee, please," Ami answered immediately. The males remained silent. "They're still deciding," Ami answered, frowning.

The waitress didn't appear to be offended. She nodded and left.

"Why didn't you answer her?" Ami asked.

"I panicked," Uriah barely murmured.

"Over a drink order?" Ami asked incredulously.

"This is my first time," Uriah whispered, his ears red in embarrassment.

"Mine too," the other three males echoed.

The realization shook Ami. Their mothers didn't let them order their own food? A lot of their social awkwardness made sense now. Her irritation and annoyance dried up. Slivers of guilt about her attitude needled her heart.

"All right, look at this part of the menu," Ami instructed calmly. She pointed to different menu sections, showing them where the drinks, individual platters, and combo meals were. By the time she finished, the waitress had returned with her coffee.

"Are you four ready for drinks?" the waitress asked, her voice still warm.

Uriah glanced at Ami for reassurance. She nodded subtly.

"I'll, um, have, um, o-orange juice, p-please," he managed to get out.

"C-coffee, please," Ados stuttered.

"Same, please," Flander said, not looking at the waitress in the eye.

"Orange juice, please," James replied quietly.

"Be right back," the waitress smiled as she took notes. When she left, the males let out a sigh of relief.

"You do know you have to give your food order to her, right?" Ami asked.

All four of them stared at her in horror.

"Can't you order for us?" Ados whined.

"Why would I do that?" Ami asked, sipping her coffee. It wasn't Logan's, but it wasn't bad.

"You did at the café," Flander pointed out.

"No, I didn't."

"You didn't?" James blinked.

Ami shook her head. "Chastity and Shayne prepared that as thanks. I had no say in it. Now, look at the menu and see what you want."

As the males perused the menu, the waitress arrived with their drinks.

"Are you ready to order?" she asked.

"We need a few minutes," Ami answered, smelling the males' panic.

The waitress nodded in understanding. Ados nearly stuffed his face in his coffee mug, choking on the hot liquid. Ami patted his back as he coughed. She had them practice saying their order and ensured they knew how they wanted their eggs. After ten minutes, the waitress came back.

"I'll go first," Ami said. She glanced at the menu and said, "I would like the blueberry pancake combo with crispy hashbrowns, wallowed and skirted, and my eggs over easy with toast. Also, the waffle combo with cheese grits and my eggs over easy."

"Is this for the table?" the waitress asked, writing furiously.

"No, that's just for me," Ami said. "Fallenleaf? Your turn."

At that moment, all the males froze. She could see the wheels of panic spiraling out of control in their petrified eyes. Ami and the waitress shared a glance. Ami signaled the Werewolf to stay silent as she turned her attention to the terrified Elf.

"Ados," Ami said gently. He stared at her, startled. "Can you tell me your order again?"

"M-My order?" Ados asked.

Ami nodded. "Yes, can you repeat it for me?" She tried to keep her tone gentle.

Ados gulped. He looked at the menu shaking in his hands. "Um, the-the pancake combo."

"Did you want any fruit with it?" Ami asked. The waitress listened attentively as she took the order.

"S-Strawberries," Ados stammered.

"Do you want hashbrowns or grits?" Ami asked.

"Hashbrowns. L-Like you did," Ados said, a blush rushing to his cheeks.

"Crispy hashbrowns, wallowed and skirted?" Ami clarified. Ados nodded. "How do you want your eggs?"

"Scrambled," Ados murmured.

"Is that all?" Ami asked. When Ados nodded, she turned to James. "James, what is your order?"

She repeated the exercise with each male. The waitress, bless her, patiently wrote their orders without interruption. With a nod, the waitress left. An odd silence gathered at their table. Ami wasn't sure what it was. Something had changed between them. She didn't know if it was good or bad.

"That was the first time you used our names," Uriah broke the silence.

Ami took a sip of coffee. "It is. Are you offended?"

Ados broke into a wide grin. "No, we've been waiting for

you to call us by name for ages."

Ami blinked. "Why?"

They looked at her with confused looks. "It's what comrades do," James pointed out.

"I'm your superior officer," Ami countered.

"You call the Head Knight Commander by name," Flander argued.

"I was his training master and sparring partner," Ami retorted, smugly drinking her nearly empty coffee cup.

"And you're supposed to teach us stuff, right?" Ados asked.

Ami considered it. "Yes."

"Then, as our teacher, you can call us by name," Uriah argued.

Their debate paused when the waitress returned to refill their drinks. Once she left, Ami replied, "There are reasons why I haven't."

"Can you explain them?" Flander asked.

"To protect you," Ami stated.

"From who?" Ados asked.

"Other males. If we're too friendly, they will think I have manipulated you like other females do," Ami explained bitterly. Military etiquette was much more straightforward in Vinci.

"We don't care." Uriah shrugged.

"I do," Ami said firmly. "My reputation can harm your career."

The males glanced at each other. Then it was as if a candle was lit.

"You don't know your reputation, do you?" James asked, his voice filled with awe.

"I'm dreading to hear of it," Ami grumbled.

Just then, the waitress and a cook came with their food. Each carefully took their hot plates. Ami inhaled the smell greedily. When the waitress and cook left, they dug in.

"You raised our reputations by selecting us," Uriah said

after a moment of eating.

"Except for Flander, I don't see how," Ami said, her mouth half full of blueberry pancake.

"Me?" Flander asked, pointing to himself.

"Yes, with my alliance with the Centaurs," Ami replied.

"We were quite excited to be selected," James said eagerly.

"No, you weren't," Ami retorted. "The three of you were terrified and wary of me."

"It was nerves," Uriah barked.

"You barely showed me respect, already letting me know how you truly thought of me," Ami snarled back. "Don't try to flatter me now. I don't appreciate fakeness."

Tense silence and the clatter of silverware filled the air.

"I was scared of you," Ados admitted. "But that was because I didn't know how to act around you."

"You still don't," Ami pointed out before stuffing her mouth with a whole egg piece.

"Can't you say anything positive?" Uriah snapped.

Ami chewed the egg for longer than it should have taken. Despite their awkwardness and lack of social interaction, they were her cover. Her males. Even though they didn't want to admit it, her words meant a lot to them. She had sworn to the voices that she wouldn't treat the males like Rascal females. What she said next would be crucial. She swallowed.

"All of you are intelligent," Ami began. They jumped at the compliment. "While we haven't been a team for a long time, I appreciate that I don't have to micromanage you on setting up tents, making a fire, or teaching you how to hunt. You take your nightly guard duties seriously, making me feel safe.

"I enjoy your questions. I like how you present different arguments or possibilities I haven't considered. All of you think outside the box, and it's refreshing. Even though we haven't spent that much time sparring, I'm eager to see where you all are and teach you what I know," Ami finished.

Ados had tears flowing down his face. Flander was blushing. James openly gaped at her. Uriah looked at her as if seeing her for the first time. Ami moved onto her other combo plate. The cheese grits were a little dry, but it was still tasty.

"Every male in Putra Helioxos cornered the cadets and interrogated them about you," Uriah said, his voice rumbling like thunder.

"What for?" Ami asked, taking a large bite of a waffle.

"Everyone heard about you saving the cadets at the expense of your life. We wanted to know what you were like," Uriah answered.

"And their answer?"

"They couldn't really answer. Most of them denied knowing much about you. A few claimed that you were just like any Rascal female," James replied. "The soldiers did the same thing at my fort."

"Same," Ados echoed.

Flander looked uncomfortable.

"What did they ask you, Flander?" Ami asked.

"They wanted to know what you were like," Flander murmured so low she could barely hear him.

"And what did you say to them?" Uriah asked, his voice full of warning.

"That you were a good storyteller, and that's all I really knew," Flander answered quickly.

Ami shrugged. "That's not the worst I've been known for."

"What stories do you know?" Uriah asked curiously.

"I'll tell one for our payment. Let's finish eating," Ami said.

They finished eating after ten minutes. The waitress gathered their plates and empty drinks. They exited the booth and went to the front counter. A few more booths were occupied during their breakfast.

"What would you like for payment?" Ami asked the waitress.

The Werewolf pondered for a while. "How about a romantic tale?"

Ami knew a good one. For thirty minutes, she told the tale of *The Bard and the Dame*. It was a story of a traveling bard who helped a female Knight travel back home. She had been ambushed and wounded when they met. Along the way, they argued, laughed, and fell in love. However, the female Knight had to serve the *Mai'po* in the capital. The bard understood and tried to become a bard of the court. The *Mai'po* wasn't impressed. The bard and the female Knight said heartbroken goodbyes, promising they would meet again one day. Unfortunately, the female Knight was killed in battle. When the bard heard the news, he continued to travel the world, singing of his lost love until the day he died. There wasn't a dry eye in the restaurant when Ami finished.

"That was beautiful." The waitress wept, drying her tears with her apron.

"Is that sufficient payment?" Ami asked.

The waitress nodded. They left the restaurant. The fog was gone, leaving the morning crisp. Unlike Talient, there were hardly any People outside.

"That was intense," James commented.

"It's one of my favorites," Ami admitted.

"You like plays, don't you?" Flander asked.

"It is my favorite form of literature. I would say poems would be my next favorite," Ami replied with a small smile.

"Lady Rose!" a voice called out. A Werewolf dressed like one of Caleb's security guards ran to them. "My lady, you are needed at headquarters," the Werewolf panted frantically.

"Is Salvador okay?" Ami demanded.

The guard shook his head. "The priests and Dali clan have arrived."

CHAPTER 17

Ami and her cover followed the guard back to the tower. Luther was pacing in front of the security front desk. The guards inside waved them in, skipping protocol.

"Where were you?" Luther hissed.

"Eating breakfast so you could talk to your godson in peace," Ami answered coolly.

Luther sighed. "I hate priests."

"Are they trying to get Sal back?" Ami asked. Luther led them to the elevators. He pushed the button hard.

"Yeah, and the matriarch is here with Deena." Luther tried to snarl, but his tone sounded defeated.

"Don't give up just yet," Ami said reassuringly. The elevator doors opened.

"What do you mean?" Luther asked as they entered.

"I'm here, and I won't tolerate anyone hurting my friend," Ami said darkly. The elevator door closed. Luther pushed the number ten.

"I don't think you realize how much power the priests have in Pluth," Luther warned.

"They haven't realized how much power they don't have over me," Ami retorted.

Half a minute later, the doors opened. Luther exited first. Ami and the cover followed. The floor was open without walls, and tall ceilings made it feel even more extensive. Thin colorful carpet covered the floor. Black leather sofas dotted the space with accompanying side tables. Each couch was occupied by several dark gray or brown Werewolves of varying ages, numbering around thirty. Hovering around the Werewolves were the priests. Their white and gold robes were a stark contrast to the dark room. Ami counted fifteen priests, far more than yesterday. The female priest Ami hit glared at her. Ami smirked at the bulging, purple swelling on the female's right side of her face. Innocently, Ami waved at her. The priests on either side of the female priest held her back from lunging at Ami. The Dragon smiled innocently. Caleb and Salvador stood far from the priests and clan members. Salvador perked up when he saw Ami.

"This is it?" one of the older Werewolves sneered. Her snide voice was like nails on a chalkboard.

"Watch your tongue, Prudence," Caleb growled.

"Watch your tone, male," Prudence snipped back.

Caleb bared his white teeth as if challenging her. Prudence bared her teeth as well, but backed down. With a "hmph," she looked down her nose at Ami. Ami stared back. She wondered how long it would take until the old wolf became uncomfortable.

"This is an odd family reunion," Ami commented offhandedly.

"You interrupted a sacred ritual," one of the priests stated in a stern tone.

"Be specific," Ami stated back.

"The one to get rid of—" the priest started to say.

"Was it Delicia, the sacred ritual to provide food for the poor? Or was it Bru'tto, the sacred ritual of cleansing?" Ami asked, observing her nails casually.

The priests looked aghast.

"How does a sinner like you know our rituals?" the swollen-faced female priest sputtered.

"Do you think the priests are only in Rascu?" Ami asked. "We have them, too, in Vinci. Unlike your sect, the ones I knew could tell the difference between demon possession and other maladies."

"Conri is a demon!" a different priest shouted.

"No, he's not," Ami said, her voice neutral. She ignored the hopeful looks Luther, Caleb, and Salvador were giving her.

"You are so absorbed in your sin that you don't realize—" the priest ranted.

"Do you not read texts besides the holy book and rituals?" Ami asked exasperatedly.

"What do you mean?" asked an old female Werewolf. She looked a few years younger than Prudence.

"What do you know about Conri? His origins?" Ami asked.

"What does that have to do with anything?" Prudence demanded.

"I've read about Conri only in Royian texts and stories," Ami added. When she realized they weren't getting it, she exclaimed, "He's not from Rascu!"

"Because he possessed Salvador," a soft yet firm female voice spoke.

From behind the priests, a young female Werewolf emerged. She was dressed in gray robes, typical for the most dedicated to the temple. Ami watched Deena's light gray eyes flicker back and forth like they did when she saw her at Old Congress five years ago.

"If Conri possessed Salvador, as you say, then why does he look like a good combination of your parents, Deena?" Ami inquired.

"Possession won't change one's physical appearance, Amaranth," Deena retorted, her eyes hard.

"That's where you're wrong," Ami said smugly.

"You act like you know everything, but you know nothing

of the spiritual world," Deena sniffed haughtily.

"You act like you're the center of the universe and jealous the sun took your spot," Ami smiled.

"For a foreigner, you almost speak well," Deena sneered.

"For a Rascal female, your speech is lacking." Ami continued to smile as if nothing bothered her.

Gritting her back teeth in frustration, Deena growled, "How does a foreigner know more about Conri than the holy priests?"

"How does a native Rascal not know he's Royian?" Ami countered.

The tension between the two females reached volcanic levels as they stared each other down. Ami's soldiers took several steps back, eyeing the females warily. Luther watched the verbal spar like he was at the stadium with popcorn. Caleb frowned. Salvador looked torn on who he wanted to defend.

After an undiscernible amount of time, Deena looked away. She sighed heavily.

"Why do you say Conri isn't a demon?" she asked, her tone curious.

"Simple. The iron rings," Ami replied.

They looked at her with confused looks.

"The iron rings were dipped in holy water and prayed over by numerous priests," one priest pointed out.

Ami shook her head. "That means nothing to a demon."

"Then what is Conri?" Luther asked.

Ami paused. She turned to Caleb. She asked, "When did you first hear about Conri?"

Caleb blinked at the question. "When Myst, my wife, and I went to Roy for our honeymoon."

"Unapproved marriage," Prudence grumbled.

"Get over it, Prudence," Caleb snapped.

"Who told you about Conri?" Ami asked, ignoring their barbs.

"All the locals. What's going on?" Caleb asked.

"When did you realize Conri was in Salvador?" Ami asked.

Caleb went quiet. His stance told her that he knew the exact moment. Salvador picked up on this too.

"Dad?" Salvador asked.

Caleb sighed as if a great weight was placed upon his shoulders. "There was a cave in the Rol'yo Mountains. Myst heard that Conri climbed that mountain often. She wanted to find the exact spot. We were halfway up the mountain when a storm rolled in. We saw a cave and took shelter. Inside was a type of shrine dedicated to Conri. Myst was looking at it while I got out blankets when she was engulfed in green light.

"I tried to get to her, but a barrier surrounded her. Out of the green light came the smell of fresh earth. Then the light disappeared, and Myst collapsed. When she came to, she immediately knew she was pregnant and believed Conri had blessed us. I think Conri took advantage of my pregnant wife and decided to take up residence."

"You never told us that ridiculous story," Prudence sputtered.

"Why not?" Ami asked. "It's just as ridiculous as your ancestor fighting a witch over a unicorn."

"That happened!" one of the younger Werewolves exclaimed. She looked to be in her twenties.

"When and where?" Ami asked.

The female Dali members looked puzzled.

"Why is that relevant?" Prudence asked, not even hiding her disdain.

"If you knew where and when, you would've found the witch by now, correct?" Ami asked. "Also, why did you wait so long to find the witch and not interrogate them more about the so-called curse if you were so worried about it? Oh, wait," Ami paused dramatically. "That's because the story involved a male heir, not a female. My bad."

"Family is everything to a Dali," Prudence snarled.

"Until the priests arrive and suddenly their word is valued

more than a member of your family," Ami said coldly.

The female clan members flinched. The priests looked smug.

"How do you know it's not a witch's curse?" Deena asked.

"I've dealt with witches before," Ami said.

"How so?" Deena asked.

Ami thought about it. "There was one that tried to take my soul." Seeing the shocked looks, she continued, "Apparently, she came out every twenty years or so to devour four or five children's souls to live. I cut off her head when she kept rambling."

"You cut off her head?" James nearly shrieked.

"Yeah, she was annoying." Ami shrugged.

Deena visibly shook off her surprise. "What other witches have you encountered?"

Ami explained, counting off with her fingers. "Then another one was killing off the local wolf packs. Another one tried to seduce the king." Ami chuckled at the memory. "That was hilarious."

"Then it's not a witch?" a priest asked hesitantly.

Ami shook her head. "No, I think it's some kind of blessing Conri put on Salvador in the womb, and we have to figure out what it is."

"There you have it," Caleb said, his tone stern. He glared at the priests. "Leave Pluth now."

"Caleb, this is my house—" Prudence argued.

"No, this is my house, Prudence! The one your daughter, my wife, left to me in her will. Per her will, I am the head of the Dali clan until Salvador marries. You're dismissed." Caleb stared down at the elderly Werewolf. Ami realized she was seeing Lord Dali right now.

Grumbling under her breath, Prudence got up and stomped out of the room, heading for the elevators. The rest of the female Werewolves followed. The priests and Deena trailed after them. Deena glanced over her shoulder, looking at Ami with an undecipherable look. Ami didn't like it.

"I'm still confused," Luther said once the clan and priests left. "How do you know what Conri did was not a curse but a blessing?"

Ami mulled over her thoughts. "It started with the story of the Dali curse. The more I thought about it, the more it didn't make sense. Why would the Dali clan not seek out the witch and kill it or get more information about the curse? Also, from my observations, Conri only shows when Salvador experiences high emotions. That's when the rings activate."

"For the rings to activate, they react to magic, not a demon?" Ados asked.

Ami nodded. "Precisely."

"Why would Salvador experience high emotions recently?" Caleb asked.

Salvador's ears went flat on his head. "My emotions have been out of sorts since Ami's death and resurrection."

"I'm sorry," Ami said softly.

Salvador gave her a small smile. "I'm just glad you're okay."

"You know what this means, right?" Luther asked, his tone solemn. "Party time!"

Caleb groaned. Salvador grinned. "Uncle Lu loves parties," Salvador supplied.

"Why aren't you guys more excited?" Luther asked, nearly bouncing up and down like a child celebrating their birthday. "Sal isn't cursed. Caleb grew a spine against his in-laws, and the priests are gone. What isn't there to celebrate?"

"Hey!" Caleb started. Then he smiled. "Yes, this does require a celebration."

"Can we get pizza?" Salvador asked eagerly.

Caleb smiled fondly. "Of course."

"Yes!" Salvador cheered.

"Pizza?" Ami asked.

"Oh, yes. You'll love it. The place we go to also has arcade games," Salvador said excitedly.

Pizza was definitely Ami's new favorite food. The place

Salvador had mentioned was owned by a family of Werewolves that were famous in the city of Pluth. Ami and her cover were amazed by the variety and how many toppings could be on one single dish. That led to an eating competition between Uriah and Ami. They tied after stuffing themselves with what the locals called "The Dumpster." Ground beef, spiced turkey slices, mushrooms, mild and spicy peppers, black olives, and three types of cheeses topped the monstrosity. Ami was amused at the astonished looks from Caleb and Luther when they saw how much she ate. Poor Uriah looked sick to his stomach.

Ami was pleased to learn that the owners also had fizz. Theirs was a different flavor, resembling cherries. Ami liked how well it paired with the pizza. Once Ami and Uriah could move without feeling sick, Salvador showed them the arcade games. Odd electronic boxes that displayed pixelated characters and backgrounds that a player could move with either a button or a control stick fascinated Ami. She was obsessed with a game titled *Starfighter*. After numerous tries, she reached the final level, only for the final boss to finish her off in two moves. She accepted her loss and moved on to see what the other males were doing.

Salvador showed Ados how to play some fighting game that involved tapping the buttons in a particular sequence to release a combo against the enemy. Uriah and James partnered on a team game with a device that simulated crossbows. Flander wandered around, unsure. She walked towards Flander.

"Let's find a game to play," Ami suggested. Flander smiled at the idea.

The game they found was surprisingly of racecars. Both were intrigued by the idea. It took Ami a while to understand the controls, but Flander took it like a fish to water. He soundly beat her in the first game. Fired up and ready, Ami challenged him to another. She defeated him in the second game. When they started their third game, the rest of the males, including Caleb and Luther, came to watch.

"Go, Ami! Make him eat dirt!" Salvador and Ados cheered.

"C'mon, Flander. Show the captain how it's done," Uriah and James cheered as well.

The tension was high. Ami and Flander punched their buttons like maniacs, their control sticks clicking noisily. In the end, Flander just barely beat her. When the screen declared her loss, Ami sagged down to her knees. Standing back up, she offered her left hand.

"Good game, Flander." Ami smiled.

"Thank you, sir." Flander took her hand with a wide grin.

"It's getting late," Caleb said.

Ami glanced at the windows. The city lampposts glowed dimly in the dark. They started to trail out of the restaurant. Caleb and Luther led the group. Uriah and James talked animatedly about the game they played. Ados and Flander spoke about the other arcade games they played. Somehow Ami and Salvador walked several steps back from them.

"Come," Salvador said quietly.

Curious, she sneaked away from the group behind Salvador. He led her to a separate street.

"What's up, Sal?" Ami asked with concern. The solemn look on the Werewolf's face was unusual.

"We haven't been able to talk since Putra Hallas," Salvador said. He looked at her shyly.

"True. Witch hunting is time-consuming," Ami said. "What did you want to talk about?"

"I don't know," Salvador said with a dry chuckle. "I just want to spend time with you. I missed you a lot."

"I missed you too." Ami smiled. "Did you want to hear more about the Jade Heron?"

Salvador smiled. "I'd love that."

"Hey, where's Sal?" Luther asked just as they got to the tower. Everyone looked around.

"Where's the captain?" Uriah asked, alarmed.

Caleb entered the tower with a determined gait. He went straight to the security booth. The three guards sat there. Two looked up and acknowledged them, while the third stared intently at a large screen.

"Karl, where are they?" Caleb asked.

"One moment, sir," Karl murmured. After several seconds, he said, "They're on Kakara Street."

Karl swirled the screen around for Caleb to see. Through one of the street cameras, they watched as Salvador and Ami walked close together. Ami said something that made Salvador laugh so hard that he clutched his stomach. Caleb's lips formed a soft smile. He could hear Salvador's laugh in his head. It was exactly like his mother's laugh, whole and free. It had been a long time since Salvador was so carefree. Rose was a good influence.

Perhaps ... "Keep an eye on them," Caleb ordered.

"Yes, sir." The guards nodded.

Caleb turned to the worried soldiers. "Your captain is with Salvador. They are safe. Return to your rooms until she returns," Caleb said.

The soldiers glanced at each other, silently debating. Caleb swore they would defy his orders, but they obeyed reluctantly.

"They're cute together, aren't they?" Luther asked fondly. He stared at the screen with a rare soft look.

"I have an idea I want to run by you," Caleb said, heading to the elevators.

They didn't speak until they arrived on the eighth floor.

Numerous large offices lined the hallway. A plaque with a name and position was posted outside each door. Caleb opened the door at the end of the hall. The office was spacious. In the middle was a large oak desk with a cushy leather chair. A loveseat sat in front of it. Luther lounged lazily in it while Caleb sat in the leather chair.

"What's the idea?" Luther asked, even though he already had an idea.

"I was thinking of proposing a courtship between Salvador and Amaranth," Caleb replied.

"I thought she only saw him as a friend?" Luther asked.

"For now. I would stipulate that they would court for at least two years to see if their relationship would progress to marriage," Caleb answered.

Luther mulled the idea over. "I could see it working, but what about her citizenship?"

Caleb raised an eyebrow. "What about it?"

"She's Vincian. That may cause problems we don't know we're getting into," Luther pointed out.

"I don't see—"

BLEEEERR! BLEEEERR! BLEEEERR!

The red emergency lights saturated everything in hues of red. Caleb picked up the phone receiver at his desk. Punching a number, he called the front desk.

"Sir, the priests have your son and Lady Rose," Karl said frantically.

"Where are they?" Caleb demanded, standing up without realizing it.

"I managed to follow them until Fourteenth Street—Wait, I see them now! They're back at the stadium, sir," Karl informed.

"Get me the chief of police and a unit of guards," Caleb growled. He hung up the receiver.

"What's going on?" Luther demanded.

"The priests captured Salvador and Rose. They're at the stadium," Caleb answered shortly.

A stormy look crossed Luther's face. Then the Werefox smiled manically. "Can I kill some priests?"

"You may have that chance," Caleb replied, picking up the receiver again. He stared at it as if trying to remember something. Slowly and methodically, he dialed a series of numbers. After hitting the last number, he placed the receiver to his ear. Luther watched with a confused frown. The phone rang four times before it was picked up.

"This is unusual, Lord Dali," a solid female voice answered.

"I have a highly unusual situation, Lady Pera," Caleb replied. Luther gaped at Caleb.

"Why are you calling?" Lady Pera asked directly.

"Have you heard of Amaranth Rose?" Caleb asked.

"I know her, yes," Lady Pera admitted.

"You do?"

"Why are you inquiring about her?" Lady Pera asked, her tone cold.

That gave Caleb pause. It took a lot to impress Ravenna's mayor. He wondered how Rose managed to accomplish that miracle.

"She's in danger," Caleb stated.

Lady Pera snarled. "Who and why?"

"The priests from Octa. They think Salvador and Rose are possessed by demons," Caleb said, his voice shaking. A jolt of memories from Salvador's previous imprisonment flooded his mind and emotions.

"How can I help?"

Ami panted heavily. The runes circled around her glowed an eerie pink. She didn't know what that meant. She didn't think she could feel this much pain. It was as if each tendon of her muscles were snapped one by one. She felt her blood heat, and her stomach revolted numerous times from her screaming nerves. Sal, bound with new chains a few feet away, watched helplessly with tears flowing down his furry cheeks. He had cried and shouted for the priests to have mercy until he lost his voice a few moments ago. The glowing pink runes suddenly went away, releasing Ami from the ritual.

She collapsed. The black chains that pinned her arms to her sides jingled in protest. Coldness crept into her fingertips and toes. The pain was so great she felt half-numb. She couldn't even sense her tail. Both of her horns vibrated an earthquake of a migraine. Blood pooled out of her mouth. Her lungs burned. Her eye was closed, too weak to open.

"Captain," a whisper reached her ears. She almost didn't think she actually heard it. "Captain." The voice was more insistent, more worried. Ami struggled to open her eye. She failed. Her body went limp as the coldness inched up her hands and feet. She was so cold. It had been a long time since she felt like this. All she wanted to do was lie in front of a fire on top of one of the furs in her cousins' room and listen to them talk. Her heart squeezed painfully. She wanted her family right now.

"Captain!" She registered the voice as Uriah. This time she was able to open her eye. She was staring at the open blue sky. When did she move to her back? Wasn't she lying face down before? What time was it? Uriah hovered over her. He looked like he was torn from crying and fighting someone.

"What?" was all Ami could ask. Words couldn't formulate in her mind. The connection between her mouth and brain was disrupted somehow.

"C-Captain, you're bleeding bad," Uriah said, his voice quick and filled with panic.

Ami somehow managed to move her hand, or at least what she thought was her hand. Uriah glanced down. Something warm wrapped around Ami's ice-cold hand. Then a jolt of warmth made her gasp. The heat fought against the creeping coldness. The numbness faded away. It was replaced with sore and frayed nerves that made Ami moan in pain. Tears ran down her cheek.

"Captain?" Uriah's voice was deeper somehow. Ami looked at him. The Werewolf's sky-blue eyes shined like the deepest lake in Vinci.

"Uriah?" Ami gasped out. Whatever shorted her brain was gone. "Where are the priests?"

"The others are distracting them. How do I get these off?" Uriah said hurriedly. He tugged at the black chains still binding her.

"Where's Sal?" Ami asked.

Uriah huffed, looking over his shoulder. "He's over there glaring at me."

Ami's body started to tremble. She could smell the priests returning. "Uriah, go. They're coming back," Ami urged.

"Captain, I'm not leaving you," Uriah stated.

"Go," Ami stated. Before he could retort, she added, "That's an order, Second."

Uriah stared at her with a look she couldn't pinpoint. With a frustrated growl, Uriah stood up and ran. Ami couldn't focus on where he went. The runes surrounding her started to glow pink again.

Here we go again, Ami thought. Then all she knew was pain.

Uriah was elated. He wasn't sure how it happened or why, but it did. He ran down the hallway, dodging random spells from the priests chasing him. There were more than from the meeting with the Dali clan. It looked like the entire temple of Octa came. He darted through the exit. As he emerged from the stadium, pain erupted throughout his whole body. Surprised, his jaw locked. His legs stiffened momentarily until he pushed through the unknown pain, stumbling back into a run.

Eventually, he met up with the rest of the cover at the designated spot. Ados looked like he had just got out of the water. James and Flander panted while smoke emitted from their clothes.

"What happened?" Uriah demanded.

"A priest tried to drown me," Ados growled.

"I'm not sure," James panted in between words, "what the priest was going to do, but it didn't work."

"Fire," Flander spat.

"I barely managed to dodge most of the spells. I think I caught something that caused me a lot of pain," Uriah said.

"Do you know what it was?" Ados asked. He ran his fingers through his hair, slicking it back.

Uriah shook his head. "I didn't see the spell."

"Let's see if that healer is still at the tower. Did the captain say anything?" James asked.

Uriah's heart sank. Remembering how vulnerable his captain was and her blood made his blood run cold. "It was bad," he whispered.

The three came closer to him.

"How bad?" Ados asked in a deceptively calm voice.

"Her hand was ice cold, and blood came from her mouth. I don't think she could understand half of what I was saying. They have her bound in black chains like Heir Dali. They're torturing her," Uriah explained.

"And they're blocking her screams," Flander stated, his tone icy.

"If no one hears the screams—" Ados started.

"Then no one can come to her aid," James finished.

For once, the law could've helped them in this instance.

"Let's get healed up and plan," Uriah ordered. A headache started to ache around his temples.

"You okay?" Ados asked as they started walking.

"Getting a headache," Uriah murmured. Pain shot through his entire body. Groaning, it brought him to his knees. It felt like needles were stabbed into his muscles and twisted like some torturous sewing session.

"Uriah, what's wrong?" James asked, coming to his side. Uriah couldn't answer. All he could do was groan. "C'mon, he needs the healer now," James urged.

Uriah faintly remembered Ados and James half-carrying him back to the tower. He briefly saw Healer van Gogh, and then the next thing he remembered was being in a large meadow. The wildflowers were in full bloom. A breeze blew by him. A familiar scent that made his heart speed up made him follow the direction of the current. Standing before him was his captain.

"Uriah!" she called out. Even though she was only several hundred feet away, her voice sounded like she was much further away.

"Captain!" Uriah called back. He tried to make his feet move, but they refused. Out of sheer will, one foot obeyed. Then the other. Then they refused to move. Uriah got on his knees and crawled slowly to his captain. She couldn't move at all. When he got closer, he saw where her feet were embedded into the earth.

"Uriah." His captain smiled at him. Uriah stared. She never gave him that look before. It was mesmerizing. Suddenly her hands gripped his furry cheeks tightly. "Uriah, listen!" she ordered. When she had his attention, she explained, "Go to the Dali archives."

"Archives?" he asked dumbly.

"The Dali archives. Go and find more information about …" Her voice faded out at the end.

"Find more about what?" Uriah asked.

"The curse!" His captain appeared to be shouting, but her voice was fading again. Now that he noticed, everything around them was fading into darkness. His captain kept a firm grip on his cheeks. He absently wondered if she liked them. "Find more about the Dali curse!" His captain's voice was loud this time. Then her grip on his cheeks loosened, and everything, including his captain, faded to black.

Uriah woke up with a jolt. His captain's words rang clear in his mind. Despite his muscles protesting, adrenaline boosted him to get out of bed. He stumbled out of the makeshift hospital room. The hallway was empty. To his left, he saw the elevator door open.

"Uriah!" Ados and James ran up to him with worried looks.

"Are you sure you should be moving?" Ados asked worriedly.

"The healer said your muscles were deeply bruised," James added.

"I need to see Lord Dali," Uriah groaned. The adrenaline was starting to wear off.

The two Elves looked at each other briefly.

"He's this way," Ados said, heading towards the elevator.

The pain was coming back. He felt it creep up his feet to his ankles. He tried to suppress it from sheer will. It fought against him fiercely. By the time the elevator doors opened, Uriah's knees had buckled.

"Uriah, this was a bad idea," Ados said, his worry doubling.

"No!" Uriah barked. Panting heavily, he forced his wobbling legs to stand. "I need to speak to Lord Dali."

Seeing they wouldn't be able to deter him, they placed an arm over their shoulders and helped him walk to Lord Dali's office. It was the longest trek in Uriah's life. He repeated over and over his captain's words. Ados reached ahead and opened the office door. Inside was Luther, Lord Dali, and a tall, imposing female Werewolf.

"What's going on?" Lord Dali demanded.

"T-The captain. S-She said to l-look in the archives. The D-Dali archives," Uriah stammered out.

The three adult Werewolves stared at him with calculating looks.

"Why the Dali archives?" the female Werewolf asked. She looked familiar, but Uriah couldn't remember why.

"C-Captain said to l-look for the Da-Dali curse in the archives," Uriah said forcibly. His strength was fading fast. Black spots dotted his vision. Then darkness engulfed him. Uriah found himself surrounded by his magic. Gold and teal glittered around him. A strong pulse got his attention. His heart pumped harder the closer he got to it. It was a string of purple and black. The string was powerful, just like his captain.

When he woke up, it was afternoon. Theo was examining a clipboard. Then the black Werefox glanced at him.

"Welcome back," Theo greeted.

"Healer," Uriah grunted.

Theo returned to the clipboard. A frown began to deepen the corners of his mouth. Uriah let out a gasp when he tried to sit up.

"What's the deal with the white-dress People?" Theo asked abruptly, looking at Uriah with a solemn look.

"The priests?" Uriah asked. Theo nodded. "They kidnapped Dali and the captain because they believe the captain and Dali are possessed by demons," Uriah explained.

"Rascals believe in demons?" Theo asked, surprised.

Uriah furrowed his brows. "Do Royians not?"

Theo shook his head. "It's unscientific."

"There's a lot we can still learn from the spiritual world," Uriah said.

Theo hummed. "How's Amaranth?"

"Not good. They have her bound in chains like Dali. Have you heard anything else?" Uriah asked, forcing his muscles to move to a sitting position.

"All I know is there's something off with Deena. I can't explain it, but the closest I can think of is that she is five pounds of crazy in a two-pound bag," Theo commented.

What if it isn't Salvador who's possessed, but his sister? Uriah thought. He would have to prove it with hard evidence. Then he thought back on what his captain ordered him to look into. Did she suspect something was wrong with Deena as well? Why did she think the answer was in the Dali archives? The urge to fulfill his orders filled him with determination. Uriah tried to stand up. Theo pushed him back down by his shoulders.

"I need to look you over, and you need to eat. It's been over a day and a half," Theo informed him as he pressed his stethoscope against Uriah's furry chest.

Uriah's heart drummed against his breastbone. Was he asleep for that long? His captain was still being tortured while he remained unconscious. Shame filled his being. He didn't deserve to be a second. Uriah's entire body started to tremble. Theo tried to calm him down, but nothing could make the shame disappear. Uriah's breathing shortened as the anxiety and worry joined forces with the guilt. The emotions battled against Uriah's weak excuses and quickly disappearing resolve. A lightning-like spark flashed out of the turbulent storm waging in his mind. It jolted Uriah out of the dark mental pit.

Uriah. The voice was solid but pained.

Captain? Uriah asked. His body was frozen, trying to process what was happening.

I'm alive, Rose replied.

Are you okay? What's going on? I'm sorry! I'm sorry—I'm sorry—The phrase repeated over and over in Uriah's mind as the whirlwind threatened to retake him.

Uriah. Rose's voice was calm and steady. It centered him.

Captain, Uriah replied timidly, ashamed that she heard

him be so pathetic.

Are you with Theo? Rose asked gently yet firmly.

Uriah blinked. The black Werefox was muttering to himself as he wrote on the clipboard. He glanced at Uriah.

"Are you back to reality now?" Theo asked impatiently.

He's here, Uriah replied to Rose. He nodded at Theo.

"Finally! You were out of it for like ten minutes," Theo said dramatically.

Tell Theo that we need his help, Rose ordered.

"We need your help," Uriah said suddenly.

"Obviously," Theo sneered. "Your muscles are strung so tight you could play them like an instrument."

I don't think he understands what I'm trying to say, Uriah said.

Ask him what he knows of rituals, Rose said.

"What do you know about rituals?" Uriah asked.

Theo stopped. He stared at the Werewolf with a wary gaze. "Where is this coming from?"

"The captain," Uriah answered.

"Amaranth is in the stadium," Theo said slowly.

"She's speaking to me through the Bond," Uriah clarified. Saying it out loud made it feel more real. Giddiness rushed through Uriah's veins.

Theo rolled his eyes. "Great. More superstitions."

Uriah took offense. "It's not a superstition."

Theo smirked. "Prove it."

"How?"

"If you're really communicating with Amaranth, tell me something that only she and I would know," Theo explained smugly.

"One moment," Uriah muttered.

Sir, Theo is asking for proof, Uriah said. He wasn't liking being the middle Person in this conversation.

Let me think, Rose said. It seemed like a long time passed until Rose spoke again. Tell him to watch his tone and I know the real reason why he wanted to be a Healer.

Uriah repeated the information to Theo. The Werefox paled until he was almost ashen.

"Did ..." Theo gulped. "Did she tell you why?"

"No, and I don't care. What do you know about rituals?" Uriah urged.

"What kind of ritual is she wanting?" Theo asked. He seemed eager to get off the previous topic.

I need to know about a merging ritual, Rose replied. Uriah relayed the message.

"A merging ritual?" Theo asked thoughtfully. He tapped his chin with a long, furry finger. "The only ones that come to mind are those for reattaching limbs. Can she be more specific?"

What about merging magics? Rose asked. Uriah asked the question.

"Magics? Is that what's wrong with Salvador?" Theo asked.

"She thinks so," Uriah repeated. He paused. "She also says that Dali may have started to reject Conri's blessing when his maternal family started to believe Conri was a demon."

"Why do they think he's a demon? He's a Royian national hero, especially for conservationists," Theo pointed out.

"How so?" Uriah asked, this time for his curiosity.

"Conri is known as the creator of forests and jungles. According to folklore, he's the one who helped protect the forests and taught the ancient Royians agriculture. He's not a bad guy," Theo explained. "His symbol is often associated with our national parks and historical areas."

"What's his symbol?"

"A wild rose," Theo stated. "When Roy had a monarchy, it was the royal emblem. Some royals even claimed to be related to Conri one way or another, but they were just stories."

"Did Conri never marry?" Uriah asked.

Theo shook his head. "He did have a love interest. She was a mysterious female. In several of the stories, it is told that she either was a Dragon or a Faerie with rainbow wings."

"What was her name?" Uriah asked, fascinated.

"That depends on the story. Some call her Sookie or Susie or Sue. I personally like Susie," Theo replied.

Can he create a ritual that will merge magic? Rose asked impatiently.

"She wants to know if you can create a ritual for merging magic," Uriah said.

"I'll have to look into it. I'll let you know," Theo said. "For now, drink these, and I'll get food." He handed Uriah three vials. Two were purple, and one was a disgusting green color. Theo exited the room.

Uriah quickly downed the potions. He shuddered violently as the vile-tasting medicine went down his throat. Theo's potions were the worst he ever tasted.

Captain? Uriah called out.

Yes? Rose replied.

Are you okay? Uriah asked.

There was a pause. I'll live.

What am I looking for in the archives? Uriah asked.

Rose started to sigh, then gasped sharply. Uriah was alarmed. He sat up straighter, not noticing his muscles didn't hurt as much as before.

Look for information on Myst, Salvador's mother, Rose said in a pained tone. She's the key.

Captain, what's—

I'll talk to you later. Then there was silence.

CHAPTER 18

Ami's body flopped like a dying fish. She didn't even fight the pain anymore. The runes were dark red now. Or maybe the pain made them appear that way? She wasn't sure.

"You're a stubborn sinner," the female priest commented casually.

"You're a hypocrite," Ami retorted hoarsely.

"We are achieving the Almighty One's desires," the female priest said haughtily. "Punishing sinners and making them repent."

Ami let out a dry chuckle that sounded more like a dry cough. "You never read the holy book, did you?"

"And a sinner like you has?" the female priest sneered.

"Love your neighbor as you love yourself," Ami quoted. "Love usually isn't this painful."

"That is towards other believers, sinner," a male priest stated pompously.

"Even if your neighbor isn't a believer?" Ami asked.

"The Almighty One decides who will be a believer and who will not," a different male priest said.

"And you think ..." Ami started to say. She paused to catch her breath. "And you think wearing the robes and acting holy will make you a believer? The Almighty One called us to love others and lead them to His truth."

"You're trying to fool us into believing you're a follower," the female priest said accusingly.

Ami shrugged. "I am not a believer. I am curious about Him, though."

"Then you should accept your punishment for your sins," the female priest urged with a bit of crazy in her voice.

Ami scoffed at her. Her bloodshot eye glared at the female priest standing over her. "The god you worship is of judgment and hate. I refuse to follow such a being." Ami bared her bloody teeth.

"Then you will suffer more," the female priest said softly. Her dead eyes lit up whenever Ami's body jumped.

Ami cried out in every Bond she had. Her pain, her suffering, all of it shot through her Bonds like purple lightning. A haunted wolf howl echoed in her head. Was that Salvador? No, it was different. It didn't sound like a wolf howl echoing from a deep forest. This howl sounded like it was when the stars came out and the tranquility of the silent night was broken by fear. Strangely, Ami beckoned it. She knew it was someone she trusted. But who?

Shouts and yells reached Ami's ears. Then they turned into screams.

"Demons!" the female priest screamed.

Ami opened her eye. Her vision was blurred. She saw a shape like one of the priests disappear with a terrified scream. At least her body stopped jumping around.

"Rose!" a familiar voice shouted in her ear.

Ami blinked. Her vision remained blurry. The figure was a dark blob. When they leaned in closer, their features became more evident.

"Pera?" Ami asked in disbelief. What was the mayor doing here?

"Rose, can you hear me?" Lady Pera demanded, her voice

firm yet urgent. All Ami could do was blink. "*Ta-bo* priests and their blasted rituals. Caleb, make yourself useful and get these chains off of her," Lady Pera ordered.

Ami passed out. After some time, she vaguely became aware of being somewhere else. Her surroundings were hazy. Her brain couldn't comprehend what she was seeing. Something echoed around her. Ami looked around. Her brain finally realized what she was looking at. It was a cave tunnel. It wasn't the northern mines. The cave's walls were roughly carved out, revealing a mixture of hard earth and granite. The echo sounded again. Ami started to walk in the direction she thought it came from. Then she was in a large cavern. Torches lit the towering room forebodingly. Ami couldn't understand why she was here. The space was empty. She didn't recognize it.

"It's been a long time, Logic," a familiar voice sang.

From the dark rafters, Serene gracefully glided down to where Ami was. Ami stared. Serene was a Siren. Her arms were longer than the average Person's and covered with long white feathers. Her feet resembled an eagle's with large black talons and grayish color. She was taller than Ami by a foot. A simple wrap-around dress covered her body's smooth skin. Serene's long wispy blonde hair and pale skin made her light blue eyes stand out.

"Serene, where are we?" Ami asked. Her voice was tired. All she wanted to do was sleep.

"We are in my prison," Serene sang sadly.

Ami didn't have the energy to ask any more questions. She lowered herself to the cold ground. She hugged her knees, wishing she was back at the Knights' Quarters in her bed.

"What happened?" Serene sang-asked.

"Since I died?" Ami asked tiredly. Serene nodded. "I was promoted to captain. I killed a witch. I got a cover, and I was struck by lightning."

"What color?" Serene sang-asked, her eyes intense.

"Purple."

Serene smiled. "So, he did contact you."

"Contact? What are you talking about?" Ami asked.

"I asked a dear friend to help after you died, and I ended up here. Are you getting on well with him?" Serene sang.

Ami stared. "Who are you talking about? I was struck by lightning and was knocked unconscious."

"He ..." Serene started. She appeared shocked. "Ai hasn't contacted you?"

"I don't know who that is," Ami replied.

Serene's pale face turned red. Her blue eyes shined brighter. She let out a string of soprano notes that sounded like curses. "That stupid bird brain!" Her voice sounded like a chorus of twenty singers.

Strangely, it didn't hurt Ami's ears. At least these dreams had some benefits.

"Who is he?" Ami asked once Serene stopped shouting.

Serene huffed. "A friend I thought you could Bond with, but now I'm unsure."

"Looks like our time's up," Ami stated. The cavern was starting to swirl unnaturally.

"Come find me, Logic," Serene sang-begged.

The cavern transformed into darkness. Ami welcomed it. She floated in tranquility for an unknown time. In the back of her mind, something tugged. It was almost like someone knocking on a door. Ami tried to ignore it. She wanted to sleep. The tug and knocking became more insistent. Getting irritated, she shoved it away. Unfortunately, that brought her closer to waking up. She groaned when she opened her eye. The room was dark. The blankets and sheets were soft. Her vision was blurry. Everything was a fuzzy blob. Something moved. She heard someone come closer.

"Rose?" Lady Pera asked, coming next to the bed. Ami opened her mouth to speak, but nothing would come out. "Don't try to speak," Lady Pera said softly. "You're still recovering from the ritual."

Ami mimed drinking water. Lady Pera thankfully understood. Ami sat up, cringing at how awful she felt. Lady Pera handed her the glass. Ami carefully sipped the water. She nearly spat it out. It tasted like vinegar.

"What's wrong?" Lady Pera asked.

Ami made a face. She handed it back to Lady Pera. Her stomach growled noisily. The door on the other side of the room opened as if on cue. Ami couldn't tell how many people entered, but from the smell, they brought food. She couldn't identify what kind. It smelled weird, like the food from Putra Hallas.

"You'll feel better once you've eaten," Lady Pera said reassuringly.

A bowl was carefully placed in her lap. Awkwardly grabbing the spoon provided, Ami took a hesitant sip and vomited over her lap. It was so sudden that she didn't realize she was vomiting until it was over. Lady Pera was shouting, and blobs were scurrying around the room, a picture of chaos. Hiccups decided the party wasn't over and made Ami feel even sicker. The soiled blankets and sheets were stripped away. Lady Pera gently guided Ami to the bathroom. Making her sit on the rim of the bathtub, Lady Pera turned the water on.

"How's your stomach?" Lady Pera asked over the thunderous sound of water.

Ami shook her head. Lady Pera helped her out of the clothes she was wearing—something she didn't register—and into the bath. The Werewolf washed her hair without hurting her and washed her with a sponge filled with soothing soap. It reminded Ami of when she or her siblings had fallen ill, and her mom would care for them. Her heart throbbed at the thought. She really wanted her mom right now. A few tears went down her cheek silently. The hiccups echoed in the bathroom.

Once Ami was clean, Lady Pera assisted her in drying and putting on fresh clothes. Ami appreciated it. Her limbs were sluggish, and she was mentally barely hanging on. New sheets and blankets were already there when they returned to the bed. Ami could tell by the smell. She went to sleep as soon as she put her head on the pillow. The next time she woke up, she felt much better and not as sick to her stomach. She didn't dream either. Her eyesight was much better. She could at least make out details this time. Lady Pera sat on a leather chair with a large matching ottoman. In her lap was a thick book. The mayor set it aside when she noticed Ami awake.

"Rose, how are you feeling?" Lady Pera asked.

"Much better today," Ami croaked.

"At least you can speak. We were worried," Lady Pera said with a relieved smile.

"Water, please," Ami pleaded.

Lady Pera brought her a glass. Ami took a sip. She relaxed when it tasted delicious.

"How long was I asleep?" Ami asked, taking another sip.

"Four days," Lady Pera stated.

"Is Salvador okay?" Ami asked.

Lady Pera nodded. "He's been trying to get into your room since he could move. We were shocked that he recovered much faster than you."

"Conri's blessing," Ami supplied.

"That's something I wanted to talk to you about," Lady Pera said. "I'm finding it hard to believe what Salvador's been going through was a blessing when we all believed it was demonic possession."

"How do you know about this?" Ami asked.

Lady Pera looked surprised. "Salvador never told you?"

Ami shook her head. "He's a private Person."

"I'm his aunt," Lady Pera stated. "Myst, Sylvia, and I were triplets."

"That's rare."

The Werewolf chuckled sadly. "And I'm the only one left. I love my nephews and swore to my sisters that I would protect their children."

But not her niece. What happened to Deena? Did she cut off everyone in her life and dedicate it wholly to the priests? Ami frowned. "When was the first incident?"

Lady Pera sighed. "It didn't start until Deena was about ten and Salvador was twelve. Salvador was home for the first time since he joined the military. When he saw Deena, his eyes went green. He said, 'The White Dragon will be coming soon. When the white rose blooms, it will be a sign from the Almighty One. On that day, we will know and turn to Him once more. Repent, sinners! Repent and return to the Almighty One.' That was when Deena proclaimed that Salvador was being possessed by a demon."

Ami had started to sit up straighter when Lady Pera recited what Salvador had said. She replayed the words in her head.

"That wasn't demonic possession," Ami stated.

"Then what was it?" Lady Pera asked.

"That was a prophecy. Salvador is a prophet," Ami explained. "A demon would not tell people to repent their sins and return to the Almighty One. As religious as Deena is, she would know that."

"Then why didn't she?"

A horrifying sinking feeling went down Ami's back like melting ice. The strange feeling she had when she first saw Deena at Old Congress. How Deena manipulated her family into believing the priests. How the priests seem to follow Deena's every command. All of it added up to a conclusion Ami wasn't happy to piece together.

"It's Deena," Ami whispered.

"What?" Lady Pera nearly shouted.

"Deena is the one possessed, not Salvador," Ami said, louder this time.

"But she's with the priests. Surely they would've known," Lady Pera pointed out.

Ami shook her head. "No, because they said I was a demon. Deena knows I'm close to finding out her secret."

"What secret?" Lady Pera demanded.

Several knocks were heard. Without waiting for an answer, Ami's cover entered, covered in the scent of dust and old books. Uriah rushed over first with a dusty book in his right arm. His Bond string was tight with tension. Ami pulsed calmness. It took until the males came to her bed for Uriah to relax. Ados glanced between the two.

"You're Bonded," Ados stated accusingly.

"What?" James and Flander exclaimed. Lady Pera raised her eyebrows in shock.

"Why him and not us?" Ados demanded. He sounded hurt.

"It wasn't my intention," Ami admitted.

Ados didn't look convinced. "I want a Bond with you, Captain."

"Me too," James added.

"Same," Flander tacked on.

"Later. What did you find in the archives?" Ami asked.

Ados twisted his lips as if debating about rebelling or not. With a frustrated growl, he answered, "We found out where the Dali curse story came from."

Uriah handed her the book he held. She noticed a bookmark. Flipping to the page, she began to read:

Today is the day. Everything that I have been planning will be set into motion. I've been dropping hints to my female relatives for the past few months. My rival is coming back soon. I need to be prepared. The story I crafted and perfected has reached the ears of the People who will convince the possessed to hate himself. The priests are too easy to please and manipulate. For holy People, they enjoy torturing those they deem sinners. Hopefully, they'll create a ritual just for Conri. Then I, Margaret, will have my revenge against all the false gods created by that blasted heretic!

Ami glanced at the date. *This was written twenty years ago.* She thought. "Who's Margaret?" Ami asked.

Lady Pera answered, "She was my mother. Why do you ask?"

"What connection does she have to Conri?" Ami asked.

Lady Pera thought for several minutes. "I don't think she did. At least she never mentioned him to us."

"Who was her rival?" Ami asked.

"There was Priya Grewner of the Most Noble Grewner family. Mother and Priya were both sculptors. Mother sculpted People from the holy book while Priya mainly did folklore," Lady Pera answered.

"Was Margaret religious?" Ami asked.

"Very." Lady Pera nodded. "She was a big influence in Deena's life until her passing."

"Did Priya sculpt anything on Conri?" Ami asked.

"I'm sure she did," Lady Pera replied. "She lived in Roy for a time before returning to Rascu."

"Is Margaret still alive?" Ami asked.

"No, she passed right after Deena's tenth birthday. Deena was devastated," Lady Pera said.

Ami gathered her thoughts. Margaret was religious. She had a significant impact on Deena's life. Did she create the Dali curse story? Is that what she was writing about?

"Did she have any influence on Salvador's life? Did she interact with him?" Ami asked.

"I can answer that," Caleb said as he entered the room. Luther wasn't with him. "I stopped her from contacting him when she started to spout utter nonsense."

"Like what?"

"She kept saying that the devil was in Salvador and we needed to cleanse him at the temples. I told her that she was delusional. She insisted that Salvador go with her to the temples so the priests could get rid of the foul darkness. I finally broke contact with her when I witnessed her making Salvador write 'I am a demon' repeatedly and convincing him for a while that he was a monster. After that, she was forbidden from contacting him again," Caleb explained.

Perhaps that's why Sal is so private about his home life, Ami surmised. She understood he felt shame and might still believe some of what his grandmother told him. "Why did you allow her to have contact with Deena?" Ami asked.

Caleb sighed. He looked like he had aged a decade. "Prudence secretly let them interact. By the time I found out, it was too late."

"How are Prudence and Margaret related?" Ami asked.

"They're sisters," Lady Pera said.

"On the Dali family side, correct?" Ami asked.

"Only Prudence came into the Dali line. She married into it since the Dalis didn't have any daughters. Margaret married a male to maintain our family line, the Masques," Lady Pera clarified.

"How is Prudence related to you?" Ami asked Caleb.

Caleb grumbled. "Unfortunately, she's my mother. She disowned me when I married Myst. Thus, I cannot call her my mother in any sense."

Ami's brain short-circuited for a moment. "Wait ..." She stared at Caleb. "You married your first cousin?"

Uriah flinched. James looked disgusted. Ados was wide-eyed. Flander looked conflicted. Lady Pera and Caleb were unfazed.

"And?" Caleb asked challengingly.

"That's incest," Ami said slowly. Now she understood Prudence's attitude.

"And this pertains to Salvador how?" Caleb asked forcefully.

"How did you and Myst interact?" Ami asked.

"What do you mean?" Caleb asked warily.

"Like, did you meet at family functions? Work in the same area? Meet up in secret because of forbidden love?" Ami suggested.

Caleb glared at her. "Family functions and occasionally met outside the city."

Ami turned thoughtful. "How did Margaret react to this?"

Caleb opened his mouth to answer, but then closed it. A contemplative look came over. "She was surprisingly supportive," Caleb responded slowly.

"I was surprised as well," Lady Pera added. "Mother was usually spouting some kind of religious doctrine down our throats. I believe it was the only time we saw our mothers argue."

"That makes sense," Uriah said suddenly.

"How so?" Ami asked.

"In her later entries, she writes about how Myst will give birth to a demon created by Priya. According to her, Myst was obsessed with Conri and Priya's statues of him," Uriah said.

"She did like the artwork and his stories," Caleb admitted. "That's why she wanted to go to Roy to learn more about him. Our elopement and honeymoon were the perfect excuse."

"Then Myst received Conri's blessing. Did Myst's obsession with him end when Salvador was born?" Ami asked.

Caleb shook his head. "No, it got worse. She even commissioned a statue of Conri to be placed in our family home."

"A statue?"

"Yes. Myst would stare at it for hours as if in a trance," Caleb said sadly.

"We tried to snap her out of it. If we tried to move the statue, she would go ballistic. I had never seen my sister act like that," Lady Pera said.

"What was Margaret's last will and testament?" Ami asked. "Did she mention Conri at all?"

"She did request the statue be destroyed. Deena and the priests went to bless the house before we removed it. However, when the movement crew arrived, they were told that the statue was already taken care of and they were no longer needed," Caleb said.

This was worse than she thought. At least getting rid of the evil was simpler than killing a witch.

"Deena is possessed by a demon inhabiting that statue," Ami stated.

"You believe Margaret's crap?" Caleb bellowed.

"I don't condone her methods. For whatever crazy reason, she wanted this to happen and the priests to have time to create a ritual that would torture Salvador. Despite this, a demon or evil spirit was invited into whatever Priya created. When Deena and the priests went to get rid of it, it possessed Deena and convinced the priests not to harm it. Where's Priya now?"

"Priya is dead. Has been for the past seven years," Lady Pera answered.

"Caleb, where is your family home?" Ami asked.

"Outside the city."

"Let's go there and get rid of that statue," Ami said, getting out of bed.

"Sir, you're still weak," Ados protested.

"Not for this, I'm not," Ami argued.

"Captain, please let us handle this. You're already swaying," Uriah pointed out. When he said that, Ami collapsed back on the bed. Her arms and legs felt like limp noodles. Sweat poured down her forehead.

"Fine," she huffed in defeat. "I need to talk to my lads in private."

Lady Pera and Caleb left. The four males gathered around her bed. Ami struggled to sit back up. When she regained her breath, she told them, "Listen carefully. There may be a witch working in the background." She raised her hand when they opened their mouths. "I've learned that witches aren't too far away wherever there are demons. Your mission, no matter what, is to completely destroy that statue. I don't mean break it into chunks and pieces. I mean, make it crumble, set it on fire, and bury it in the earth. It cannot be recreated. That is the only way for the spirit to leave."

"What about Deena and the priests?" Ados asked.

"Try not to kill them. Knock them unconscious. If they continue to fight you after you destroy the statue, you can kill them," Ami said.

"Why only after?" James asked.

"Then they are no longer under the demon's influence. They are acting on their own free will," Ami stated. "Do you understand your orders?"

"Yes, sir," they chorused.

"Very well. Good luck, lads." Ami saluted.

They saluted back and left. Ami laid back down. She hated feeling so weak. Her lads were in for a hard battle if a witch was nearby. She hoped her soldiers were prepared enough to handle this kind of battle. She lay there for what felt like days until a polite knock on her door interrupted the silence. Forcing herself to stand, she staggered to the door like a drunk Person. The knocker was Salvador.

"Hey," Salvador greeted her shyly.

"Hi. What's up?" Ami greeted him back.

"I brought you some new clothes," Salvador said, handing her a brown bag. Rubbing the back of his neck, he asked, "I was wondering if we could eat together after you changed."

That was when Ami noticed Salvador's outfit. He was dressed in a black T-shirt and dark denim jeans. The dark leather sandals spoke of the Dali wealth.

"Where are we eating?" Ami asked, taking the brown bag.

"There's a covered balcony on the twentieth floor. I can order food from there," Salvador said.

"Give me a minute," Ami said. She closed the door. The outfit was like Salvador's, except Ami's shirt was purple. The leather sandals were stiff. Ami wondered how he got her shoe size and when he had time to put in the order. Exiting her room, she followed Salvador to the elevator. She was forced to lean on Salvador when they reached their floor because her knees gave out.

"Can I carry you?" Salvador asked. His ears were dark pink.

"Yes," Ami muttered.

Salvador held her as if she was a precious doll. Ami was uncomfortable. The floor was bland, with light tan carpet and matching colored walls. Large windows showed the vast blue sky. Next to the windows were various tables and chairs. He gently set her down at a table.

"Thank you," Ami said gratefully.

"You're welcome. What would you like to eat and drink?" Salvador asked.

"I want soup and bread, please, with water," Ami answered.

"What kind of soup?"

"Onion, if they have it. Broccoli and cheddar are good, too," Ami said.

"I'll be back." Salvador nodded.

Ami closed her eye. Her head was swimming. The world around her swirled like a whirlpool. Her stomach lurched at the sensation. The smell of food paused the dizziness briefly. She opened her eye. Salvador carefully placed the large bowl of onion soup in front of her.

"Thank you," she whispered.

"It's no problem," Salvador said with a blush. He, too, had soup.

They sat for a while, quietly slurping their soup. Ami enjoyed it. It didn't taste weird, and she felt some of her energy return.

"Dad told me you figured it all out," Salvador stated.

"With Conri?" Ami asked.

Salvador nodded, wiping his mouth with a napkin. "I'm glad it's not a curse, but I'm still confused about what he told me."

Ami tore a piece of bread and stuck it in her mouth. She held it there, wracking her brain on how to word what she wanted to say without being crass or insensitive. Nervously, she swallowed the bread.

"Has your father or uncle told you about the situation?" Ami asked.

Salvador's eyes dimmed. He slumped in his chair. "Yeah. It's Deena, isn't it?"

"I'm sorry, Sal," Ami murmured. She reached over the table

and gently placed her hand on his.

"Me too," Sal said mournfully. "I wish I could've saved her sooner. I keep looking back and seeing if there were signs of help from her, but I can't find anything." He looked up at her with tears in his eyes. "Am I a bad brother?"

"No, you're not," Ami said. "Remember what you told me? How would you sneak her out for ice cream or tell her stories of your mother away from your female relatives? I believe you did the best you could in the situation. I know Deena remembers those moments." She retreated her hand.

Salvador nodded, but didn't look entirely convinced.

"Do you mind if I pray?" Salvador asked.

"I don't. Do you need privacy?" Ami asked.

"I'd rather you be here," Salvador admitted.

He offered both of his hands, palms up. Ami hesitantly placed her hands into his. She'd never done this before. Gently gripping her hands, Salvador bowed his head, closed his eyes, and began to pray:

"Almighty One, we come before you. We raise our grievances to you. There is darkness around us, and it's hard to see the light right now. Creator, we ask you to show us your light. Show us out of this darkness. Take the darkness that has overtaken my sister, Deena. Great One, I don't know her circumstances or what she is going through, but I know you have the power to take the evil away. Cast it out of her! This evil has nothing against you, Almighty One. Cast it out! Destroy the house the evil is resting in. Cast it out! Shine light upon her so she can leave the darkness. We trust you to guide her with your shining lamp. In all this, we pray in your holy name. Amen."

Ami opened her eye. She hadn't thought Salvador was going to pray out loud. She only knew of silent prayers in the private confines of one's room. This was a new experience. She rubbed her arms with her hands. Goosebumps had bubbled on her skin during Salvador's prayer. A heady presence of something was in the room with them. Ami didn't know what it was, but it was comforting. Strong, yet she knew nothing would harm her.

"That was interesting," Ami said quietly. She didn't want to break the atmosphere. Inwardly she was craving it. She couldn't identify what it was exactly. It was like a dessert she tried once and couldn't find the chef to make it again.

"Thanks," Salvador said nervously. "We just have to trust the Almighty One to help Dad and the others with Deena."

"I didn't realize you were religious," Ami commented.

Salvador shook his head. "I'm not. I have a copy of the holy book from my mom that I read when I can't sleep."

"How is that different from being religious?" Ami asked curiously.

"You met the priests, right?" Salvador raised an eyebrow.

"Point taken."

"Not all of them are bad. It's just sad that many are," Salvador said. "There was a priest my mom knew in Octa that talked me through her passing. He helped me a lot whenever we visited the temple growing up."

Ami hummed to herself. Maybe this priest could answer some questions she had?

They murmured about minor things like poetry and their favorite writers. The blue sky turned yellow, bright orange, and red as the sun began to set. Their dinnerware had crumbs and faint remnants of soup. Salvador refilled their water glasses several times, refusing to let Ami get them on her own. When the sun disappeared below the horizon, exhaustion smacked Ami against the side of her head.

"I believe it's time for us to sleep," Ami said, yawning halfway.

"I'll walk you to your room," Salvador said.

Ami was glad he did. She nearly fell asleep standing up on the elevator. When they reached her door, they hugged.

"Thank you," Salvador whispered.

"You're welcome," Ami whispered back.

They separated. Ami turned and entered her room. Closing the door, she leaned against it. She felt her knees threaten to give out on her.

We're almost there. Let's change into pajamas, and then we can sleep. Ami tried to encourage her remaining working limbs. It seemed to work. Slipping under the covers in fresh pajamas, Ami lay there. Her body was exhausted, but her mind wasn't ready for slumber. She sunk down into herself. Her Bonds thrummed pleasantly. Ami scrutinized each one.

Rikardi's was slithering like a snake. The vibrations gave the impression of anxiety. Ami gently grabbed it. The Bond stilled immediately. She tried to send calmness. The Bond vibrated with irritation, not buying her calm waves. Ami shrugged it off. The gangs' Bonds were rigid, as if bracing for a natural disaster to hit. Ami placed her hands around the Bonds. As soon as she did, they loosened in relief. Rune pulsed with excitement. The string beat a light, almost like a signal. Shayne, Benton, and Philip sent something along the lines of smiles. It made Ami smile.

I need to test out the limits of the Bond with the males, Ami mentally noted.

Giving the impression of moving on, the males professed their yearning for her to return. Ami hoped it would be soon. She missed them. She missed Talient. Then Ami came Uriah's Bond. It was teal mixed with red. A strange color mixture. Ami wondered if one's color indicated their magical strength or affinity to a particular element. Does teal mean water or wind or both? Was the red fire or something else? Perhaps once she Bonded with the other males, they would trust her to teach them magic.

Without warning, she returned to reality with a sharp gasp. Opening her eye, she saw the bedside lamp was lit. Uriah sat on the bed next to her. Ami stared. Uriah looked like he went to the Pits, fought his way back, and didn't even get a

T-shirt for his efforts. His clothes were torn. Minor cuts covered his arms and shoulders. What troubled Ami the most was his eyes. They were haunted. Whatever innocence Uriah had carried had been torn away.

"Uriah," Ami called out softly.

"Captain," Uriah answered monotone.

"You're hurt," Ami said. She moved to get a first aid kit. Uriah's hand on her shoulder stopped her. Uriah's eyes looked far away, deep in his memories. Ami gently placed a hand over the one on her shoulder. "Uriah?"

Her voice snapped him out of whatever consumed his mind. "Sir?" Uriah cleared his throat.

"What happened?" Ami asked.

Uriah let out a shaky breath. "Deena and the priests were waiting for us at the manor. They had already placed various ritual circles all around, making it impossible to get close to them. Then Lady Pera did something that made a gale of wind move some priests out of the way. Caleb followed up by pelleting them with large rocks. I ... I don't know where they came from," Uriah said uncertainly.

"He more than likely created them or used the earth outside with magic," Ami supplied. "Were you able to advance?"

Uriah shook his head. "The rituals were still active somehow. That was when Ados noticed how interconnected they were, and powered by Deena and a few priests. He told Caleb and Lady Pera. Deena and the priests were able to shield themselves from their magic. James then saw a fountain filled with water. He grabbed an urn, and we filled it up with water. We then threw the water at the ritual circles. It made them fade."

"They probably used chalk to create the circles. At least that part was easy," Ami said.

Uriah nodded. "Once we noticed that, Lady Pera and Caleb distracted them while we poured water over the circles until they were useless. Then the witch appeared." Uriah paused, the haunted look returning to his eyes. "The air around us was sickening," Uriah whispered. "It was like breathing in a plague. She smelled like sweet poppies and death. She used some kind of black lightning bolt to paralyze us, including Deena and the priests. Then she started to brag about how she would use us in a sacrifice to her lover.

"Weirdly, it didn't affect me like the others. I noticed I was able to move. The witch didn't like that. She attacked me with magic. I could only dodge her attacks. I dodged a big fireball, which hit something that made her scream in agony. I looked, and it was a wolf statue. It absorbed the fireball. Then these creepy black tentacles reached out of the statue and grabbed the witch. A terrifying voice said, 'This is how you repay the contract?' She screamed as the black things pulled her into the statue. When she was gone, the stone cracked and crumbled to the ground.

"Once the statue was destroyed, everyone else was able to move. I told everyone your instructions, and we followed them to the letter. Deena seemed confused about what was going on. I'm not sure what happened with the priests. Caleb and Lady Pera seemed relieved. Then we headed back here," Uriah explained.

Another witch, Ami thought with a frown. Why were they popping up in Rascu all of a sudden? She could understand Vinci and parts of Goya for their remote mountains, but Rascu was often viewed as untouchable. *That's probably what made it enticing for them.* Ami thought bitterly.

"Did the witch say her name?" Ami asked.

"Priya. She had told Margaret she would take the Dali line and was almost successful," Uriah replied.

If another so-called dead Person is a witch, I'm going to dig everyone up and burn their bodies, Ami thought with irritation. "Are you okay?" she asked.

Uriah looked at her with tears filling his eyes. "Are they all like this?"

Ami nodded solemnly. "Unfortunately, yes. Sadly, there are

worse ones than her."

She felt their Bond throb. Uriah stared at the foot of her bed. A yearning for something tried to translate over their Bond. It took a moment for Ami to recognize what it was. Without hesitation, she reached with both arms and hugged Uriah. The Werewolf flinched before relaxing. Realizing she wasn't letting go, he firmly wrapped his arms around her. His body shook in suppressed tears.

"Let it out," Ami whispered, her chin resting on his shoulder.

Uriah obeyed. His fear, terror, horror, and reality of the situation flooded their Bond. Ami absorbed it, tears flowing down her cheek as Uriah shared his pain. A sky-blue string was added to their Bond as the flood ebbed away. Feeling emotionally raw, they reluctantly pulled away. Both wiped their faces with their hands.

"Will you guard me tonight?" Ami asked. Guarding a superior officer was a sign of trust amongst the Rascals.

Uriah blinked at her. "Yes, sir."

"Let's deal with your wounds. Grab the first aid kit," Ami ordered.

She dressed his wounds methodically. Once it was done, Uriah left briefly to change. When he returned, he wore only sweatpants. Ami eyed his body critically. She needed to get her lads into better shape. Uriah's lean physique cautiously sat at the foot of the bed.

"Get over here. You can't guard me from there," Ami teased.

Uriah visibly gulped. Ami scooted over to make room. Uriah took the hint. He slid beside her on top of the covers while Ami remained under. The Werewolf was still a statue.

"Don't forget to guard me," Ami warned as she turned off the light. She thought it would take her a while to get to sleep with Uriah next to her. Surprisingly, she fell asleep quickly.

Ami returned to the waking world from the sound of her door opening. Cautiously using a tiny bit of magic, she identified Salvador. While it was nice of him to wake her for breakfast, Ami wasn't ready to get up. The bed was comfortable for once, and she was in the best position. It was like sleeping on a warm cloud. Salvador came next to her bed.

The weight on the bed shifted drastically. Ami opened her eye in surprise. Uriah hovered over her on his hands and knees. Only he wasn't looking at her. He was glaring at Salvador. Deep, threatening growls emitted from his chest.

"Why are you in my captain's room without permission?" Uriah demanded, his lips curled back to bare his teeth.

Salvador bared his teeth as well. "Why are you here in the first place?"

"I was asked to guard her," Uriah answered. Ami thought she heard traces of pride in his answer.

"Why you?" Salvador sneered.

"I'm her second," Uriah stated.

"And I'm awake," Ami announced.

Uriah swiftly got off of her. He kept his eyes on Salvador, though. Salvador's glare melted into a softer expression. Ami sat up.

"Why are you here, Sal?" Ami asked.

"I was going to wake you for breakfast," Salvador said.

"Knowing how exhausted I was yesterday, wouldn't it have been better to let me sleep?" Ami inquired.

"I-I thought you'd be hungry," Salvador stuttered.

"I am now," Ami growled. She moved to stand up. Taking a step, she stumbled. Uriah caught her by the arm first. He snapped at Salvador, who also reached over to grab her. The two started to growl and bare their teeth at each other. Ami had enough.

"Enough!" she shouted. She yanked her arm out of Uriah's grasp. "I will not be in the middle of this male posturing and will not tolerate it. Both of you, get out of my sight!"

Both males ran out of the room with their tails tucked between their legs. Ami growled in frustration. She needed to talk to Salvador about their *friendship* before they left for

Talient and to make a training plan for her cover. Military and societal etiquette was at the top of the list.

Belladonna shrieked in anger. She threw the pieces of her makeshift chessboard across the room. That pest killed Priya! Her lover and beloved follower, a genuine witch in every sense. Belladonna admired how Priya would entice demons into her statues and use them to control various Nobles in Rascu. With her dead, the contracts were voided, and Belladonna couldn't use Priya's statues to collect sacrifices. Even Priya's puppets were free and under protection.

Belladonna's beautiful face morphed into a hideous sneer. The pest was to blame. It had a hand in this somehow. The witch looked around her destroyed room. She was losing power. Most of her followers had abandoned her once her lieutenants were killed, and even the ones she initiated into becoming witches had bailed. Even Mother was becoming concerned.

I need to get rid of this pest, Belladonna thought desperately. Then she thought of her chess pieces. Thoughtfully and carefully, she gathered the tossed pieces and replaced them on the chessboard. She eyed the board with a meticulous eye. Ideas and plans filled her evil mind.

"Very well, pest," Belladonna hissed to the empty room. "Since you want it, you shall have it. I declare war."

ABOUT ATMOSPHERE PRESS

Founded in 2015, Atmosphere Press was built on the principles of Honesty, Transparency, Professionalism, Kindness, and Making Your Book Awesome. As an ethical and author-friendly hybrid press, we stay true to that founding mission today.

If you're a reader, enter our giveaway for a free book here:

SCAN TO ENTER
BOOK GIVEAWAY

If you're a writer, submit your manuscript for consideration here:

SCAN TO SUBMIT
MANUSCRIPT

And always feel free to visit Atmosphere Press and our authors online at atmospherepress.com. See you there soon!

ABOUT THE AUTHOR

SAMANTHA DAVENPORT grew up in South Carolina and remained there to set up her roots. When not writing, she is baking, cuddling with her three dogs and playing some sort of Pokemon game on her Switch while binging Mystery Science Theater 3000 for the one millionth time.